the cauldron's curse

COLLEGE OF WITCHCRAFT BOOK THREE

ALICIA RADES

This book contains characters with the following medical conditions. The information included is meant to educate readers on disabilities featured within the College of Witchcraft series.

RHEUMATOID ARTHRITIS

Rheumatoid Arthritis, or RA, occurs when the immune system mistakenly attacks the body's own healthy tissue. RA commonly affects the joints, causing painful swelling, stiff joints, and fatigue, among other symptoms. RA can occur at any age.

CROHN'S DISEASE

Crohn's Disease is a condition that causes chronic inflammation in the gastrointestinal tract. Symptoms may include fatigue, abdominal pain, severe diarrhea, and malnutrition. Symptom severity varies by patient.

ONE

Fighting for justice could be hell.

The last three months had felt like an eternity—yet had passed in the blink of an eye. For three months, I'd been investigating nightshade within the Miriamic Coven. Three months, and I hadn't found one damn answer. Three months, and I still hadn't spoken to *her*.

Three months…

The words echoed in my mind as I strolled along the dark street, my hands shoved into the pockets of my hoodie. How had so much time passed by already? How had I failed to gather any answers?

Something was going on with the coven's magic—unexplained bouts of magical suppression. I'd dedicated the last three months to hunting down answers about Black Ivy—or nightshade, as it was called on the streets. It was a magical drug brewed by Alchemists, intended to boost magical powers. But as soon as you went off it, withdrawals set in, and your magic didn't work quite the same. I suspected there was a connection. I just didn't know what it was yet.

It was my duty to find answers. I'd been the one to give up Nadine's secret, to let it slip to the Imperium Council that she was a Curse Breaker. Now they wanted her to find the Oaken Wands, powerful relics created to restore Miriamic magic should it ever be stolen, though the wands themselves had been lost years ago. I had to help Nadine find out why this was happening in the first place—even if she wasn't my girlfriend anymore.

I stopped at the end of a long driveway and stared through the trees at the house beyond. The quarter moon cast the abandoned Gothic house in shadows. It was the end of August, and yet the night air sent a chill down my spine.

The house always had a sense of loneliness about it, but it'd never felt abandoned—until now. It was Professor Daymond's old residence. It had been empty since the night he was arrested for possession of nightshade. The whole place had been cleared out after everything went down, and it hadn't sold yet. It didn't matter how many times I'd scoured the property —there were no more answers here.

I knew it, but I kept finding myself drawn back here. It was where Daymond had told me about the drugs, and where I'd found his notebook containing his drug contacts. But the book was long gone, as was everything else that ever belonged to the old man. The house was nothing more than a shell, a memory.

I heard the sound of a car approaching. I turned as it slowed along the street. The passenger window rolled down, and Grant leaned across the middle console to call out to me.

"Lucas, I thought I might find you out here." Grant sighed, before adding, "Why do you insist on torturing yourself?"

"I'm not *torturing* myself," I insisted. "I'm looking for clues."

Grant gestured toward the house. "You've been over this property a hundred times. There's nothing left."

I walked up to his car and leaned my elbows on the open window. "I suppose you have a better idea?"

Grant smirked, like he knew something I didn't. "I do. Get in the car."

I had to admit, he had me intrigued. I opened the door and slid into the passenger seat.

Grant stepped on the gas. "I don't understand what you think you're going to find out here."

I watched out the window as the house disappeared from view. "Something—anything. Daymond was the one lead I had, and now he's dead."

It had happened the night following his confession. Daymond had been found dead in his jail cell. The official report called it a heart attack, but everyone knew what really killed him. He'd been cursed.

There was no way to prove it. Curses that could kill were incredibly difficult to cast, which meant someone was fucking *pissed* at him. It was pretty obvious to anyone with a brain that it'd been someone within his drug circle, someone who didn't want the information getting out and pointing back to them. When the Imperium Council caught the guy orchestrating this illegal trade, there would be hell to pay.

"Daymond wasn't your *only* lead," Grant pointed out. "We know other people at the school were dealing."

"I have no doubt the Tarantulas were in on it," I agreed. "We already know they've been dealing drugs since Freshman year and that they stole from the Alchemy department last year."

Grant and I had investigated their old hideout, but it'd been totally cleaned out.

"But it's not a great lead if I can't find them," I added.

Everyone had their own plans for summer vacation. Nadine had been staying with her grandmother. I hadn't seen her all summer, and didn't know what she'd been up to. Talia had spent the summer composing music for her brother's band, and Grant had spent most of his break at the pool.

As for me, I'd been crashing on Grant's couch, as I did whenever the dorms were closed. When I wasn't there, I was scouring the town for clues about what the hell was going on in this place.

But the Tarantulas? I had no idea what they were up to. After news broke of Professor Daymond's involvement, it was like they'd vanished, along with anyone else we suspected of dealing drugs on school grounds.

"The Tarantulas will be back," Grant stated confidently, though we couldn't be sure.

The best theory we had was that they were traveling, probably transporting drugs and making deals with other magical races. We already knew the Elementai were trading unicorn hair for nightshade, thanks to Professor Daymond's confession. But the Elementai tribe was all the way across the country, in California. *Someone* had to transport the goods, and who better to use than a bunch of kids who had nothing to do all summer?

But just because all my leads had vanished didn't mean the drugs had. They'd just gone underground, where the Imperium Council couldn't find them—and neither could we.

"In the meantime, I think I found a lead," Grant said with a smile.

I sat straighter in my seat. "You're kidding."

Grant traced two imaginary lines over his heart. "Cross my heart and hope to die."

"That's great!" I cried. "What's the story?"

Grant placed both hands back on the wheel and smirked confidently. "I was lifting weights at the gym when I heard Frederick James say something about nightshade. I gave him my whole story about my broken arm and how I had to skip out of the championship swim tournament last semester. I managed to convince him I needed the nightshade energy boost for training."

"You said *Frederick James?*" I asked. "That Mentalist who accused Nadine of hexing the school last semester?"

Grant frowned. "Yes, unfortunately. But he's our only lead. Are we going to take it or leave it?"

I sighed. "Take it."

"Good, because he should be at the school any minute." Grant turned down a familiar road, which led to the gates of Miriam College of Witchcraft.

"The school?" I asked.

Grant shrugged. "It's summer vacation. No one's there this time of year. Oh, and I got you something."

He reached into his middle console and tossed me a small electronic device. I caught it and looked over the buttons.

"It's a voice recorder," Grant said. "I figured it'd come in handy with your Journalism major."

"Can't I just use my phone?"

"This is better," he assured me. "It's easier to use and picks up more sound. And the design is super simple, so it's less likely to get any interference from magic. It'll pick up everything."

I smiled. "Then let's make sure we catch a confession on tape."

Grant pulled into the parking lot of Miriam College. The Gothic mansion was huge and stood out from the trees surrounding it. It was late

—near midnight already—but I was used to seeing college kids roaming the grounds. It seemed eerie that we were the only ones there.

We'd just pulled into a parking space when a pair of headlights swept by us. Grant stepped out of the car. The other car sped through the parking lot and came to a screeching halt beside us. James jumped out of an old, beat-up sports car, and the hinges squeaked as he slammed the door. I quickly pressed *record* on my device and shoved it in my pocket.

"Grant, my man!" James sang, as if the two of them had been best buddies since grade school. He was already approaching Grant, but stopped when he saw me climb out of the car. He eyed me, as if trying to decide if I could be trusted or not. "I see we have company."

"Relax," Grant said smoothly. "Lucas wants a vial, too. I assume you have enough for both of us?"

James relaxed and straightened his leather jacket. "Yeah, I've got enough. What's your story, Lucas?"

"A bad breakup," I told him, without missing a beat. "I need to forget."

That wasn't quite a lie, either. I'd spent the summer trying to get Nadine out of my mind. Nothing—not even throwing myself into this investigation as a distraction—had done the trick. Every morning I woke up, the memory of her was there, seeded into the forefront of my mind. Every night I fell asleep, I dreamt of her. I'd been pissed when we broke up, certain I couldn't forgive her for the choices she'd made to protect her friends. Now I knew I'd been wrong, because if I truly thought I could never forgive her—never be with her again—it wouldn't hurt so damn much.

James smiled. "Nightshade can help with that. The euphoria is quite something. How much are you looking for?"

"Depends. What do you have?" Grant asked.

"I can do two vials each," James offered. "You got the money?"

Grant nodded and conjured a wad of cash. "The price we agreed on," he said. My eyes went wide as Grant handed over several twenties.

"That's... quite the price tag," I remarked, choosing my words carefully.

James narrowed his eyes. "That depends on how desperate you are to forget about this girl."

I chuckled, playing along. "Oh, believe me. I want the nightshade."

I conjured what little money I had and began slowly counting out the bills. James's eyes grew hungry at the sight of cash.

"I was just wondering… is there any chance we can get in on dealing?" I asked.

James frowned. "I'm afraid not."

I stopped counting my bills, but he never took his eyes off the money. "There's gotta be a way to get us in. How did you get involved?"

"Can't say," James replied curtly, before quickly adding, "It's boss's orders. Ever since Daymond was busted, someone's been poking around looking for answers. Did you know his house was broken into after he died?"

Guilty, I thought, though I hadn't been the first person to think of it. By the time I got there, all clues about Daymond's ties to nightshade were gone. Someone really wanted to cover this up.

"Who would do that?" I asked innocently.

James shrugged. "Someone hell-bent on getting the drugs out of Octavia Falls, I guess."

Huh. So they had no suspects of their own.

"Is there someplace we can go to get more nightshade, after we run out?" Grant asked.

A good question. They had to have some sort of headquarters… right?

"Two vials should last you a while," James said. "When you're ready for more, you talk to me."

"What if we can't get ahold of you?" I pressed. "Is there someone else we can get in contact with?"

James chuckled. "It's not like I'm going anywhere. I'm not stupid enough to overdose or some shit like that. Look, I don't have all night. I realize you've probably never bought drugs before, but you're going to have to get quicker on the exchange. The last thing you want is to get caught buying nightshade."

I pressed my lips together. I was getting nowhere with this guy. Perhaps money was the only way to get him to talk.

"Will this do it?" I waved a few bills at him.

"Sure will." James took the cash, then conjured four small vials of nightshade. A purplish-blue liquid sloshed around inside them. Grant and I each took our respective vials and subconjured them.

"You sure we can't get in on this?" I gritted my teeth. I was starting to get frustrated with this guy.

"Positive. Boss says no newbies." James pocketed the money. "Before you leave, a word of caution, since you've obviously never used before. No more than a few drops under the tongue at a time. You don't want to overdose."

I narrowed my eyes. "What happens if we do?"

James scoffed, like he found my ignorance amusing. "What happens if you take too much of *any* drug? You'll die."

My mouth went dry. It wasn't like I was going to *use* the nightshade we'd just bought, but the thought of anyone dying over this chilled me. No drug was worth your life.

"Thanks for your business," James said, with a nod of his head. "Oh, and I'm sorry things didn't work out with your girlfriend—Nadine, was it?"

My stomach twisted at the sound of her name. "Yeah," I replied flatly.

James got a distant look in his eyes. "It really is too bad. I hope you tapped that before you broke up."

My hands instantly curled into fists. *"Excuse me?"*

James laughed. "Nadine's totally hot. I mean, she's not really *my* type, but I'd still do her. Since she's single, I might just—"

Thwack!

My fist cracked into James's jaw, and he stumbled sideways.

"Lucas!" Grant gasped.

I already had a battle orb aimed at James's face. "Don't you *dare* talk about Nadine like that! If you even *think* about touching her—"

"Back off, man!" James thrust his hands outward, and a spell erupted from his palms.

It rammed into my chest and flung me backward. My back slammed into Grant's car, and my elbow cracked against the back window. I hadn't been stunned, but I'd be damned if that wasn't one hell of a spell.

I gasped for breath, but reacted quickly, tossing a stunning spell at him. James was fast and ducked out of the way. I didn't waste a second. I swung my knee upward while he was ducked down. It connected with his nose, and he let out a cry of pain.

Grant grabbed for me. "Lucas, stop. This is unnecessary!"

But I'd already lost it. I shrugged Grant off and grabbed James's collar, shoving him against the side of his vehicle. Blood dripped from his nose. He laughed like the fight was nothing short of amusing.

"You were already pissing me off, but *no one* talks about Nadine like that and gets away with it," I growled. "Where are the drugs? Who are you working for? Tell me now, or so help me—"

"Go fuck yourself, loser!" James shoved me off of him, and another spell blasted from his hands, more powerful than the last. It blew me backward so hard I flew off my feet and rolled across the pavement a few times, accumulating bruises. Something clinked to the ground.

James's eyes darted between Grant and me. "You can forget about buying any more nightshade off me. Consider this your final purchase."

I groaned as I pushed myself to a sitting position. It wasn't until James's eyes landed on the ground that I realized with horror what had slipped from my pocket. *My recording device.*

James's eyes went wide, and he flicked his wrist at me. An ungodly pain overtook my body, as if my bones had been set on fire. My back arched as a scream tore from my lungs. Every organ in my body seemed to be ripping apart beneath his spell.

I was vaguely aware of Grant rushing to my side. I heard the sound of tires squealing as James sped out of the parking lot.

"Fuuuck!" I screamed, the blazing inferno tearing through me.

All at once, it was gone. The fire stopped, though every inch of my body trembled.

"Lucas, Lucas!" Grant repeated my name over and over. He slapped my face a little, until I tore my gaze from James's car to look at him.

"W-what the hell happened?" I demanded.

"James is a Mentalist," he reminded me. "It must be one of his specialties—tricking you into thinking you're in pain when you're not."

I drew in a greedy gulp of air. "That was one hell of a spell."

Grant helped me up, though I was still shaking. "Come on. We should get out of here before anyone comes to check it out. I bet the whole coven heard you scream."

I stood on shaky knees, then bent to pick up my recording device. I turned the recording off and waved it at Grant. "Thanks for the recorder, but we got nothing."

His shoulders sagged. "I'm sorry. I was sure we'd learn *something.*"

"It's not your fault this night was a bust," I told him. "I'm the one who lost it."

I just hoped it hadn't cost us everything. James knew now that I was a threat. He knew I was coming for him—for all the witches and warlocks involved in the coven's drug trade.

Which meant I had to get creative if I was going to beat them—before I ended up like Daymond, and the drug ring killed me for messing with their operation.

nadine
TWO

S ummer was a cursed season.

Three months had passed, and I'd barely seen my friends. I'd been too sick, but it was more than that. I hadn't seen Lucas since the night we broke up, and that hurt more than any physical ailment. This wasn't just a lupus flare-up—I was suffering from a broken heart.

I'd spent most of the summer in bed. As my magic grew stronger, so did my lupus. The worst of it started when I'd performed a locator spell with the Imperium Council to track down the Oaken Wands—powerful relics that could retrieve lost magic. For months, our magic had been disappearing in waves. People would lose their magic for a few days, then it'd come back. Sometimes, it would disappear again, but there was no consistent pattern. Anyone could become a victim.

The Waning—the term the *Miriamic Messenger* had coined for the event affecting our magic—was only getting worse. Eventually, we could lose our magic for good.

We intended to stop the Waning before things got even worse. The Imperium thought that together, our magic would be strong enough to find the Oaken Wands, but they couldn't be tracked through magic. It was one of the traits that made them so powerful and kept them protected, and why the Imperium Council hadn't found them yet. I'd asked Grammy about the Wands, too, but she didn't know anything that would help us locate them.

The Imperium and I attempted a second locator spell to track whoever was behind the Waning. But without knowing specifics, we couldn't trace the culprit.

The spells—though ineffective—had knocked me on my ass. I was tired all the time, and my joints were swollen and painful.

What truly did me in, though, was the space-bending spell I'd assisted with at one of the cider mills. The council intended to expand the factory to create new jobs, and we had—but at my expense. I couldn't get out of bed after performing the complicated spell. I'd avoided magic for a few weeks, but as soon as I performed the simplest spell, my symptoms flared. My hair was thinning, and I'd developed nose sores. I hadn't been back to normal since, and no potion seemed to help. Dr. Yonker had urged me to continue using my magic, because I was supposed to be getting used to it.

"It will get worse before it gets better, Nadine," he'd pressed. "Trust me."

Hell, I wanted to. I was just sick of waiting for things to get better already. I didn't know why the Imperium Council still wanted my help with the Wands, considering I could barely get out of bed most days.

Scratch that. I knew exactly why they wanted my help. They thought my family still had the Curse Breaker Wand. Each of the Oaken Wands was powerful on its own, but like the Casts, they were strongest together. The council needed all five Wands if they hoped to stop what was coming. It was the only way to restore our magic—before it was gone completely.

Returning to school after summer break felt like taking a breath after three months of suffocating. If there was a clue to all of this, it had to be here.

My first day back at Miriam College, I woke with more energy than I'd had all summer. I was excited to get back to classes, and I'd been itching to explore the library for more information on the Wands. At school, I felt free. It didn't feel like the Imperium was watching my every move. I'd felt the scrutiny every time they called me to a meeting.

I wasn't officially a priestess yet—not until my induction on Halloween—so I wasn't invited to every meeting. But I'd been to a few, and they'd asked about my progress in finding the Curse Breaker Wand each time. I had to tell them time and time again that I hadn't found it, and that it was no longer in my family's possession.

Priestess Lilian insisted I try harder. She didn't believe me.

At school, things were different. It used to be that classes were the worst of my problems. Now they felt like a welcome reprieve to the real issues plaguing the coven.

But I couldn't hide from my problems, no matter how hard I tried. When I returned to the school, it was evident that these problems followed each and every one of us wherever we went.

I stepped out of my car and grabbed my bag from the back. Isa prowled at my side. As I passed by another vehicle, I heard a girl sobbing through an open window. I glanced toward the car to see two girls from my meditation class sitting in the front seats—Ashley and Christine.

"It will be all right," Christine said.

"It's gone!" Ashley cried. "I can't conjure anything. I've lost it."

"Your magic will be back in a couple of days," Christine assured her.

Ashley wiped her tears. "You don't know that. This is the third time I've lost my magic this summer. It's getting worse."

My stomach twisted as I continued walking toward the school. I reached the front doors and caught sight of a guy fumbling with various textbooks that came out of nowhere. They appeared in his arms one after the other, piling into a teetering stack. He struggled to balance it.

"Whoa!" he cried as the stack fell and crashed to the sidewalk.

A guy who looked identical to him scoffed. "Stop being so dramatic, Alex."

"I'm not being *dramatic*, Shane," Alex shot back at his twin. "I can't control my conjuring!"

More items began to spill out of Alex's stash and into his arms—clothes, notebooks, and coins. They clinkered to the ground, sounding like a slot machine.

I eyed the brothers curiously. Shane caught me staring, and he nudged his brother. The two gazed at me, and I heard Shane whisper lowly, "That's her."

"*She's* the new priestess?" Alex gaped.

Oh, great. Here we go.

Shane shoved his twin, and the two scrambled away before I could say anything. I wasn't even sure what I'd say. *Yeah, bitches. I'm the latest priestess. If you've got a problem with it, bring it up with the Imperium Council, because it wasn't my idea.*

Shane and Alex weren't the only ones who noticed me. The whispers seemed to follow as I entered the school. I resolved to ignore them. I was sure people had been talking about me all summer. My secret was already out there, and nothing I could say would change that.

Instead, I remained on high alert for signs of other magical issues. I had to pay attention, because it was up to me and the Imperium to stop this.

The Main Foyer was crowded, but most people seemed to perform magic just fine. As usual, a group of Alchemists huddled around the fireplace and brewed a potion. One of the group members stood over the cauldron and funneled sky-blue magic into it. On the other side of the foyer, a group of Mortana girls used their magic to tweak their makeup until they were all sporting dark eyelashes and red lips. Two Seers passed by me, and I heard one of them telling the other about a vision she'd just had. Apparently, she was going to miss her first class due to oversleeping. A Mentalist avoided the crowd near the grand staircase and levitated himself over the balcony with telekinetic powers.

Nearby, I spotted Onyx, my previous Alchemy lab partner, conjure a leash for her cat and clip it to his collar so he wouldn't get lost. It was a black long-hair with a white patch of fur on its forehead. She must've gotten a cat over summer break, because I'd never seen her with one before.

Though most people still had a firm grasp on their magic, others weren't so lucky. I heard one girl tell her friend she couldn't conjure her schedule and didn't know what classes she had. A Seer complained that the ghost she'd been talking to all summer break had vanished that morning and she was worried about him.

My stomach sank. I'd been called to become a priestess, which meant I had to stop this. I didn't know how yet.

I climbed the stairs and dropped my bag off in my room. I saw that Talia's piano was already set up, and a collection of candles and crystals had been laid out atop her dresser. I pulled my phone from my pocket and sent her a message.

Meet you downstairs, she messaged back.

I brimmed with excitement to see my best friend again, and I cocked my head at Isa. "Come on, girl."

Isa scurried out of the room behind me and down the hall. I noticed several students shooting glances at me in the hallways. It seemed like everywhere I walked, people kept at least ten feet away. I made my way downstairs and glanced around the Main Foyer until my eyes landed on Talia.

"Nadine!" she called in a bright voice. She wore her hair in a high ponytail and had on a cute pink top. Her cat, Gus, practically skipped next to her. A girl with matching eyes walked beside her, but the facial structure was where the similarities ended. While Talia was all about pink and glitter, the girl beside her dressed in a tight black clothing and fish-net stockings. She had a rebellious look about her.

"Hey, Tal!" I cried as I gave her a hug. She squeezed me tightly. We'd seen each other over the summer, but it'd been a few weeks, since Talia had been busy making music with her brother's band. Isa and Gus looked thrilled to see each other and started licking each other's fur.

Talia drew away. "How are you? How's your magic? I hear tons of people are having problems today."

I could tell Talia was asking about more than just my magic. She made it a point to check on me all the time, to see if I needed help getting through the day. I really appreciated it. "I'm all right," I told her honestly. I turned to the girl beside her. "Hi, I'm Nadine."

The girl smiled brightly. "I'm Tate, Talia's younger sister. I've heard so much about you."

"Tal talks about me?" I teased. "Only good things, I hope."

"Absolutely," Tate said.

I'd met Talia's brother Tyler before, but I'd never met Tate. This was her first year at Miriam College of Witchcraft.

"As fate would have it, Tate's our next-door neighbor," Talia said. "We moved her in this morning, and we were just on our way to the lawn to play some games. There's a whole welcome-back thing going on. Want to join us?"

"Sure." It was great to finally get out of Grammy's house.

Tate started rambling as we headed outside, but it couldn't drown out the whispers.

"She's a Curse Breaker," someone hissed.

"More like a *Curse Maker*," another replied.

I looked around for the source of the voices, but there were so many students, parents, and professors around that I couldn't tell who said it.

"I love my dorm room," Tate raved. "It's so big. I can't believe I get so much space all to myself."

"Um… you have a roommate," Talia chuckled.

We stepped out into the sunlight. Gus and Isa wove between our legs as they chased each other around.

"It can't be any worse than sharing a room with *you* growing up," Tate teased.

"I was a delight!" Talia shot back. Tate frowned and glanced at me for confirmation.

"She really is," I said, looping my arm through Talia's. "She's mine now, and you can't have her back."

"Just on weekends," Tate offered with a wink.

Talia placed a hand on her heart. "Aw, my sister wants joint custody."

Tate laughed. "Well, you're still my big sister. I'm going to need a shoulder to cry on every now and then."

Talia rolled her eyes and turned to me. "Tate has vowed to break as many hearts as possible during her four years here."

"I did *not* say that," she defended. "I only said I *might* sleep with a couple guys and girls." For my benefit, Tate added, "I'm pansexual, if Talia didn't mention."

"She didn't, but that's cool," I said with a shrug.

A high-pitched voice came from behind us. "Nadine! Talia!"

The three of us stopped and turned to see Mandy and Amy waving at us. Mandy's long black braid swayed over her shoulder, and she wore her usual skater dress, which swirled around her knees as she walked. Amy wore a green tank top with tight jeans. Her cat, Stormy, followed beside her. She gave a cheerful smile as they approached.

"We've been looking for you guys!" Mandy said brightly. "We checked out your room, but you weren't there. Amy and I are just a few doors down."

"You're roomies this year?" I asked.

"Absolutely," Amy said. "I couldn't stand another semester with my last roommate. She was a homophobic bitch."

Tate scrunched up her nose, but her eyes roamed over Amy's slim figure. "Homophobes are the *worst*!"

Talia placed a hand on her hip and glared at her sister. I'd lived with

Talia long enough to read that look. *If you're going to be breaking hearts all semester, don't go anywhere near my friend.*

Tate read the look too, and she dropped her shoulders.

"We missed you guys!" Mandy threw her arms around me.

I squeezed her back tightly. "I know. It was a long summer. It feels like we haven't talked in ages."

Mandy sighed as she drew away. "My summer abroad in India was great, though. I earned six credits for my counseling major and learned *so* much about my Indian heritage."

I pulled Amy into an embrace. "How was your summer internship?"

"It went better than expected," Amy said. "I had a wonderful time studying supernatural history."

"Where'd you intern at?" Tate asked.

"I actually got to travel to a couple of different places," she replied. "I mostly stayed near the Grand Canyon and learned a bit of hypnotherapy with a small group of hypnotists there, but I also visited a pod of Atlanteans based in Hawaii, and I spent a few weeks in Canada with a really nice vampire couple."

Tate's eyebrows shot up. "Vampires? Now that's a kink I could get used to."

Talia rolled her eyes. "Goddess. Someone please remind me the dorm walls are soundproof. They are, right?"

Tate nudged her sister. "I'll make sure to scream just so you can hear it."

Talia turned up her nose. "Please don't."

"Sexual jokes aside…" Mandy raised an eyebrow at me. "Why didn't you *tell* us you were a Curse Breaker?"

"Yeah, we would've kept it a secret," Amy agreed, sounding a bit hurt.

My shoulders fell. "I didn't tell *anyone*—only the people who were at my ceremony and saw the mark. I *did* want to tell you, but the fewer people who knew, the better."

Amy frowned. "I'm sorry you felt you had to keep it from us."

"From *anyone*," Mandy added. "I think it's awesome you're a Curse Breaker."

Amy's eyes lit up. "Can we see the mark?"

My heart warmed to see my friends so enthusiastic about my Cast. It made me feel as if they'd already forgiven me for keeping it from them.

"Sure." I glanced around the property, but the closest people were way off by the parking lot. I lifted the hem of my shirt and showed them the crescent moon tattoo on my hip.

Mandy's eyes widened. "Ooh, that's hot!"

"Can I?" Amy gestured to my arm, and I nodded. She ran a finger over the cauldron tattoo on it, as if trying to find evidence it was fake. "So this…?"

"It's just an ordinary tattoo," I explained. "I went to a tattoo parlor after my Evoking Ceremony."

"Damn, you are badass, girl," Mandy said approvingly. "You fooled everyone."

I frowned. "Well, for a while at least."

Talia seemed to notice my unease, because she quickly stepped in. "We were headed to play games. You in?"

Mandy shrugged. "I'm up for it."

"Me, too," Amy added.

Outside, several canopies had been set up in the lawn, where we could grab snacks and drinks. Several games were in action throughout various portions of the school's property, including a match of flag football, soccer, and ultimate Frisbee. People shot stunning spells across the field at opposing team members.

"What are you guys up for?" Mandy asked. "Amy has a hidden talent for flag football."

"Yeah, if I don't want to be crushed beneath three hundred pounds of muscle!" Amy objected. She pointed to the guys on the field. I noticed Ryan and several of the other Treacherous Tarantulas running around.

"I'm not going anywhere near *that*," I agreed. "What about soccer?"

Mandy laughed. "The most talent I have with my feet is walking in heels. I can't kick a ball to save my life."

"Ultimate Frisbee, it is," Tate chuckled.

I was all for it, though I knew I wouldn't be able to get around the field like my friends. But when I turned to the game of Frisbee, my stomach sank, yet my heart lifted at the same time. I suddenly felt hot all over.

Lucas.

I'd tried to think about Lucas as little as possible over the summer, but I was unsuccessful. The truth was, I hadn't stopped thinking about him since we broke up. Seeing him again made all these feelings I thought I'd gotten over come rushing to the surface. I became a statue as I drank him in.

Lucas had gone shirtless for the game, and damn it, I'd forgotten how fucking hot he was. The sunlight glinted off his muscled chest, and my mouth went dry. His hair was longer than I'd ever seen it, and it fell into his gorgeous green eyes.

The Frisbee flew toward one of the players on the opposite team, but Lucas jumped from out of nowhere and caught it mid-flight. He tossed it to Grant halfway across the field, and it flew in a perfect arc over to him. Grant was nowhere near any of the opposing team members, and he caught it with ease.

Amy nudged me and pointed to the edge of her lip. "You've got a little drool there."

I snapped my mouth shut and nudged her back. "I do not. I think I'm going to sit this out."

"Because of Lucas?" Mandy asked kindly.

I shook my head. "The sun's too strong today."

It wasn't a lie. Sometimes, the sun made my skin tingle and feel like it was on fire. But the truth was, I was *absolutely* avoiding the game because of my ex-boyfriend. Goddess, I just wanted to run across the field and jump into his arms.

I yearned for him, but I was still pissed—mostly at myself, for letting him go. But there were reasons for that, reasons I didn't think we could ever resolve.

You're not the Nad I fell in love with, he'd said the night we broke up. The words still haunted me, slicing like a knife through my chest. I thought Lucas knew me better than anyone, but he only saw the good in me. He hadn't accepted all parts of me, and it was unfair of me to ask him to. Even after I broke my family curse, he couldn't understand why I killed those witches at Pinewood Manor.

I'd done it to save my friends. I wouldn't change a thing I did, but I worried that Lucas was right. I acted impulsively. I'd gotten away with *murder*.

I didn't blame him for being terrified of me. Hell, sometimes I scared myself.

I couldn't ask him to be with me after everything I did—and every-thing I'd said. I'd been a bitch. If I could take it all back, I would. But the damage was already done. We broke each other's hearts, and there was nothing we could do to change that.

How could we repair what was already broken?

"I'll sit out with Nadine," Talia offered, pulling me from my thoughts.

"You don't have to—" I started to say, but Talia wouldn't let me finish.

"It's fine," she insisted. "I don't want to play anyway."

Talia and I went to sit under the shade of a tree while Amy, Mandy, and Tate went off to join the game. Isa, Gus, and Stormy batted at butterflies in the grass. I couldn't keep my eyes off Lucas as he raced across the field. The air moved through his tousled brown locks, and my eyes locked on the perfect curve of his ass. He seemed so carefree. Perhaps we *were* better off apart.

Grant spotted Talia, and he jogged over to the sidelines. He grabbed a water bottle, then plopped into the grass beside us. "Hey," he said brightly. He breathed heavily and took a swig of water. "Great to see you guys."

"You, too," Talia replied with a smile. I was pretty sure she was blushing.

I liked Grant, but he spent a lot of time with Lucas, so I hadn't seen him all summer. "How was your summer?" I asked.

"It was pretty good. Got better once my arm healed." He rolled his shoulder. He'd broken his arm fighting the horrible witches last semester. "I'm back to swimming, but I've gotta build up my strength again. And you ladies?"

"It was okay," I said vaguely. "Talia spent a week out in L.A."

Grant turned to her. "Yeah, I heard. You and the Wicked Warlocks rented a recording studio?"

"Just for the day," she said. "They recorded three of my original songs. They sound amazing. Want to hear?"

Talia conjured her phone with earbuds and handed them to Grant. He bobbed his head to the beat of the first song. "That's *really* good, Tal," he said. "The lyrics are... wow."

He wasn't just saying it to be nice. Talia *was* a really talented songwriter.

"So, uh..." I didn't know how to approach the topic, but I had to know. "How has Lucas been?"

Grant's shoulders fell, and he gazed onto the field, where Lucas ran for the Frisbee. "I'm not going to lie to you. It's been rough."

My stomach sank. "He looks like he's doing well, though."

Grant scoffed, like there was so much more to tell than he could really say. "He's gotten good at hiding it, but I know him too well. He's hurting."

I was imagining the worst. Grant must've noticed my fallen face, because he was quick to clarify. "He hasn't done anything bad."

Grant was talking about self-harm. It was a relief to know Lucas hadn't hurt himself, but I worried about him. I'd blame myself if something happened.

"We don't talk like we used to—not about things that matter, anyway," Grant admitted. "At least he's doing *something* about the whole nightshade thing."

"Nightshade?" I felt the blood drain from my face. "He's taking drugs?"

"Goddess, no!" Grant said quickly. "He's investigating for an article, trying to uncover who's behind the whole thing."

My guts twisted. "That's good that he's still writing, but doesn't he realize how dangerous that is?"

Grant frowned. "He won't take no for an answer."

Lucas was treading in dangerous territory, and I worried he was going to get hurt. I felt solely responsible, and it tore me up inside.

"Well, I'm gonna get back in there," Grant said as he stood. "See you girls around."

He handed Talia her phone back, then raced onto the field. My eyes locked on Lucas.

Talia must've noticed me staring. "Do you think you want him back?"

I bit my lower lip. "I thought I was getting over him. It was easier when we didn't see each other all summer, but seeing him now…"

His eyes caught mine for a brief second, then moved over me—like I was nothing more than a distant memory to him. I tore my gaze away from the field.

"I don't think I'm over him like I thought," I admitted.

"Would you take him back if he asked?" she asked curiously.

I snapped off a blade of grass and stared down at it. "I used to think maybe I would, but I don't think I regret breaking up." I took a long breath, then continued. "I realize I was scared when I broke up with him, and that I'd been a total bitch about it. I know I handled it poorly and said things I shouldn't have. It hurts that we broke up, and I've always loved him, but I don't think we can be together."

"Why not?" she asked softly. "If you still love him."

I sighed. "It's not that simple. I treated him poorly, and it's unfair of me to be with him if I'm a terrible girlfriend."

"You're not a terrible girlfriend," Talia argued.

I frowned. "You didn't hear the stuff I said to him. I blamed him for spilling my secret about being a Curse Breaker. The Imperium Council never would've found out otherwise. But I know he didn't do it intentionally, and it's unfair of me to blame him. I've had to make tough choices, and I can't keep hurting him with those types of decisions. Plus, I can't serve on the Imperium Council if I'm worried what he's going to think of me. That's not fair to him or the coven."

I sighed. "Besides, I can't sit around and watch someone I love continue to sink into a hole. He *said* he was doing better last semester, but I think he was using our relationship as a crutch to avoid his depression. Being with him was worse for him in the long run, because using me to keep himself upright could only last so long. Being together was a distraction for him rather than a solution."

"You don't want to be with him because he's depressed?" Talia asked, trying to understand.

"It's not that. I'm okay with being with someone who's depressed, but I need to know he'd be okay even if I wasn't around. And I truly think he'll be better off without me. I can't watch him fall back into his depression. It's too painful."

Ultimately, all I wanted was for Lucas to be happy.

I tried to steer the conversation away from myself. "How are you feeling being back?"

Talia took a deep breath of fresh air. "I feel great."

"Because Cody graduated?" I asked carefully.

She was slow to answer, but she nodded. "I didn't realize how much he held me back. I'm still trying to get over what happened between us, but I've vowed to make this year better than last."

I wiggled my eyebrows. "Do I detect a date with Grant in the future?"

Talia shrugged. "I've been trying not to rush into anything after Cody. I feel like I need to be single for a while and find myself, you know? I got so obsessed with Cody, and I just don't want to let anyone control me again."

"Grant's nothing like Cody."

"I know," she said quickly. "It's not that I think *he'd* control me. Just that I need to learn about myself first. I could never speak up with Cody, and I don't want to be like that with anyone else."

"I understand."

"I don't even know if I like Grant," Talia said, but I was almost certain she was lying. She quickly added, "I don't want to rush anything."

I smirked and threw my blade of grass at her. "Rush, my ass." The two had known each other for a year.

"Hey!" she objected, tossing a blade of grass back at me. "I'm sure Lucas would like to *rush your ass.*"

I frowned, but I got hot all over at the same time. "I don't want to make things worse than they already are. I think it's best if we just both move on."

"Maybe it will help to have something to distract you," she suggested. "There are tons of clubs on campus. Maybe you could pick up a hobby this semester."

"Like what?" I asked. "I've never been good with *hobbies.* Sports and stuff like that aren't my thing. That's probably why I watch so many mystery shows."

Talia frowned. "It doesn't have to be sports. You're really good at a lot of things."

I furrowed my brow at her. "Good at what?"

"At puzzles," she started.

"Tal, there's not a club for *puzzles,*" I pointed out.

"I wasn't finished," she insisted. "You could join the music club with me, or the debate club, art club, LGBTQ alliance, Community Service Club—"

"The Community Service Club sounds fun," I stopped her, but I quickly frowned. "But I don't know if I can keep up. I'd tried joining a Community Service Club at my high school, but I couldn't walk for miles picking up trash."

"They do *way* more than that," Talia told me. "They made blankets for foster kids last year, and they visit the nursing home a lot. Oh, and they're always helping out at the pet shelter."

I thought about how nice it'd be to surround myself with cats all day. "I'll have to check it out."

Talia and I spent the next half hour talking about our upcoming classes. She must've noticed I couldn't stop eyeing Lucas, because she finally said, "Do you want to get out of here? We could grab something to eat in the Lounge?"

"Yes," I answered, almost too quickly.

Talia and I called our cats over, and we went inside. In the Lounge, we ordered two Peppy Parfaits, which were new to the menu. They were supposed to put you in a good mood. As the barista handed mine over, I turned around and ran into a solid wall of muscle.

I stumbled back a step and tilted my head up at the guy. He was at least a head taller than me, and his black slicked-back hair grayed at his temples. He was old enough to be my father. He frowned down at me as recognition crossed his features. Something in his dark eyes shook me, and I had the sudden urge to run far away.

"Sorry," I muttered.

I went to step around him, but he stopped me, his gaze roaming over me curiously. "Nadine Evers."

My mouth went dry, but I didn't let my unease show on my face. I tilted my chin up at him. "What's it to you?"

He ignored my question. "You're the Curse Breaker they've called onto the council. My daughter told me *all* about you."

I didn't know whose father this was, but by the way he looked at me, I suspected he hadn't heard anything good. Talia stepped closer to me, until we were almost touching, like she was ready to defend me if needed.

"And who might your daughter be?" I asked.

He laughed in a way that made my skin crawl. "You *must* know who I am."

"Can't say that I do," I stated dryly. I felt a little unsettled by this cocky old man, but I didn't let it show.

"Magnus Knight," he introduced, holding out a hand. "Surely you've heard the name."

I'd never heard of him before, but the last name was unmistakable. He was *Gwen's* father. That girl had made my Alchemy 101 class miserable. I glanced down to his hand and noticed a cauldron tattooed on the back of it, marking him an Alchemist like his daughter.

He noticed my hesitation and sneered, "Surely Faith didn't raise her daughter to be so rude."

My nostrils flared at the mention of my mother. "No, she didn't," I said through gritted teeth. "But she also told me never to talk to strangers."

Magnus dropped his hand and huffed. I'd obviously offended him, which I suspected was the *last* move I should have made with a man like him. Power and pride seemed to radiate off him in waves. "I'd hardly call a member of your own coven a stranger," he said bitterly. "Though for an outsider, I suppose that's the truth."

I swallowed the lump in my throat and tried to keep an even tone. "What is it that you want from me?"

He certainly wanted *something*, because he wouldn't still be standing here if he didn't. He leaned in closer, and I spotted the threat in his eyes. "I want you to leave my daughter alone."

Before I could reply, Talia shot back at him, "Nadine never touched Gwen! It was Gwen who—"

"Is that any way to talk to your father's employer, Miss Murphy?" Magnus snapped.

Talia's cheeks went bright red, and she dropped her head. Holy hell, this guy was frightening.

He turned back to me and growled, "Just because the priestesses want you on the Imperium Council doesn't mean the rest of the coven does. It's unfortunate that an outsider like you would be allowed such a high position in the first place. They only want you so you can break this curse."

"It's not a curse," I stated. At least, the council didn't seem to think so.

"Don't be so naive," Magnus snapped. "The Elementai in California suffered a plague a year ago. Someone in the coven handed them the Omnimotus Curse. It tampered with their magic—just as we're experiencing now. This is the Elementai getting back at us. It's all just a political show."

I cocked a challenging eyebrow at him. "If it *is* a curse as you say, then perhaps you shouldn't threaten the single Curse Breaker who could save you from it."

Magnus's features faltered. He could try to intimidate me all he wanted, but I had him there. As long as I was in line to become a priestess, he couldn't touch me.

His eyes darkened. "That may be the case—until they find the *real* culprit behind this."

There was something in his tone that sounded accusatory.

"What do you mean by that?" I demanded.

"Witches have left the coven before," he reminded me, clearly talking about my mother. "Perhaps someone has returned to finish something for them—revenge on the coven, if you will."

"That's not true!" I snapped. For a second, I'd forgotten how much he frightened me.

Magnus stood straighter and chuckled. He seemed amused that he got a reaction out of me. "No matter the cause, I will not stand to see my daughter get hurt. So help *anyone* who gets near my family."

"Daddy!" Gwen whined from across the Lounge, capturing his attention. He looked up to see her waving him over. "I need help with my bags."

I noticed Chloe beside Gwen. When my eyes caught hers, I witnessed a softness in them I hadn't seen before. Chloe had always been so cold and threatening toward me, but after we'd resolved our feud and broke our curse last semester, she seemed warm and welcoming. She waved to me, and I shot a smile back—but it was only half-hearted, because I was still shook by what Magnus had said.

Talia's eyebrows shot up once Magnus departed. "That was intense."

"No kidding. I've got goosebumps." I held up my arm to prove it. "What an asshole."

Talia rolled her eyes. "Believe me, he gets worse."

"Worse how?" I bit my lip.

"My dad works for him, and he's horrible."

"Really? What does your dad do?" I asked.

"He's in retail. Mister Knight owns practically half the town. Remember that alchemy shop on the Catwalk we took you to last semester?"

"Wicked Alchemy? Yeah, I remember."

"Mister Knight owns it," Talia told me. "Along with at least a dozen other businesses."

I winced. "No wonder he's so threatened by me."

She cocked an eyebrow. "A teen girl in a position of power? Yeah, that would *really* mess with his ego."

I sighed. "This is why I intended to keep my true Cast a secret. My first day back and I'm already being threatened because I'm a Curse Breaker."

Talia looped her arm through my elbow and began leading me to an empty table. "*No one* threatens my bestie and gets away with it. He can't touch you."

I shot her a smile. "Thanks, but if Magnus Knight really wanted to hurt me, he wouldn't need magic. He could crush my head between his hands."

Talia chuckled. "He'd have to get his hands on you first."

Problem was, Magnus wasn't the only person who wanted to get their hands on me. The Imperium already had me searching for the Oaken Wands. There was no telling what—or who—I might face to restore the coven's magic.

THREE

When I spotted Nadine across the lawn, my heart fucking stopped. For one split second, it was as if the world had stopped turning. Truth be told, my world had stopped turning three months ago when she'd called things off between us. *She* had been my world, and it'd been shattered to bits. Seeing her now was a painful reminder of that. If I thought I'd made any progress in getting over her, I was kidding myself.

I didn't let my steps falter as I ran across the field. She looked so radiant and happy surrounded by her friends. A lock of brown hair drifted in the breeze, and though I was thirty yards away from her, all I wanted was to reach out and caress it.

My heart crumbled into a million pieces all over again. That evening on the Catwalk, the night we broke up, came back to me. Every word, every memory replayed in my mind.

I regretted bringing up the Reaper's Shadow curse. I'd told her we couldn't be together, because I couldn't stand people dying for me. I couldn't stand *her* dying for me if the curse claimed her. I knew now that I was only pushing her away because I was scared. I couldn't handle seeing her in danger.

And it had broken us. Maybe if I never said anything, we'd still be together.

Goddess, I missed her so much, and she had obviously moved on.

Sweat dripped down my forehead by the time the game finished. Grant and I headed off the field, and I grabbed my t-shirt from where it lay in the grass. I wiped the fabric across my forehead and took a swig from my water bottle. My gaze roamed the lawn, but I'd lost sight of Nadine.

"She went inside with Talia," Grant stated, snapping my attention to him.

"Huh?" I asked.

He pulled his t-shirt over his head. "I saw that look. Nadine went inside."

"Oh," I replied flatly. "I—uh—wasn't looking for her."

"Sure you weren't," Grant said skeptically.

Tate ran up to us, waving the Frisbee. "You guys up for another round, or are you too scared to be beaten by girls again?"

Mandy and Amy snickered, along with a few other girls who'd played on their team.

Grant frowned. "We'd have won if my star player here hadn't been so *distracted.*"

"I wasn't distracted," I shot back.

Tate's eyebrows shot up, and she teased, "Oh, so we won by pure skill?"

"Wait, no," I said quickly.

"Your loss." Tate shrugged and tossed the Frisbee at Mandy, who threw her hands up to block it instead of trying to catch it. Tate went running onto the field, leaving Grant and me alone on the sidelines.

"Who is that?" Grant asked as he watched her run.

"Don't ogle her too hard," I joked. "That's Talia's sister."

Grant threw his sweaty shirt at me. "I wasn't *ogling* her. Shut up."

"Who are we ogling?" a male voice asked.

I turned to see a guy our age standing there with a calico cat at his heels. He looked a lot like Grant, with the same dark eyes and Latin American features, but his hair was longer and his smile cockier. I barely recognized him at first. He'd grown up a lot.

My eyebrows shot up. "Miles?"

It was Grant's younger brother. They were two years apart in age, but Miles had easily surpassed Grant in size. He'd always been such a string bean as a kid. Before their parents split and they moved away from Octavia Falls with their mom, I'd spent almost as much time with Miles as I had with Grant. Grant had returned to attend college, and now Miles had come back for classes, too.

Miles beamed back at me. "Hey, Lucas. It's been a while."

"At least a decade!" I reached out my hand, and he grabbed it and pulled me into a one-armed hug. His cat must've decided I was friendly, because she nudged her head into my leg and started purring. "How the hell are you, man?"

"Better than this old crank," he cracked as he nudged Grant.

Grant jabbed Miles in the gut, and the two started to wrestle like they did when we were kids. "Who are you calling an *old crank?*" Grant quipped. He locked his younger brother into a headlock, and Miles surrendered.

I laughed as Miles straightened his shirt. "Just like old times," I said. "I can't believe you're a freshman already!"

Miles smiled. "I'm thrilled to be back. Been dreaming of this day my whole life. How've you been?"

The sadness was evident in his eyes. He knew what had happened to my brother, but obviously didn't want to bring it up. Miles hadn't been back to Octavia Falls in years, so he never had a chance to talk to me about it.

"It's okay," I said, but my throat closed around my words. "You can talk about him."

Miles frowned. "I always thought he'd be here when I got back, you know? I miss him."

Grant clapped Miles on the shoulder. "We all do, bud."

I got it. Eric had been *my* biological brother, but he'd been like a big brother to all of us.

"Hey," Miles said brightly to distract us. "Grant told me you followed through on that bet."

I laughed as the memory came back to me. "You mean when I bet Grant that toad was actually a person who drank a transfiguration potion, and I epically lost? Absolutely. I went through with my Evoking Ceremony in the abandoned mausoleum."

Miles laughed. "Grant kept that toad in his room for six months!"

Grant narrowed his eyes. "*That toad* had a name."

"I know, I know," Miles chuckled. "Toad-o."

"Toto," Grant corrected.

Miles shook his head. "It was Toad-o."

Grant changed the subject. "You said you wanted a grand tour of campus before classes. You up for it now?"

Miles shrugged. "Sure. What's the best place to see on campus?"

I pulled my t-shirt on. "Depends on what you like, but you'll probably enjoy the Lounge best. It's got a café, TVs, pool, bowling lanes, and arcade games."

Miles's eyes lit up as we started inside. "Oh, hell yeah. I'm a champ at Skee-Ball."

Grant frowned. "I hate to admit it, but he really is."

"There's also the greenhouses if you're into botany, and the pool if you want to swim," I listed off.

"Grant got all the family swimming genes. Selfish jerk," Miles joked.

"Ah, well, if you get too jealous of him, you can toss him into the Vanishing Stairwell," I teased.

"Ha ha," Grant said dryly. "If I know my brother well, he'll be spending most of his time in the Penthouse Suite."

"What's the Penthouse Suite?" Miles asked curiously.

"It's a myth," I stated bluntly.

Grant wasn't so convinced. "Legend has it, a red door will appear when you want… *some privacy*. No one else can enter as long as someone's already inside. And it always appears in a different spot, so no one ever knows for sure where to find it."

Miles smirked. "So it's the perfect place to hook up. I'm guessing neither of you have had the pleasure of taking a girl there."

"Because it's a myth," I insisted. "It's not like we haven't had the chance."

Grant cocked an eyebrow at me. "Have you?"

I frowned. Nadine and I had never had sex. "Shut up and show your brother to the Cat-fé."

"What's that?" Miles asked.

"It's the new cat café on campus. Kiki will love it," Grant explained as he gestured to Miles's cat.

"Then by all means, show the way," Miles said.

We started around the side of the school. The Cat-fé was on the other side of the building, and with the space-bending spell that made the school bigger on the inside, it was faster to cut around the outside of the mansion.

"What classes are you guys taking this semester?" Miles asked.

Grant started rambling about his Advanced Magical Plants class on our way. "I have to take care of a black pothos plant for my final project. They need constant watering and are really hard to keep alive. They're magical plants that bleed black liquid. It sounds creepy, but it's actually really useful. They make great anti-allergy potions."

He was describing all the plants he'd learned about last semester when we arrived at the Cat-fé. We stepped inside, and Miles's cat, Kiki, pranced ahead of us in delight. Her eyes darted every way, like she couldn't decide which part of the café to run to first.

The café was small, with about a dozen tables for patrons and a counter to order tea and snacks in the back. The walls were painted a midnight blue, and tiny twinkling lights had been set into the ceiling and made to look like stars. In the center of the room was a huge cat tower that reached a wooden beam at the ceiling. The beam stretched from one end of the café to the other, and cats prowled along it and climbed down connecting cat towers along the walls. There must've been over two dozen cats lazing along the cat towers or roaming the room, waiting for patrons to pet them.

Various stations were set up—a toy station with strings, feathers, and balls for the cats; a treat station with all flavors of cat treats imaginable; and a grooming station with brushes, nail clippers, and more. All the decorations, including the hooks for jackets at the entrance, were in the shape of cats. I'd never seen anything quite like it.

Miles rushed over to the treat section first. "Kiki," he called in a high-pitched voice. She tore her gaze from the cat tree she'd been eyeing and pounced over to him. "Want a treat? It's salmon flavored! There you go. Such a good girl."

He stroked the top of her head, and she purred as she crunched down the treat. The second she swallowed it, her eyes went wide. The treats had obviously been made by Alchemists, because the magic took effect immediately. Her feet rose from the ground, and she floated into the air like she was as light as a balloon. Grant laughed and poked her in the side. She meowed loudly as she spun through the air in slow motion.

Miles couldn't keep it together as the magic faded and she landed back on her feet. He bust a gut laughing as she stumbled and her eyes darted around, obviously dizzy. He fed her another one, and her calico fur changed color, fading into blues and purples, before returning to normal.

"What about me?" Grant teased. "I want a treat."

Miles grabbed another salmon-flavored treat from one of the containers and waved it at him. "You gotta do a trick first."

Grant smirked. "I've got a magic trick for you. Hold on. What's this?"

Grant dug into his pocket, then pulled his hand out with the middle finger raised. Miles burst into laughter, startling one of the sleeping cats on the cat tower nearby.

Kiki was already on her third treat, which must've created some sort of illusion, because she was batting at something we couldn't see.

"I meant I want to order something," Grant said. "The croissants here are supposed to be better than the ones downtown."

"Let's grab a table while we look over the menu," I suggested. The café was already a bit crowded, and there weren't many tables left. We claimed one, and Grant conjured his insulin to get to work checking his blood sugar levels.

Kiki meowed up at Miles. "Go on, girl," he encouraged. "Go play."

Kiki took off running toward a group of cats, and they started tackling each other. Kiki held down a tabby, until it surrendered. She jumped off of it, and they went right back to playing.

I laughed while I watched her. "Your cat is tougher than she looks."

"Yeah, she can be a bit of a handful," Miles admitted. "She's really friendly, though."

I glanced around at all the cats. I spotted a munchkin cat with short legs, and a gray tabby that must've been nearly twenty pounds.

"You don't have a cat?" Miles asked me, noticing me glancing around at the others.

"No, not yet," I told him.

Cats were extremely common pets in the coven, but not everyone had them. In the coven, cats were very respected, as they were considered the reincarnation of our loved ones and were here to guide us. You didn't just go to a pet shop and pick out any cat. Your cat found you whenever you were ready.

I wasn't ready, apparently. I'd never admit I was bitter about it, though.

Miles must've noticed something in my tone, because he quickly changed the subject. "So, I heard you're studying to become an investigative journalist."

I laughed lightly. "Yeah. Who would've thought?"

Miles leaned forward. "Grant tells me you're investigating something right now, but he won't spill the details."

"You know I said it's not my story to tell," Grant protested.

I trusted Miles, so I lowered my voice and said, "We're *trying* to investigate nightshade, but we've gotten nowhere all summer. We got our hands on two vials. Grant's going to try reverse-engineering the formula."

Miles's eyebrows shot up, and he looked at his brother in shock. "You can do that?"

Grant gave a half-hearted smile. "I'm going to try. It's advanced alchemy, especially with a drug like this. But we figure if we can break down the formula, we might be able to narrow down where they're getting the ingredients, and figure out who's brewing it."

"Clever," Miles remarked. "Why investigate this, though? It sounds like nothing but trouble."

"I think it might be connected to the Waning," I told him.

He tilted his head. "In what way?"

"We know that nightshade boosts your powers when you're on it, and that it messes with your magic once you're off it," I explained. "That confirms the formula is powerful enough to manipulate magic. My question is, where does that magical boost *come* from?"

Miles looked thoughtful. "You think people on nightshade are siphoning magic from everyone else?"

I shrugged. "Even if it's unwitting, it could explain all of this."

"But Elves were the only magical race who could ever take someone's magic, right?" Miles pointed out. "How could anyone in the coven do that?"

"I don't know, but we need to figure it out," I said. "It would make sense why the Waning affects students more—because there are more drug users at school. It also explains why the Waning is getting stronger."

Miles's eyes lit up with understanding. "Because the drugs are spreading. There are more users."

I nodded. "That's our theory."

"Whoa," Miles breathed. "I've waited my whole life to get my magic, and *this* is what I come back to."

Grant smirked. "Perfect timing, huh."

"Perfect," Miles said with a frown. He eyed the menu one last time, then drummed his fingers on the table. "Well, I'd like to experience magic while I can. I'm ready to order whenever you are."

We approached the counter and ordered, then returned to our table. Grant ordered a Ball of Yarn—which was really a croissant baked into the shape of yarn—and a kitty cocktail. Miles ordered a Fur-tunate Frappe, which was supposed to give him luck, and I got a Purr-fect Peppermint Tea.

A cat came up to me as I was sipping my tea—a tiny kitten with black and white marbled fur. "Aren't you precious?" I said as I bent to pet it. The kitten nuzzled into my hand, and I picked it up. It licked my nose. I found I was really enjoying myself. It'd been hard to have fun lately, when all I'd felt was numb.

The kitten jumped off my lap, and I took a sip of tea. My bright mood lasted only a split second, because the bell above the door snapped my attention to the latest patrons entering the café. I froze with the teacup in my hand. My heart lifted momentarily, then immediately sank, when I caught sight of Nadine walking in.

She was accompanied by Talia and their two cats, but I only had eyes for her. The others might as well have not been there. Nadine smiled at something Talia had said. She moved through the café without noticing me, but my heart hammered as she neared my table. Her eyes locked on a group of cats playing on the other side of the room. She didn't notice me, until she bumped into my chair.

Hot tea jumped from my cup and splashed all over the front of my shirt. I jumped from my chair so fast that it knocked over. The hot liquid burned my skin, and I did the first thing I could think to do. I yanked my t-shirt off over my head, and my skin instantly began to cool.

"Dear Goddess!" Nadine cried. She glanced around frantically, then grabbed a stack of napkins on the table and turned to me, but she cut off when her eyes connected with mine. It was like she hadn't noticed she'd run into *me*.

I turned into a statue, and everyone else went quiet. The warmth of her body against mine when she'd bumped into me, even for just the briefest of moments, sent my nerves working in overdrive. Her eyes on mine made my heart come alive, as if she hadn't totally forgotten me. For the first time in months, I felt *something.* I didn't know if that was a good thing or a bad thing. Being next to her was heavenly, but at the same time felt like hell—a torturous reminder of what I'd lost.

"Lucas," Nadine said breathlessly. Suddenly, I was crumbling at the sound of my own name. I wasn't sure whether to fall to the ground at her feet, or make a run for it.

Nadine's eyes darted down to my chest, and whatever spell seemed to be forming between us broke in an instant. She took one look at my red skin and began apologizing profusely. "I'm *so* sorry!"

Nadine began dabbing the napkins across my chest to soak up the hot liquid. My skin had become red and tender, but I barely felt the pain, as every ounce of my attention was on her. The air left my lungs when she touched me, and for a second, all I could do was stand there and let her fingers graze over my skin.

But it was too much. I grabbed her wrists to stop her, and she gasped, like she too felt the electricity between us.

"Don't worry about it," I said, though I secretly *liked* that she cared.

"I didn't mean—" she started.

"Thanks, Nad." I cut her off as I took the napkins from her. I internally cringed at the nickname. I forced my tone to remain even, though the rest of my body quaked. "I hope you're enjoying your first day back."

I only said it to ease the tension between us, but it seemed to make it worse.

She gave a friendly smile. Goddess, how did she remain so calm? It was like we'd never been together in the first place… like I'd made it all up in my head. Maybe she'd never really liked me and just *tolerated me.* If that was true, that would be the worst.

"It's great." She glanced around the room, looking uneasy. "The Cat-fé is cool."

"Yeah, it's, uh…" *Fuck.* "It's neat."

Her gaze roamed over my chest. "Are you sure you're okay?"

"It's fine. I barely felt it." I barely felt *anything* these days.

"Well, um, again, I'm really sorry." Nadine waved, then hurried off toward the treats section with her cat. It was like she couldn't get away from me fast enough. She turned to Talia and whispered something, but I couldn't hear what it was. I watched her go, and though there were mere yards between us, it felt like a million miles.

"Fuck," I groaned once she and Talia were out of earshot.

"That went… well," Grant said flatly.

"There's literally nothing you can say to make this better," I told him, before gesturing to the red spots on my chest. "I need to deal with this."

I hurried out of the café. Grant must've thought better of chasing after me—or Miles had talked him out of it—because he didn't follow.

I returned to my room and slumped to my bed, trying to wrap my head around the encounter with Nadine. I'd never been so nervous in my life. What the hell was wrong with me?

Apparently, I really liked to torture myself, because I opened the top drawer of my nightstand. Inside sat various mementos I hadn't thrown out yet, though I knew I should toss them. I pulled them out of the drawer one by one. First was the ticket I'd kept from our Valentine's Day date last semester, from the time we'd had dinner on The Hearse. It'd been a magical night, one I hadn't wanted to forget even after we'd broken up.

Next, I grabbed a vial of liquid and popped the cork off. I inhaled the rose and lavender scent, and nearly broke down then and there. It was an essential oils mixture Nadine had suggested when we'd visited Wicked Alchemy.

Lavender and rose? Why these two? I'd asked her.

So that every time you smell it, you think of me, she'd said.

And it worked. Every fucking time.

Finally, I pulled a key from the drawer. The old key hung from a chain and was rumored to be enchanted with a protection spell. Nadine had given it to me the night we snuck into the swimming pool a year ago. I knew I should've given it back to her and tossed everything else away, but I just couldn't bring myself to do it. It was like if I let go, I'd forget the time we'd had together. And even though I didn't have *her* anymore, I still had these memories. I couldn't give them up.

I didn't know why I tortured myself like this. On some level, I felt guilty. I'd made a mistake giving her up to the Imperium Council, and I couldn't undo it. I was scared for her—of what they wanted from her—and it was my fault.

The door creaked open, and my heart lurched. I immediately shoved the mementos back into the drawer and slammed it, but it was too late. Grant had already seen.

His eyes darted to me. "You doing okay?"

I swallowed the lump in my throat, though my voice still came out a pitch too high. "Fine. Where's Miles?"

"He's still down at the café," Grant said.

I frowned. "You didn't have to come after me."

His shoulders fell, and he sat on the couch, facing me. "I'm worried about you."

"It's not a big deal," I stated. "I haven't seen her since we broke up. It was bound to be awkward."

"That's not what I'm worried about," Grant said softly. His gaze darted toward the drawer. "It's been three months."

My stomach twisted. "So, you've known for a while, then?"

He cocked an eyebrow. "That you keep a box of her things? Yeah. I saw you pull them out a couple of times at my dad's."

I hung my head. "I don't know what to do. Everything I touch breaks. Loving Nadine was my one chance to escape that, but I broke that, too."

I got to my feet and started pacing around the room. "It scares me how much I love her. I'd do anything. I'd walk through the Abyss to be with her again. There's nothing I want more. I feel fucking crazy."

"You're not crazy," Grant insisted.

Frustration bubbled to the surface, and I felt my face turning red. "Maybe I am. I push everyone away, like Nadine said. I've even pushed Eric away."

"What do you mean?"

"Why hasn't he come back for me?" I asked. "He could've reincarnated by now. I could have *really* used a companion these last two years. Having him here, even as a cat, would've helped."

"There are a lot of reasons he might've not come back," Grant reassured me. "Perhaps he has an important job in Alora, or maybe he's still working through his own stuff in the afterlife."

I dropped my gaze. "I guess you're right."

"Or maybe he didn't think you were ready," Grant added.

I scoffed. "Ready? I've needed help for a long time."

"But when was the last time you accepted it?"

I paused. My initial reaction was to be offended. All I ever wanted for over a year was to have Eric back. But would I have accepted his guidance?

Probably not, to be honest. I'd been trying so long to figure things out on my own, to *prove* I was strong enough to do it on my own. I didn't know who I was trying to convince, other than myself.

"I want to help you," Grant said. "But I can't if you don't let me."

Accepting help wasn't one of my strong suits. I'd been raised to believe no one was ever coming to my rescue. As kids, Eric and I had to fend for ourselves.

But maybe Grant was right. Maybe there *was* an escape from this hell I'd created for myself. If only I was willing to accept it.

"What do you suggest?" I asked.

He shot a glance at my nightstand. "First, we need to get rid of anything that reminds you of Nadine. You've *got* to stop living in the past. It's not doing you any good."

I agreed with him, but I wanted to hurl at the suggestion. "I can't."

Grant stood from the couch, and his voice turned irritated. "If you won't do it, I will. I can't sit around and watch you mope over her like this anymore!"

He started for my nightstand, but I flung myself in front of him. "Stop!" I cried as I wrestled him away.

He fought hard to get past me. "This is getting ridiculous!"

"I can't just throw them away!" I protested.

"Why not?"

"Because I can't throw *her* away!" I screamed.

Grant stopped fighting against me, and he took a step away.

I sank onto the bed. "If I throw this stuff away, it's like admitting she doesn't matter to me anymore, and she does."

His tone softened. "You know that's not what I'm suggesting. I know she matters to you, but *you* should matter to you, too. If I was the one standing in your shoes, what would you say to me?"

I tried to picture Grant where I was. I thought of what it'd be like if he and Talia got together, then broke things off—how horrible it'd be to watch him fracture and break down when he had so much life left to live. I could see the hollow look in his eyes. I imagined what would happen when he forgot to eat, or slipped up and didn't take his insulin. The heart-break could literally put him in the hospital.

The image of him in a hospital bed began to morph in my mind, until I saw myself there. It wouldn't be because of a diabetic coma, but something just as real and very serious. I'd be lying if I said harming myself hadn't crossed my mind. If I didn't get myself together, I could end up there.

"I'd tell you that it hurt to see you that way," I realized.

"Exactly," Grant said. "I gave you space over the summer to grieve, but we're back at school now. Something needs to change."

"I want to," I told him. And I truly meant it.

No matter how much it hurt.

Throwing away Nadine's things was worse than anything I could imagine. But Grant was right. I had to do it. I kept the key, because it was valuable, but I tossed everything else into a bag. It hurt to throw away the blanket we'd laid on the night we'd camped out at the abandoned mansion behind the school. I almost held on to the Ouija board we'd used to summon Old Man Keller the first time we met, but I couldn't keep looking at it. I even threw out the matus tea she'd gifted me, because even though it was useful, it was a painful reminder of what we had. I sealed the bag up tight, then walked down to the dumpsters.

This was good. It felt safe. If I regretted it in an hour, I could come back down and dig the bag out.

I realized how dangerous that was. If I truly wanted closure, I had to get rid of all this for good. The dumpster wasn't good enough. The only way to get rid of it all was to burn it.

I snuck into the trees, until I could no longer hear any noises from campus. I cleared an area of brush and conjured a lighter, then watched as my memories of Nadine faded to ash and drifted away in the wind.

I wished I could say I found the closure I'd been seeking, but I merely felt empty. Letting go of these possessions didn't get rid of the memories. Those I would keep, no matter how much I tried to forget them.

I slumped back to my dorm room. By the time I arrived, Grant had already left. I opened the door and stepped inside. Something crinkled beneath my feet, and I looked down to see an envelope that someone must've slipped under the door. I reached for it and noticed my name had been sprawled across the front in smooth handwriting. Curiously, I opened the letter.

A message from the spirits beyond, it read at the top. Below that, the handwriting changed—the letters became twisted and jagged, like someone had jotted it down quickly and without looking. As my eyes scanned the message, my blood ran cold.

By fire and noose
The coven will fall
Division and suffering
Destruction to all

Great power of the chosen
The coven be made whole
By the only witch of her kind
And a reaper bound to her soul

It read like a prophecy—a warning from a Seer.

This had to be some sort of joke. It was obviously talking about Nadine and me—the only witch of her kind and the reaper.

But Nadine and I were done. We weren't getting back together. It hurt too much to be near her.

Screw the coven. Someone was messing with me, and it was cruel.

Even if this prophecy were true, I couldn't tell Nadine about it. Breaking up had nearly killed me, and this prophecy wanted us to work together. I couldn't imagine doing that.

Grant was right. I had to move on.

The coven was just going to have to save itself.

nadine

FOUR

What a disaster. The first time I ran into Lucas post-breakup, I literally *ran into him*. He rushed out of the Cat-fé so fast, I worried that I'd burnt him really badly with the tea. I wanted to go after him, but I stopped myself. For the briefest of moments, I'd forgotten that we were no longer together.

I didn't see Lucas again until I walked into my first class of the semester—Wand Theory. My breath stalled when I saw him sitting there, next to the last available seat in the class. He scribbled something down in a notebook and didn't notice me at first.

I scanned the room for any other empty seats, but a girl quickly walked by me and claimed the last one. I noticed it was Avery, a bitch from my Thoughtography class last semester. She caught me eyeing her, then whispered something to the girl next to her.

I didn't realize who it was until she turned. *Lena*, Lucas's ex-girlfriend. She shot me a dark glare from across the room.

Isa nudged my leg with her nose, and I returned my attention to Lucas.

I can do this, I thought confidently. But damn it all, this semester wasn't going to be easy if I had to sit next to him three times a week. *We can be mature about it. We're both adults.*

Steeling my nerves, I walked across the room and slid into the seat beside him. Isa jumped into my lap and began purring. Lucas continued writing, but after a moment, his pen stilled. His gaze shot up to mine, and his features paled.

"Nadine? What are you doing in this class?" he asked, sounding shocked. I didn't know what his reaction meant. Maybe I was trying to find meaning that wasn't there.

I spoke in a low whisper. "I thought I might learn something about the Oaken Wands."

"Maybe, but I mean, Wand Theory is a Junior-Level class," Lucas pointed out.

"There aren't any classes on Curse Breaking, so I had to fill my schedule with other classes," I explained. "The school board had to approve me. At least I'm getting a bit of a head-start on my major with my Miriamic Law class. The Imperium Council wanted me to take it early, since I'm going to be a priestess..."

I trailed off when I realized I was rambling. I *tried* to talk casually to him, but it wasn't like it used to be between us, back when I could tell him anything. The tension between us was so strong, I bet the whole class could feel it.

"You'll do great in this class," he assured me. "I know it."

I chuckled lightly, but it felt stilted. "Thanks for the vote of confidence."

Our professor entered the room. He was an older man with gray hair who wore black glasses and a thick sweater. A tiny white kitten was tucked into his breast pocket, purring while she slept. He turned, and I noticed a cauldron tattoo poking up beneath the collar of his shirt.

"Welcome, students, to a new semester," he said kindly. "I'm Professor Blackbird. I hope you all had a lovely summer."

I'd never been in one of his classes, but I'd seen him around campus before. He usually sat with Professor Wykoff and Professor Daniels in the cafeteria at lunch.

"In this class, we will be studying wand theory and spellcasting," he continued. "One of your assignments will be to purchase your first wand, so that we may practice using it in this class. Though many witches and warlocks settle on a favorite wand, it is a misconception that you must only choose one. Some witches choose to use a separate wand for various tasks. One for protection magic, and another for defensive magic, for example. For some, this helps keep the energy around the wand purer to the intention of the spell. As you get better with your magic, you may come to rely on your wand only when performing complicated spells, the same way you can grow out of using incantations."

He began pacing around the room. "Though wands can help you in casting spells, they can be tricky. This is why we wait until your Junior year to teach you these concepts. In order to use a wand effectively, you must be confident in the spell you are casting—otherwise, the wand itself is ineffective."

I shifted in my chair, and my leg brushed up against Lucas's under the table. My heart leapt, and I quickly pulled away from him, so fast that my chair squeaked across the floor. Lucas cleared his throat. Crap—he'd definitely noticed. I tried to focus on the lecture, but I hardly caught what Professor Blackbird said, as all my attention was on Lucas. He was just *breathing*, for Alora's sake, and all I wanted to do was lean over and kiss him.

Damn it.

Professor Blackbird began ticking off on his fingers. "When shopping for a wand, there are several things you want to consider. The first is the wand's magical properties. Do not misinterpret this to mean that wands hold magic for spellcasting themselves. Rather, the properties of one may resonate with you more than that of another. For some of you, your magic may be more compatible with animal-based wands, such as those that contain the hair of a unicorn or the scale of a dragon. For others, solely plant-based wands will be easier to work with. You may have to test several wand compositions before you find one that directs your magic effectively."

He continued his lecture. I did my best to focus, and I took notes on how the size, shape, and color can affect the way you interact with your wand.

"You want something that feels authentic to *you*," Professor Blackbird explained. "Wands *can* be used just as effectively from one person to another, but only if you allow yourself to *feel* it. As this is your first introduction to wand usage, your first wand should be something that makes you feel safe, yet powerful."

I know a magic wand that makes me feel safe, I caught myself thinking. And yeah, it was *that* kind of magic wand—specifically, Lucas's dick.

Fuck.

I was practically on the edge of my chair, as far away from Lucas as the table would allow. Did he *feel* that energy between us? It had to be my imagination.

Professor Blackbird conjured over a dozen wands to show us examples. They were all very beautiful. Each was a different length, and they varied in color from pale wood tones to dark mahogany. Some were simple, with smooth handles, while others were intricately carved with swirls up and down the entire length. One of the wands even had rhinestones set into its base.

I immediately started picturing what I wanted my wand to look like. Something with a cat carved into the handle would be cool. But Professor Blackbird's comments gave me pause.

"I suggest you begin searching for your wand with no expectations," he said. "What you truly connect with may surprise you."

That was his last comment before he dismissed the class. I started toward the front of the room as everyone else was leaving. I needed to get as far away from Lucas as possible, because that whole hour had been uncomfortable.

Ahead of me, I heard Avery sneer, "What good is a wand going to do us if we can't use our magic? Especially with the *Curse Maker* in this class?"

I stopped dead in my tracks. Was *everyone* calling me that?

I stepped forward to give Avery a piece of my mind, but Lucas had already stepped in front of her and Lena. He didn't notice me in the sea of students.

"What did you just say?" Lucas demanded.

Lena scoffed. "Everyone knows Nadine is a Curse Breaker. It makes sense she's the one who created this curse. The Waning won't stop until she's gone."

Lucas narrowed his eyes. "In what twisted way does that make sense? You're just scared, because she's more powerful than you'll ever be."

Lena chuckled. "Don't be so dramatic, Lucas. If she's *that* powerful, I'd like to see it."

"She doesn't owe you a damn thing," he growled. "If you didn't believe she was that powerful, you wouldn't believe these stupid rumors that she started this curse. We all know it would take a damn powerful witch to cause what's happening, but it wasn't Nadine. Don't be so naive."

Lena opened her mouth to reply, but Avery nudged her and the two hurried out of the room, whispering to each other. Lucas looked up, and his eyes connected with mine. I quickly ducked my head and turned toward Professor Blackbird, as if Lucas might believe I hadn't heard everything he'd just said.

But I had. Lucas had stuck up for me, and I didn't know what to make of it. Did this mean he still liked me? He had to still *care*, or he wouldn't have said anything… right?

I was doing it again—trying to find meaning where there wasn't any. Lucas was just like that. He stood up for people.

I tried not to analyze it too much as I approached Professor Blackbird. "Professor?"

He looked up from the wands he was organizing. "Ah, yes. Miss Evers, is it? How may I help you?"

I glanced toward the door to confirm everyone else had left the room. We were alone. "I ran across some information about wands, and I was wondering if you could help."

"Sure," he said brightly. "What questions might you have?"

"Do you know anything about the Oaken Wands?" I asked. I honestly didn't know if I could trust Professor Blackbird, but I had to at least *try* to get some information from him. He was the wands professor, after all. If anyone knew anything, he would… right?

His eyes lit up in recognition, but his shoulders fell. "I'm afraid I've only heard the term in the context of lore. I don't teach about the Oaken Wands in this class, as the rumors surrounding them have been largely regarded as false."

"You don't think they exist?" I questioned.

"If they did, the Imperium Council did a fine job of hiding them," he remarked. "No one has ever seen them."

He apparently didn't know their connection with my grandfather.

"We believe in all kinds of things we've never seen before, though," I pointed out. "I mean, we have magic."

"Yes, but this is different," he said. "Many Miriamic historians believe it to be nothing more than a story to keep witches and warlocks from abusing their magic—like how parents use the story of Santa Claus to get their children to behave."

I frowned. Regardless of what Professor Blackbird believed, the Wands were real. The Imperium Council knew it, Grammy knew it, and I knew it. I wasn't going to learn anything from this old man.

"Thanks for your help," I said.

He shot me a smile, like he thought he'd actually been helpful. "Anytime."

I wasn't satisfied. I needed to know more, so I drove to Grammy's after class. I had to review everything she'd told me about the Oaken Wands if I hoped to figure out where to go next.

We sat on her porch, sipping tea. "The Oaken Wands are a legend," Grammy said.

"A legend you believe," I stated. I'd asked Grammy about the Wands months ago, but I couldn't shake the feeling that there was something I was missing. "I want to hear the story again."

Grammy stopped swinging in the porch swing and looked at me from where I sat in the patio chair. "Yes, I believe they're real. Your grandfather learned of them during the short time he served on the Imperium Council."

I leaned forward in my seat. Even Isa, who purred at my feet, perked up. "What did he learn about them?"

Grammy went back to rocking. "The Oaken Wands are a collection of five wands cut from a branch of the Protection Tree. There was one Wand created for each Cast. Their power allows them to attract the magic of their Cast, so that it can be restored if it were ever stolen. When all five Wands are united, the owners have complete control over all Miriamic magic—defensive spells, protection spells, conjuring... all of it. Like the Casts, the Oaken Wands are more powerful together."

"That's what the Imperium Council told me," I said thoughtfully. "Do you think someone could have all five Wands already? Could that be what's happening to our magic?"

She shook her head. "The Wands' effects would be sudden, if the owners chose to use them in that way. The Waning is gradual, and whoever's behind it doesn't have enough control to make it permanent... yet."

"Lucas told me that our magic comes from Alora, our afterlife," I thought aloud. "How can it be stolen?"

"It is true that our magic can be replenished," Grammy agreed. "But we're also able to harness magic within ourselves. It is no one's right to take from our own reserve. Stealing one's magic is stealing from Alora itself, and is a great offense. That magic belongs to the coven as a whole."

Grammy paused for a moment to let me absorb the information, then she continued. "But the implications get far more complicated when you consider the possibilities. If someone can steal your magic once, what's to keep them from stealing it over and over again? Think of it as someone taking the air from your lungs. Yes, our air supply is virtually limitless. There is air all around you. But you have to recover before you can take in another breath. If your air is stolen at the next breath, and the next, and the next, it doesn't matter how often you recover or how much air you breathe in. You will never have enough to support yourself."

I sipped my tea and furrowed my brow. "So even though our magic is limitless, our ability to access it can be limited, such as by someone with ill intent toward the coven?"

Grammy nodded.

I continued thoughtfully. "So when the Oaken Wands are used to draw that magic back to its rightful owner, the person literally takes back their power. They keep it from being stolen again."

"Precisely," Grammy said.

Grammy's analogy made sense. The more our breath—or magic—was stolen, the less we could support ourselves. Eventually, the coven could lose its magic altogether. That's why I'd agreed to help the council find the Wands—not for *them*, but for the coven. I couldn't live to see the coven lose their power.

"Grampy had one of the Wands, didn't he?" I asked.

Grammy dropped her gaze. "He did."

"I need to know the real story," I begged. "Chloe gave me one version, and the Imperium Council mentioned a few things, but I need to know what really happened—from someone who was there."

Grammy finished her tea and set the cup and saucer beside herself on the porch swing. "I agree. You've proven to me that there is no need to keep this from you any longer—to keep *anything* from you. Clearly, I've let my fears get the better of me, and you deserve to know everything."

She drew a deep breath. "As you know, your grandfather Nicholas was the only Curse Breaker of his time, just like you are. As such, he was the only eligible witch or warlock to serve as a Curse Breaker on the council."

"Is there a reason there's only one Curse Breaker at a time?" I asked.

"Hundreds of years ago, there were many Curse Breakers. I do not know why Mother Miriam has not chosen more in modern times." She sighed. "After your grandfather became a priest, he was let in on many of the coven's greatest secrets."

I opened my mouth to ask which secrets, but she held up an index finger.

"Before you ask, you should know that he didn't share these secrets with me," she stated quickly. "Much of it he was sworn to secrecy for the safety of the coven. However, there was one thing he became obsessed with."

"The Oaken Wands?" I asked.

Grammy nodded. "Your grandfather admitted to me that the council showed him the Wands, and that they spoke of using them to control magic. He didn't agree. He believed—as do I—that we reserve the right to our free will and therefore our magic. Nicholas believed he had been chosen as a Curse Breaker in order to protect the Wands from the power-thirsty council of our time."

Grammy drew a long breath, then continued. "Nicholas stole the Wands from the Imperium Council and intended to destroy them. He believed they were far too powerful. But he quickly learned that they could not be destroyed, and so, he decided to hide them."

I sat at the edge of my seat. "Hide them where?"

Her lips turned down. "I'm afraid he didn't share that information with anyone—not even me. However, he was unable to hide all the Wands before the Imperium found out what he'd done. Jeb Olson, the late husband of Priestess Lilian and Chloe's grandfather, went after Nicholas. He stole the Mentalist Wand from him. The two dueled—Jeb with the Mentalist Wand and Nicholas with the Curse Breaker Wand. It was the duel that killed your grandfather."

My mouth went dry. "Grampy did what was right, though," I argued. "The Imperium was going to steal magic for themselves. He was only protecting the coven, as he promised Mother Miriam he would."

Grammy frowned. "In some way, the Imperium believed they were protecting the coven, too."

"You agreed with Grampy, though, right?" I asked.

"Of course I did!" Grammy quickly assured me. "I just wish there'd been a better way for the Imperium Council to agree on how to protect the coven. If there had been... perhaps Nicholas would still be here today."

Grammy's eyes glistened, and I quickly asked another question to distract her. "So Grampy managed to hide the other three Wands before the duel—the Mortana, Seer, and Alchemy Wands?"

"I believe so," Grammy replied. "But he never told me where."

"What happened to the Mentalist and Curse Breaker Wands after the duel?"

"I took the Curse Breaker Wand and kept it hidden for many years. But it was lost from me long ago."

"Someone stole it—again?" I asked.

"Yes." Grammy quickly added, "But recall that the Wands can only be used by their own Cast. No one can use the Curse Breaker Wand but you."

It sounded like Grammy was trying to convince herself I was in no danger from the Curse Breaker Wand—as if she was racked by guilt over losing it.

"I'm going to find it," I stated confidently.

She wiped her eyes, but she couldn't hide the worry in them. "I wish I could do more to help."

"You *have* helped," I assured her. "I know where the Curse Breaker Wand was last. It gives me a starting point. Do you know anything else about the Mentalist Wand?"

Grammy shook her head. "Last I knew, the Olsons had it."

I pressed my lips together. "Priestess Lilian swears they don't. Maybe Jeb did something with it and never told her. Or maybe she's lying."

Grammy took my hands in hers. "Whatever happened to them, they must be found. The coven is losing magic, and we can't wait until it's too late. I hate that it's my family wrapped up in this again, but perhaps Nicholas was right. Perhaps he was chosen as a Curse Breaker to protect the Wands. I've always believed that Mother Miriam chose you for a reason. It must be to save the coven."

"I will save them," I promised, squeezing her hand back. "I'll do everything I can."

I really meant it. The only problem was, I still hadn't figured out what the hell I was supposed to do. Find the Wands or not, I didn't have any further clues on where they might be. It didn't matter how many spells I'd tried or how often I prayed to Mother Miriam.

I knew gods didn't interfere with things here on earth, but I hadn't received so much as a clue. It was like Mother Miriam was waiting for something—like there was something I was supposed to *learn* from all of this. But if that were the case, I felt like I'd walked into a class far beyond my skill level.

And I had no idea how to master my powers.

☾

I REPLAYED Grammy's story in my mind the following day, wondering if I missed anything. I didn't think I had. I needed more pieces of the puzzle to solve this one.

I was on my way to Headmistress Verla's office, because she'd asked to see me after class. I didn't know why, but it must've been important. Verla was a powerful witch, and very busy.

I knocked on the door, and a kind voice answered. "Come in."

I stepped inside. Isa prowled in front of me and narrowed her eyes at Odin, who lazed on his cat tower beside Verla's desk.

"You wanted to see me?" I asked.

Verla had all kinds of books, crystals, and tarot cards spread over her desk. She wore a look of concentration. She looked up and smiled at me. "Yes, come in."

She quickly swept up her belongings and placed them neatly in a drawer. She shut her books and slid them into place on the bookshelf behind her.

"Have a seat." She gestured to the chair across from her desk, and I sat.

Isa curled in my lap, but I shifted under her weight. I always felt a little uncomfortable in Verla's office, as if I'd been called to the principal's office because I'd done something wrong. But Verla wasn't wearing that disappointed frown I'd seen her use before, so I figured this was about something else.

"It's good to see you, Nadine," she said. "I trust that you had a good summer."

I stroked Isa's fur. "It was okay. I was sick for most of it."

"Yes, I heard," she said sadly. "Your grandmother mentioned it. Did you get the cookies I sent you?"

"Yes, they were lovely. Thank you."

Verla had sent a care basket more than once. It was obvious she was concerned. It felt so motherly of her.

"Excellent," she said brightly. "You're probably wondering why I wanted to talk to you. Don't worry—you're not in trouble. I actually have an offer for you."

My curiosity piqued. "What kind of offer?"

Verla crossed her hands and rested them on the desk. "An academic one. As you know, our curriculum is limited for Curse Breakers like yourself. It's been a long time since we had a Curse Breaker enrolled at Miriam College. The previous courses have since been retired. Unfortunately, resurrecting them would be difficult, even for a necromancer."

She chuckled at her own joke, then continued. "What I mean is, none of our professors have experience with Curse Breaking, so it would be difficult for anyone to teach you."

"So… how will I learn?" I asked.

"That's what I want to help you with," she offered. "I would like to continue being your mentor, if you'd like. I know I don't have Curse Breaking experience myself, but I'd like to learn with you. Perhaps we can develop a system inspired by the other Casts, catered specifically to you."

My heart surged with excitement. I felt like I had so much to learn, and that I was doomed to fall behind the rest of my classmates. Headmistress Verla was giving me an opportunity to learn and grow—and providing me a safe place to do it. She knew so much about the other Casts. Surely some of that knowledge would apply to me as well.

"It will, of course, count as a credit," she added. "We'll meet three times per week for private tutoring sessions. My hope is that we can work together to unlock your potential."

"Yeah, that sounds great," I told her. "When can we get started?"

Her eyes lit up. "Right away, if you'd like."

I shifted in my chair to get more comfortable, though my body ached no matter how I sat. It wasn't anything new. "Sure, but can I ask you something?"

Verla was already reaching for a book on the shelf behind her. "Ask away."

I chose my words carefully. "Did you... know? That I was a Curse Breaker, I mean?"

She gazed down at the book in her hands and took a deep breath. After a moment, her eyes met mine. "Why would you think I knew?"

I bit my lower lip. "There were some things you said last semester that made me think maybe you suspected something. And then you caught me looking for books on Curse Breakers in the library, and I thought maybe you'd guessed. But you never said anything."

Verla wore a calculating look. "I suspected something was going on, but I didn't know what it was. I thought perhaps..."

"Perhaps what?" I asked when she trailed off.

"I thought maybe you were researching spells beyond your capabilities," she admitted. "Now I see you are capable of so much more than I ever would have thought."

"What exactly do you think I'm capable of?" I asked. "I mean, besides breaking curses."

"The Curse Breaking title can be a bit misleading, because your power has far more potential." She smiled lightly and glanced down to the permanent cauldron tattoo on my arm. "Though I suppose you've already figured that out."

"Yeah, kind of." As a Curse Breaker, I could move magic from one place to another. It's what allowed me to break curses, though I could use it for other purposes as well. I'd been posing as an Alchemist last semester, since I could brew potions using Alchemy crystals.

"Perhaps we can continue your Alchemy study throughout your time at Miriam College," Verla suggested.

I nodded. "I think learning to brew potions is a good skill. Will you be teaching me?"

"Not in our mentorship," Verla said. "I'd like our sessions to focus specifically on learning more about your abilities. We don't know much about Curse Breakers, because they've always been a rare Cast. I'd like to see how we can push the boundaries of your magic and what we can learn together. For example, if you can manipulate Alchemy magic, could you do the same with telekinesis or necromancy?"

"I've tried that," I admitted. "I used crystals from the other Casts last semester, but they didn't give me any new powers."

Verla thought about it for a moment. "I don't imagine they would. My theory is that perhaps you can enchant objects with magic. Take a powerful Mentalist, for example. They can infuse their telekinesis into a broom, so that any witch can fly it, regardless of whether they have telekinesis or not."

"Really?" I questioned. "Why don't I see more people riding brooms then? Forget my car. I want to ride a broom."

Verla smirked. "Enchanting is complicated magic for a witch, but it *can* be done. And I believe you'll be able to do it with some practice. This is one of the ways in which the Casts are stronger together. A witch might be unable to enchant an object herself, but it should be easier with your help."

My heart lifted. I loved the idea of using my magic for more than just breaking curses. The dark magic could get depressing. "What other things do you think I could do?"

"If you can break a curse, you should be able to break wards," Verla said.

"Wouldn't that be unethical?" I questioned.

"That would depend on the ward," she pointed out. "If a ward holds after the spellcaster dies, you may be the only one who can remove it. It could help out families who have lost valuable possessions to wards, for example. I think you'll find there's more potential than you realize. Curse Breakers are also said to be able to absorb magic. It would be interesting for us to explore that angle once you have a firm grasp on simpler concepts."

I felt really hopeful. "Where do we start?"

"I'd like to start with transference. It's similar to enchanting, but transferring magic into crystals is easier than enchanting a regular object, though the two are both advanced techniques." Verla placed several crystals on the desk between us, all different colors. "I don't expect you to get this on your first try, but we have to start somewhere."

"Oh, I've done this before. This is easy." I picked up an amethyst point.

Verla's eyebrows shot up. "Many students graduate Miriam College without ever mastering transference. You've already done it?"

"Isn't it basically the trademark of my Cast?" I tested the weight of the crystal in my hand. "Though I don't feel any magic in this."

"Well, you have to *put* magic in it," Verla said. "That's the point of transference."

I set the crystal back on the desk. "I've never done it with my own magic. I've just moved magic around that came from a crystal. But my own magic... what would I even *put* into a crystal?"

Verla looked confused. "What do you mean?"

"Well, do I really have my own magic? Or do I just manipulate the magic of others?"

"Of course you have your own, Nadine. How else do you think you conjure items or cast orbs?"

"I suppose, but everyone can do that, regardless of their Cast. That's just generic witch magic. Does a Curse Breaker really have their own Cast magic?"

"You must. Otherwise, everyone would be able to do what you do," Verla answered. "Let's see if you can find that magic within yourself and put it into a crystal."

I gazed down at the crystals scattered across the desk, then picked up a midnight blue one. I closed my eyes and concentrated on finding my magic within me. An energy I'd become accustomed to buzzed in my chest and swirled around my belly. I tugged at it and tried to put it into the crystal, but nothing happened.

"Why don't you try this one?" Verla suggested, handing me a rose quartz crystal.

I concentrated again, but it was like my magic met a wall when I tried pushing it outward. I tested three more crystals, but none of them worked.

The crease between Verla's eyebrows deepened, and she pressed her lips together. "Perhaps a different crystal would be more effective."

I tilted my head. "Does it matter which one I use?"

"It can," she said. "Different crystals resonate with different types of magic. It's why, even without magic infused into them, various crystals are used in different rituals, or used to amplify different powers. Seers often use shattuckite for clearer visions, for example, so it's one of the stones Seers usually start with in their transference lessons. Alchemists use different crystals to amplify the power of their potions—rose quartz for love potions, or agate for concentration and balance. But versatile crystals tend to work better for Alchemists when it comes to transference —crystals like clear quartz and amethyst. Clear quartz is probably our best place to start."

She reached into her desk drawer and handed me a clear quartz point. I tried again, but my magic didn't budge.

"It's not working," I told her as I set the crystal back on the desk.

Verla took a long breath, as if thinking deeply. After a few moments, she stood. "Follow me."

She didn't say where we were going, but I followed her out of her office with Isa at my heels. Odin slowly climbed down from his cat tower and waddled after us. We wove down a few hallways, until we descended a flight of stairs and reached the basement of the school.

Verla stopped at a door marked *Crystallary*. She conjured a ring of keys and unlocked the door.

"This is our Crystallary," Verla said as she flicked the light on. "It's the school's crystal storage."

I gasped as I stepped into the room. The room was long and skinny— more like a hallway than a room. I expected rows of shelving, but there weren't any shelves in here. Instead, thousands of holes had been cut into the wall, fit perfectly for every single crystal. Crystal points and smooth stones were set into the walls, and they seemed to glitter in the light. It was like stepping into a magical cave.

"Go ahead," Verla encouraged, gesturing me further into the room. "Have a look. See if any stone calls out to you."

My jaw dropped as my gaze roamed over all the beautiful stones. I stepped further into the room, hoping something might jump out at me, but I was a bit overwhelmed by the beautiful rainbow of colors.

Isa sniffed at one of the crystals near my feet, and it fell out of the wall and clinked across the ground. She jumped back and hissed, then hid behind me.

Verla grabbed the crystal before I could and returned it to its spot on the wall. I took another step into the room, looking up and down the walls. The crystals were arranged in clusters, with identical crystals set together and labeled, so they were easy to find.

I ran my fingers across various crystals, reading the labels as I passed by. *Citrine, aventurine, fluorite, obsidian*—the list went on. As I touched them, I could sense that they didn't have any magic within them, but each of them *felt* different. It was like Headmistress Verla had said—that crystals could be used to amplify certain powers, emotions, or abilities.

"What exactly am I looking for?" I asked her.

"Anything that speaks to you," she said. "It may not be obvious at first, but see if something sticks out, even if there's no rhyme or reason for it. Follow your intuition."

I turned to a collection of light bluish-green stones. The label beside them read *Aquamarine – Communication, Courage, Calming*. Intrigued, I pulled one of the crystals from the wall. I held it for a moment, testing how it felt in my hand. Something about it didn't feel quite right, like it wasn't what I was looking for at that moment. I had no reason to think that, other than a simple inner knowing.

I put the crystal back, then did the same thing with several others. I must've picked up a dozen stones before my eyes landed upon a collection of beautiful white crystals with a blue shimmer. My breath caught, and I began reaching for the stones before realizing it. The moment I touched the crystal, I felt an instant connection. A calm, inner knowing spoke to me, telling me I'd found it.

"This one," I announced to Verla as I pulled a round stone from the wall. "This one feels right."

"Rainbow moonstone," she said thoughtfully. "This is a stone of balance, creativity, and feminine energy. Shall we try it?"

"I'll give it a go," I said.

I curled my fingers around the crystal and concentrated. My magic resisted at first, and I wasn't sure why. Verla remained silent, and I worried I was taking too long.

After taking several deep breaths, I opened my eyes. "I don't think it's working."

Verla studied me. "You're thinking hard. About what, if I may ask?"

I shrugged. "I thought you might be getting impatient, like I was wasting your time."

"I assure you, you're not. Let's try again, but this time, I want you to become aware of how *you* feel."

I nodded, then closed my eyes again. A weight settled in my gut. After a few moments, I realized something. "I think I'm scared," I admitted. "I'm afraid to get it wrong."

"This isn't a test, Nadine," Verla promised. "We have plenty of time. Relax and trust yourself."

"I'll try." I drew in a deep breath. Instead of focusing on my magic, I focused on my reservations.

It's okay, I told my magic. *It's safe to perform transference. Nothing will go wrong. No one expects anything from me. I won't disappoint anyone if I don't get it.*

Something shifted as I began to communicate with my magic. The nerves began to melt away, and that wall my magic had hit before seemed to crumble. My magic flowed into the crystal and stayed there.

"I did it!" I cried to Verla.

Her eyes lit up, and she held her hand out. "May I see?"

I handed the crystal to her, and she examined it from every angle.

"There certainly seems to be some magic in here," she said, sounding excited. "Can you keep going?"

"I don't know," I admitted. "I don't want to push myself too far. I get really tired if I use too much magic."

Verla frowned. "In order to learn your powers, you must be willing to push yourself, Nadine. Growth does not occur inside your comfort zone."

I hesitated. I really wanted to learn more about my powers, and she had a point.

"I can try again," I offered.

Verla handed the moonstone back. "See how much magic you can place into this crystal. If we're to learn about your powers, we must know how much can be harnessed."

I took the crystal and began funneling more magic into it. Verla had been right; I still had more to give, and the magic within the crystal hadn't pushed back yet.

But the more magic I used, the more fatigued I became. My head started to spin, and I steadied myself against the wall. Isa meowed, sounding concerned for me.

"I'm not sure I can do this anymore," I admitted.

"I believe in you," Verla encouraged. "Keep trying."

Verla understood the limits of magic better than I did. If she believed in me, then I could believe in myself. But I thought if I kept doing it standing up, I might pass out. Instead, I sat on the ground cross-legged and continued transferring magic into the stone.

"I really don't think I can do much more," I said after a few minutes. Every muscle in my body was starting to ache.

"You're doing great, Nadine," she said. "You've almost charged the whole crystal. You're almost done."

Verla's encouragement was infectious. I was so close to completing this task, and I really wanted to impress her, so I continued. But the more magic I pushed into the stone, the more my body fought against it. My bones started to ache, and my breath grew heavy, like I was in the midst of running a marathon.

But marathon runners didn't quit. I was close to the finish line. I gritted my teeth and pushed on—

I lost all sense of time. The next thing I knew, Verla was kneeling over me, shaking me. I lay on the ground with a throbbing pain in the back of my skull. Isa meowed loudly next to me, and the crystal lay beside her. I was so disoriented that it took me a moment to realize what had happened.

"Ugh. I passed out," I groaned.

Verla helped me sit up. Her lips pursed, and I couldn't quite read her expression. "I had no idea. I thought—"

"It's not your fault," I interrupted. I was so embarrassed. I just wanted to disappear. "I'm sure most witches could handle that just fine. It's my lupus. My magic and my body don't always get along."

Verla conjured a water bottle and shoved it in my direction. "Drink something. When we're done, I'll walk you to the infirmary."

"That's really not necessary," I protested.

"Yes, it is," she insisted. "It's important that you feel better before we continue any further."

I took the water bottle and sipped on the water. "Thanks."

After a moment, I stood on shaky knees and followed Headmistress Verla to the infirmary. She walked close to me, like she feared I might pass out again and she might be able to catch me.

I hated being treated like I was a porcelain doll, ready to shatter into a million pieces at any moment. The problem was, it wasn't too far off from the truth.

Verla had said growth didn't occur inside your comfort zone, but that implied that discomfort could benefit you. But sometimes discomfort indicated that things were bad for you.

I had to start learning the difference, or my magic could end up breaking me.

☾

It was clear over the next two weeks that keeping up with my classes was going to be harder than ever. My lupus flared, and I could hardly get out of bed. I thought I was doing better on Wednesday, but I got halfway through a shower before realizing I just didn't have the energy for anything more that day. On Thursday, I managed to get to one class, but my brain fog was so bad I didn't absorb anything the professor had said. I'd gone back to my dorm room for a nap and slept through my alarm for my next class.

On Friday, I was feeling a bit better and managed to get to class. Amy and I had Moonology together, and she'd saved me a spot. We covered the phases of the moon, which was pretty basic stuff that would set the foundation of the lunar spells we'd be learning the rest of the semester.

"Hey, you like bowling, right?" Amy asked as we were leaving class.

"Yeah, I love it," I told her. "I haven't had many chances to play recently, though."

"Tate invited me to play after class," Amy said. "Do you want to come?"

I hesitated. I had to be careful where I put my physical energy. If I went bowling now, I wouldn't have the energy for homework tonight. Even if I sat on the sidelines and watched, I'd drain my energy. But I really didn't want to miss a game with my friends. I decided my homework could wait until the weekend. I hoped I felt well enough to complete it then.

"Sure, I'd love that," I told her.

Amy ran her fingers through her hair as we headed toward the Lounge. "How do I look?"

I smirked playfully and wiggled my eyebrows. "Are we trying to impress someone?"

She visibly blushed. "I might be crazy, but I swear Tate's been flirting with me.'

"Ah, so that's why you invited me along. Emotional support," I teased.

She snickered. "Maybe just a little. Tate's just so outgoing and fun. I don't want her to think I'm boring."

"You're not boring," I assured her. "Plus, you're smart and creative and really supportive. Tate would be lucky to date you. Just be yourself. If it's meant to be, it will."

Amy smiled, and I was glad I could alleviate some of her fears. When we stepped into the Lounge, though, her face dropped. Stormy stopped in her tracks, and Isa ran into her butt.

Tate sat on one of the couches next to the TVs, sandwiched between identical twins—Shane and Alex. She threw her head back in laughter and touched one of their legs.

"My brother isn't *that* funny," Shane teased, reaching over Tate to punch Alex in the shoulder.

She laughed so hard that she doubled over and struggled to catch her breath. "Oh, come on…" she gasped between breaths. "You know me… *everything's* hilarious when I'm around you two—"

Her eyes caught Amy's, and her laughter quickly settled. "Sorry, boys," she said. "I've got a hot date. I'll catch up with you later."

Tate winked at the twins, then hopped to her feet. Shane grabbed her by the wrist before she could get too far away. "Aw, can't you stay?" he begged playfully.

She pouted, playing along. "I'll be back later. I promise."

"You should be careful," Alex said in a low voice, though we could still hear him. "Stick to your own Cast."

Tate rolled her eyes. "I don't have a Cast yet, silly. My Evoking Ceremony isn't for months."

"But you're *going* to get Seer, like us," Alex insisted. "That's what you said your family is."

"Yeah, but it's no guarantee," Tate pointed out. "Look, if I get the mark of Seer, you can have me. Until then, I'll go where I please."

Shane dropped her arm, and Tate held her head high. She practically danced over to us.

"What was that about?" I asked, confused.

Tate rolled her eyes. "It's stupid. Everyone's being dumb."

Amy frowned. "A bunch of people in my Alchemy class were talking about this—how we had to *stick together*."

I furrowed my brow. "Like, the Casts have to stick together? Not the whole coven?"

Tate waved her hand, like it wasn't a big deal, but I was bothered by it. "You've heard the rumors. *Something's wrong with Alora. There's one Cast responsible for it all, so we have to stick to our own.* I can't keep up with the gossip."

"Are you kidding me?" I asked. "People are dividing into their Casts now because they're *afraid*?"

Tate sighed. "I said it was dumb."

"Don't worry," Amy said firmly, misreading my frustration. "I'm not scared of my friends. No one is going to leave you for being the only one of your Cast."

"I'm not afraid of that," I replied. "I just think it's immature to say who you can and can't be friends with based on your magic."

"Exactly," Tate agreed. She turned to Amy with bright eyes and looped her arm through hers. "Hey, sweet thing. How are you?"

Amy must've immediately forgotten about the twins, because her features lit up. "Good. And you?"

"Fab-ulous!" Tate sang. "Who's up for bowling? Both of you? Excellent. We can share a lane. I think Talia already claimed one. What ball do you want? I have this black one I absolutely adore."

Tate rambled a million miles a minute. The girl radiated energy, which I found both admirable and a tad annoying. I didn't know how to take her yet.

Tate skipped past the arcade and pool tables, to the back of the Lounge where the bowling lanes were. Talia sat at one of the lanes next to Mandy, putting names into the scoreboard.

"Perfect timing," Talia said. "Let me just put in Nadine's name, and we'll be ready to go."

"I'm just going to watch," I said.

Talia opened her mouth, but she must've noticed something in my features. She could always tell when I was feeling bad. She was the only one. Usually, I hid it really well. She snapped her jaw shut and hopped to her feet, taking the attention off me. "I'm up first!"

Talia knocked over nine pins, but missed the last one on her second try. I cheered for her and gave her a high-five.

Mandy stood, smirking. "Great job, girl, but let me show you how it's done."

Mandy chose a sparkling black ball, then narrowed her eyes at the lane. She stood there a few seconds, as if calculating her strategy. Finally, she stepped forward and swung her arm back. The moment she let go of the ball, a shield blasted out of her palm, sending the ball shooting down the lane insanely fast. It hit the pins so hard that one of them spun through the air and landed in the next lane.

"That's cheating!" Amy teased.

Mandy tossed her dark hair over her shoulder. "Hey, you can't blame me for using my natural talents."

Amy went next, refusing to use magic to boost her score. She split the pins. I hated that I couldn't participate. They looked like they were having so much fun. Still, this was better than sitting in my dorm in pain, bored and lonely. So I put on a happy face and pretended that I was all right.

Tate was up after her and laughed at herself when she only knocked down three pins. She swayed her hips and teased, "I'm a natural."

Fuck it. I wanted in.

"Tal, mind if I give it a shot?" I asked, since it was her turn.

"Go ahead," Talia said. She picked up a lightweight ball and handed it to me.

"I'm telling you, you can use magic," Mandy encouraged me.

"I can try, but I haven't perfected shields yet," I said.

Mandy scrunched up her nose. "Yeah, it's kind of an upper-classman spell. Just go with it."

The ball was only a few pounds, but felt like a hundred pounds. My hands really ached today, but pain be damned. I wanted to bowl with my friends. I positioned myself in front of the lane and concentrated on my magic, but I couldn't feel a thing. After a few moments, I dropped the ball to my side and turned to my friends. "Something's wrong. I can't feel my magic."

Talia's face paled. "You think you've been affected by the Waning?"

"I don't know." I lifted my hand and tried to conjure a pen—something light and easy—but nothing happened. "Shit," I mumbled.

"It… it's okay," Talia stammered. "Your magic will be back soon." She was trying to reassure me, but she sounded nervous.

I bit my lower lip. "Yeah. I guess."

"Hey, I bet you can't bowl a strike," Mandy challenged. She was trying to distract me. And it worked.

"I'll take that bet," I told her. I took my shot and was confident in my swing, until the last second when the weight of the ball became too much. A twinge traveled through my hand, and I winced. I accidentally twisted my hand, and the ball thudded to the ground and landed in the gutter.

Mandy started laughing. She hadn't noticed what had actually happened. No one did, because I'd become so good at hiding my pain. "Pay up, girl," she said.

"Think I can get a spare? Double or nothing?" I asked.

"You're on," she agreed.

I tried again, but the same thing happened. My stomach twisted as the ball rolled down the gutter. I plastered on a smile as I turned to my friends. "I meant to do that."

"Sure, you did," Tate teased.

Inside, I was crushed. I used to be so good at bowling. I knew I could hit a strike if my symptoms were under control, but it didn't matter what I did today. My body just wasn't going to cooperate.

"I gotta go to the bathroom," I announced, though it was a lie. "I'll be back."

I turned and started out of the Lounge. Isa meowed and followed behind me. It wasn't until I stopped in the hall that I realized she wasn't the only one who'd followed. Talia emerged from the Lounge behind me.

"Hey, Nadine," she said softly. "Are you okay?"

"It's nothing," I lied.

I leaned my back against the wall and scowled. I didn't want Talia to think I was overreacting. It was, after all, just a game of bowling. Except I knew it was bigger than that. I just didn't know how to explain it to her.

"You can talk to me," she encouraged.

"I know I can. I just…" I blew a breath. "It's not a big deal."

"It obviously is," she pointed out.

I chewed my lower lip, then lifted my gaze to look at her. Her eyes were so soft and welcoming. Maybe Talia *would* understand.

"Okay, so you know when you're reading something, and you just *can't get it* because of your dyslexia?" I asked.

Talia chuckled lightly. "All the time. Sometimes, it doesn't matter how many times I read a passage. It just doesn't make any sense."

"Right. And for me, it does. I don't even have to think about it."

Talia nodded along.

"My lupus can be like that sometimes," I said. "Like things that just seem easy to you guys are a big deal to me. I freaking *love* bowling, and I just… can't do it today. There's nothing I can do to force my body to do it. I'm sorry. It probably feels like I'm upset over nothing."

"No," Talia assured me. "I appreciate the metaphor with dyslexia, because that's something I can understand. And most people don't get that, either. So I understand that you have trouble where I don't."

I relaxed. "Thanks for understanding, Tal. I just really wanted to enjoy myself, and I couldn't. I feel so out of control with my body, and it can be devastating sometimes. Bowling used to be easy for me, when my symptoms were under control. I could bowl strikes every game. I felt in control, and now I don't."

Talia frowned, like she felt bad for me. I wasn't searching for pity—just understanding.

"Maybe it would help to find something you *can* control," she suggested.

"Like what?" I asked curiously.

She pressed her lips together thoughtfully. "I'm not sure yet. Start with something small, like getting your nails done."

I smiled. It was a good idea—a middle-finger to my aching joints. If I couldn't *use* my hands properly, at least I could control what they looked like.

"I might do that," I said. "I still have that gift certificate to the spa Lucas gave me for Valentine's Day. I could get a massage and a manicure."

"There you go," Talia said brightly. "I know it's probably not the answer you wanted, but it's a start."

I shook my head. "No, it's fine. I need to focus on the things I can handle, and I can handle a day at the spa."

Talia snickered. "Can't we all?"

Talia offered to tell our friends why I'd left. Meanwhile, I called the spa, though I had to use Talia's phone because I couldn't conjure mine. The receptionist said they'd had a cancelation and I could get my massage in an hour. I was shocked to get in so soon, and I *really* wanted that massage right now. I booked the slot, and Talia drove me into town after bowling. I was worried about driving on my own right now. The spa was located in a strip mall and surrounded by various alchemy and crystal shops.

Talia dropped me off in front of the spa. "I want to do some shopping while you're in there. I'll park over there and meet you out here when you finish. Sound good?"

"Yeah," I told her. "I'll see you soon."

Inside, the spa was quiet and peaceful. It smelled of citrus and cinnamon, and orange light orbs floated overhead. It was so relaxing.

The massage therapist was gentle with me and really nice. She asked me a little about school and my major, and I told her about how I was planning to apply to the Criminal Justice program. She thought that sounded cool.

The massage ended, but I didn't feel any better physically. It was always a toss-up if a massage would help my flare-up. I was disappointed that the pain persisted.

By the time my nails were done, I was feeling better emotionally. I could really get used to spa treatments all the time. I hoped being a priestess paid well, because I could do this every week.

When I left, a group of six students stood outside the shop next door. I noticed Avery in the mix of them. Talia's car wasn't far from them, but I had no interest in a confrontation. I decided to loop around the parking lot, so I didn't have to pass by them, but as soon as I stepped off the sidewalk, they noticed me.

"Hey," one of the guys barked.

I kept my head down and kept walking, pretending I hadn't heard him.

"Hey, Curse Maker! I'm talking to you."

Fuck.

I glanced up. It was Frederick James, an asshole who'd accused me of cursing the coven more than once. "I'm not interested."

James started toward me, and I began to panic. I knew a few defensive spells, but I'd only just started my Defensive Magic class this semester. James was a year ahead of me, and surely knew more spells than I did. I increased my pace. His friends must've thought it was funny, because they started cackling.

Adrenaline shot through my system, and even though we were out in the open in the middle of the day, I suddenly felt very unsafe. I remembered what my mom had taught me as a kid. *It's better to be safe than polite.*

I took off running toward Talia's car. My body ached and protested, and I thought I might puke. If I could get to her car, I could lock myself inside, and hopefully he'd leave me alone. I reached for the passenger-side door, but James was faster than me. Before my fingers touched the handle, he slid in front of me. His back pressed against my door, blocking me from getting into the car.

I took a shaky step back. "What the hell do you want?"

"The truth," he snarled. "Everyone knows there's something different about you."

"So I'm a Curse Breaker. Do you want a medal for being the first to figure it out?"

"Yeah, a Curse Breaker," he spat. "That's quite a step up from an Alchemist, wouldn't you say? If you're so innocent, why'd you lie to everyone about what you were?"

"So that assholes like you wouldn't harass me," I shot back.

I tried to shove him out of the way so I could get in the car, but he barely stumbled a step. He grabbed my wrist. Though my heart hammered, I stared him down, as if daring him to do something about it.

"What are you going to do?" I scoffed. "Hurt me in front of all your friends?"

His nostrils flared. "I'd be doing them a favor. And trust me, honey. I'd do more than that."

I wanted to puke, but I spoke dryly. "To a member of your own coven? How noble."

He scoffed. "You weren't born here. You have no right to call this your coven."

"Yeah, yeah, I know," I said with an eye roll. "You all need someone to blame, so you target the new girl who has no other Cast members to protect her. Why don't you just admit that you're scared as fuck and that this has nothing to do with me?"

James's features paled, and I knew I'd hit a nerve. "I'm not scared of you."

"Oh yeah? Then let me go," I growled. "You want to call me a Curse Maker? I *will* curse your ass if you don't let me go."

James just squeezed my wrist tighter, and I gasped at the pain. To anyone else, it might just feel uncomfortable, but with my flare-up, it was agonizing. I tried to conjure a battle orb to distract him, but my magic still hadn't returned fully.

The second sparks flew from my fingers, he created a shield that sent the sparks flying toward my face. I pulled back on my magic and curled my free hand into a fist. I swung my fist toward him, and it connected with the side of his abdomen. My fingers ached, but James looked like he barely felt it. Near the shops, his friends roared in laughter.

James's features contorted in rage. My heart leapt to my throat as he shoved me up against the side of my car, pinning me there.

"Help!" I screamed, but the only response was the laughter coming from James's friends. They were enjoying the show.

Relief flooded through me when Talia walked out of a crystal shop. Her features paled when she saw me pinned against the car.

"Talia!" I cried.

She reacted quickly and conjured her phone. "I'm calling the police!" she shouted. Talia began racing across the parking lot, but James's friends stepped in front of her, blocking her path.

My stomach twisted. "Don't hurt her!"

James chuckled. His disgusting breath brushed across the side of my face. I squeezed my eyes shut and turned my face away from his, holding my breath.

"You think you're so tough," James said. "You're nothing but a—"

He cut off as someone yanked him off of me. I breathed a sigh of relief and opened my eyes to see that no one was nearby. James had fallen to the ground and clawed at the asphalt. He screamed as he was dragged across the parking lot by an unseen force.

My breath stalled, and my gaze darted around. The Imperium Council hurried toward us, their robes billowing around them. Priestess Stella dropped a pile of shopping bags she'd been carrying. Priestess Lilian's gaze locked on James, and I realized *she'd* been the one to pull him off of me with her magic. Her fingers twitched at her sides. James's body yanked upright, until his toes hovered a mere inch off the ground. The Imperium Council surrounded him, and in unison, they drew wands from their robes and pointed them at his throat.

"A *what?*" Priestess Margaret snapped, waving her wand at him. She was shorter than James by at least a foot, but she held her head high and fucking *owned* her authority over him. "Go on. Finish your sentence."

"A… a…" he stammered. Fear overtook his features.

"A coward, perhaps," Priestess Lilian suggested. "If you were looking for a word to describe yourself."

His nostrils flared. "I'm just trying to get answers. Someone needs to do something."

The council exchanged a glance, then spoke in unison. "*Silentium.*"

Magic shot from their wands at the same time, and James's jaw snapped shut. His eyes went wide in fear, and he moved his mouth like he wanted to speak, but nothing came out. They must've cast some sort of muting spell on him.

"Answers will be found," Priestess Margaret stated confidently. "If you so much as threaten Nadine Evers, you *will* answer to us. And so help me, the Imperium Council does not take threats to future priestesses lightly."

"We trust your friends to know better as well," Priestess Stella added. "Or they shall expect a death far worse than the one I've foreseen for you."

James said nothing, but he whimpered as Priestess Lilian released her hold on him. He crumpled to the ground, then scurried to his feet and raced toward his friends. They'd all gone completely silent and shared a wide-eyed look.

When they were out of sight, I finally felt like I could breathe again. My whole body sagged as I steadied myself against my car. Talia ran over to me.

"Are you okay?" she asked, looking me over. "He didn't hurt you, did he?"

I cradled my aching wrist. "I'll be all right."

The Imperium Council approached, and I turned to them. "Thank you."

"The council does its best to protect its people," Priestess Charlotte said.

Lilian crossed her arms. She shot a look at Talia. "Leave us."

Talia hesitated.

"It's okay," I told her. "You can wait in the car."

"I'll be right here if you need me." Talia looked apprehensive, but she went to the driver's seat anyway.

Priestess Lilian scowled at me. It was like she wasn't pleased with having to step in and save my ass—like a soon-to-be priestess should be able to protect herself. Hell, I would if I could.

"You're lucky we were here," Lilian sneered. "We can't defend you at all times."

"I understand that," I said, still reeling from how fast it all happened.

Priestess Margaret glanced in the direction James and his friends had gone. "Luckily, I think we got through to them. No one else will think to lay a hand on you anytime soon."

My shoulders relaxed. I didn't quite meet any of their gazes. I was very grateful they'd helped me, and I suddenly felt like I'd underestimated them. "I appreciate the help."

Priestess Lilian tilted her nose upward. "Yes, well, we've done our job. You may thank us by doing *yours*."

I gaped at her. She was going to bring up the Oaken Wands *now*, after I'd just been assaulted? I got defensive. "I'm doing my best. I have little to no information to go on. And forgive me if I'm not motivated to help a coven that doesn't even want me here."

Priestess Margaret gasped. "Of course you're wanted. Who would dare say otherwise?"

Chloe. James. Magnus Knight. Pretty much everyone but my friends.

I didn't get a chance to answer before Priestess Stella said, "Anyone who doesn't want you in our ranks is an ignorant fool."

"And you can prove them wrong," Lilian added. "Once we discover where your grandfather hid the Oaken Wands, and we restore our magic, the coven will see the truth."

She said it like it was supposed to motivate me. But I felt bitter as all hell.

"I don't have anything to give you," I told her bluntly. "I don't know what more you want from me."

"We need proof," Lilian demanded.

"Proof that I… don't know anything?" I asked.

Lilian pursed her lips. "Bring us everything you can find on the Oaken Wands. Perhaps there's something to be found in your grandfather's records."

What records? I wanted to ask, but I didn't trust that I'd get anywhere with Priestess Lilian. She was sure I was hiding something.

"I'll do my best," I promised.

"Very well," Lilian said. "We'll be waiting."

The council whirled around in unison, the hems of their robes billowing around their ankles. I climbed into the passenger seat.

"That was intense," Talia said.

As the Imperium Council walked off, it became clear to me why they came to my defense.

"They don't care about me," I said. "All they want is for me to find their damn wands. They'll protect me, but only as long as they need me."

I didn't want to find out what would happen once they no longer deemed my presence necessary.

FIVE

Classes passed by at an agonizing pace. I couldn't concentrate, and all I wanted to do was sleep. Then came the weekend, which was even more torturous. I couldn't get out of bed for anything, and I wasn't sure what had triggered it.

Let's face it. I was a failure. The coven was losing magic, and I'd failed to come up with any answers. Investigating nightshade was proving to be useless. There was nothing I could do to help.

I told myself I'd make it to class on Thursday, but sunrise came, and it didn't matter how much I talked myself into it. I already knew it wasn't going to happen.

You're being an idiot, I told myself. *You've been stuck in bed for a week for no reason. You're pathetic.* I needed help, but I was too fucking proud to ask for it.

The end is finally here, a voice that wasn't my own cut through my thoughts. It sounded like an older woman. I wasn't sure if she felt relieved by her death or not, but it felt more depressing than anything. The voices always got louder when I slipped deep into my depression.

I curled the pillow around my ears, like that might quiet the thought echoing in my mind.

The door to my room opened, and I buried myself deeper under the blanket. I figured it was Grant coming back from class. He probably wanted to talk again. I didn't want to talk. If we did, he'd know how pathetic I truly was. He couldn't help me.

"Wakey, wakey, sleepy head!" someone said, tugging on my ankles.

I groaned and curled into a ball. "Go away, Grant. I'm sick."

"I'm sick, too. Sick and tired of not seeing you in class. You've got half an hour until Magical Plants and Herbs. You're not skipping today. We're dissecting *spira cacti*. They're cactuses shaped like—"

"Whether or not I go to class is none of your damn business. Go away," I snapped.

"It's my business when you're my lab partner, and I'll fail the class without you."

"You're not even in that class—" I cut off as I tossed the blanket off my head and realized it wasn't Grant standing there.

It was Miles, along with his cat, Kiki. He *was* my lab partner. Magical Plants and Herbs was required for all Casts, since the coven didn't want people accidentally eating things they shouldn't or shit like that. Plus, there were a ton of plants used in different coven-wide rituals we had to learn about. Alchemists were the only ones who took advanced plant classes, though.

I groaned and sank deeper into the bed. "Your brother let you in?"

Miles smiled proudly, then yanked the blanket the rest of the way off of me. Cool air swirled around me, and I swear it was the worst feeling in the world.

"Fuck off," I growled, before burying my face in the pillow.

"Grant's been trying to get you out of bed all week, and he's gotten nowhere," Miles said. "He thought maybe I could help."

I snorted. "If he can't, neither can you."

"I might surprise you." Miles sat on the couch, waiting. Kiki sat at his feet, and she stared at me with piercing eyes. The silence was agonizing.

"If you're just going to sit there all day, you might as well leave," I said.

"I have a better idea," he replied. "I'm going to help you, the same way someone helped me when I was in your position."

I lifted my head to look at him. "What do you mean?"

"I've been where you're at, Lucas."

I scoffed. "No, you haven't."

"Don't act like you know me," Miles objected. "I've been depressed."

"Yeah, right. You're one of the happiest people I know."

"You missed a few years of my life," he reminded me.

I eyed him curiously. He wasn't lying.

"It was a few years ago," Miles said, even though I hadn't asked. "I was in a lot of pain from rheumatoid arthritis, and I hadn't been diagnosed yet. I lost interest in school, and I fell behind. I thought I was just stupid, so I started skipping. My mom and I fought all the time, and our whole house was just... dysfunctional. I went to this really dark place that made no sense at the time. It really freaked me out. I didn't know what to do."

I finally sat up. "What *did* you do?"

"I found a friend who helped me," Miles admitted. "She tutored me, got me back on track, and helped me fight for a diagnosis. She encouraged me to make up with my mom."

"Was she your girlfriend?" I asked curiously.

He shook his head. "Just a really good friend. We still keep in touch."

Miles sighed. "I'm not gonna sit here and tell you to buck up and be a man, because that never worked for me, either. I'm not gonna tell you that you've gotta get over this today, that if you just get out of bed everything will feel great, because I know it's a lie. But I *am* going to make you come to class. You don't have to like it, but you've gotta do it."

"No, I don't," I said.

"Yes, you do, because if I don't help you do it, you'll never do it by yourself," he insisted. "It's too hard with this disability."

I scoffed. "Depression isn't a disability."

My depression was nothing like Nadine's lupus. She was actually disabled. I wasn't.

Miles raised his eyebrows. "It affects your daily life. It prevents you from doing basic tasks. It may be a psychiatric disability, but it *is* a disability. It's important to learn how to work with it. Just do *one* thing today. I'm willing to compromise how we make it happen, but it's gotta happen."

"It's too much," I admitted.

"I know how it feels," Miles said. "Getting out of bed... it seems so simple, but it's the hardest thing in the world when you've got depression. You just want to sleep until it's over... or until you die."

"That's the thing, though. I *don't* want to die—not the way Eric did. I don't even know if that counts as depression."

Miles frowned. "The longer you lie to yourself, the harder it will be to figure out a solution. You don't eat, all you do is sleep, you don't hang out with friends. Grant told me all about your pessimism and irritability. You look like you haven't showered all week. It's a classic symptom."

"I've showered—" I started to say, but I realized I couldn't actually remember the last time I had.

"Okay, I'll make you a deal," Miles offered. "You only have to do *one* thing today. You can either shower or go to class."

I didn't want to do either of those things. "Or what?"

"I'll sic a ghost on you," he joked.

I rolled my eyes. "Like you could."

"I can," he said proudly, lifting his sleeve to show me a tattoo on his shoulder. "You missed my birthday. I got Seer."

I sat up straighter to look at the image of an eye on his arm. "Really? That's great."

"Yeah, it turns out I can see and talk to ghosts. Pretty neat, huh?"

I was really happy for him. "Yeah, man. That's awesome. No one's haunting my room, are they?"

"Just you and your stinky-ass feet," he cracked.

"Yeah, yeah, I know," I grumbled. "I really *could* use a shower."

"So that's your decision?" Miles asked.

"It's better than going to class," I grumbled.

"Agreed." Miles crossed his arms and leaned back on the sofa.

I cocked an eyebrow. "You're gonna sit there the whole time?"

He grinned widely. "Moral support."

"Not if you actually want me to accomplish anything." I yanked off one of my dirty socks and threw it at him. It hit him in the face. "I don't need a babysitter."

His shoulders fell, and he spoke genuinely. "Fine. If you feel that way, I'll leave."

Miles clapped me on the shoulder as I got out of bed. He was perhaps the only person who understood how great of a feat it truly was. His encouragement meant the world to me.

"Thanks," I told him.

"No problem. If you decide you want to come to class later, I'll have a *spira cacti* ready for you," he offered.

Miles left the room with Kiki, and I dragged my feet to the bathroom. The hot water felt good on my shoulders, but all I could do was stand there. Even washing my hair seemed like a monumental task. Soon, standing became too much, and I sat in the tub. I brushed my teeth in the shower, because it was easier than making a second task out of it.

By the time I finished, the whole room was a cloud of steam. I thought about tossing on a pair of boxers and crawling back into bed, but I forced myself to put on a t-shirt and a pair of jeans. Once I did that, putting on socks and shoes didn't seem so hard, either.

I'm already dressed. I might as well go to class, I thought. Truth was, I knew that if I crawled back under the covers, I'd never leave.

But going to class right now was like asking myself to move a mountain. Instead, I took it in steps. All I had to do was open the door, then step out into the hall, then walk down the stairs. Professor Warren passed by me in the hall and gave a polite nod, like he was happy to see me up and about. He knew I struggled with depression, since he'd tried to help me with it more than once.

As much as I appreciated his effort, he was no therapist. He couldn't help me.

Eventually, I made it to the greenhouse. Miles's features lit up when he saw me, and that almost made coming to class worth it. I sat next to him and looked over the dissection kit laid out in front of us.

"Good to see you," Miles said.

"Thanks," I told him, but it was more than just a pleasantry. I really meant it.

Class passed by quicker than I expected. Miles cracked jokes the whole time to keep me entertained, and we finished our report before class let out.

"All I'm saying is if Professor Lewis didn't want people making penis jokes the whole class, she should've chosen a less phallic plant," Miles said as he walked beside me in the hall.

"What else would we possibly use to ward off evil spirits?" I teased.

Miles stopped outside an open doorway. "Hey, perfect timing. Isn't this your next class?"

I glanced into the classroom, where Professor Daniels stood, writing things out on the board before class. I'd had her once before for Demonology. Her Bengal cat slept on the edge of her desk, so close that it looked like it was about to slide onto the floor.

I sighed. "Journalism Ethics. You walked me past here on purpose, didn't you?"

Miles plastered a look of innocence on his face. "I didn't do anything. It's not like I know your schedule by heart."

I frowned. "Grant told you."

Miles didn't give up the façade. "If you don't want to go to class, you don't have to. I'm proud of you for making it to Magical Plants and Herbs—"

"Lucas, good to see you!" Professor Daniels called. Her long brown hair flowed around her as she turned from the board. "You're here early. Did you have a question about your report?"

My mouth went dry. There was a report?

"That's due today?" I asked.

"It's due next week," she said kindly. "You have plenty of time."

Miles nudged me forward, and I entered the room. I couldn't exactly ditch class now.

The classroom was empty, as I was the first one there. I slumped into a chair at the front of the room. There weren't many people in this class, and Professor Daniels always wanted us to fill the front rows first.

Professor Daniels went over to her desk and began shuffling through papers. After a few moments, she looked up. "Did you happen to hand in your proposal for your final paper? I seem to have lost it."

My shoulders slumped. We were supposed to write an article for our semester final, to practice what we were learning in class. Then we were supposed to follow-up with a report on our experience, and how we'd incorporated five ethical lessons learned throughout the semester. I should've handed in my idea for the article already, so it could be approved and I could get to work on it. I hadn't even thought about it.

"I'm a little stumped on a topic," I admitted. I'd reached a dead end on my nightshade article, so I couldn't submit that for my topic.

"There are plenty of interesting topics to write about," she said brightly. "Several of your classmates have chosen to write about the Waning, but there are many other ideas to explore. I'm working on a piece myself for the *Miriamic Messenger* on the topic of drug use among college-aged students."

My spine straightened, and I chose my words carefully. "How would a journalist go about finding information about something like that?"

"Interviews, mostly," she said.

Hell, I'd tried talking to people, and it'd gotten me nowhere. "But who do you start with?"

"I've been interviewing faculty who have some insight," she admitted. "It's quite an interesting topic. Have you ever heard of Black Ivy, sometimes referred to as nightshade?"

My mouth went dry. "Nothing more than whispers. Do you think it could have anything to do with the Waning?"

Professor Daniels smiled, with a gleam in her eye. "Perhaps that's a topic you'd like to investigate for your final."

"I might," I said thoughtfully. "Could I interview you?"

She smirked. "That would be cheating. I think it's best if you get your information from direct sources. I can help you find a few."

"Really?" I asked, feeling a spark of hope enter my chest.

"Sure. I'm happy to help out with whatever you need," she offered.

Just then, a group of girls entered the classroom, and Professor Daniels greeted them. She turned back to me. "I'll get you a list of sources after class."

My heart lifted. For the first time in months, I felt hope. I might actually be able to help the coven.

Professor Daniels didn't speak to me again, since other students had started arriving for class. She dove into a lecture, discussing the ethics around making promises and deals with your sources. She emphasized to always exercise caution when making promises, but that journalists must *always* keep their word.

The longer I sat in this class, the more I realized I broke a shit ton of journalism rules last semester when I was investigating the missing kids. I'd broken a lot of promises—like telling my friends things I'd vowed to keep private. Hell, I'd promised an article I never even finished writing. It just didn't seem to matter after I discovered my journalism advisor was the one behind it all. I was determined to get things right this time.

I left class with a list of sources in one hand and a renewed sense of purpose in my heart. I read over the list Professor Daniels had given me. It wasn't very long, and was mostly filled with names of different professors.

The first name on the list looked promising—Professor Clarke, a Seer who taught counseling and criminal justice classes. According to the notes, Professor Clarke had written his master's thesis on drug use and addiction.

I was walking through the halls when I overheard Nadine's name from around the corner. My heart stopped, and I paused. I didn't *mean* to eavesdrop, but I couldn't help it.

"James did *what?*" a girl squeaked.

"I'm serious," a guy replied. "He pinned that Curse Breaker up against a car and threatened her."

"When?" the girl asked.

"Last week or something. I can't believe you didn't hear about this."

My hands curled into fists. This was the first I'd heard about it, and it royally pissed me off.

The girl snorted. "Good for James. I hope he scared the shit out of her."

"Well, we would've, if the Imperium Council hadn't stepped in. No one's allowed to touch Nadine, or they'll answer to the council."

My blood boiled. Frederick James had *assaulted* Nadine? That asshole was about to learn a lesson, and not just from the Imperium Council. He had a reaper to answer to.

I stomped down the hall, hungry for blood. I spotted Tate walking in my direction. She had her nose buried in her phone.

"Hey, Tate," I said, stopping her in the hall.

She came to a halt and looked up at me, narrowing her eyes a bit. "It's Lucas, right?"

"Yeah. Any chance you know Frederick James?"

She eyed me skeptically. "I might. Why?"

"I'm looking for him. Have you seen him?"

"Last I saw him, he was at the Cat-fé," she said. "But that was a while ago."

"Thanks," I told her, before rushing off.

I made my way to the cat café on campus. It wasn't too crowded, but James wasn't anywhere in sight. That fucker.

The atmosphere was strange when I walked in, though I couldn't put my finger on it right away. Then I noticed that there was no one sitting in the middle of the café. Everyone stuck to the outer walls, as if avoiding each other. The Treacherous Tarantulas sat at a table across the room, laughing loudly at some disgusting joke, I was certain. My gaze roamed over various tattoos, and I realized that everyone had segregated themselves by Cast. It was a bit eerie.

My eyes landed upon my friends at a table near the window. They were the only group in the whole room whose members were from multiple Casts. Grant, Talia, Amy, and Mandy crowded around each other, staring down at the front page of the *Miriamic Messenger*.

I approached their table. "Has anyone seen James?"

They looked up from the paper. Talia must've noticed the murderous look in my eyes, because her features paled. "Oh, no. You heard."

"Hell, yeah," I growled. "Why didn't anyone tell me what he did to her?"

Talia bit her lower lip. "The Imperium took care of it."

"Speaking of the Imperium, take a look at this!" Mandy cried, slapping the newspaper.

"What's going on?" I asked.

"The Imperium Council has issued a curfew," Talia said, sounding disgruntled. She stood behind Grant and read over his shoulder. "*Effective immediately, all individuals ages twenty-two and younger must adhere to a curfew of 10:00 p.m. to 6:00 a.m. daily. Students found outside their living quarters during nighttime hours will be subject to a fine, with possible jail time for repeat offenses. Fines are double on weekends. This curfew remains in effect until further notice, pending the investigation of the Waning.*"

My friends were trying to distract me from James, and it worked. "This is ridiculous," I protested. "They're deliberately targeting college students. We're adults. We should be able to come and go as we please. How can they do this?"

Grant frowned. "They're the Imperium Council. They can do anything."

I crossed my arms. "They're going to piss off a bunch of people in the process."

"Town curfews aren't uncommon," Amy pointed out.

"Yeah, but that's for noise and shit, isn't it?" Mandy countered. "This makes it sound like we can't leave our dorm rooms at all. I know people who work later than ten o'clock. How are they supposed to do that if they'll be fined for leaving campus?"

"I get having a curfew," Talia said. "I'm sure the Imperium Council is just trying to protect us while they figure out what's going on. But ten o'clock seems too early. I've had study sessions go later than that."

Mandy placed a hand on her hip. "You know what this means, right? *Pending the investigation of the Waning.* They think college kids are responsible."

"Do you think they could be?" Grant asked.

Mandy frowned. "If they are, they're certainly not doing it alone. No one graduates with enough knowledge or power to cause the Waning."

"We know students can't brew drugs as strong as nightshade, either, and they're still getting into the school," I pointed out.

Mandy bit her lower lip. "True."

Grant folded up the newspaper, then tossed it onto the table between us. "Either way, I don't like it. What if this doesn't help the Imperium learn anything new? What measures will they enact next?"

"It's just a curfew," Amy said, trying to sound reassuring. "Do you spend that much time out of your dorm at night anyway?"

Grant looked at her sideways. "Not really, but I'd like the option."

"Same, but what are we going to do about it?" Talia asked. "There's nothing we *can* do. This is the Imperium."

"Maybe when Nadine's inducted, she can advocate for us," Amy suggested. "Wait till she hears about this."

Just the mention of Nadine made my stomach flip. I tried not to let it show. I still wanted to beat James's ass for what he'd done to her.

"I'm going to protest," Grant announced. "I'll write a poem for the talent show. *Slam* poetry. The Imperium Council won't know what hit them."

Talia eyed him. "Have you ever written slam poetry before?"

"No," he admitted. "But the talent show isn't until the end of the semester. I have plenty of time to learn."

"What's this about a talent show?" Mandy demanded. "Why didn't you tell me? I could design a dress and show off my fashion skills—like on a runway."

"That's a great idea," Grant said. "You should sign up. Meanwhile, what do you think of this? *You give us a curfew in the name of justice, but what you call justice, I call a disservice. You talk about fairness, but I call it a lie. You'll just fuck us over till the day that we die.*"

"Not too bad. I'm honestly impressed," I admitted.

"Isn't it a little… dramatic?" Amy asked.

"Well, it sounds better when it's dramatic, right?" Grant said. "Maybe I can tone it down. *You think you're so great. You think you're the man. But I'm an adult. I'll do whatever I… want.*"

He trailed off, looking at a loss for a rhyme. He blushed, obviously embarrassed.

"It's good," Talia assured him. "We can work on it."

I think that embarrassed Grant more, because he stood quickly and abandoned the table. "I'm up for a coffee. Anyone else?"

"No," I told him. I didn't think I could eat anything right now.

As he walked away, Mandy leaned forward. "Do you think you'll enter the talent show, Tal? You could play your keyboard."

"Yeah, it might be fun," she said. "I've actually been composing a new song. It might be ready in time for—"

Talia cut off as her eyes locked on something across the room. I followed her gaze to see that the Tarantulas had stood from their table and gotten in line behind Grant. My stomach twisted, and I knew this couldn't be good. I was on my feet in a second.

Ryan spoke so loudly that his voice projected across the café. "I heard your little poem. Pretty impressive."

"Really?" Grant asked, sounding shocked.

"Yeah. Maybe you could make money off it back in Mexico," Ryan taunted.

I stepped between him and Grant. A couple of the Tarantulas started laughing, like they couldn't wait to see a fight break out between us.

"Back off, Ryan," I snapped. I was already pissed off about James, and Ryan was making it worse. I was two seconds away from breaking.

"Look who it is. Lucas has come to save the day again," Ryan laughed. "What is it with you? I was being *nice*."

"You were being an asshole, like always," I shot back.

"You really want to do this here?" Ryan challenged, puffing out his chest.

"Yeah, I do," I said. "A warlock's duel. Right here, right now."

It was obvious I meant business. You didn't suggest a warlock's duel unless you intended to do real damage. But I was sick of the way the Tarantulas treated Grant, and I was determined to end it.

"Lucas, you really don't have to," Grant protested.

"Yeah, I do," I countered. If I won this duel, they'd finally leave Grant alone.

"I'll enter the duel," Grant offered.

Ryan stared me down, smirking. "Nah, Taylor's the one who challenged me. I want to fight him."

Nobody with a pair of balls turned down a warlock's duel, but it had rules. It wasn't like the time the Tarantulas beat the shit out of Grant and me. A warlock's duel could only be fought between two contenders, and with magic only. The Tarantulas couldn't outnumber me this time, because if any of them stepped in, Ryan automatically forfeited. He'd live with the shame until we graduated —at minimum.

"You're on," I growled.

"Warlock's duel outside!" Nolan shouted, cupping his hands around his mouth.

The girl behind the counter gasped, but a few other people scurried out of their chairs to follow us outside. Talia froze in her seat, looking worried, before scrambling to follow behind Amy.

Mandy rushed to my side as I stepped outside. "Are you really going to do this?"

I cracked my knuckles. Anger stirred in my belly, and I knew there was no way I was backing down. "Hell yeah, I'm going to do this. I've wanted to for years."

"You realize how dangerous this is, right?" Amy asked, her tone shaky. "If Ryan's pissed enough, his battle orbs could kill you."

"Then you all better stand back," I warned.

A wide stretch of grass lay between the entrance to the café and the forest. I stomped out to the middle of the clearing, then turned to face Ryan. Over a dozen people had followed us outside, and several others who'd been passing by came over to watch. We were surrounded on all sides.

"Let the warlock's duel begin!" Corbin yelled.

The Tarantulas began cheering, and several other onlookers joined in. I just barely caught the look of worry on my friends' faces before Ryan lifted his hands. A crackling ball of black magic shot out of his palms, but I was ready for him. I threw up a shield, and the battle orb bounced off of it and fizzled out.

I scoffed, though I felt alive inside. "You call that magic? Show me some real power."

Ryan twitched his fingers. In the blink of an eye, he conjured a knife. He didn't have to draw his arm back before it went spinning through the air, straight at my face. He was using his telekinetic powers on it. I ducked, but only enough to avoid being impaled straight through the eye. The tip of the blade nicked my ear, and I felt the warmth of blood trickle down my neck. Several people behind me gasped.

Heat swept across my skin as fury flared in my bones. I retaliated quickly and swiped my palm through the air while muttering an incantation. The skin on Ryan's cheek split open, like he'd been sliced by a blade. A line of blood several inches long began to seep from his skin.

"Motherfucker!" he cried as he clutched his face.

I smirked in satisfaction. It was an advanced spell I'd never tried before. We weren't supposed to use it on other members of the coven, but I was too pissed to care.

Ryan swore loudly, then spoke an incantation I hadn't heard before. Battle magic surged from his palm like a lightning bolt. It came so fast that I didn't have a chance to get out of the way. The magic struck me in the chest, sending a jolt of electricity surging through my entire form. It blasted me backward, and I rolled in the grass several yards from where I'd been standing. The air left my lungs, but I didn't let it slow me down.

I leapt to my feet, nostrils flaring. "Asshole!"

A battle orb whipped out of my palm, striking Ryan in the shoulder. It must've hit him pretty hard, because he screamed, and his arm went limp at his side.

"You've dislocated my shoulder, you jackass!" Ryan seethed.

I saw the battle orb forming in his hand, but I reacted faster. I pulled the same trick Professor Carlisle had on me the night at Pinewood Manor. I created a shield around Ryan, encompassing him inside. He didn't notice, and he threw his battle orb as hard as he could. The orb bounced off the shield and whizzed by his head before ricocheting off the other side. It slammed into the back of Ryan's skull, and he collapsed.

A collective gasp traveled around the group of onlookers, but I ignored them. I rushed over to Ryan and jumped on top of him, conjuring my scythe in the process—a weapon I'd picked up at Pinewood Manor. It was infused with magic after I'd used it to slice off the head of a hellish monster. Since it was magical, I wasn't breaking any rules of the duel by using it.

I knelt on top of Ryan and aimed the point of my scythe at his neck. He came to, but it took him a moment to process what had happened. When he saw the scythe, his eyes went wide. The crowd around us cheered, but I didn't pay them any attention.

"That's cheating," Ryan growled.

"Not if it's magical," I countered. "Tap out."

"Like hell," he snapped. "You'll have to cut my throat open with that thing before I submit. You don't have the balls to do it."

"Don't I?" I leaned closer to him, until the point of the scythe pressed into his skin, threatening to break it. "Give up. Leave Grant alone, and tell me what you know about nightshade."

"Like I'd tell you," he scoffed. He didn't sound scared, but I could see it in his eyes.

"I know you're dealing," I stated confidently. "Who's brewing it? You have to know, or you wouldn't have stolen all those Alchemy supplies last year."

Ryan narrowed his eyes. "Who've you been talking to?"

"Doesn't matter," I snapped. "Answer my questions, or lose the duel. Who are you working for, you prick?"

Ryan stretched his neck, distancing himself from the point of the scythe, but I pressed it into his skin harder.

"Stop embarrassing yourself and finish this already," he challenged.

"I'd be happy to slit your throat," I said. "I'm sure one of your buddies will talk. I know how shitty Declan is at keeping secrets. Shall I use this scythe on one of them?"

Ryan didn't like that. "Burn in hell, you damned reaper!" he screamed. A shield ballooned from his chest, blasting me off of him. I flew so far away that I landed in the arms of several onlookers, who helped me stay upright when I stumbled backward. My scythe landed in the grass several feet away, and I dove for it. I jumped for Ryan, who was getting to his feet—

Someone leapt between us, catching me before I could gouge Ryan's eyes out.

"You're dead, Tarantula!" I screamed. "Mess with my friend again, and you're dead!"

"I'll lay you in a grave!" Ryan snapped back.

"STOP!" the newcomer shouted. He shoved me, and I finally realized who had stepped between us.

Professor Warren drew his wand, pointing it at me. He held his other palm up in Ryan's direction. The two of us froze as Professor Warren's threatening gaze shifted between us.

"What the hell are you boys thinking?" Professor Warren growled.

"It was him!" Ryan pointed an ugly finger at me.

"Oh, like you didn't do a thing," I snapped back.

"I don't care who started it. I'm ending it," Professor Warren said, sounding a bit scary. I'd never seen him like that.

"Thanks so much, pops," Ryan said with an eye-roll. "Goddess, you sound just like my father."

"I mean it!" Professor Warren roared. "You should all know better. Let's break it up!"

Warlock's duels were prohibited on campus. Professor Warren was going easy on us. He shot a glance around at the onlookers, and people started to disperse immediately.

I caught Grant's eye, and he looked bummed. He obviously felt like this was his fault. Talia placed a hand on Grant's shoulder, then turned away. All the blood drained from my face when I saw who stood behind them.

Nadine. Hell, she'd been here for the whole thing.

She looked angry, like she was disappointed in me for starting a brawl. Or was she worried? I wasn't sure. She looked like she wanted to give me a piece of her mind, but Amy nudged her, and the girls turned away.

"Am I going to have to report you two to the Headmistress?" Professor Warren threatened.

Ryan cleared his throat. "No, sir."

Professor Warren shot me a look, as if to ask what I thought of this. There was no point in getting the Headmistress involved. If she knew we'd agreed to a warlock's duel, we would both be suspended.

"It was just a friendly sparring session," I said flatly, never taking my eyes off Ryan.

"Don't let it happen again," Professor Warren demanded. "Get back to class."

Ryan huffed, then strode away. The duel had ended in a draw, and we were both pissed about it. I grabbed my scythe and subconjured it. I started back toward the school, but Professor Warren stopped me.

"Lucas," he called.

I turned around. My hands curled into fists at my sides, but I steadied my tone. "Professor."

He stepped toward me. "Is everything all right?"

"Of course," I lied.

He eyed me skeptically. It was like he could sense everything that was wrong, even when I didn't fully understand it myself.

"Nothing… *upsetting* has happened lately?" he asked.

Hell, did he know something?

Who was I kidding? He knew *me*. He could tell something was wrong.

What was I supposed to say, though? *My best friend is being bullied by a pack of losers, and I can't seem to help him. I've got all these feelings that make no sense. Oh, and I'm still pining after the girl I broke up with months ago.*

What a load of bullshit. It was no excuse.

"Everything's fine," I lied again.

"Okay," he said like he believed me, though I knew he didn't. "May I offer a word of advice?"

I shrugged. "You'll give it to me whether I want it or not."

Professor Warren ignored my rude remark. "When I have a lot weighing on my mind, I find that resolving *one* thing can help with all the rest. You don't have to do it all at once, Lucas. Start somewhere, and see where it takes you."

At that, Professor Warren walked off, leaving me to think about his comment. But I didn't want to think.

All I wanted to do was forget.

I returned to the school, but I nearly ran into Nadine when I entered the back door. She was alone, like she'd been waiting for me. I took a step back.

"If you're here to give me a lecture, save it," I said. "Professor Warren beat you to it."

"I actually wanted to make sure you were okay," Nadine said.

She reached up with a clean tissue to wipe the blood from my ear. I winced, but my heart softened beneath her touch.

"It doesn't look like it needs stitches," she remarked.

"I'll be fine," I told her. "Are you okay?"

"Well, I'm shocked, to be honest," she admitted.

"I'm not asking about the fight," I said. "I'm talking about James. I heard he threatened you."

Nadine sighed. "He was just trying to intimidate me."

"And someone needs to intimidate him!" I insisted.

"The Imperium Council already did," Nadine reminded me. She crossed her arms and frowned. "Lucas, what are you doing?"

"Um, trying to protect you?"

"You're looking for fights," she countered. She could see straight through me. "You just fought Ryan, and now you want to fight James. You're going to get yourself hurt."

"So?" I challenged.

"So you could get yourself killed!"

"Why do you care? We broke up." The words slipped out of my mouth before I could stop them.

She looked at me in disbelief. "I'm not allowed to care? Do you really think I'd rather see you dead?"

"I don't know what you want," I snapped. All I knew was she didn't want to be with me.

"Promise me you won't go after James," she insisted. "He's not worth it."

I swallowed the lump in my throat. That wasn't a promise I wanted to make. "Nadine," I sighed.

"Please, Lucas," she begged. She wasn't taking no for an answer.

I held her gaze for several seconds, before I finally caved. "Okay, I promise I won't go after James."

I could make this one promise, but I couldn't promise I'd stay out of danger.

SIX

Witnessing Lucas hold a scythe to Ryan's neck was both terrifying and—dare I say it—sexy. There was something about a man standing up for his friend that made me want to jump him.

But at the same time, I was worried. Lucas was already putting himself in danger by investigating nightshade. He couldn't keep starting fights on top of that—and certainly not for my sake. It was one thing for him to stand up for Grant, but I couldn't bear it if he got hurt because of me. That's why I made him promise not to go after James.

I did my best to put Lucas out of my mind the following day.

I sat in the Main Foyer between classes, reading my Miriamic Law textbook. I assumed word had spread about the Imperium Council's threats toward James, because no one had bothered me since. People had been avoiding me, so I was surprised when someone plunked down into the seat next to me. I started and looked up to see it was Grant. Isa jumped off my lap and started rubbing up against his legs. He sagged in his chair and scratched her head.

"Hard week?" I asked, eyeing his defeated features.

Grant's eyes darted across the foyer. "I'm trying to avoid the Tarantulas. They insist on making my life a living hell."

I frowned. "What'd they do this time?"

"Finn and Corbin kept throwing these tiny, piercing orbs at me in the cafeteria. I mean, I couldn't be *sure* it was them. They were facing away from me. But those fuckers hurt like hell."

"Raise hell back," I offered.

Grant shook his head. "I'll get in trouble."

I sat up straighter. "Well, we have to do something. The warlock's duel obviously didn't scare them away. These fights like this can't continue. How can I help?"

Grant sank deeper in his chair. "You can't. Look, just forget about it."

I wasn't going to, but I wanted to cheer him up. "Want to head down to the pool and talk?"

"Coach Campbell says I'm working too hard," Grant said with a frown. "He wants me to give my arm a rest. I'm just trying so hard to get back in shape, you know? I've been pulling extra practice sessions."

"Which is probably *why* he wants you to take it easy," I pointed out. "You need to listen to your body. Trust me."

Grant offered a kind smile. "You're right. I know I'm pushing myself hard this semester. I just feel like I lost so much time when my arm was healing."

I subconjured my textbook. "It sounds like you need the night off."

"And sulk in my dorm room? No, thank you."

"You like musical theatre, right? It's a Friday night. I'm sure something's playing at Starlight."

Grant's eyes brightened. "That's a good idea. Do you… do you want to come with me?"

I noticed his cheeks flush, and I eyed him curiously. "Are you asking me on a date?"

Grant averted his gaze. "If, uh, that's what you want it to be. I mean, we're both single… It, uh, doesn't have to be. I just thought…"

"What about Talia?" I asked.

His eyes widened. "What do you mean? Did she say something about me?"

"Not really," I admitted.

Grant sighed. "Nothing's happening between Talia and me. I think she wants to just stay friends, and I need to be okay with that."

It didn't feel right, because I knew despite what Talia said, she liked Grant. But she hadn't made a move, which meant Grant was free game.

He looked really sad, like he could really use a friend right now. All I wanted was to help.

"You know what? A date sounds great," I said.

It felt strange agreeing to a date with Grant—almost like... I was betraying Lucas in some way. After all, he and Grant were best friends. But Lucas and I weren't together anymore.

Grant's spine straightened, like he hadn't expected me to say yes. "You really want to go on a date with me?"

Truth was, I didn't want to date *anybody*. But I didn't want to sit around pining after Lucas the rest of my life, either. I had to move on.

"Yeah," I told him. "I really do."

"Goddess, I haven't planned anything," Grant started to ramble. "We could go to the lake—I think there's a party there tonight—or get dinner at Applewood Brewery. They have the *best* burgers. Or there's the café with the pies that change flavor with every bite."

"How about we think on it for a few hours, until classes finish?" I suggested. "We'll meet up around sundown and see what ideas we come up with."

"Sure," Grant said. "That sounds great."

I left the foyer shortly after for my mentorship with Verla. I was nervous the whole time, anticipating the date tonight. But part of me was excited, too. I was sure we would have a good time.

When I returned to my room to change, Talia was there. My stomach twisted into knots, and I knew I couldn't go on this date without her permission.

"Hey, Tal?" I said. "Something weird happened today."

She looked up from her sheet music. "You're not flaring up again, are you?"

"I actually feel pretty good," I assured her. "Actually, it's about Grant."

Her features changed at the mention of his name, but it was so subtle I couldn't really read her. "What happened?"

I sat on the couch next to her. "Grant asked me on a date."

"Oh," she said, looking stunned, though her tone was difficult to read.

"That's okay, right?" I asked. "I mean, I know he likes you, and you might like him, but you're giving it some time—"

"I don't like him," Talia stated.

I was skeptical, but she was so firm about it. "You're sure?"

"I mean, if he wants to ask you on a date, that's fine. I don't own him."

"Really?" I wasn't sure if I believed her. "Because if you don't want me to go, I won't go."

"I'm not going to tell you what to do," she said, but she was acting weird. She wouldn't look me straight in the eye.

"Um, okay. If that's how you really feel—"

"It's fine," she interrupted.

I still wasn't sure, but Talia seemed insistent, so I got ready to go. I changed into a cute orange dress with pockets and boots. I brushed out my hair, then darkened my makeup a bit with my magic. When I felt I looked cute, I left the room, leaving Isa behind—she'd already fallen asleep on my bed.

Grant was waiting for me when I reached the main foyer.

"I have the whole night planned," he said. "We'll start out with a show at Starlight, then have dinner at Red Apples. They have amazing pumpkin pie. Unless you had any ideas?"

I didn't really, since I didn't know the town as well as he did. I was up for anything.

"No, that sounds great." I gestured toward the doors. "Show the way."

Grant led me to his car, and we drove into town. When we arrived at Starlight, the line was really long, and we couldn't find parking. By the time we made it to the doors, the show was already sold out.

Grant's shoulders fell. "Shoot. Well, I guess we can go to dinner early."

"That's fine. I'm not in a hurry," I said.

But when we made it to Red Apples, they told us it would be a forty-five-minute wait.

"There's this really good diner on the lake called The Witch's Brew," Grant said. "They make the greatest desserts. It's chocolate, layered with chocolate, layered with whipped cream, layered with chocolate, and so on. Each one is served in a mini smoking cauldron, and they're enchanted to make you feel hungry so you can just keep shoving your face."

"That sounds amazing."

"Oh, they're low calorie, too," Grant added.

My stomach growled. "Perfect. Let's do that."

Grant and I drove to the Catwalk. He seemed a little out of his element now that his plans were ruined, but I kept assuring him it wasn't his fault and I didn't mind.

"What would you say is your favorite food?" Grant asked as we started down the Catwalk. The trail twisted and turned through the trees. He seemed a little uncomfortable—like he'd only asked to make conversation.

"I don't know if I can pick," I admitted. "I like variety."

"Huh, interesting," he replied. "I like bread."

I laughed. "Bread? That's so *boring*."

"No, it's not!" he argued. "You can have all types of different bread—flatbread, sourdough bread, banana bread, zucchini bread, pita bread, rye bread…"

"Fair enough. Then I'll choose salad," I decided.

Grant scrunched up his nose. "That's like, the most tasteless thing on the planet."

"Is it?" I challenged. "While you're over there eating your rye bread, I'll be shoving my face full of potato salad, fruit salad, macaroni salad, Snickers salad—"

"Now you're just making things up," he accused. "Snickers salad?"

"Don't tell me you've never had Snickers salad," I said with a frown. "My dad used to make it all the time. It has apples, pudding, whipped cream, and Snickers candy bars."

"Don't forget that I grew up on a steady diet of Latin American cuisine," Grant reminded me. "My mom mostly cooked rice, beans, tamales, and stuff like that."

"That's right. Your mom owns a restaurant, doesn't she?" I asked.

"Yeah. We're here." Grant gestured ahead of us.

A diner sat next to the lake, with a bunch of tables set up outside and lights strung overhead. The water lapped against the shore, and the crickets sang as night fell.

A host seated us at a table, and we both got lost in the menu. I didn't think either of us knew which topic to bring up next, so we just sat in awkward silence. It was pretty quiet around us, too, since there weren't very many people here tonight.

After a few minutes, our waitress brought us a basket of garlic bread. Her name tag read *Sadie*. I was sure I'd seen her around school before. Her eyes locked on Grant, like I wasn't even there. She was *definitely* checking him out, though Grant didn't seem to notice.

"I guess you don't have to order anything else," I said after she left. "Here's your *bread*."

Grant scowled at me. "Maybe you should stick to *this* section of the menu."

He pointed to the section labeled *salads*.

I laughed. "I'm thinking of maybe getting the Friday fish fry."

"It's a lot of food," he warned me.

I shrugged. "With our magical dessert, I'll have plenty of room."

"Well, if you want something magical, check out this page." He opened to another page and pointed out a section of magical entrees. "Oh, the walking crab sounds good. I haven't had it yet. It's infused with necromancer magic, so it dances around your table, even though it's fully cooked."

"I'd like to see that," I said.

"Then it's settled. That's what I'm getting." Grant closed his menu, and we ordered shortly after.

Grant didn't seem to know what to do while we waited, so he started playing with his straw wrapper. I excused myself to use the bathroom, and stayed in there longer than I probably should have, just to kill the time.

Finally, I returned to our table just as the waitress was bringing our food. My fried fish smelled delicious, and Grant's crab really did dance around on his plate. Grant poked at him, and the crab snapped its pinchers at his fingers.

Grant yanked backward so fast, he nearly knocked his chair over. "Whoa, he's a feisty one."

"Be careful he doesn't get away from you," the waitress teased. Her eyes sparked down at Grant.

"He's not going anywhere," Grant stated confidently. He poked his butter knife at the crab, like he was preparing for a sword fight. The crab snapped its claws at him.

I laughed. "Hurry up and eat him, or he'll get you."

Grant frowned. "He's not going to *get* me. He's just a harmless—OW!"

Grant squealed like a child as he sprang up out of his chair. The crab had jumped toward his face and clung tight to his ear with his pinchers. Grant shook his head and swatted at the crab, but the devilish little crustacean held on *tight*. The pinchers broke skin, and blood oozed out of Grant's ear and dripped onto the ground.

"Goddess!" I gasped. I leapt out of my chair and grabbed a stack of napkins from the table. I reached out to yank the crab off his ear, but Grant spun away from me.

"No, don't!" he cried. "It hurts."

"Then let me get him off," I insisted.

Grant swatted at the crab, which hung from his ear like a giant earring. *Everyone* in the restaurant turned to watch Grant flail around with a reanimated crab stuck to his earlobe. People across the restaurant began laughing, and I felt bad for Grant.

"Grant, stop," I begged. "I'll get him."

Grant practically whimpered as he stopped moving so I could help. I grabbed the crab around the middle with one hand, then pinched its leg in my other and yanked the two apart. The leg ripped off and went limp, though the crab in my hand was feisty as hell. He still had one claw left and used it to nip my hand. I squealed as I dropped him, and he went scurrying away toward the lake.

"Hey, that's my dinner!" Grant cried while holding one hand over his ear.

I handed him the napkins so he could soak up the blood. He held them up to his ear as he sank into his seat in defeat. Our waitress rushed over and began apologizing profusely.

"This almost never happens," she assured us. "Let me get you a first-aid kit."

"Ugh, why do these things always happen to me?" Grant complained as he pulled his napkins away from his ear. Blood started trickling down his neck, and he groaned as he placed the napkins back in place.

"I'm sorry," I said. "We can order something else."

Sadie, the waitress, returned with a first-aid kit for Grant. She tried patching up his wound, but only used a tiny bandage. I dug inside the kit, which she'd set on the table, then taped gauze to the side of Grant's face to stop the bleeding.

All the while, Sadie couldn't stop apologizing to him. "I'm so sorry. I'll get you another one on the house—no magic this time."

Even though Sadie brought out another crab—that didn't move at all —Grant seemed a bit wary of it and didn't touch it the whole meal. He just ate his French fries.

By the time I started eating, my fish was cold, and my fries tasted like

Styrofoam. We were both pretty disappointed in the meal, so we didn't order dessert.

"I'm sorry," Grant said after we left The Witch's Brew. "I ruined dinner, didn't I?"

"Well, it was entertaining for sure," I teased.

Grant started laughing. "Yeah, I guess it was… a little. Hey, girls like guys with scars, right?"

I grimaced. I didn't think he'd pick up any dates with *that* story. "I doubt it'll scar. You don't even need stitches."

Grant frowned. "Too bad. Wanna stop into Wicked Alchemy? I need to pick up some fertilizer for my plant."

"Your plant?"

"It's a project for my Advanced Magical Herbs class. I have to keep it alive the whole semester."

"And *that's* why I'd never pass as an Alchemist," I stated as we headed toward Wicked Alchemy. "I'd kill the plant in the first week."

"Nah, I'd help you out," he teased.

We entered Wicked Alchemy. It was a small shop, with various potions ingredients lining the walls, along with a fountain in the center that various essential oils flowed out from. A woman with a crooked lip sat behind the counter, her feet propped up near the register. She flipped through an old spell book and didn't even glance our way when we walked in.

There was a lot of neat stuff here for brewing potions, including cauldrons of various sizes, decorative glass potion vials, and magic crystals. I picked up a black candle and smelled it. It had a sort of sweet smell, but with something unpleasant underneath, like black licorice. I made a face and put it back on the counter.

"Don't go messing with black candles," Grant warned.

"Why? Is it related to black magic?" I questioned.

"Not really, but the plants used to make them have… questionable properties," he said. "The magic can be tough to work with, and spells go wrong really fast, unless you're a master."

I nodded. "Noted."

We browsed a while longer, until Grant found the fertilizer he needed. We ended up in line behind the only other customer in the store, a man with a long ponytail.

"Ah, David," the woman behind the counter said brightly. "I suppose you're here for your pickup."

She placed a box on the counter, which I noticed smelled a lot like the black licorice candle. She looked behind the counter a few moments longer before saying, "The rest must be in the back. Just a minute."

She disappeared into the back room. While we waited, Grant poked at a scale on a display nearby. The man in front of us tapped his shoe impatiently.

Several minutes of silence passed, before David must've decided he'd waited long enough, because he grabbed the box and whirled around—straight into me. I stumbled backward, right into Grant and the scales. One toppled over into another one, and a series of *crashes* sounded through the shop as the scales clanged together. They toppled into a pile of glass vials, and those shattered all over the ground. My eyes went wide at the destruction, and Grant's features paled.

"Watch where you're going," the man sneered. "You're gonna pay for those."

I froze for a second. The entire display must've cost several hundred dollars. I couldn't replace all of it.

"I'm not paying for that," I said. "It wasn't my fault."

David smirked. "It's my word against yours."

The man gave me chills. I was almost certain he could convince the cashier he had nothing to do with this. And seeing as Grant and I were the only other two in the shop, she'd make us pay.

"Hold up," Grant said. "I think I know how to solve this."

"You do?" I asked.

"Yeah. Run!" Grant grabbed my arm, and we raced out of the shop. He left his fertilizer behind, and we hightailed it out of there. I caught a brief glimpse of the woman racing out of the back room as we ran away.

We ducked into the shop nearby. I kept watch out the window, but the woman was glancing up and down the Catwalk, like she hadn't seen where we'd gone. David stepped out of the shop beside her. He must've said something to her, because she turned back inside, like chasing down a couple of college kids wasn't worth her time.

After a few moments to catch my breath, I turned to Grant. "Is it just me, or was that guy crazy?"

"No kidding. He gave me the creeps," he agreed. "But I think we're safe now."

I took a deep breath and looked around. Glass cases filled with wands lined the walls of the small shop. There were a couple of patrons here, but it wasn't crowded.

"Oh, this is perfect," I said. "I'm taking Wand Theory this semester. I'm supposed to shop for my first wand."

Grant's eyes lit up. "I haven't taken that class yet. I'm supposed to next semester. Maybe we can both find something."

I started browsing near the first case, but all the wands there had gems set into the handles. They were a bit too over-the-top for me. I wanted something pretty, but sensible.

Grant leaned over and lowered his voice. "How's the search for the... um, *Wands* going?"

I frowned. I didn't want to talk about the Oaken Wands. "I've talked to my grandma, and I've tried searching the library. No one knows anything. Sometimes I wonder why I'm even helping the council."

Grant tore his gaze from a wand with feathers carved up the blade. "Well, why *are* you helping them? I thought you wanted to be a homicide detective, though I don't know if that's possible now that you're going to be a priestess."

"I can be whatever I want, priestess or not," I said simply, keeping my gaze on the wands.

"You obviously don't know anything about the Wands," Grant added.

I sighed. "Some days, it makes no sense. No one wants me here. I don't know why I'm trying to protect everyone. But then I think of you and Talia, and I know I'm doing this for you guys."

Grant ducked his head and blushed. "I don't know how you do it. I think I would've given up by now."

I must've made him uncomfortable, because he suddenly became intrigued by the wands across the room. Their handles were designed to look like the hilt of a sword.

I was eyeing a wand with a braided design on the handle when a woman came up to me. "Can I help you with anything?" she asked.

I pointed to the wand. "Can I see that one?"

"Certainly," she said kindly. She opened the display case and handed it to me.

I wasn't sure what I was looking for in a wand, so I turned it over in my hands.

"How does it feel?" she asked.

"I like it," I remarked.

"Why don't you give it a try?" she suggested.

"Sure, I'll give it a go." I waved the wand over a dirty spot on the display case and spoke a cleansing incantation. *"Ask it once, ask it twice. Make this glass as clear as ice."*

I was confident in the incantation, as I'd learned it in one of my classes last semester. But I must've been wary of the wand, because a huge puff of black dust blew out of the end of it. The whole display case became covered in what looked like soot. I couldn't even see the wands beneath it.

The woman coughed a few times. "Perhaps we should try something infused with magical properties. We have a selection over here."

She led me over to another display case. The wands were very pretty, with twisting swirls all over the blade, and intricate designs on the handles. Some of them seemed to shimmer under the light. She handed me one with a blue stone on it.

"Let's start with something simple," she suggested.

"I could try subconjuring something," I offered.

She laughed. "Oh, no, honey. There are too many wards on this place to prevent theft. Perhaps try a glamour spell. There's a mirror right here if you'd like."

She turned a tabletop mirror toward me. I looked into it as I waved the wand around my face. I'd been trying to darken my makeup, but nothing happened. "It's not working," I remarked.

"Let me see," she said kindly, offering her hand.

I handed back the wand, and she flicked it a few times. I gasped when her features changed. Her makeup had gone from looking light and natural to so dark that she looked like a clown. Red, glittery eyeshadow covered her lids, and her eyebrows turned into a unibrow.

She noticed the horrified look on my face and turned the mirror toward herself. Her reflection must've scared her, because she stumbled back a few steps. "Dear Goddess."

She waved the wand a couple more times, but she couldn't get her face to go back to normal. Whatever spell I'd cast must've stuck. I hoped it didn't last long. Nearby, Grant was trying to stifle his laughter.

I bit my lip. "I'm sorry."

She looked a little ticked off, but took a breath to calm herself. "Perhaps if we find a compatible wand, you can reverse the spell. Try this one."

She handed me a smooth, simple wand with no special carvings. I thought it was kind of ugly, but I figured I'd give it a go.

"Let's try another simple spell," she suggested. "A light orb, perhaps?"

"I can do that." I swished the wand through the air, intending to create a simple light orb. Instead, a blast shot out of the end of the wand. My magic smashed straight into the display case in front of me, shattering it to bits. The woman gasped as glass rained down on her feet, and I winced.

She pursed her lips and just stood there a moment, like she couldn't believe what just happened. "OUT!" she snapped. "Get out of my shop. I can't help you."

Grant and I exchanged a wide-eyed glance. *Whoops.*

We hurried out of the shop as quickly as we could. It was dark outside, and we could hear music booming in the distance. Once we were out of the shop, Grant finally let himself laugh. "Oh, my goddess! Did you do that on purpose?"

"Of course not!" I shoved him. "Stop laughing."

"I thought you were supposed to be *good* at magic," he teased.

"Not with wands, apparently," I grumbled. "I guess this means our date is ruined."

His shoulders slumped. "It wasn't really what I envisioned. But it wasn't all that bad."

I frowned. "You're just saying that."

He wrinkled his nose. "Yeah, a little. I'm sorry, Nadine."

"I'm sorry, too."

"Well, if it went according to plan, we wouldn't have these wonderful stories to tell," he joked. "Maybe we can still salvage this. There's that party across the lake I mentioned earlier."

I thought about it for a moment and decided I really wanted to try salvaging the date. "Let's head over there."

We climbed in his car and drove around the lake, until we reached a bunch of cars parked along the side of the road. Loud party music and laughter could be heard from near the beach.

"Are you up for dancing?" Grant asked.

I smiled. "Always."

Grant took my hand and guided me down to the beach. I think he was trying to make it romantic or something—to try saving the date—but his hand was sweaty, and the whole thing just felt a little awkward.

This beach was different from the one I'd been to before, the night Lucas drove me home when I got too tired to drive myself. I caught myself glancing around the beach for him, and I put a quick end to it.

We're broken up, I reminded myself. *Plus, I'm on a date with Grant.*

I focused on my surroundings to take my mind off Lucas. The beach was small, and there was no bonfire this time, but someone had driven their car onto the beach and left the headlights on so we could see. Music played, but I didn't see anyone dancing. People mostly stood around drinking, and a couple of guys swam in the lake. To our left stood a large rock formation. It jutted into the lake and stood fifteen feet high. Three guys climbed on top of it, then launched themselves into the water.

"Cannonball!" one of them called. Their screams of delight carried over the music.

"Did you still want that dance?" I asked Grant.

He glanced around. "No one else is dancing."

"Should that stop us?" I asked.

He shrugged, then took my hands and started twirling me around. I laughed as we spun and swayed our hips to the music. People were probably looking our way, but I didn't care. Dancing on the beach was so much fun. I kicked my boots off, enjoying the feeling of the sand on my toes as Grant led me in circles.

"Want to see something?" Grant didn't wait for an answer before spinning away from me. He got down on the ground and tried to break dance, but it looked more comical than anything. All he really did was kick up sand. I covered my mouth and doubled over laughing.

Grant blew a breath as he stood up, like all that dancing was hard work. "I need some practice, but it was pretty good, right?"

"If you were trying to entertain me, sure," I teased.

"Date officially salvaged," he said proudly, puffing out his chest.

I smiled at him. "To be honest, I *did* have fun with you tonight, even though most of it was a disaster."

"But a *good* disaster, right?" he asked, taking a step toward me.

I nodded. "A good disaster."

Part of me wanted this date to work out—because if it did, I could finally say I was over Lucas. I could stop thinking about him all the time and move on. After all, why couldn't Grant and I work out? We were good friends. Maybe we could be something more.

Grant and I were so close that we were nearly touching. I didn't really know how it happened. It just seemed like the right thing to do at the time—like I needed to experiment to see just how good the date actually went. I reached out and took his hands in mine, and he came even closer to me. I tilted my chin up to him. He hesitated a moment, and I had no idea what was going through his head. For a moment, I thought he was going to back off, and I caught myself thinking I hoped he did.

If this date ended horribly, I didn't have to let go of Lucas. I'd never admit it to myself, but I was so freaking terrified of letting him go.

I almost backed away, because I didn't think I could do it. I couldn't move on. It was wrong. But then Grant closed the distance between us, and his lips connected with mine. I couldn't turn back.

My breath hitched in surprise. I didn't think we'd actually kiss. But we *were* kissing...

Except it was *all wrong.*

Our hands hung limply in one another's. There was no passion, no surge of excitement. Just the sinking of my gut as I waited for the kiss to end.

I wanted to feel something, but I just... didn't.

Grant took a step closer to me, except he got too close and stepped on my foot. He tripped, and we fell into the sand. Grant landed on top of me, and for a second, the two of us just froze. After a beat, I burst into laughter. Grant looked totally embarrassed at first, until he started laughing, too.

"Nope, can't be salvaged," I teased.

Grant chuckled. "Friends?"

My laughter quieted, and I nodded. "Friends."

Grant pushed himself off of me, but his belt buckle snagged on my dress. "Sorry," he said as he fumbled to unhook himself from the threads. We were in the shadows, so he couldn't really see what he was doing. This date was turning out to be hilariously sad, if anything.

"Oh, no. Help! Help!" I joked with a laugh.

Grant looked a bit uncomfortable as he tried to free himself. "I'm getting it. I just don't want to—"

Thwack!

Something came out of the darkness and connected with Grant's stomach. I gasped as he was flung off of me. The threads in my dress snapped. Grant rolled across the sand, into the shadows where I could hardly see his face. I hadn't realized what happened at first, until I looked up to see a tall, shadowy figure above me.

"Nadine?" he asked breathlessly. My heart skipped a beat at the sound of his voice.

Lucas. I was too shocked to say anything.

He walked around me and straight up to Grant. "What the hell do you think you're doing?"

Lucas grabbed Grant by the collar, then slammed his fist into the side of his face. The air left my lungs as I scrambled to my feet.

"Whoa, man—!" Grant started to say.

Lucas hadn't heard him before he punched him again. A sickening *crack* sounded across the beach.

"Stop!" I screamed, racing over to grab Lucas's shoulder. "Stop it, Lucas!"

Grant scrambled to his feet, then tackled Lucas to the ground. The two ended up in a scuffle in the center of the headlights lighting up the beach. Fists flew in all directions, and everyone turned to stare.

"What the hell's your problem!?" Grant snapped.

Lucas stilled in the sand. It was like he hadn't realized who he'd been fighting until then. It'd been too dark to see his face. Now that they were in the headlights, though, I could see the damage Lucas had done. Grant's left eye was already starting to swell up, and blood coated his teeth. It looked like he'd hurt him pretty badly.

Grant shoved Lucas. "It was *just* a kiss."

Lucas's eyes went wide, and his gaze darted between Grant and me. The look on his face felt like an arrow to my heart. I shouldn't have felt guilty. We weren't together, which meant I could kiss whoever the hell I liked. But I couldn't bear to watch him get hurt, either.

And that just pissed me off, because I shouldn't care what the hell Lucas thought of me. I was trying to move on, and he was coming in here starting fist fights.

"You guys *kissed?*" Lucas growled. "What the hell, man? We're best friends!"

"Nadine and I are friends, too," Grant said. "I didn't think—"

"Yeah, you didn't think," Lucas fumed.

"Oh, so *you* get to decide who I can date?" I snapped. I didn't care who was watching. I helped Grant to his feet, but I didn't take my eyes off Lucas. "You can't go around punching my dates! I don't care if I was dating the devil himself."

"I was *defending* you!" Lucas yelled. He stood, and I saw that Grant had gotten one good punch in. Blood trickled out of a cut on Lucas's cheek. "I thought—"

"I don't care what you thought!" My nostrils flared. "I'm not your girl-friend anymore, and your possessive behavior isn't cute."

"You were yelling for help!" he screamed, throwing his hands into the air. "I guess I'm just not supposed to help people who ask for it anymore, huh?"

"I was joking!" I insisted. "Grant and I were laughing and having a good time."

"That's not what it looked like," Lucas snapped back.

I crossed my arms. I was so mad at him for attacking Grant that I'd say anything to get Lucas to admit he was wrong. "I don't care what it looked like. If I wanted help, I'd take it from anyone but *you.*"

"What's that supposed to mean?" he demanded.

Something about speaking to Lucas again—even though we were yelling at each other—enthralled me. I felt more in my element, more *alive*, than I had all night.

"I don't need your help, Lucas!" I yelled. "I need you to stay away from me."

Even as I said it, I knew it was a lie, because all I wanted was for him to take me in his arms and calm me down. I longed for him to smooth down my hair and kiss the top of my head like he used to do. I wanted to cry and scream and make a scene, because it was easier than facing the truth.

I *missed* him. And it sucked that we weren't together.

Lucas gritted his teeth. "Fine, Nadine. Next time I see someone attacking you, I'll sit back and watch it happen. Would that make you happy?"

Hell, no.

"Yeah, it would," I lied. "I can handle myself."

He rolled his eyes. "What are you trying to prove, Nadine? That you're *so* independent you don't need a guy?"

I lifted my chin proudly. "I don't need *you.*"

But hell, I wanted him, even though I wasn't supposed to.

"What are you even doing here?" I demanded. "You don't like parties."

"Why should you care?" Lucas shot back. "I could ask you the same thing. Since when did you and Grant start dating?"

"We're not," I stated bluntly. "I came to strip down and skinny dip for fun."

"Then by all means, go right ahead," he challenged, gesturing toward the water. He was calling me on my bluff.

I cocked an eyebrow. "Is that a dare?"

It hurt to ask, because that used to be *our* thing. We didn't dare each other anymore.

Lucas's face paled when he realized I was serious. "What? No."

I whirled away from Lucas, but Grant caught my arm. "You don't have to do this."

I pulled away. "If Lucas thinks he can tell me what to do, he's wrong."

I started across the sand, well aware that there were plenty of eyes on me. Lucas hurried after me, but I shrugged him off when he tried to stop me.

"Nadine," he insisted, reaching for me.

"Get away from me!" I snapped.

I ran ahead of him, to the rock formation at the edge of the beach. There was a rocky trail on the backside, with large boulders I had to use my hands to crawl over.

"Nadine, get down!" Lucas insisted. "You're going to hurt yourself."

I didn't look back at him as I climbed up higher. "That's the fun of it."

"Everyone's watching," he hissed, like that was supposed to get me to stop.

I could see Lucas's shadow at the base of the rock formation, shifting from foot to foot like he was fighting whether to chase after me or not. Part of me wanted him to walk away. Another wished he was right behind me, jumping in with me.

But more than anything, I wanted to prove that he didn't own me. I was a free woman.

I yanked my dress over my head, until I was standing in just my bra and panties. Several people cat-called me from below, and I just smirked and tossed my dress over the rocks. It fluttered downward, until it landed in the sand next to Lucas.

"Okay, you've proven your point," he said. "Now get down before you—"

I didn't hear what he said next, because I took a running start and screamed in exhilaration as I jumped off the end of the cliff. For a moment, I was flying, my heart flip-flopping in my abdomen as I took the plunge. It felt *so* damn good.

I squeezed my eyes tightly shut and held my breath. Cold water enveloped me from all angles, but it felt great. I kicked my feet and stroked my arms through the water.

Panic set in when after a few strokes, I still hadn't surfaced.

Fuck! I didn't know which way was up and which was down. My eyes shot open, and I frantically looked through the water, but all I could see was darkness.

My heart hammered. I'd made a terrible mistake.

The pressure in my lungs rose, until I thought I couldn't take it any longer. My head spun, and I feared I was going to drown...

Strong hands landed on my arms, and I was suddenly being dragged through the water. I was almost certain it was a reaper, dragging my soul from my body—

Then my head surfaced, and I gasped a huge breath. I must've been in shock or something, because when I tried to move my arms through the water, I couldn't get them to move right. I was terrified and shaking, still trying to recover from the terror I'd put myself in.

Those hands never left my body as someone dragged me toward shore. I was vaguely aware of people shouting and screaming my name, but I barely processed it. I was just relieved to be alive.

Someone dragged me onto shore and laid me on my back in the sand. We were so close to the water that it still touched my toes. I coughed up water.

"Nadine!" Lucas called, his silhouette hovering above me. Water dripped from his wet hair and onto my chest. It was only then that I realized he'd been the one to drag me from the water.

Relief flooded through me, and my heart surged in my chest. I didn't think about what I was doing when I flung my arms around him. "Goddess, Lucas."

"That was stupid, Nad—" he started to say, but I must've squeezed too hard, because he grunted in my ear.

The sound brought me back to reality, reminding me that I was half-naked and far too close to him. I pulled my arms away quickly and glanced around. My chest heaved in deep breaths, and everyone stared.

Grant rushed up to me and handed me a towel. I didn't know where he'd gotten it—probably from one of the other people who'd been swimming—but I took it anyway and covered up. "You all right?" he asked.

I glanced at Lucas, who had a worried look on his face. "I will be."

Lucas started to reach out for me, but he seemed hesitant. It broke my heart a little.

I may be a free woman, but at what cost? I still needed Lucas to rush in and save me. And I hated that, because it wasn't fair of me to rely on him anymore.

"I should get you back to school," Grant said.

I pulled the towel around myself and let Grant help me to my feet. I kept my eyes on Lucas. He brushed his wet hair out of his eyes, watching me go. I wanted to say something, but I was so conflicted, I didn't even know how to feel anymore. There was no pride left, that was for sure. Whatever I'd been trying to prove… I hadn't.

I just felt immense gratitude for him being there. And I knew I couldn't expect that from him.

I hung my head, unable to stop throwing glances back at him. The look on his face was heartbreaking, like for a moment, he actually thought he might lose me.

And the terrifying thing was… we'd already lost one another.

LUCAS

SEVEN

I didn't know what I'd been doing at that party.

Hell, that was a lie. I was drinking away my feelings, if I was being totally honest. I'd made it through Professor Daniels's list of contacts in a day, and I'd interviewed them all except one. The last lead was out of town. But these people knew nothing. It was all expert opinion and speculation regarding general drug use, but nothing solid about nightshade. I needed to find the real people behind this crime. I felt useless.

And worse, I couldn't stop thinking about Nadine. I told myself I went to the party to get out there, to try moving on like Grant suggested. All while he swooped in and took care of Nadine when I couldn't.

The asshole.

He wasn't the one who'd jumped into the water to save her. He'd never care about her the way that I did.

Then again, he wasn't the reason she'd jumped, either. Maybe it was better this way. Nadine wasn't in danger when I wasn't around.

I didn't speak to Grant the rest of the weekend. He'd tried more than once to explain to me what happened, but I couldn't be bothered to hear it.

I made the mistake of opening the drawer to my nightstand, and I caught sight of the enchanted key Nadine had given me. I was too broken up to wear it, because it reminded me of her, and I hadn't had the guts to face her and give it back yet. I was about to shove the drawer closed again when I caught sight of an envelope.

It was the letter that someone had slipped under my door a few weeks ago. I didn't know why I hadn't thrown it out. After all, it was nothing more than a prank. I was certain of it.

So why hadn't I let it go?

I pulled out the envelope and reread the letter.

By fire and noose
The coven will fall
Division and suffering
Destruction to all

Great power of the chosen
The coven be made whole
By the only witch of her kind
And a reaper bound to her soul

I eyed the handwriting, and it suddenly hit me that I recognized it. I hadn't realized it before. I conjured a piece of paper from my stash. I'd kept it there for months. I hurried over to the desk and slapped both pieces of paper side-by-side on the tabletop, then turned on the lamp next to me. My eyes darted from the letter that'd been slipped under my door to the paper I'd conjured. It was the transcript of the encounter I'd had with Eric almost a year ago—from when I'd turned to Everly Hall, the Seer with automatic writing powers.

The handwriting was identical.

My knees shook as I stood up straight. I couldn't deny it any longer. This was no joke.

It was a *prophecy*.

Nadine and I had been chosen. If we didn't work together to save the coven, everyone would perish.

I had to do something.

It was nearing sunset when I left the school. Grant's car sat parked in the corner of the school's parking lot. He'd given me a key a few weeks ago, with an open invite to drive his car whenever I wanted. I think it was his way of helping me with my depression by giving me options. He was mad at me now, but he'd never revoked the invite, so I hopped inside and drove into town.

The car tires squealed as I skidded to a stop along Main Street. I did a shitty job parking the car, but I didn't really care. I jumped out of it and hurried inside a psychic shop. A couple of teenage girls giggled in the corner as they flipped through this month's edition of *New Moon Horoscopes*. Nearby, a woman arranged a tarot display behind the counter. She gave a start when I whipped the door open.

"Out!' I growled at the girls.

They both went dead silent and shot each other a look, before dropping the magazine and scrambling out of the shop. I was pretty sure they were nearly in tears.

The woman behind the counter straightened her spine. "Lucas."

"Everly," I said, sounding less than pleased.

She didn't seem affected by my shitty mood. "What can I do for you?"

I conjured the sheet of paper she'd left at my dorm room and slammed it onto the counter. "You can give me answers. What does this mean?"

Everly took the paper and scanned the prophecy. It was like she was seeing it for the first time. She didn't say a thing until she handed the paper back.

"I'm afraid I can't help you," she said in a soft tone, like we were discussing nothing more than the weather.

"You have to know!" I insisted. "You wrote this, didn't you?"

"It looks like my handwriting," she admitted. "But my understanding only goes so far. My powers of automatic writing allow me to convey messages, not to necessarily understand them."

"This isn't just any old message," I stated. "This is a prophecy, isn't it? It's going to come true one way or another."

Everly swallowed. "I believe so."

"It's talking about me, right? I'm the reaper. And the only witch of her kind? That's Nadine, the Curse Breaker."

"That's my assumption as well," she said, looking slightly worried.

"What do we have to do?" I begged. "What's this *great power*? How do we save the coven from destruction?"

"I don't have those answers," she said.

I sensed my phone ringing in my stash, but I let it vibrate without answering it.

"I need to know!" I snapped, slamming my fist against the counter.

Everly didn't seem phased by my outburst at all. She simply blinked and said, "All will be revealed if you are patient. Please understand that I don't even remember writing this. I wrote it and gave it to you in a trance. This message came from someone on the other side—not me. If you want answers, you'll have to ask the Goddess yourself. I cannot help."

"That's not good enough," I insisted. "If I'm to fulfill this prophecy, I need guidance."

My phone continued to vibrate. Someone was desperate to get a hold of me. Whoever the hell it was better have a damn good reason. I conjured my phone and answered.

"What?" I snapped.

A woman sobbed from the other end of the line. "L-Lucas."

My blood ran cold. "Mom?"

"It's the house," she cried. I could picture her shoulders shaking as she sobbed. I'd seen it too many times before. "It's—"

She said something, but I didn't catch it.

I turned away from Everly, the prophecy forgotten. All that mattered was my mother. I worried that dad had gone on a rampage again and wrecked the house. I just hoped he hadn't hurt her in the process. My stomach hollowed at the thought.

"Mom, I can't understand you. What happened?"

"It-it's gone," she sobbed.

"What's gone?" I demanded. "Mom, *what's gone?*"

"The house! It's in flames! There's nothing we can do to save it."

My stomach dropped from my abdomen. This couldn't be happening. For a moment, my mind went blank. Surely, I hadn't heard her right.

"The house burnt down?" I repeated in a raspy tone.

"It's burning right now!" she cried. Her sobs snapped me back to attention.

"Where are you?" I asked, panic evident in my tone.

"I'm right outside the house," she said. "What's left of it, anyway."

"Don't go anywhere," I told her. "I'll be right there."

I snatched up the prophecy page and subconjured it, then raced out to the car. Tires squealed as I tore out of my parking spot and onto the street. Someone honked at me as I cut them off, but I held tight to the steering wheel and sped through town.

I smelled the fire and heard the sirens before I reached my street. A huge black cloud of smoke billowed into the sky. I could barely see the setting sun behind the ominous cloud. The street was so crowded that I couldn't get through as firemen and onlookers filled the area. I slammed on the brakes and parked the car in the middle of the street, abandoning the keys inside as I jumped out.

"Let me through!" I snapped as I pushed past people.

They must've noticed the vengeance in my eyes, because people parted until I reached the edge of a barricade. A fireman caught me by the chest and pushed me back. A shield ballooned from his palm, keeping me at bay.

"I need everyone to stay back!" he yelled.

My knees went weak as my eyes locked on the scene before me. Orange flames engulfed the tiny house I grew up in, and smoke billowed out broken windows. The front door had been knocked off its hinges, and I could see furniture inside ablaze. Every single one of my mother's possessions had been inside.

My soul felt as if it was burning along with the house. There weren't many memories of that house that I cherished, but there were enough that the sight shot bile into my throat. I wanted to puke, scream, and weep all at the same time. The shock of it all riveted through me, until my whole body shook.

A crew of firemen used hoses and spells to try to kill the flames, but it was already too late. There was nothing left to salvage.

Nearby, a woman wailed, and my stunned gaze snapped in her direction. I saw my mother on her knees beyond the barricade, holding a shawl around herself and shaking. My father was nowhere to be seen.

"Let me through!" I shouted at the fireman. "That's my mom!"

His features fell, and the shield dropped. "Come on through, kid."

I immediately jumped over the barricade and raced to my mother. I dropped to my knees beside her and wrapped her in my arms. She shook against me as tears streamed down her cheeks.

"There's n-nothing!" she sobbed.

"How did this happen?" I demanded. "Where's Dad?"

"H-he's on his way home," she said, though she didn't mention where he'd been. Out drinking his feelings, I was sure.

I gritted my teeth. "He's responsible for this, isn't he?"

Smack!

Her palm cracked across the side of my face. It took me a second to realize she'd slapped me.

"Mom!" I gasped. My hand came up to cradle the side of my face. I expected this kind of reaction out of Dad, but *never* from my mother. It happened so fast that I could barely process it.

"How *dare* you," she growled. "How dare you accuse your father of this!"

"It's something he would do!" I cried. "He's careless like that."

She glared at me. "Your father has made mistakes, but he would never do something like this. He wasn't even here. It was someone else."

She sounded so certain, like she *knew*.

My mouth went dry. "You're talking arson. You know who's responsible?"

Her lips tightened, and she shoved a crumpled piece of paper into my hands.

"What's this?" I asked as I unfurled it.

"A message," she stated.

The street seemed to spin as my eyes roamed over the paper. My hands shook so fiercely, I could hardly read the words typed in big, bold letters.

Belladonna has come for you, Lucas.

Fuck. This was my fault.

Belladonna was another name for deadly nightshade, an ingredient in poisons that were only brewed by the coven for warfare. It was a message from the drug dealers. They were warning me that I was dead if I kept pursuing answers. They must've found out that I'd been asking around.

Fuck, I'd stirred up some serious shit by pursing those contacts and demanding answers from Ryan. The dealers had gone after my parents as a warning, and it was doing one hell of a job scaring me away. If they were willing to attack my parents like this, what else would they do to the people I loved?

"Where did you find this?" I demanded.

Mom swallowed. "It was attached to the mailbox when I ran outside. Lucas, are you doing drugs?"

I ignored her question and bellowed, "You were inside the house when this happened!?"

She nodded solemnly.

My hands curled into fists. These fuckers couldn't mess with my family like this! I shoved the paper back in her direction. "You have to turn this into the police."

"So these people have more reason to hurt us?" she asked. "No."

"So they can be caught!" I cried. "They have to be stopped, before they can hurt anyone else."

Mom gazed down at the paper, her hands shaking. "Just leave."

My jaw dropped. "What?"

"I said *leave*." She finally lifted her gaze, and her eyes glistened with tears. "I called you because I thought you'd want to know what *you* did. Now you know, and you can go. It's your fault the house is gone, Lucas. I don't know what it is, but you got involved in something you shouldn't have, and now we all have to pay the price. I'll clean up this mess, like I always do."

"Mom…" My stomach hollowed, and my face heated. I wasn't sure I believed what I was hearing. "Let me help."

"Like you helped Eric?" she snapped.

My whole body trembled. She didn't blame me for that, did she? She couldn't mean it.

But it didn't matter. The accusation stung like a motherfucker.

She shoved me away. "You've helped enough."

My lungs must've been collapsing, because my chest became so tight I couldn't breathe. The pain of rejection permeated into my bones, and I couldn't think straight. My mother blamed me, and she didn't want my help—or my apology. I didn't know how to fix this. I didn't know if I *could*.

I couldn't handle the pain… so I did the only thing I knew how.

I shut down.

I barely remembered returning to the car. Even when I got back to school, I felt like a zombie, just going through the motions. My consciousness was somewhere else entirely. I'd let myself go numb again, because that was easier than facing the emotions welling up inside of me.

I stepped into the Main Foyer, and my feet carried me up the grand staircase. I reached the second level when a voice caught my attention. It was low, nearly a whisper, but I honed in on it.

"We heard you're the guy to go to for nightshade."

I stilled and turned in the direction of the voice.

"I sure am," a nasally voice replied. Gregory Walker stood beside a group of girls, smirking proudly.

Of fucking course Gregory was dealing. I should've known.

If these drug dealers wanted to mess with me, they had one hell of a death wish. They wanted to scare me off, to show me exactly what they were capable of. But I was a reaper, a symbol of death. I'd show them just how deadly I could be.

I was dead set on murder when I stomped up to Gregory and grabbed his shoulder.

"Whoa!" he cried as I whirled him around to face me.

"We need to talk," I demanded.

Gregory's eyes went wide. "About what?"

I rolled my eyes. "I need some fucking alchemy supplies. I know you deal."

He shot a glance at the girls. "Sure. I can get you alchemy supplies. But I'm in the middle—"

"*Now*," I growled. I wasn't giving him a choice, and Gregory knew it.

"Step into my office." He gestured down the empty hallway.

I blew a breath but followed him away from the girls anyway.

He stopped halfway down the hall. "Before we do business, I have to ask who referred you to me."

"The fucking ashes of my childhood home," I snapped.

Gregory's face paled. "I don't know anything about that."

"You sure as hell know where to find someone who does," I growled. "Maybe be a little more discreet next time. Your clients just blew your cover. Tell me what you know. Who's your boss?"

"I have no idea what you're talking about," he said innocently, but he was a terrible actor.

"Yes, you do," I accused. "Give me the info, or I'll report you for dealing nightshade."

His voice came out a pitch higher than normal. "Nightshade? Never heard of it."

I was sick of this game. I didn't just sit with my sobbing, homeless mother to come back here and talk circles with this guy. I snapped. I grabbed Gregory by the collar and shoved him hard against the wall.

"Don't play dumb with me!" I growled. My fist slammed into the wall next to his head. It was only a warning, but he shook in fear.

"Get off of me!" he yelled. "If I weren't affected by the Waning right now, I'd shove a battle orb up your ass."

His attempt at intimidation fell flat. There was nothing terrifying about this guy. I'd get him to fold. We were attracting the attention of everyone in the hall, and people lifted their phones to record. I didn't care.

"I *just* heard you, and I saw you last year with Ryan," I accused. "He said you owe him money. It was for the nightshade, wasn't it? I don't care if you're dealing or buying, but you know something, and you're going to tell me now."

Gregory whimpered. "I don't know anything, I swear."

The guy was a liar, and I was going to prove it. Fury blazed through my veins, and I acted without thinking. I curled my fingers in Gregory's shirt and yanked him behind me. At the end of the hall stood an archway that no one dared step into.

Gregory must've noticed where I was headed, because he began to flail and scream. "No! You can't!"

He tripped as we reached the Vanishing Stairwell. I yanked him forward and forced his head through the doorway. I held him so tightly that he couldn't move. He squeezed his eyes shut tightly, and his lips trembled.

"Who was it!?" I seethed. "Who's behind all of this? The drugs, the arson! Give me a name!"

"I-I don't have one," Gregory whimpered. "They contacted me, knew I needed the money for my medical bills. I've got all sorts of shit wrong with me. I was born with a heart condition and asthma. I get the night-shade from pick-up locations all throughout town. It's never the same place twice. Same with the cash. I never talk to anyone. I've never seen a face."

It sounded like he was telling the truth, and I was pissed. My first real lead in months, and it turns out to be a dud—just like all the contacts Professor Daniels had given me. What a waste.

"You're useless," I said in disgust. "I want a phone number. Let me find this guy myself."

"It changes every time," he said. "I-I couldn't get ahold of them even if I wanted to."

"Then try harder!" I yelled so loud that my voice echoed down the hall.

"Lucas!" someone snapped, and a hand landed on my shoulder.

They yanked me away from Gregory, and he fell into the middle of the archway. He scrambled to his feet so fast, I was sure he'd pissed his pants.

I whirled toward the newcomer, and all the blood in my body drained to my toes. She was like an angel, so beautiful and majestic. But angels and reapers didn't belong together.

"N..." I couldn't even say her name.

"What the hell is wrong with you!?" Nadine shouted.

"Everything!" I seethed.

She didn't like that answer. She crossed her arms and glared at me. "You said you wouldn't get into any more fights."

"I said I wouldn't go after James," I reminded her. "Why should I do what you say, anyway? *You* won't listen to me."

"You're putting other people in danger!" she cried. "You don't know when that staircase will disappear. You could've killed Gregory."

"Like you didn't do the same thing to Chloe," I snapped.

"I never meant to!" Nadine growled back. "Thank the Goddess that Chloe got lucky. Gregory might not have."

"Gregory needs a fucking wake-up call."

"And you should be the one to give him it?" she challenged. "Where'd you earn that right?"

"Today! When he and his buddies tried to kill my mom!"

Nadine opened her mouth, but her words stopped dead on her tongue. Her tone softened. "What happened?"

My shoulders shook. "They burned my house down."

Her eyes went wide. "Who?"

"I-I don't know," I admitted, shoving my hands into my hair. I was a fucking mess. "I don't know a damn thing. That's the problem!"

"Lucas—" Nadine started to say, but she cut off when the crowd gasped.

"It was *him*!" someone shouted.

Gregory burst through the crowd with Headmistress Verla behind him. He visibly shook as he pointed a finger at me. Verla wore a tight-lipped expression. She was not pleased.

Gregory, you fucking tattle tale. What is this? Grade school?

"Lucas," Headmistress Verla said. "Gregory tells me you held him over the Vanishing Stairwell. Is this true?"

I tugged hard at the strands of my hair, wishing to just pull them out. That pain would be far more bearable than the turmoil swirling in my gut right now. But instead, I dropped my arms to my sides.

"Yeah, it's true," I admitted between gritted teeth.

"Very well," Verla said. "Come with me."

I huffed a breath, but I followed her. Might as well get my expulsion over with. I shot one last glance back at Nadine. She wore a sorrowful expression that broke my heart to pieces. It was almost easier to bear her presence when she was mad at me. Now I just had her pity.

Nausea hit me when I noticed the wall behind her. The wall was flush, the Vanishing Stairwell gone. If Nadine hadn't stopped me, Gregory might be dead. I was a fucking idiot.

Verla didn't even wait until we were in her office to interrogate me. She stopped in a quiet hall and turned on her heel. "Do you want to tell me what's going on?"

I couldn't meet her gaze. "Not really, to be honest."

"I heard a rumor of a warlock's duel that occurred several days ago. You wouldn't happen to know anything about that, would you?"

I swallowed the lump in my throat, but I didn't answer.

Verla pursed her lips. "You do know that threatening another student is grounds for expulsion."

"Yes," I answered flatly. "Might as well just get rid of me. I'm not going to pass this semester anyway."

I expected her to tell me to go pack my bags, but instead, her features softened. "Are you all right, Mister Taylor?"

My fists shook at my sides. "Well, my parents' house just burnt down because I'm a royal fuck-up."

The sympathy in her eyes deepened. "I think you need to take some time off."

I furrowed my brow. "You're not expelling me?"

"I'm suspending you," she said with pursed lips.

"You're... what?" I couldn't blame her for punishing me. I'd screwed up. But I didn't have anywhere to go.

"Take a week off to help your parents," she said, like she was going easy on me. And she was, to be honest. She could've expelled me.

"I know you're trying to help, but my parents don't want me around," I admitted.

"Then take some time for yourself," she said kindly. "I hope you feel better when you return."

"Yeah, me too." The thing was, I wasn't lying this time.

Headmistress Verla was giving me a chance to redeem myself. I told myself I was grieving, but all I was really doing was letting myself go. *Something* had to change. I didn't care what the fuck it was. I just couldn't keep going on like this.

I returned to my dorm room to gather my things.

"What's going on?" Grant asked.

"I fought with Gregory. I've been suspended," I said flatly, feeling embarrassed. "I hope your dad will be okay with me crashing at his house for a week."

"Yeah, of course he will."

I must've looked like a mess, because Grant seemed really concerned. He didn't ask too many questions, and part of me resented him for it. I wish he'd just yell at me or something. It'd be better than the silence.

Neither of us mentioned his date with Nadine, though I was sure we were still pissed about everything that happened.

Mister Bryant was more than happy to let me stay in Grant's childhood room. He was more of a dad to me than my own father.

I slept on the floor that night, knowing full well that if I crawled into bed, I'd never leave. Besides, it was *Grant's* bed. It didn't feel right.

Sunlight streamed in through the window the next morning, casting light across my face. By the time I woke, Mister Bryant had already left for work. My whole body felt stiff as I rolled over and stretched.

My eyes caught sight of something under the bed. It was a few of my things Grant had let me store there when I'd moved out of my parents. I noticed a skateboard, which reminded me of Eric. He'd bought it for me years ago, back when we were dumb kids who would take our boards up the mountain trails and ride them all the way down on the twisting roads leading into town. The adrenaline rush had been incredible. I'd never forget the way the wind whipped through my hair as I sped down the mountainside—

My heart gave a start as an idea struck me. Eric and I used to do all kinds of extreme sports together. It's what made us feel alive and free when Dad wasn't screaming his head off at us. I knew how to handle my grief, because I'd been doing it for years.

I'd forgotten all that. I'd given it up once Eric wasn't around anymore.

It was time to feel something again.

I didn't think it through as I grabbed the skateboard and my backpack, tossed on some clothes, and headed outside. It was a nice day for a hike—cool, but clear skies. The hike could take hours, but I didn't mind.

There was a trailhead not far away. I blasted music in my earbuds as I took in the scenery along the trail. It helped keep me from overthinking things.

Hell, who was I kidding? I wasn't thinking at all.

I didn't know how long it took me to get to the top of the trail, but it seemed like no time at all. The trail ended at a scenic outlook, which gave a perfect view of the town below. Octavia Falls was beautiful this time of year as the trees began to shift from green into shades of orange and red. Peak autumn beauty was only a few weeks away.

Below me, the peaks of Miriam Mansion rose above the trees. In the distance, Lake Santos spread several miles across the landscape. The trees were so thick that most of the town was hidden beneath them. It was gorgeous.

But the view didn't seem to matter to me right now. I came here for one thing. I was hungry for adventure.

I walked across the parking lot next to the scenic outlook. There was no one here but me. It felt as if endless possibilities lay ahead of me.

I took my skateboard from my bag and placed it on the pavement. I put my foot on it, testing the wheels under my weight. They glided with ease, just like I remembered. My gaze locked forward on the winding road ahead, which dipped downward and disappeared into the trees. A smirk stretched across my face, as I was already anticipating the thrill.

"Let's do this," I said aloud.

I kicked off. My skateboard rolled forward, picking up speed within seconds. I sped down the road faster than most would dare, knowing I couldn't stop my momentum until I reached the bottom. My heart hammered as adrenaline kicked in. I crouched down and kept my eyes forward, controlling the board around twists and turns. Air swept through my hair, which was getting so long that it fell into my eyes. I laughed in exhilaration. I felt all-powerful up here on this mountain, like if I could take on these twists and turns, I could take anything life threw at me.

I guided my board around another turn, then spotted the next bend ahead. It turned so sharply that a guard rail bordered the outer edge. It was dangerous for sure, but that's what made it fun.

My pulse quickened as I approached the bend. Something inside of me begged to be let free, and I was done pushing it downward. I screamed and laughed, all at the same time. My thrilling cry echoed off the mountains around me.

I reached the bend and shifted my weight. The skateboard moved to my command, breezing past the curve faster than I could blink. The road straightened for barely a moment before the next curve came. I had a mere moment to calculate my movements before I was twisting around the bend at record speed. I moved to the rhythm of the road, feeling on top of the world as I took on the dangerous challenge.

"Woo-hoo!" I screamed.

I kept my eyes on the curve ahead, knowing this was going to be an easy one. I barely had to shift my weight.

The road beyond came into view, and my hammering heart suddenly stalled in my chest. All I remembered was the sight of a vehicle headed my way, Nadine's wide eyes staring back at me from the driver's seat—and a second of indecision.

☾

THE NEXT THING I KNEW, I was blinking my eyes open to fluorescent lights above me. I had no idea what had happened, or if any of it had even been real.

"It's good to see you awake," a woman said.

I tried to move, but my back ached like a motherfucker. Cuts and bruises covered my entire body, and my hip throbbed. I glanced toward the voice to see a woman in scrubs changing my IV. It took me a second to realize I was in a hospital room.

Fuck.

I laid my head back on the pillow. "What happened?" I asked in a scratchy voice. "How long have I been here?"

I glanced to the window to see it was already dark out. I must've been here for hours, if not days.

"You were brought in eight hours ago," she said. "You're going to be all right."

"Was I hit?" I asked. I honestly couldn't think straight to determine how much pain I was actually in.

"The car clipped you," she said.

"And the driver?" I asked. Had it really been Nadine?

"She's fine," the nurse said. "She was here for a while. She seemed pretty upset about the whole thing."

I wasn't sure whether to appreciate that she cared or be pissed that she hit me.

"I don't remember anything," I admitted.

The nurse looked worried. "I'll have the doctor come in and explain your injuries."

As she left the room, I did a quick assessment of my body. I could move my toes, which was good, but I had bandages all over my arms and legs, along with one hell of a pounding headache.

After a few minutes, a man stepped into the room. "I hear you can't remember what happened to you," he said.

"Is that concerning?" I asked.

He dodged the question. "Let's see what we can do about that."

The doctor shone a light into my eyes and asked me a bunch of questions, like if I felt nauseous or had ringing in my ears. I told him all I had was a headache.

"It doesn't look like you have a concussion," he told me. "But you weren't wearing a helmet, so I am concerned. I'd like to run some more tests. As far as your other injuries, nothing's broken, so that's good. Just a bit of road rash. You got very lucky. Your split-second decision to abandon your skateboard made the difference between a few injuries and something more serious."

I heard it in his tone. I could've died.

"The Goddess really was looking out for you today," he said.

This had nothing to do with the Goddess. This was all thanks to my own stupidity. *Way to go, Lucas.*

"Yeah, I guess so," I said anyway.

"I'll get those tests ordered," the doctor said. "We'll do our best to make sure you're okay to walk out of here."

"Thanks," I said before he left the room.

My head spun as I lay there, going over what had happened. I wished I could remember, but no matter how much I tried to recall what happened after I saw the car, nothing came back to me. The doctor ran a bunch of tests, but he didn't seem to think I had a head injury, which didn't make a damn bit of sense.

I must've fallen asleep at some point, because when I woke, the sun was shining. Someone knocked on my door, and I looked up to see Grant enter the room. Something seemed different between us, like we were both sad we'd been fighting when I very well could've died before either of us apologized.

Grant never took his wide eyes off me as he sat down. "You okay?"

I offered a light smile, though it was clearly forced. "I'm fine, considering the circumstances."

"I'm sorry for everything that's happened recently," he said. "For dragging you into the shit with the Tarantulas, then your house, that thing with Gregory, and then this. And, well… for dating Nadine without asking you. It was a really shitty thing of me to do."

I sighed and lay back against my pillow. "I wish you would've asked me first, but Nadine and I broke up. It's not my place to tell you who to date. Besides, *I'm* the one who should be sorry for starting the thing with the Tarantulas in the first place. And there's nothing you could've done about the rest of it."

A beat passed before I added, "You know Ryan only picks on you because we're friends, right? They can't stand that I left their group and chose you over them. They're jealous of you."

"You really think so?"

I scoffed. "I know so. If they can lose me, they can lose anything. It scares them."

"I guess I never realized how close you guys used to be."

"We were like a band of brothers in high school," I admitted. "Ryan was my best friend. That was before they all became assholes."

"Thanks for stepping in. I just wish it wasn't necessary. I wish I had the courage to stand up for myself." He hung his head.

"That's not what this is about," I assured him.

"I know. You were just standing up for me. It's what you do."

"Are you mad?" I questioned, unable to read him.

He knotted his hands together. "I feel like I should be, but it's not your fault. It's just so... emasculating that I can't fight my own battles."

"I can't just sit there and let them pick on you," I said.

"I know," he sighed. "I'm glad you're okay."

"Are you still mad at me?" I asked.

"Not if you're not mad at me. You know, about Nadine."

The thought of them kissing made my stomach twist, but I knew it was unfair. Didn't change how I felt, though. I couldn't stand back and watch Grant fall in love with the woman I cared about.

"Do you like her?" I asked. I couldn't help it. I needed to know.

Grant shook his head. "Nah, we're just friends. There's nothing between us."

That was a relief.

"I'm sorry," he said. "It was a spontaneous thing. I didn't really think about it."

"There's a lot I don't think through, either," I said with a chuckle. I winced, since it hurt my face. I hadn't had the balls to look in the mirror yet, but I could tell the cuts were pretty bad.

"Yeah, haven't been thinking anything through lately, have you?" Grant teased.

I smirked. "Not for a second."

"I'm just glad it didn't turn out worse than it did. You're lucky."

I practically snorted. "I'm something."

Grant frowned. "Why'd you go by yourself? You knew it was dangerous."

I frowned. "I had to do *something*. I just don't want to be miserable anymore. The only person I'm hurting is myself."

"What can I do to help?"

I shook my head. "I don't honestly know."

"Well, if you think of something, I'm here for you," he offered. "I mean it."

"Thanks. Are we good then?" I was honestly a little worried he might not want to deal with me anymore.

Grant nodded. "Yeah, we're good."

Eventually, Grant left to get some food. It wasn't long after that someone else arrived. I didn't know how long she'd been standing there, and I jumped a little when I saw her. She stood in the doorway, watching me with a soft expression as if trying to assess how I was feeling.

"Helena?" I said, shocked.

Nadine's grandmother smiled as she stepped into the room. "I heard what happened."

"How's Nadine?"

Helena took a seat next to my bed, placing her purse on her lap. "She feels awful."

"It wasn't her fault," I said. Something about talking to Helena was easy. She knew all about my anxiety and depression, and she'd never judged me for it.

"Perhaps you two can talk about it soon. Here, I've brought you a gift." Helena took a thermos from her purse and pressed it into my hands.

"Tea?" I asked. "I appreciate it, but I can't keep using matus tea and shrub leaves to try to fix myself. I need a lasting solution."

She frowned. "I'm not here to drug you, Lucas. I'm here to listen. It's chicken noodle soup."

"Oh," I said flatly. I opened the thermos, and the most delicious scent hit my nose. "Thank you. It means a lot."

I sipped on the broth, and I practically melted into my pillow, it was so good.

"Do you want to talk about it?" Helena asked. That's how she had always used to start our conversations, back when I first started coming to her for the matus shrub leaves that helped soothe me. I'd opened up a lot to her the year after Eric died. There wasn't much Helena didn't know about me.

"Part of me doesn't want to talk," I admitted. "Part of me wonders, what's the point? I hate that I've slipped back into these old habits. I feel like I made so much progress last semester, and now it all seems like it was for nothing. What if I put in all this work *again*, and I end up right back here?"

"You might," Helena said thoughtfully. "But what if things *do* change?"

I shook my head. "You were always an optimist."

"Life is easier that way," she said with a wink. "I know you can't see it now, but that progress you made is still there. It will compound over time. You're just facing different things now, learning new lessons."

"I don't remember the accident," I blurted. "The doctor said my head's fine, though."

Helena looked thoughtful. "Sometimes, we forget things to protect ourselves. From what I hear, you've been through a lot lately."

"You think I blacked out so that I had one less thing to deal with?" I asked.

She shrugged. "It's been known to happen. The question is, what are you going to learn from this?"

I thought about it for a moment. "All I know is I can't keep going on like this. If blacking out and getting hit by a car is what it takes to show me things need to change, then it's already gone too far."

She considered my words. "A radical change such as this one requires a radical choice."

"Like what?" I asked.

She sat back in her chair. "I think it's time for you to see a therapist. I want to help you get the professional support you need."

My initial reaction was to reject the idea. I didn't need a therapist to tell me something was wrong with me.

But deep down, I knew the real reason I'd never pursued therapy. I didn't want to admit to myself that I couldn't do this by myself. It was shameful if I couldn't pick up the broken pieces of my life.

But it was worse if I let myself break any further. I was so fractured, that maybe asking for help was the only way to pull myself back together again.

And I had to. Not to save anyone else, but to save myself.

"Okay," I agreed. "I'll go to therapy."

After Helena left the room, another visitor arrived soon after. I was apparently very popular today. I noticed the black cat first. When I looked up, my heart stalled.

Nadine held a gift bag in her hands, but I barely noticed it because I was too busy staring into her soft eyes. I didn't think she'd come.

"I'm sorry," Nadine said immediately. "I feel terrible."

"It's not like you ran me down on purpose," I said. "Though I am curious, what were you doing on that road?"

"I just… wanted to be alone," Nadine admitted. She fidgeted with the strap of the gift bag. "I was going to check out the scenic outlook. When I saw you, I panicked. I thought—"

"I'll be okay," I said quickly. "You don't have to blame yourself. I'm the one who put myself into danger."

Nadine gazed down at her feet. The tension between us was palpable. Neither of us really knew what to say, now that we weren't yelling at each other.

"I got you this," Nadine blurted. She gingerly approached me and handed me the gift bag.

I took it from her. "You really didn't have to."

"It's the least I could do. I *did* hit you with my car," she reminded me.

I smirked. It seemed a bit comical when she said it out loud. "So, this gift makes us even then?"

She chuckled. "I mean, *you* could run me over with a car."

"Never," I said, reaching into the bag. I pulled out a wad of tissue paper to reveal an array of care items. Inside sat magical salves to help with the road rash, painkillers, shampoo, and warm socks—anything that could help during recovery.

Tears welled in my eyes, but I blinked them back. "Thank you, Nad."

The sound of her nickname made me pause, but she didn't seem to notice.

"I hope it helps," she said.

"I'm sure it will. Consider us even."

She smiled, and though I could tell it was forced, it was welcome. Her apology gave me hope.

Nadine and I were over. We were never getting back together—but maybe it didn't have to hurt so much anymore.

EIGHT

"Lucas is out of the hospital," Talia told me later that week. We were on our way to the cafeteria for lunch. Our cats ran on ahead, batting at each other playfully. "Grant told me this morning."

I picked at my fingernails, just to do something with my hands. "That's good to hear."

"I'm going to visit him after class, if that's okay," she said.

I furrowed my brow. "Yeah. You don't need my permission."

"Well, I wanted to make sure."

I eyed her curiously, but she wouldn't look at me. I stopped in the lunch line and turned to her. "Hey, are we good?"

"Sure, why not?" she asked.

"You've hardly spoken to me since I went on that date with Grant," I pointed out. "Are you mad at me?"

Talia bit her cheek. "No. I just… I don't know. Maybe."

"You said you were fine with it."

"Well, I guess I lied," she admitted. "I didn't know at the time that it would upset me."

I *knew* she liked him! "If it makes you feel any better, Grant and I agreed to be friends," I said.

"I guess that helps, but I didn't want to say anything, because it's not like Grant and I are going to start dating. I'm still not ready."

"You're still allowed to feel something for him," I offered. "I'm sorry I went out with him."

"I'm sorry I lied about how I felt."

"We're okay, then?" I asked.

She nodded. "Yeah, we're good. So, do you want to come with? To visit Lucas, I mean?"

I bit my lower lip. To be honest, I wanted nothing more than to see how he was doing, but I had mentorship with Verla after lunch, and I didn't think I'd have the energy afterward for anything else.

"I'm honestly not feeling well today," I admitted. "My back is killing me, and I can't think straight today, but I can't skip my mentorship with Verla. I've already missed two sessions."

"I thought your magic was getting better," Talia remarked as we started filling our plates. "Didn't Dr. Yonker say your symptoms would improve as your magic got stronger?"

"Yes, but my body better get with the program pretty damn quick, because this is a far cry from a walk in the park." I piled my plate full of salad, a baked potato, and beef tips. "My stress levels have improved now that I'm not worried about Chloe all the time, but my magic is still triggering symptoms. It's like my body thinks my magic is foreign, but my immune system doesn't know how to get rid of it, so it attacks my other organs. Once I get used to my magic, my immune system will calm down. Dr. Yonker thinks I'll be in remission soon. I've just gotta get past the worst of it, then my magic won't affect me like this anymore."

Talia turned toward an empty table, and our cats followed. "I really hope you start feeling better soon."

"Me, too," I agreed with a sigh. "I just hope I don't fail the semester."

"That would be unfair," Talia stated as she popped a French fry in her mouth. "You're disabled. The school has to give you some sort of accommodations."

I stabbed my salad. "I've visited the disability office, but the paperwork is insane."

"We need to do something to push them," Talia insisted.

"I can talk to Verla about it at my lesson."

Talia agreed that was a good place to start. I intended to bring it up right away, but when I entered Verla's office, my attention was stolen entirely by the array of carcasses laid out over Verla's desk—two fresh mice, a bird, and the skeleton of a cat. My stomach twisted when I saw the dead creatures. It looked as if Odin had caught the mice fresh this morning.

"Uh… what's going on?" I asked Verla.

She punched a few keys on her computer, then turned to me. "Nadine, great to see you're feeling better today."

Not really, I thought, but I didn't tell her that.

"Have a seat," she invited.

I scooted the chair further away from her desk so I wouldn't have to sit so close to the dead creatures. Isa stood on the arm rest, sniffing the air. She reached a paw toward the desk, but I pulled her back.

"I thought we could play with necromancy magic today," Verla said brightly.

I had to admit, I was a bit intrigued. "You want me to try to reanimate these creatures? How would that work?"

"I've explained how we might be able to achieve this through enchanting," she reminded me.

I remembered she'd mentioned it, but for some reason, I couldn't quite remember all the details. "Can you remind me?"

"The necromancy magic resides in a crystal," she explained. "You would simply have to transfer the magic from the crystal into the carcass. If we can get it to stick, you've effectively enchanted the animal."

It seemed simple enough.

"This is just a theory for now, but I think this will be the easiest place to start," she said, before sliding a dark crystal across the table. "Go ahead and take your time with the magic. When you're ready, try funneling it into one of the creatures, just as you've done with transference into crystals."

"Um… okay." I picked up the crystal and tested the weight of it in my hands. I could sense the buzz of magic inside of it. Mortana magic was just as I remembered it—chaotic and unpredictable. I wondered why Verla had chosen this type of magic to start with, but I didn't ask. I figured it was easiest to tell if necromancy was working, as opposed to other enchantments.

I didn't know how long I sat there before Verla suggested, "Let's start with one of the mice."

I nodded, then reached out to grab the bird. Verla gave me an odd look, and I realized my mistake. Fuck, brain fog could be a real struggle. It was part of my lupus, which like my other symptoms, came and went on its own.

My cheeks flamed as I set the bird back down. "You said the mouse, didn't you?"

"Yes, but if you'd rather start with the bird, that's okay," she offered.

"The mouse is fine," I said. I took the limp creature in one hand and the crystal in the other, focusing on shifting the magic from the crystal into the mouse. I found that the magic moved through me effortlessly, but when I tried to funnel it into the mouse, it simply sprang back into the crystal.

"What do you feel?" Verla asked, looking hopeful.

Tired, I wanted to say, but I knew that wasn't the answer she was looking for.

"It feels like it's resisting me," I said. "Or… maybe I just need more practice. This kind of—um—magic…"

I paused, because I'd totally forgotten the word. It happened all the time with brain fog, and it could be really embarrassing.

"Necromancy, you mean?" Verla pressed.

"Yes, necromancy. Sorry." I cleared my throat. "Necromancy magic seems harder to control. Maybe if we tried enchanting something else to start with, I could work up to this."

"I fail to see the difference," Verla said. "This is a perfectly good place to start. Why don't we try…?"

I didn't hear what else Verla said, though she continued to talk. Instead, my attention fell upon a bird that landed on the branch outside her window. Both Odin and Isa noticed, and they perked up at the same time. Isa balanced on my arm rest, moving her weight from one foot to the other, like she was ready to pounce on it.

"Nadine!" Verla snapped.

I jumped a little and tore my gaze off the bird preening its feathers.

"Are you even listening to me?" she demanded, sounding upset. I didn't blame her; I was being a bit disrespectful. I just couldn't seem to focus on anything.

I sank into my chair. "I'm sorry. What were you saying?"

"I'm saying you must *focus,*" she emphasized. "This is important work we're doing here."

A lump rose in my throat, but I swallowed it down. The last thing I wanted was to disappoint Verla and fail the semester. It was so hard for people to see how difficult things could be for someone with a disability, because the things that were easy for everyone else were a chore for someone like me. I shouldn't feel ashamed for the way my body worked, but it was hard sometimes not to. I felt like I should be able to keep up, when I knew I couldn't. This couldn't be fixed with willpower. I placed my hand over my mouth, and my shoulders shook. A sob broke from my chest.

Verla's features fell. "Nadine, what's wrong?"

"I-it's just so hard," I admitted, my voice cracking. "This semester is so hard. My class schedule is packed. I've missed so much class already, and it's only been a few weeks. I'm already falling behind. I *can't* focus. I can't think straight."

"Is it something you're stressed about?" she asked.

I wiped at my eyes. "I'm just having a really hard time with my lupus. I hate to say this, but I need help."

Verla reached for her phone. "Do you want me to call Dr. Yonker?"

I sniffled. "No, not that kind of help. I just… I need understanding. I need to be able to miss class without fearing that I'm going to fail the whole semester."

Verla looked sympathetic, but she didn't seem to understand. "Nadine, you still need to learn your material. You can't pass without doing your work."

"I know. I don't want to miss out on anything," I agreed. "But part of my grade is based on attendance, and I can pretty much kiss that part of my grade goodbye. Even if I attended every lesson until the rest of the semester, my GPA's already gone to shit."

Verla looked skeptical. "If your attendance was forgiven, how would this help you? You need to learn the material."

"Yes, but I need some way to do it on my own time," I said. "If I can devote my time to it when I have the energy, I feel like I'll actually learn the material better, rather than trying to force myself to go to class when I can't absorb the material. Maybe my friends can record the lectures for me, and I could watch them outside of class."

Verla frowned. "This is not standard practice."

I swallowed the lump in my throat. "No, but I'm not your standard student, either."

"Because you're a Curse Breaker?" she asked.

"No, because I'm disabled," I replied, a bit bluntly.

I witnessed a calculating look in Verla's eyes, though I couldn't quite read her. After a few moments, she leaned back in her chair. "I may never understand what you're going through, but your education is important. I'll do what I can. There is, of course, paperwork you'll have to fill out with our Student Services office. Dr. Yonker will have to sign it as well."

"I just want to pass the semester without killing myself," I said desperately.

"Very well," Verla said. She gathered the paperwork I needed, then excused me. Before I left, Verla stopped me and added, "I expect to see your grades improve with these accommodations."

I did, too. I just hoped it was enough.

AFTER MY APPOINTMENT with Dr. Yonker later that week, I was feeling a lot better. He had no problems signing my papers to prove to the school that I was, in fact, disabled. Verla had made sure my paperwork was processed quickly. Dr. Yonker also prescribed me new meds, which seemed to help my symptoms. For the first time in a long time, I didn't feel like passing out after class.

"Mandy invited me to the library after class today," Talia said on our way out of Defensive Magic. "She's working on a jewelry design for one of her classes and wants to go through some magazines for inspiration. You up for it?"

"Yeah, that sounds like fun—" I started to say, but I cut off when we turned the corner.

Lena, Camille, and Gwen were walking our way. Lena immediately noticed me, then turned to whisper something to the other girls. In unison, the three of them conjured miniature wooden crucifixes and held them up in my direction, like they were repelling a vampire or something. Isa hissed at them, and Gwen hissed back as they passed us.

"Curse Maker," Lena sneered.

Talia and I both stopped in our tracks. The girls walked away laughing. Were they fucking serious? Honestly, it was more comical than anything. If they thought it hurt my feelings, they were nuts.

Talia's lips pursed, and her hands curled into fists. "I'll show them a Curse Maker—"

She started forward, but I grabbed her wrist. "Hold on."

Talia raised her eyebrows at me. "They're tormenting you! I want to give them a piece of my mind."

"Yeah, but beating them up isn't going to do us any good," I pointed out. "I learned my lesson with Chloe."

Talia narrowed her eyes. "You sound like you have a better idea."

I held my head high. "I know exactly how to deal with them. I'll meet you in the library. Bye!"

Talia must've been too shocked to follow me, because she just stood there with her mouth agape, like she was still trying to process it.

Isa followed me back to my room, where I dug through my closet until I found a tight black crop top and a pair of low-rise jeans. I brushed my hair into a high ponytail and shot myself a look in the mirror. It was perfect.

Heads turned as I walked down the hall, midriff on full display. The crescent moon tattoo above my hip was fully visible, and boy, did it draw the eyes. I'd never shown people my Curse Breaker mark before, and it was one hell of a *fuck you* to my bullies.

James and Avery sat with a group of students in the Main Foyer. James spotted me coming down the grand staircase and smacked Avery's arm. I smirked as the two of them watched me breeze through the room, unaffected by their stunned gazes.

Outside the library, Gwen, Camille, and Lena were surrounded by half the dance team. They looked into a trophy case and argued about which alumni in the photos wore the best costume.

"Our outfits for the next recital have to be the *best*—" Lena said, but she cut off when she saw me coming.

I saw her jaw drop as her gaze locked on my tattoo, but I otherwise didn't spare her a glance. I breezed straight into the library with Isa on my heels.

"What is she *wearing*?" Camille hissed from the hallway.

I spotted Talia and Mandy at a study table nearby, and I waved to them. Mandy's jaw dropped, and she whistled.

"Wow, that is one sexy tummy," Mandy said.

"You like it?" I teased.

"Nice tattoo," Talia added. "Where'd you get it?"

I tossed my ponytail over my shoulder. "Only the best tattoo artist around."

"Shh!" the librarian hissed from across the room. We lowered our voices.

Mandy rested her chin on her fist and stared at me with dreamy eyes as I sat. "Forget these magazines. I think I know where I'm getting my inspiration for my design project."

I blushed a little. "Oh, come on. You don't have to do that."

Mandy sat up straighter. "No, I'm serious. You look freaking hot. I could draw on some of that confidence. I think I'm going to build off a crescent-moon design. I just need to pick a stone to start off my color scheme."

"How about a rainbow moonstone?" I suggested.

Mandy's eyes lit up. "That would be perfect! Oh, my gosh. I'm so excited."

She shuffled around her magazines, until uncovering a sketch book. She immediately opened it and started drawing out designs. I'd never seen her in such deep concentration before.

"This is going to be so hot," Mandy mumbled to herself.

Talia smiled at me from across the table. "I guess my work is done here. I see you didn't let those mean girls get to you."

I shook my head. "Not a chance. If Lena thinks she can shut me down, she's wrong. I'm proud to be a Curse Breaker."

"You handled it much better than I would've," Talia praised.

"It takes practice," I joked.

Mandy finished a quick sketch and turned it to me. "What do you think? I might have to change the way this wire swirls around the stone." Her imagination was the perfect blend of complicated and elegant.

"I love it," I told her honestly.

"I think this might be the start of the ensemble I'll create for the talent show," she said proudly. "Are you signing up?"

I shook my head. "I don't really have a talent that I can show off on stage."

"You're great at puzzles," Talia pointed out. "You could solve a Rubik's Cube on stage."

"Is that really a talent, though?" I asked.

"Sure it is," Mandy said. "Hold on, I think I have one."

Mandy conjured a Rubik's Cube and placed it on the table in front of me.

I laughed lightly. "You just wanted to get rid of that, didn't you?"

Her shoulders sagged. "I've been carrying it around forever. Amy bet me I couldn't solve it, and she was right. It's best we just… forget about that bet."

I picked up the cube and eyed it from every angle before I started twisting the squares around. "I'm not sure about this…"

"You could try poetry," Talia suggested. "Grant says he's going to try stand-up comedy instead of slam poetry, so the show could use a poet."

I wasn't much of a writer, not like Lucas was. He could improv a poem like it was nothing.

My heart sank, and my fingers froze on the Rubik's Cube. I remembered all too well the night we'd shared at the abandoned mansion my first semester here, when he'd opened up to me and shared an impromptu poem. It'd been so sweet and romantic. At the time, it made my heart swoon. Now it just made me sad.

"Are you stuck?" Mandy asked, eyeing the cube in my hand.

I snapped out of my thoughts and glanced up at her. "No, just… thinking."

"Maybe poetry was a bad suggestion," Talia said.

She went on to suggest several other ideas, but I didn't hear her, because my mind was on one thing only, and that was Lucas. It was so hard to think about anything but him these days, and when I tried, all I felt was a heavy weight in the pit of my stomach. The guilt I felt every time I *wasn't* thinking about him was unbearable. It was like I had to think about him constantly, or I'd forget how much I'd loved him. It was like admitting the time we'd shared together didn't matter.

But it did matter. And it was all the time we'd get. We didn't get any more, because we weren't getting back together.

"Nadine," Mandy prodded, snapping her fingers in front of my face. "You've been staring down at that thing for a full minute. You okay?"

I'm miserable, I thought, though I didn't say it out loud. The truth was, I knew hanging on to Lucas was doing no one any good, and yet I couldn't seem to let go. I had to start learning how to enjoy myself—Lucas or no Lucas.

I shook my head, as if that might help clear my mind. "I'm fine," I said, before twisting the Rubik's Cube a few more times until I had all the red squares on one side. Mandy looked impressed. "I just think if I'm going to pick up a hobby, I need something more active, if that makes sense. Something to take my mind off things."

Mandy chuckled. "But you're so good at resting. I wish my hobbies included sleeping."

My eyebrows shot up, and my jaw dropped. Mandy had *no* freaking clue. "If you had lupus, you'd have no choice but to rest as much as I do," I snapped. "It's not like resting is a hobby or a passion. It's not all I care about. I care about my family, my friends, and the coven. I care about social justice and helping people. I care about solving problems, not just puzzles."

I tossed the Rubik's Cube back on the table, abandoning it.

Mandy reeled back, looking shocked. "Oh, Nadine, I'm so sorry. I didn't mean it that way."

"I don't care how you meant it. It wasn't funny," I said. I loved Mandy to death, but her joke had really hurt me. I sighed and stood. "I just need to do *something*. I'm sick of sitting around being miserable."

"What are you going to do?" Talia asked.

"I'm going to do something that matters," I told her. "I'll catch up with you guys later."

I left the library and found my way to Professor Daniels's office. She taught my Demonology class my first semester, though I hadn't had her since. She sat behind her desk with her door open. I knocked lightly, and she looked up with a smile.

"Nadine, good to see you," she said brightly. "What can I help you with?"

I stepped into the small room. "You're the advisor for the Community Service Club, right?"

"I am," she said with a nod.

"I was thinking about joining. Can I still do that?"

"Sure. We'd love to have you." She reached for a form behind her desk, then handed it to me. "Our next service project is this Saturday. We'll be baking cookies in the kitchen starting at nine a.m. Just fill out this form to sign up for the club, and we'll see you there."

My heart swelled as I filled out the form and handed it back to her. "Thank you so much. I can't wait to help."

I left the room feeling really good that I'd taken a step in joining a club on campus. Even better, I got to do something that mattered. I hadn't been able to do much lately, and I finally had a chance to prove to myself that disability or no disability, I could still help others.

I showed up in the kitchen at nine o'clock on the dot Saturday morning. I felt pretty good and ready to get to work.

Students weren't usually allowed in the kitchen, so I'd never been there before. I had to admit, though, it was pretty cool. The walls were made of brick, and the room housed three brick ovens. A cauldron hung over the ashes in a huge fireplace. It reminded me of a cottage.

I witnessed students opening cabinets, and I saw that they were bigger on the inside. They must've been enchanted with Mentalist magic, because when a girl listed off ingredients, they floated to the front of the cupboard for her to retrieve with ease.

Several students had already arrived and were setting out ingredients. I was a bit surprised to see Chloe on the other side of the room donning an apron. A black and white kitten followed her around. It was the first time I'd ever seen her with a cat. She noticed me, but we didn't exchange anything more than a glance.

The only other person I knew was Grant's brother, Miles. He was accompanied by a cat, who seemed very interested in Isa. The two cats eyed each other curiously.

"Need an apron?" he asked, holding out a black one with a cauldron embroidered into it.

I took it and began tying it around my neck. "Thanks. I don't think we've met yet. I'm one of Grant's friends."

"Nadine, right? He's mentioned you." Miles wiggled his eyebrows.

My cheeks flamed. "Oh, Goddess. He told you about our date, didn't he?"

"Only that it was a disaster." Miles beamed.

I laughed. "Just a bit."

"Don't worry. This will be a piece of cake," Miles said as he slid a container of flour toward me.

I smirked. "Very funny."

He shrugged. "I'm told I'm a genius."

"A very humble genius, I hear," I cracked back.

"What can I say? The rumors are true."

Professor Daniels came by, shuffling through a pile of index cards. "Let's see, how many people do we have? I need three on chocolate chip cookies. Chloe, why don't you come over by Miles and Nadine? You three can work together."

"Um… sure," Chloe agreed, but she sounded apprehensive.

"It's okay," I told her. "I don't mind."

"Perfect," Professor Daniels said, handing us a recipe card. "We need three batches. Let me know if you have any questions."

As Professor Daniels walked off, Miles glanced between Chloe and me. "I'm sensing some hostility."

I honestly wasn't sure how Chloe felt after everything that happened last semester. We hadn't really talked about it.

"Nope," she said, though she didn't meet my gaze. "Everything's fine. Let's get started."

Chloe used her telekinesis to gather our ingredients. They floated out of the cupboards and across the room. Miles and I began measuring out the ingredients. I tried twisting off the cap to the vanilla extract, but it wouldn't budge. I'd always had weak hands, thanks to my lupus, but it was kind of embarrassing that I couldn't even open a tiny bottle.

Miles noticed. "Do you need help with that?"

"Would you?" I asked, handing it to him. "My hands are weak as fuck."

He chuckled. "Same, but I can try."

He made a face as he tried twisting off the cap, but he couldn't get it, either. He shook out his hand and tried again. "It's my RA. Bottle caps will be the death of me."

"You have rheumatoid arthritis?" I asked. I was shocked, but I felt a little flutter in my belly. It was always a bit exciting to meet someone with an autoimmune disease, because they just *got* something about me that no able-bodied person could.

Miles handed the vanilla to Chloe, who took it without saying anything. She just shot a glance between the two of us.

"Yeah, it's a pain," he joked.

"I hear you," I told him. "I have lupus, so my symptoms are very similar."

"Aw, man," he groaned. "That totally sucks. I've just got stiff, painful joints. How many pickle jars have you broken by getting frustrated and slamming that sucker against the counter just so it'll open?"

I laughed. "Luckily none. I did throw a water bottle across the room once and broke one of my mom's vases."

"Ah, the infamous water bottle," he said in understanding. "I steer clear of anything with a twist-cap."

"Wise advice," I joked.

"Almost done," Chloe announced. The ingredients appeared to swirl together in the bowl on their own, though I knew it was from Chloe's powers. "We're missing chocolate chips, though. I couldn't find them."

"I'll hunt some down," Miles offered.

He walked off, and a momentary silence stretched between Chloe and me. Her manicured fingernails tapped against the countertop, but I couldn't take the silence.

"Do you mean it?" I blurted.

Her wandering gaze darted to mine. "Do I mean what?"

"That we're fine," I clarified. "I mean, I know what happened between us last semester was… intense. I'm not asking to be friends or anything, but I don't want us to hold anything against each other anymore."

Chloe sighed. "Thank the Goddess. I don't want that, either. Honestly, I wish I could take it all back."

"Same," I told her. "You seem… different."

"Really?" She raked her fingers through her hair. That was the first time I noticed her black locks had a bit of a blue shimmer to them, like she'd dyed it. "I'm trying something new with my hair. Do you like it?"

"It's kind of cool," I admitted. "But there's something else."

Chloe chuckled. "You mean I'm not acting like a raging bitch?"

I laughed and joined in on the joke. "Maybe that's it."

"Eh, I'm trying. It's why I joined the Community Service Club, after I was kicked off the dance team."

My jaw dropped. "Are you serious?"

"I guess *technically* I quit," she admitted. "I just couldn't handle those girls anymore."

"Even Gwen and Camille?" I asked.

"*Especially* Gwen and Camille," she said.

"But you were so close to them."

"I know." Chloe dropped her gaze, like she was sad about it. "But I couldn't handle the drama anymore. I thought maybe I could make up for all the horrible shit I did by helping people, you know?"

I was surprised, to say the least. "That's good. I've actually been wanting to ask you something, if you're willing to help me."

She eyed me. "That depends. What do you need?"

I lowered my voice. "Information. I'm not trying to dig up old wounds, but it's about our grandfathers. The Imperium Council has asked me to figure some stuff out."

Chloe's eyes sparkled with intrigue. "Ooh, priestess stuff. I'm all in."

"We know our grandfathers fought over the Mentalist Wand. Your grandma swears she knows nothing about what happened to it afterward, but is there any chance anyone else in your family knows?"

Chloe shook her head. "I wish I could help, but I don't think I can. If my grandmother doesn't know anything, no one does. All she ever told me is that it was lost after the feud. My only guess is the council seized it when my grandpa was arrested for murder."

"But wouldn't the council know where it is now, if that were the case?" I questioned.

"You'd think so, but if I've learned anything from my grandmother, it's that even the council members keep secrets from one another."

I scrunched up my nose. "Ew, that's gross. How can the council do their job if they're always waiting to be stabbed in the back?"

"It causes problems, for sure," Chloe agreed.

"Let's not do that," I said.

She tilted her head at me. "You mean if I'm on the council with you?"

"You said the priesthood is usually passed down through families, right?" I asked. "So you'll be a priestess, right?"

She smiled. "For sure."

Miles returned then, tossing a bag of chocolate chip cookies on the counter between us. "That only took *forever* to find. But we can finish up now."

We mixed in the chocolate chips, then began scooping spoonfuls onto cookie sheets. It smelled so sweet and delicious.

"When do we get to deliver these?" I asked.

"Deliver them?" Miles questioned.

"Yeah, like… where are we taking these?" I asked. "I mean, I thought we were making these for sick kids or the nursing home or something."

"Oh, no," Miles said with a shake of his head. "These are for the bake sale. You know, to raise money for new equipment for the fitness center."

I gaped, and Chloe must've noticed.

"Lame, right?" she asked, before turning and sliding her full cookie sheet into the oven.

"If you think it's lame, why are you doing this?" I asked.

She shrugged. "I thought it'd be a fun service project."

"This isn't a service project," I protested. "This is free labor. I signed up to make a difference, not to fund the athletic department."

Miles shoved a wad of raw cookie dough in his mouth. "They're paying me in cookies. They just don't know it."

"Yeah, it's dumb," Chloe agreed. "The trash cleanup, the fundraisers, it's all really just free stuff for the school. But at least I'm doing *something*."

I shook my head. I wasn't here for this. When Professor Daniels wasn't looking, I yanked off my apron and threw it on the counter, before stomping out of the room.

Community Service Club was an absolute joke. If I wanted to help people in this coven, I needed to step up and be the priestess they expected me to be. Any good priestess would be doing all she could to understand and resolve the Waning. I hated that I couldn't help with the last investigation with the missing boys, but I was sick of being ill. I wasn't going to sit this one out.

If I was being honest with myself, I knew exactly why I'd avoided pursuing answers—because the only person I knew who'd give them to me was Lucas, because he was investigating nightshade. I just didn't want to deal with him right now.

Screw Lucas. If he could find answers on nightshade and its connection to the Waning, so could I.

And I knew exactly where to start.

☾

I SLIPPED into the shadows in a corner of the Main Foyer that night. Isa sat beside me, her eyes darting around the foyer like she was watching for threats. I paid close attention to each student passing through, awaiting my target. The sun had dipped below the horizon, and the sconces in the Main Foyer had been lit before I saw him.

Gregory stepped out of the hall behind the grand staircase, glancing around as if to make sure no one was watching him. There were a few other groups in the foyer, but no one paid attention as he exited the building out the main doors.

"Come on, Isa," I hissed.

I followed behind Gregory, keeping a safe distance so that he wouldn't spot me. I hugged the side of the building, staying in the shadows as he turned the corner of the building. Isa and I hurried forward, and I peeked around the corner. Gregory stopped at the edge of the trees, then shot another glance around the lawn. He didn't see me watching him.

I moved quickly but quietly across the grass and entered the forest behind him. Gregory wasn't particularly good at sneaking around. I could hear the crunch of leaves and the breaking of sticks up ahead. I was stealthy, though, and my feet didn't make a sound as I followed behind him.

We must've been walking for fifteen minutes by the time the trees cleared. The sound of trickling water met my ears, and I crept behind a tree as I watched Gregory step out of the forest. We'd reached a river bend of one of the small creeks that flowed into Lake Santos. I conjured my night vision goggles and watched him through the darkness. Gregory shot a quick glance behind himself, but I was well concealed.

Assuming he was alone, Gregory stepped forward and bent behind a large boulder. I swore I saw him grab something, but I didn't see what it was before it had vanished. He must've subconjured it.

Isa growled, just loud enough for me to hear, and she took a step forward. My foot shot out in front of her to stop her. "Not yet," I whispered.

I had no intention of confronting Gregory. Lucas had already tried that, and he'd gotten nothing out of him. What I wanted to know was where his drop-off point was, and who was coming for his supplies. But this wasn't a drop-off location, I realized with frustration. This was his pick-up.

Didn't mean I wouldn't find any answers, though.

A stick broke from behind me, and my heart lurched. Gregory must've heard it, too, because his head snapped in the direction of the forest. A moment of hesitation passed, and then he took off running.

Fuck.

My heart hammered, and magic tingled in my palms, ready to fry a mother if they spotted me. I flattened myself to the tree, listening closely. If it was one of Gregory's contacts, I had to figure out who was involved.

I listened for the footsteps, but I didn't hear any. Then came the sound of a voice that turned my blood to ice and fire all at the same time. I wasn't sure whether to be relieved or royally pissed off.

"It's all right, Nadine. It's just me. You can come out now."

My breath caught. I kept myself pressed against the tree as I asked, "Is that a dare?"

"Do you want it to be?" he challenged.

I blew a breath as I stepped out from behind my tree. Lucas stood in the middle of the forest, looking as tall and handsome as ever in the dim light. I wanted to slap him as much as I wanted him to hold me.

"Are you kidding me?" I demanded. "What are you doing out here?"

He shoved his hands into his pockets. "I could ask you the same question. I saw you follow Gregory out of school."

"Oh, so you're following me now," I huffed.

"What? No." He sounded genuinely hurt by the accusation.

I crossed my arms. "It sure sounds like it."

"I came to tell you that Gregory's a useless lead."

I lifted my chin. "Oh, and I suppose you have a better one?"

"Actually, I do," he said proudly. "Professor Daniels gave me a list of sources. Most were a total bust, to be honest, but I'm hopeful about this one. Apparently, she's seen nightshade first-hand. She's been out of town for a few weeks, but she's back tonight, and I think I can finally get some answers."

I hesitated. I wanted to go with him, but my feet remained rooted in place. Working together would be too painful—for both of us.

"What's wrong?" Lucas asked.

"I don't know if we can work together," I admitted.

"We can still be civil, Nad."

"But can we trust each other?" I asked. "You heard my mom's last thoughts, and you kept it from me because you thought it was too dangerous. Investigating nightshade, the Waning, and the Oaken Wands is *far* more dangerous. How can I trust that you'll tell me the truth, even when things get difficult?"

He looked taken aback. "The last thing I want is for you to get hurt, but I also know I can't save you from everything. We need to figure something out, because we're going to have to work together one way or another."

"What do you mean?" I demanded.

Lucas hesitated, like he hadn't meant to say anything. "The fire at my parents was started by the drug dealers. I don't know who they are yet, but they made it pretty damn clear they were coming for me unless I stayed away. Problem is, I can't seem to do it. And I don't know if you can, either."

He yanked a piece of paper from his pocket and handed it to me.

I furrowed my brow. "What's this?"

"It's a prophecy. About us."

My heart pounded as I unfurled the piece of paper. "Is this some sort of joke?"

"Unfortunately, no," he said with a frown. "A Seer gave it to me."

By fire and noose
The coven will fall
Division and suffering
Destruction to all

Great power of the chosen
The coven be made whole
By the only witch of her kind
And a reaper bound to her soul

I read over the prophecy several times. Each time, my knees grew weaker and weaker. I steadied myself against a tree, and Isa meowed in concern.

"*Bound to her soul?* What does this mean? We have to get back together?" I shoved the paper to his chest. "I'm not taking relationship advice from some cryptic message from the beyond."

I stomped away from him, but he followed.

"What? No," he insisted. "Nad, please. We need to talk about this prophecy."

I whirled back toward him. "What's there to talk about? We both already know our magic is special. We both want to help the coven. What else is there to know?"

"The prophecy says we have to do it *together*," he pointed out. "Please, just do me this favor and come check out this source with me. Maybe we'll find something."

I was getting frustrated. I didn't want some prophecy telling me what to do. "Why should I do *you* any favors? The last time I tried, you blew up at me and we broke up. I saved your life."

"That was unfair of me," he admitted, so calmly that I wasn't even sure I was talking to Lucas.

"W-what?" I asked.

"You were right," he admitted. "When you killed those witches to save everyone, you did the right thing."

His confession caught me off guard. I eyed him up and down. "Who are you, and what have you done with Lucas?"

He drew a deep breath. "I'm the same guy. I'm just… trying to do better. I really am. Look, I'm not going to push you away this time. You're right. If I want your help, I have to get comfortable with you getting your hands dirty."

"Well, that's… unexpected," I said. "You really think we can work together?"

"I'd like to try."

Silence stretched between us. I hadn't made up my mind.

Lucas sighed. "I wish magic could fix all this."

I chuckled lightly. "No kidding."

Lucas held up his palm, as if he were trying to conjure an orb. Nothing but a spark came from his fingers. "I'm all out tonight."

My shoulders fell. "The Waning?"

He frowned. "Unfortunately. Magic or not, I do want your help, Nad."

I eyed him curiously. "Even if it's safer for me to just go back to school and stay there?"

"I couldn't stand to see you get hurt, but I'd be lying if I said I didn't believe in you," he admitted. "I can run around pretending like I've got the guts and know-how to uncover the coven's secrets, but it's you who knows how to piece this shit together. And I know you won't sit back and play it safe anyway. At least if we do this together, you won't be alone."

Lucas would never know it, but what he just said meant the world to me. Just the thought of diving into this investigation further gave me a thrill. And that Lucas believed in me and wanted me here made it all the better.

"But you should know how dangerous this could become," he added. "If they find out you're poking into this, they'll go after you, too. I'm not okay with that."

"Then let's make sure they don't find out," I stated confidently. "Where do we find this next lead?"

lucas

NINE

The sun had set by the time Nadine and I made it into town. She parked her car outside a shop with a big sign that read *The Jolly Pumpkin*. The shop itself was painted to look like a pumpkin, with an orange exterior and a green roof.

"So, what can this lady tell us?" Nadine asked as she climbed out of the car.

I shrugged. "The history of nightshade, hopefully."

Nadine quickened her step, like she was determined to beat me to answers. Even though we'd agreed to work together, I was certain she was more than a little sour about what had happened between us. Couldn't say I didn't taste the bitterness, either. We were obviously working together because it was our only option, not because we wanted to. It was painful, to say the least.

I slipped in front of her and held the door open. She frowned, though she didn't say anything, as if she found my chivalry insulting. I realized I enjoyed irritating her with kindness.

Isa followed her inside. The shop housed all kinds of witchy items, from crystals and wands to maple syrup and candy apples. I felt like I could wander the shop for hours, taking in the variety of potions and oracle cards.

The shop was empty of patrons. I almost didn't see the shopkeeper until her head popped up from behind the main counter, next to a sign that advertised specialized tarot readings. She had a basket in her hands and was arranging a display behind the glass at the main counter.

"Can I help you find anything?" she asked kindly. The woman was old, with long white hair that contrasted against her darker skin.

"Are you Hattie?" I asked.

She gave a smile that met her bright eyes. "I am. What can I do for you?"

"Leila Daniels sent me," I said. "She said you might be able to help me with a paper I'm writing on nightshade."

I held my breath, hoping I'd chosen my words well.

"Ah, yes," she said mystically. "I have many stories to tell. Come, take a seat."

Hattie gestured to a small table nearby, which had a vase of flowers upon it. Nadine and I sat beside each other, almost so close that we were touching. I eyed her hand resting on the table beside me, but I resisted the urge to reach out and take it.

"Do you mind if I record our conversation?" I asked, conjuring the voice recorder Grant had given me.

"That's fine," Hattie said. "Anything to help with your report."

Hattie hobbled around the counter with the use of a cane. It was only when she stepped around the counter that I realized she was followed by a companion—not a cat, like most witches, but a canine.

"That's an interesting dog," Nadine commented.

"She's a gray wolf," Hattie said as she sat. "And she's more than just a companion. She's my Familiar. Go ahead, you can pet her."

The wolf sniffed Nadine's outstretched arm, then started sniffing Isa. Isa sniffed her back, and the two looked like they'd get along just fine.

"Familiar? That's from the Elementai culture, isn't it?" Nadine asked.

"Yes," Hattie confirmed. "I'm half witch, half elemental. I have both witch powers and the power to control Earth."

She waved her hand over the vase of flowers, and they wilted before our eyes. Another wave of her hand, and the flowers were back in full bloom.

Nadine's eyes brightened. "That's amazing. The Elementai seem like such an intriguing people."

Hattie frowned. "They are, when they aren't in the midst of a civil war. That's why I had to leave."

"You grew up there?" Nadine asked.

"I grew up in many places," Hattie said. "I lived with the Elementai for many years, but they never knew of my witch heritage and empathetic powers. Things became too dangerous there, especially if my secret were to come out."

Nadine exchanged a glance with me before turning back to Hattie. "What do the Elementai have against witches?"

Hattie sighed. "A year ago, a plague took over our home—a terrible illness that affected our Familiars, and in turn, our magic. Many people died. We discovered that the plague was caused by a curse, which was sold to us by someone within the Miriamic Coven."

I gaped. "Who would do that? That's cruel."

Hattie shook her head. "Cruel indeed, which is why I didn't flee right away. I just couldn't stand the thought of being in Octavia Falls with someone who might seek to hurt my Familiar. I went off the grid, waiting to emerge once the war between the elementals ended. But things kept getting worse, and I had to leave before they found out what I was, or I'd be blamed and executed. The priestesses welcomed me back to Octavia Falls, and I was lucky enough to open this shop, which is what I've always dreamed."

"You've been gone for several weeks," I mentioned. "Did that have anything to do with what's happening with the Elementai?"

"No. I was traveling and sourcing magical items from the mermaids," Hattie said. "But that's neither here nor there. During my time off the grid, I met some wonderful people, but I also saw some terrible things. I even witnessed nightshade spread among my own tribe, the Nivita House, which is where my Earth powers came from."

"That's what Professor Daymond's confession said, before he died," I pointed out. "That the coven was trading nightshade with the Elementai for unicorn hair."

Hattie frowned. "Unfortunately. I heard many rumors about nightshade while in hiding. Would you like to hear them?"

I leaned in closer, curious. "What can you tell us about nightshade? I need to know everything."

"It begins with the Crock of Death," Hattie said ominously. "This story is one of fae legend, which I learned many years ago during my travels to Malovia."

"You visited the fae?" Nadine asked. "I thought they didn't like witches."

"Oh, I've traveled to many places," Hattie said. "Of course, they thought I was a full-born elemental."

"What's the Crock of Death?" I questioned.

"The Crock of Death is a cauldron belonging to Milonna, the fae goddess of love. It was in the possession of the fae for many years, until it was stolen during the Great Supernatural War eighty years ago. Legend says that treasures can be hidden inside the cauldron—and later retrieved. The caveat; the fae can only *guard* this treasure. They cannot possess the treasure themselves. It was said that long ago, the fae were protectors of this treasure."

"Someone other than the fae could retrieve the treasure, then?" Nadine sounded engrossed by the story.

"Yes," Hattie confirmed. "But as the legend goes, the treasure can only be retrieved by brewing a specific herb."

Nadine wore a calculating look. "So someone inside the coven stole the Crock of Death from the fae, and they're brewing nightshade in an attempt to retrieve the treasure locked inside?"

"That's the rumor," Hattie said. "No alchemist in Elementai society has been able to replicate the nightshade brew, which suggests they're missing something. If it's not ingredients, then it must be something else."

"The Crock," Nadine said brightly. "You think nightshade gets some of its properties directly from the cauldron?"

Hattie smiled. "I'd bet my cane on it."

My jaw dropped. It was a lot to take in, considering a deity's cauldron was involved. This wasn't the kind of thing you heard every day. "What's this treasure that's supposedly inside?"

Hattie shook her head. "I'm afraid I can't answer that, as I do not know."

"Where could we find out?" Nadine asked, looking toward me.

"We'd have to dig into fae lore," I replied thoughtfully. "The coven keeps some records on the fae, so that we know how to fight them in times of war. I'm sure we can find some books in the library or talk to some professors."

"It's not that simple," Hattie said. "Old tales won't give you an answer. If you know how to use the cauldron—if you know what herb to brew—

then you can put whatever treasure you want into it. It's possible that in the eighty years since the Crock went missing, someone removed the old treasure and added something new."

"So there's no way to know who might be motivated to find the treasure," I said.

Hattie leaned forward. "I'll tell you one thing. You're looking for someone motivated by material possessions."

"That's the point of treasure, isn't it?" Nadine pointed out.

"Perhaps, but that is not the point of the Crock," Hattie replied. "The Crock symbolizes spiritual attainment. Material treasures *can* be found within it, but not if you are motivated by the material need. Which makes you wonder... if someone is brewing nightshade to obtain this treasure, why haven't they found it yet?"

Hattie's question hung in the air. Only someone who had been searching for the *specific* treasure for material gain would've been trying this long to get at whatever was inside. Otherwise, they'd have retrieved it by now.

"Thank you for the information," I told her. "Is there anything else?"

"Be careful," Hattie warned. "I sense whoever is behind this is much more powerful than you realize."

A shiver ran down my spine. We thanked Hattie and returned to Nadine's car. I tapped my fingers on my knee as I gazed out the window on our way back to school, thinking.

"We have to destroy the cauldron," Nadine blurted, breaking the silence between us.

"What?" I practically choked on the word. "This is a *deity's* cauldron. I don't know if we *can* destroy it."

"Well, we have to try," she insisted. "If this cauldron is the only way to brew nightshade, and that's somehow tied to the Waning like you think, then we have to cut these people off at the source. If we destroy the cauldron, we destroy nightshade for good."

"That's *if* it can be destroyed. But I'm down for a little theft." I smirked, and Nadine shot me a mischievous glance. "We unfortunately have to find it first. There are thousands of cauldrons in Octavia Falls, and even more people who'd want one for its treasure."

"True," she said thoughtfully. "But it must be an Alchemist who took it, right?"

"Yeah, it would have to be," I replied. "Only an Alchemist can brew potions."

Nadine sighed. "That hardly narrows it down. I mean, how many Alchemists are in the coven? Thousands?"

"Ten thousand, at least." My shoulders sagged.

Nadine pressed her lips together. "I think I need to talk to Grammy about this. She might know more about the Crock of Death. I bet she's heard of it."

"Good idea," I said.

She pulled into the school's parking lot. "And you? What's your next step?"

"If the Crock is used to brew nightshade, then my goal is to learn what nightshade is made out of," I said. "I have a hunch that figuring out the ingredients might lead us somewhere."

Nadine pulled into a parking space and cut the engine. "How are you going to do that?"

"I'm already on it. Well, Grant is," I clarified. "He's been trying to reverse engineer the ingredients all semester, but it's a long-ass process."

She narrowed her eyes. "Where'd he get nightshade to reverse engineer?"

I sucked air between my teeth. "It's probably best if you don't ask."

"You went undercover," she said flatly. I wasn't sure if she was teasing me, or was trying to hide how impressed she was. "This investigative journalism stuff is getting really serious."

I shrugged. "Not sure I can call it that, considering how many rules I break."

"Ah, so you're a *bad boy*," Nadine teased, nudging me.

I chuckled. "You like bad boys."

She smirked. "Is that a question?"

"Are you willing to answer?"

She winced playfully. "Ooh, sorry. Only my diary knows the answer to that one."

I rolled my eyes. For a moment, it was easy to forget that we'd broken up. But then I remembered that we had, and it was like a knife to my stomach. It was a far cry from the metaphorical sword that once impaled me every time I looked at her, and I counted it an improvement.

"Bummer," I said, before redirecting to our previous conversation. "I'm going to follow the Tarantulas. Let's see if we can find out who they're working for."

Nadine wrung her hands.

"What is it?" I asked.

She lifted her gaze to mine. It was hard to tell in the moonlight, but I swore her eyes sparkled with tears. "I was going to say you shouldn't, because if they find out you're following them, it'll be worse than a house fire next time. But I did the exact same thing, so…"

"So who are you to tell me what to do?" I finished for her softly.

She nodded, gazing back down at her hands. "I don't want them setting *you* on fire next."

"Valid point, but we gotta take this risk, Nad. For the sake of the entire coven."

She nodded, gazing up at me past a waterfall of hair. "I know. But… stay safe, ckay?"

I tucked her hair behind her ear before realizing what I'd done. "I promise that nothing's going to happen to me. After all, they already burnt down my house. What more can they do?"

Nadine looked doubtful. "I don't know. Just be careful."

TEN

I called Grammy the second I got back to my dorm room that night.

"I've heard of the Crock of Death, yes," she admitted. "Why do you want to know? Is this for a class?"

"It's something I'm researching," I said vaguely. "Where did you learn about it? I'm trying to find sources so I can learn more."

"Your grandfather was obsessed with it years ago—almost as obsessed with it as he was with the Oaken Wands," she huffed. She sounded grumpy, like the very thought of the Crock made her uneasy. "It's all he ever talked about for months. Crock this, Crock that. His obsession nearly ended our marriage."

That must've been why Grammy had never mentioned it. If she thought it was important to finding the Wands, she would've said something.

"I asked him what treasure he thought he might find inside," she continued. "He'd always say, *It's not about the treasure, Helena. It's about the potential.* Whatever that means."

My heart stuttered at the potential to learn more. "Grampy never found it, did he?"

"Of course not! What do you think, I'm hosting the Crock of Death in my attic? The closest he ever came was those drawings."

I clutched the phone tighter. "What drawings?"

She sighed. "He had a journal he'd draw in. The same cauldron, over and over. I told him to burn the pages and end his obsession once and for all, because there was no way he was getting his hands on a fae goddess's personal cauldron."

"Rumor has it the coven stole it," I told her bluntly.

"No. We can't possibly have it. Your grandfather would've found it if that were true."

"Why do you think Grampy was so obsessed with it?" I questioned. "Perhaps the council knew someone in the coven had their hands on it. Maybe he was trying to protect it, like he did the Oaken Wands."

The other line went silent.

"Grammy?" I prodded. "Are you still there?"

"I'm here, I just…" She trailed off. "If the coven had it, why didn't your grandfather ever mention it to me? He spoke of the Crock so often."

"Maybe he was bound by secrecy," I pointed out. "The council must have secrets, right? He must've told you as much as he could."

"Mm…" she mused.

"Grammy, you don't happen to still have those drawings, do you?" I asked.

"I doubt it," she said. "Eventually, your grandfather gave up on the Crock—just stopped talking about it one day. I never heard about it again until now. I figured he'd burned the sketches and gave up, like I'd suggested."

"Didn't he leave *anything* behind?" I was ready to beg on my knees for any clues that could lead us to that cauldron and bring an end to the Waning.

"I have boxes in the attic, but I doubt you'll find anything."

"Can I at least come and look?" I asked.

"Sure, but I'll have to clear the stairs. They've become terribly crowded over the years with storage. Come by after class on Monday, and we'll take a look."

I beamed. "Thank you so much, Grammy."

I could barely pay attention in class on Monday, as I kept thinking about the Crock of Death and what it could possibly mean for our investigation. By the time I finished with class, I was more eager for answers than ever. When I arrived at Grammy's, the house appeared to be empty.

"Grammy?" I called as I stepped inside. Cornelius came running down the stairs, and he sniffed Isa curiously. The two cats started licking each other.

No answer came, so I called for Grammy again.

"Up here, darling!" she called from somewhere in the house.

The stairway looked like a mountain to my swollen, aching joints, but I wanted answers more than I wanted a nice long nap. I slowly climbed the stairs to find boxes piled up and down the hallway. At the end of the hall, a door stood open, with an ascending staircase beyond it.

"You up there, Grammy?" I called into the doorway.

"Yes. I've been cleaning all day. Come look at what I found."

I grabbed the railing and pulled my aching body up as I climbed the dusty stairwell, which creaked beneath my feet. Isa followed behind me. I emerged into a large attic, which was piled high with storage boxes that looked like they hadn't been touched in years.

Grammy sat on an old rocking chair, her form illuminated by a small window beside her. She held a book open in her lap, and tears filled her eyes as she stared down at it.

"Grammy, what's wrong?" I asked curiously as I stepped toward her. I eyed the book, wondering what had upset her.

She wiped her eyes. "Nothing's wrong. I thought I'd lost this."

She gazed up at me with sparkling eyes. It was an old scrapbook with pictures of a young couple in it. In one of the photos, they stood in front of a large, pale house with a big turret. The man had his arm around the woman, and they both wore a big smile. The yard looked different, as there weren't any bushes growing in the photo, but the wrap-around porch was undeniable. It was Grammy's house.

"Is that you and Grampy?" I asked.

She smiled, before standing from her chair and offering it to me. "Here, take a seat. Look through it. I think you'll like it."

I sank into the chair and placed the scrapbook on my lap. I flipped to the front page and began thumbing through the scrapbook. There were so many pictures of my grandparents at a young age. Grammy had been such a beautiful woman, with long brown hair that she wore in curls. Grampy was an attractive man, too, with a charming smile.

Grampy had the same look on his face in every picture. His eyes never met the camera, because he was always staring at Grammy with this starstruck look in his eyes.

I ran my fingers over the photographs. It was like a portal back in time. My grandparents stood in the Main Foyer at Miriam College, posing in front of the big fireplace. The carpet had changed since then, but the painting of Mother Miriam remained. In the next photograph, they were crowded around the Protection Tree with their friends, reaching around the large base and hugging the thick oak. Another photo showed them laughing in front of the abandoned mansion Lucas had taken me to more than once, only it wasn't abandoned in the photograph. The lawn was well manicured, and the windows were all intact. It was so beautiful.

"You've been to this house?" I asked her.

"It was our headmaster's," she said. "Nicholas and I were in the Honor Society. Every year, the headmaster would host a dinner for honor students at his house. It was always so much fun. You've seen it before?"

"Lucas showed me," I said.

"You're very lucky," Grammy told me. "Rumor has it, there's a spell upon the house to conceal it. Very few people have been there since it was abandoned."

"That's too bad that no one fixed it up," I said sadly. "It's a really beautiful place."

"It was." Grammy stared down at the photo fondly. "Nicholas and I always said we'd love to live there, but we graduated and bought this place before the headmaster died."

"*You're* the lucky one," I joked. "I can't imagine owning a house like this right after graduation."

"Yes, well, times were different then." She stared back at the photographs as I continued flipping pages. In one, Grampy stood on a dock, holding up a big fish. He had the proudest smile on his face.

"He has the kindest eyes," I told Grammy. "It looks like you guys had a lot of fun."

"We did," she said fondly. "He was truly the best partner I could ever ask for."

"Is that why you never remarried?" I asked softly.

She nodded solemnly. "Nicholas was it for me, in a romantic sense. But I had so many other people in my life that I've loved. I have plenty of friends, and for a long time I had your mother. Now I have you."

She smiled sweetly, but it couldn't mask the tears rising to her eyes. I set the book aside and wrapped my arms around Grammy's waist, leaning my head into her belly from where I sat on the chair.

"I love you, too, Grammy," I said.

She stroked my hair and sniffled, before saying, "Let's see if we can find anything that might help you on this… research."

Grammy moved some boxes toward me, and I rocked on the chair as I went through them. I quickly learned why Grammy's attic was so full. She didn't throw *anything* out. She had boxes full of Grampy's old things, even down to his old razors. All of my mother's old stuffed animals from when she was a kid were in boxes, along with jewelry, worn birthday cards, and even clothes that my mother must've worn as a teenager.

"Ooh, I'm kind of digging this dress," I told Grammy as I held up a long gown with puffy sleeves.

"That was your mother's Midnight Formal gown. She cleaned houses all summer before college to save up enough money to buy it." Her features turned sad. "That was only a few weeks before her Evoking Ceremony. She only got through one semester of college before she left town."

I ran my fingers over the fabric. "I bet she felt like Cinderella."

"It's funny you say that, because her friends found a spell to transform a pumpkin into a carriage that night." She laughed. "They couldn't get the mice to turn into horses, though, so they had nothing to pull the carriage."

I chuckled. "That sounds like Mom. For my fifth birthday, I asked for balloons, and she bought them, but forgot the helium. I think she was more upset than I was."

I turned back to the box and grabbed another dress. "I wonder what else she—oh, my Goddess."

I turned to a statue when I saw what lay beneath the dress. At the bottom of the box sat a long, intricately carved piece of wood. I reached down for it, my hands shaking. I could sense the magic within it before I touched it. The magic felt smooth and calm, and tasted like honey in my mouth.

Grammy turned from the box she'd been going through. "What is it?"

"Is this Mom's wand?" I lifted the wand, rolling it around to view the carvings from every angle. The blade of the wand was made of maple, with swirling designs all the way down to the handle. At the base of the wand, the wood wrapped around a rainbow moonstone crystal. The stone was set deep into the wood, as if the branch the wand was cut from had grown around it naturally.

My eyes widened as I stared down at it in wonder. I was so engrossed in the design that I could've teleported to the Arctic and never noticed. I barely remembered I was sitting in Grammy's attic at all, until she broke the silence.

"That *was* your mother's wand, but something tells me it's yours now," she said.

My gaze snapped up to hers. "I can keep this?"

"If you'd like." She nodded, looking curious. "I'm not sure how it got there. I thought for sure she would've taken it with her when she left. She had it designed before she even got her magic."

"Maybe she found one she liked better and left this one behind." I tested the weight of the wand in my hand. I couldn't imagine a better wand for me. "There's something magical inside the wand. Is it the crystal?"

Grammy took a deep breath, and her features turned serious. "You must never tell anyone this. Such magic is demonized in the Miriamic Coven."

I leaned forward in my chair, intrigued. "It's not black magic, is it? It doesn't feel dark."

"No. Everything used to make this wand was ethically sourced," Grammy said. "But it was designed by a friend—a wandmaker who had some… unconventional ideas. If anyone asks, you say it contains unicorn hair."

I shook my head. "That can't be right. I've touched wands with unicorn hair, and none of them felt like this."

"That's because it's not unicorn hair," Grammy said. "It contains hair from a faekin."

"Fae hair?" I balked.

"No, *faekin*," she clarified. "Faekin are companions to the fae, which share their blood."

I eyed the wand skeptically. "But witches don't like fae magic."

"Which is precisely why the coven has failed to explore its potential," Grammy pointed out. "Witch and fae magic are far more compatible than most would believe. It's just that the coven and the fae aren't willing to explore their magic together. They'd rather slaughter each other."

"So how did the wandmaker find faekin hair?" I asked.

"You must never repeat this, do you understand?" Grammy said. "I will not tell you his name, in order to protect him."

"My lips are sealed," I promised.

"This friend of mine… he was half fae. The faekin was his own companion."

My jaw dropped. "But if fae and witches hate each other, how did they have a kid?"

Grammy chuckled. "The same way everyone does, Nadine. Sometimes enemies become lovers."

Or lovers become enemies, I thought, though I quickly pushed it out of my mind.

I looked back down at the wand. "This is really incredible. You're sure I can keep this?"

"Yes, of course. It's yours," she said with a smile.

"Can I test it out?" I asked.

Grammy shrugged. "Have at it."

I stood and swished the wand through the air, muttering a simple incantation under my breath. Bubbles floated out of the end of the wand, and I beamed. Isa jumped at the bubbles, popping them with her paws.

"So far so good," I told Grammy, before trying another spell. I swirled the wand in circles, and tiny little light orbs swirled around me. I laughed as I swished the wand in the opposite direction. The orbs began to float through the air the other way, dancing to the motion of my wand.

Isa's eyes lit up as the orbs began flashing above her head. She tried to catch them, but they blinked out before she could.

"Watch this." I giggled. I drew a heart in the air, and it hung there like a neon sign for a few moments before fading away.

"And this," I added. *"Light of sun on summer's day, make all this dust go away."*

I flicked my wand. All the dust in the attic swirled together in a whirlwind, then swept out of the room through the tiny window behind me. I watched it go, enjoying the ease at which I performed the spell.

Thwack!

I jumped as a loud sound filled the room. I whirled around to see that a box that had been teetering on top of a pile had been knocked off by the gust of wind. All sorts of belongings spilled out of it, and I rushed to help

Grammy pick it up. I handed her old salt and pepper shakers, a pocket mirror, and a watch that no longer worked.

"These all look really old," I remarked. "I wonder if Talia would want any of this."

"She's welcome to come look—" Grammy started.

She cut off when I gasped. An idea suddenly struck. "What if Talia could get a vision from some of these things? Maybe she'd see a conversation, the journal pages—anything that could lead us to the cauldron or the Wands!"

Grammy frowned. "I knew this was more than just a school project."

I bit my lower lip. "I didn't want you to worry. I technically never said it was for school."

Grammy looked thoughtful, then said, "I guess you didn't. If you want to take any of this back to school, you can. I'll find you an empty box to put it all in."

Grammy left the attic while I finished cleaning up the contents of the spilled box. I tossed a few more items inside before my gaze landed on an old, tattered piece of paper. My heart stopped.

The paper was thick and ripped on one side, like it'd been torn out of an old journal or sketchbook. The page had yellowed over the years, but I could still make out the prominent image in the center—a sketch of a cauldron. It was unique, with handles shaped like tree branches.

I reached out with shaking hands to inspect the drawing. Beside the cauldron was a drawing of a wand. Below that was a symbol of another very specific cauldron that I'd seen many times before—specifically, the mark of an Alchemist.

My heart hammered as my gaze darted over the page. Most of the words had faded, but there were several words I was still able to read, all capitalized: *Crock, Death,* and *Wand.* In the bottom right-hand corner of the page, I could barely read the word, *Finished.*

That's when I realized what piece of the puzzle I'd been missing. All my blood drained to my toes. Isa nudged me, but I was so dumbstruck that I couldn't move.

The sound of Grammy's footsteps on the stairs snapped me back to attention. She gave me a weird look. "Everything all right?"

I swallowed the lump in my throat. "I found something."

I showed Grammy the page, and her eyes widened. "He did it," she breathed. "He found it."

"He must've," I said. "Which means I need to find it."

Grammy wore a mask to hide her worry, but I saw it in her eyes. I didn't want her to worry about me.

"It's getting late," I said. "I think I should head back to school and see if Talia can find anything in her visions."

"You don't want dinner?" Grammy asked.

"I ate before I came," I said. "I'm getting tired."

She nodded in understanding. "Stay safe, Nadine."

"Thanks for your help, Grammy." It was all I could say, because I couldn't make any promises.

She helped me pack a few things into the box, and I hurried out of her house as fast as I could. Isa jumped into the back seat, licking her leg and purring. I couldn't stay calm.

I conjured my phone and dialed Lucas's number. I hated to admit that I'd memorized it by heart. Deleting him from my contacts hadn't done me one bit of good.

"Nad, is everything okay?" he asked, sounding worried. Apparently, he hadn't forgotten my number, either.

"I'm on my way back from my grandma's," I told him. "Can you meet me at my dorm? I have something to show you. Make sure Grant and Talia are there."

"I'm on my way," he said quickly, before I hung up.

I could barely think on my way back to the school. I made it back as quickly as I could. Lucas *had* to know what I'd found. I walked into my dorm room to find Lucas, Grant, and Talia sitting on the bed.

"Did she say what she had to show us?" Talia asked Lucas.

"She didn't. It sounded—" Lucas cut off as Isa and I walked into the room.

I barely had the energy to explain to him what I'd found. Instead, I conjured the page and handed it to him, before plopping down onto my bed.

Lucas stood from the couch and began pacing as he looked over the sketch. "What is this?"

"Is everything all right?" Grant asked. His eyes darted between me and the page, searching for an explanation.

"I found it in a box of my grandpa's old stuff," I explained. "Grammy says my grandpa was interested in the Crock of Death, but that he just stopped talking about it one day. I think I know why."

Lucas's face paled. "You think he found it?"

I nodded firmly.

"Wait. Hold on. What's the Crock of Death?" Talia asked.

"That's a fae legend, isn't it?" Grant said. "I read about it in one of my alchemy books, though it didn't go into detail."

"Yes," Lucas confirmed. "We're pretty sure it's tied to nightshade."

Lucas dove into an explanation of what we'd learned from Hattie—how the Crock of Death could hold treasure inside, which could be retrieved by brewing a specific herb.

Talia furrowed her brow. "If your grandfather found it, who could have it now?"

"Anybody," I answered. "Just because he found it doesn't mean he took it."

"But he used it," Lucas theorized.

I nodded. "It says *finished* in the corner, which means he wasn't just making plans. He actually carried them out. I think he found the Crock, and he traded the treasure inside. That drawing is of the Alchemy Wand."

"We're not just looking for this Crock to end nightshade production," Lucas realized. "We're looking for this pot to retrieve one of the Oaken Wands."

"Exactly," I stated. "This means whoever is brewing nightshade is looking for the Alchemy Wand, too. They're close to beating the priest-esses to it, so that they can control magic."

Grant paced around the room, running his fingers through his gelled hair. "This isn't good. Whoever possesses the Alchemy Wand could take all Alchemy magic for themselves. The Waning is just a precursor. At least with the Waning, our magic returns after a few days. That won't be the case if someone uses the Wand. If the entire Alchemy Cast loses their powers, the coven's health infrastructure will fall apart. All the medication we brew will be useless."

"You're working on something, aren't you?" I asked Grant.

He swallowed, looking worried. "I've been trying to identify the ingredients used in nightshade, but it's a complicated and timely process. The nightshade I have is almost gone."

"We need to do something else in the meantime," Talia suggested. "We don't even know if finding the formula will lead us anywhere."

Grant chewed on his thumb nail. "I'm worried about that, too. I don't want to keep wasting time."

"It's not a waste," Lucas insisted. "We'll find something."

"Is there anything I can do?" Talia asked.

I handed her the box I'd taken from my grandma's. "I need you to see what kind of visions you can get from these. Maybe we can find clues in my grandfather's past."

Talia's eyes brightened, looking happy to help. "I can work on that. What will you do?"

"I have to take this information to the priestesses," I said. "It's what I signed up for. I have a meeting with them tomorrow, so I can tell them everything we've learned. Hopefully they can find the Crock and bring an end to all of this."

Lucas got an excited look in his eyes. "If the priestesses catch who's behind this, nightshade will be off the streets, and it could bring an end to the Waning."

"Right," I agreed. "Which means we wouldn't even have to find the other Wands."

"In the meantime, I'm going to read up on the Crock of Death legend," Lucas offered. "I might find something Hattie missed that can lead us to answers."

"By the Goddess, I hope we find some," I said.

We had no other option. We had to find the cauldron and retrieve the Wand—before the Alchemists lost their magic completely.

☾

THE SUN HAD ALREADY DIPPED below the horizon by the time I arrived at Octavia Hall. I parked out front and waved to the new guard stationed at the doors. Ever since the council learned they couldn't trust their own people, they had instituted new security measures. The guard, Lincoln, let me through, and I climbed the stairs to the Imperium headquarters. Isa followed behind at my heels. The door was open when I arrived.

Priestess Margaret turned when she heard my footsteps. "Nadine. Come inside, please."

She gestured me forward, then shut the door behind me. The room was dark, with nothing but five flickering candles illuminating the attic. The candles were arranged in a circle on the meeting table, encompassing a crystal ball in the center. Next to each candle sat a bowl of herbs. The other priestesses sat around the table, but their expressions were hard to read. Priestess Lilian had a stone-cold look on her face like normal. Stella appeared a bit excited, while Charlotte looked apprehensive. I had no idea what was going on.

"Have a seat, dear," Priestess Margaret invited. "We have something to discuss."

I sat, and Isa jumped on my lap. "I have something to discuss, too."

"We'll get to that," Priestess Margaret assured me. "First, we have business to attend to."

"But this is—" I started to say, but Margaret was already speaking over me.

"As you know, our tracking spells have failed to identify who is behind the Waning. Whatever magic the culprits are using is strong enough to conceal themselves from us. However, we have been working on a spell that should help us narrow down the perpetrators."

"In what way?" I asked curiously.

"While we may not be able to identify the *specific people* behind this, we've developed a spell to read the *energy signature* behind the Waning," Margaret explained.

"So you can narrow it to the Cast," I realized.

Margaret nodded. "Or if it's coming from outside the coven. After tonight, we'll be able to confirm once and for all where the threat is coming from."

I glanced between the priestesses, my stomach twisting. "I'm guessing this is a spell that can only be performed by all five Casts together?"

"Yes. It's very advanced," Priestess Margaret said.

Priestess Lilian stared down her nose at me. "You're hesitating. Why?"

She made it sound like she suspected me of something.

"Last time we tried advanced spells like this, I couldn't hardly get out of bed for three months," I reminded them.

Lilian scoffed. "Don't be so *dramatic*, Nadine. Do you really think your health is more important than the safety of the entire coven?"

"If I'm going to keep helping you, it's pretty important," I snapped back. "Or would it be better if I die and you lose all access to my powers?"

Lilian gaped, but Priestess Stella quickly stepped in. "No one is going to die," she said quickly.

I wasn't entirely sure how her powers worked, but I'd heard she could foretell death. Maybe I could trust her judgement.

Lilian smirked. "Then Nadine should be perfectly capable of performing this spell with us. She looks healthy to me."

"I didn't say I wasn't capable," I started. "I only meant—"

"Ladies," Priestess Margaret said sternly, cutting me off. "We cannot perform this spell when there is such contention among us. Nadine, *of course* we do not want to overwhelm you, but this spell is crucial to our investigation. We cannot do it without a Curse Breaker. It is your duty to help the coven."

My chest compressed, and guilt rattled around in my chest. *All* I wanted to do was help the coven. "I wasn't suggesting otherwise. I just wanted to take precaution, so I can *continue* helping wherever I'm able."

Lilian blew a breath and rolled her eyes. It was obvious she had no faith in me. She clearly thought I was *weak*—but she couldn't do anything about it, because I was her only option.

Stella caught Lilian's expression and quickly spoke up. "I believe in Nadine. She can perform this spell. We'll get the person behind this."

I shot her a kind smile. It was nice that at least *one* of the priestesses was sticking up for me.

Priestess Margaret locked her eyes on me. "Are we ready to begin?"

"Yes," I told her.

"Very well," she said. "Everyone join hands."

I took Priestess Stella's hand on one side of me, and Margaret's hand on the other. Isa stood on my knees, looking alert. I was glad she was here, because I wasn't sure if I could do this without her. The tension in the air was palpable, and I was certain the priestesses could feel my racing pulse.

"We will begin with a prayer," Priestess Margaret explained. "Then we will light the sage to cleanse this space. When the cleansing is complete, we will speak the incantation we've written and light our herb mixtures." She gestured to bowls of herbs set in front of each of us. "If successful, symbols will appear in the crystal ball to identify the magic behind this. Let's begin."

The priestesses all bowed their heads in unison, and I followed their lead.

"Mother Miriam," Margaret prayed. "We welcome you into our presence, to clear our minds and cleanse our hearts. We seek to identify the threat plaguing the coven. We pray for the power and strength to complete this spell, and protect the coven as we've all pledged ourselves to do. So shall it be."

"So shall it be," the rest of us repeated in unison.

We dropped our hands, and the priestesses reached for their bundle of sage in their herb bowls. I copied them and held my sage to the candle in front of me. The scent of burning herbs filled the attic. Everyone remained silent, apart from the deep, heavy breaths they took. I drew a long breath and dropped my shoulders, feeling a little more at ease.

After several minutes, Priestess Margaret announced, "You may light your herb bowls now. Repeat after me: *The Waning is spreading. We must overcome. Reveal to us where this magic came from.*"

In unison, we took our candles and lit our herbs, then began chanting in unison. My herbs smoldered, filling my nose with a sweet scent. Margaret reached out for me again, and we joined hands as we continued chanting.

As the other priestesses continued, Margaret spoke directly to me. "Nadine, you must channel our magic into the crystal ball."

I nodded firmly. "I've got this."

She closed her eyes and joined the others in the chant. "*The Waning is spreading. We must overcome. Reveal to us where this magic came from.*"

I spoke the incantation with them, but my focus remained on the crystal ball in front of me. I narrowed my eyes, gazing deep into the clear glass. As we continued the incantation, our magic began to swell. I could feel it pulsing around the circle, moving in and out of me in multiple directions. It was a lot of magic to manage at once, and if I lost my focus, it could very well break me.

I took several minutes to get a feel for the energy of the magic surrounding me. It was powerful, but chaotic. Getting a handle on it and directing it wasn't going to be easy. I drew a deep breath, then gave it a try.

The magic stabilized for a mere second before slipping from my grasp. Instead of moving in all directions, it began to move clockwise around the circle. It appeared as a white light—dim at first, but it slowly grew in intensity as the chanting continued. The energy swelled within me, before moving through Priestess Margaret, and so on. I tried to control it again. This time, I gained control of the magic for a few seconds longer, but as more magic pulsed through me, I lost control.

My head spun as I tried to capture the magic and make it my own. There was so much at once. I tore my gaze from the crystal ball and closed my eyes. I had to stop chanting to gain my focus back. I tuned everything out, until all I could sense was the magic flowing in and out of me, swirling through our circle over and over again.

Our magic was like a spinning top, ready to topple over at any moment. My brow furrowed as I concentrated, reading the energetic patterns of our magic. Heavy. Light. Heaviest. Lightest.

The pattern continued surging through me. I had to even it out, so that the magic flowed effortlessly. I had to time it perfectly, but how?

After a few more moments of observation, I realized it was nothing more than a puzzle. I waited for the heaviest of the magic to hit me, and I held on to it for a second before letting it go. When I touched it, it was like grabbing on to a spinning merry-go-round. My whole body yanked to the side, but the priestesses held on tight to me so that I wasn't knocked out of my chair. I sat upright again, but my shoulder hurt from the sudden force. The magic sprang out of me, surging through our circle like an electric current. As the magic swelled through me again, I realized it had stabilized, but it wasn't perfect.

I timed the magic again, moving it and rearranging it until the current flowing around us evened out, becoming one constant stream of magic that I could manipulate with ease.

I opened my eyes again and gazed into the crystal ball. When I felt confident, I guided our magic into it. Colorful smoke began to swirl in the ball, shifting from green, to red, to midnight blue, like it was shuffling through its options.

"It's working," I announced.

Everyone opened their eyes to watch as images formed within the crystal ball. The smoke turned completely black. It twisted, creating the solid image of an animal-like skull with long, curved horns.

The priestesses gave a collective gasp, and a shiver traveled down my spine.

That was all we saw before the image turned into smoke again, then dissipated.

Priestess Margaret stopped chanting, and the room went dead silent. For a moment, we all sat there, staring at the crystal ball like it might show us something else. Margaret's hands shook as she drew away from me. My shoulders sagged, and I swayed in my chair.

"What did that mean?" I asked, breaking the silence. "Are they Mortana?"

"It's not my Cast," Priestess Charlotte said, her voice shaking. She wore a wide-eyed, horrified look.

Priestess Margaret swallowed. "It's not Cast magic at all."

"It's someone *outside* the coven?" I questioned.

Margaret blinked a few times, like she was still trying to process the symbol. "It could still be happening inside the coven."

"So this means… what?" I wondered. "The Waning is being caused by…?"

"Demon magic," Lilian spat.

My mouth turned to sandpaper. I'd learned in my Demonology class how dangerous that kind of magic could be.

"Someone made a deal with a demon?" Priestess Stella sounded disgusted.

"That's one theory," Margaret said. "We can't know for sure. There are many other ways to get your hands on demon magic—though they're all forbidden."

"How?" I asked.

"A demon artifact, for one," Margaret said.

"Or a demon themselves could be behind this," Lilian added.

"What? Like, they want *revenge* on the coven?" I asked.

"It could happen," Lilian replied. "The question is, how do we stop such a thing?"

I sat there, dumbstruck. I wished I had an answer.

"The Wands," Margaret said. "When we find all five Wands, we'll restore our magic, and defeat this demonic force."

I snapped to attention at the mention of the Wands. I quickly conjured the journal page I'd found in my grandfather's stuff. "I found the Alchemy Wand," I blurted.

Stella's gaze snapped in my direction, like she couldn't believe it. "You *have* it?"

"Not quite," I rushed to explain. "But I learned where it is."

I placed the drawing on the table, and the priestesses leaned in to view it.

"There's a legend of a fae goddess's cauldron called the Crock of Death," I explained. "It's said to hold treasure. I believe my grandfather hid the Alchemy Wand inside of it."

Margaret placed her reading glasses on the end of her nose, then picked up the paper to inspect it. "Yes, we've heard of the Crock of Death. It once belonged to the Imperium Council. I was meant to inherit it as the Alchemy priestess, but it was lost before my induction. The last priestess's family was questioned, but they didn't know anything about it. Your grandfather found it?"

"I believe he did, but I don't think he kept it," I admitted. "I've never seen a cauldron that looks like the one in his drawing."

"May I?" Lilian asked, holding her hand out to Margaret. She retrieved the paper and eyed it skeptically, like she thought it might be a fake.

After a few moments, she relaxed and looked up at me. For the first time, I saw something other than disdain in her features. I swore I had actually *impressed* her. "Well, this is… useful information."

"Do you have any idea where to find the Crock?" Stella asked.

I shook my head. "I'm afraid my grandfather didn't leave those clues behind. I believe it's tied to nightshade, though. As the legend goes, you must brew a specific herb to retrieve the treasure. I think that herb is nightshade, which means whoever is brewing nightshade is looking for this Wand."

Stella's eyes went wide, like she couldn't believe the connection.

Priestess Charlotte looked disgusted. "Then whoever is brewing nightshade shall be considered a traitor to the coven. When we find them, they shall suffer the death sentence."

"I agree," Priestess Margaret said. "Nightshade is a threat against the coven. We've already seen three overdoses in the last six months."

My jaw dropped. This was the first I'd heard of it.

"Not to mention our relations with the Elementai are strained over this," Margaret added.

"We must get nightshade off the streets of Octavia Falls," Lilian said firmly. "We've spent so much time dealing with the Waning that nightshade has lost priority. Given this new information, we must consider this our number one priority, in order to get our hands on the Alchemy Wand."

I titled my head to the side. "You think the Waning and nightshade are two separate events? You don't think they're connected?"

"We've considered that, but we can't be sure until we have more information," Priestess Margaret admitted.

"Knowing the Waning involves demon magic, it's unlikely they're connected," Charlotte pointed out. "The Crock of Death is a different type of magic entirely."

"Yes," Stella agreed. "Nightshade doesn't seem like demon magic. We know from Professor Daymond's confession that it's brewed using unicorn hair. Such an ingredient couldn't be used with demon magic."

"That's true..." Margaret looked thoughtful. "I see we have much to consider. If that's all you have for us, Nadine. You may go."

"Isn't there anything else I can help with?" I asked.

"You have done all you can for now," Margaret said. "You should get back to your dorm before curfew."

My stomach sank as she ushered me out of the room. The way she spoke of curfew suggested I was nothing more than a child to her, and not a real priestess. After everything I'd done, I expected more than that.

I didn't object, because I was exhausted after performing that spell. My shoulders ached from when the magic had yanked on me. I felt like I could curl into a ball at the bottom of the stairs and sleep until morning. Isa purred against my leg and looked up at me, as if offering me encouragement.

"At least I did *something* to help," I told her on my way downstairs. "That's all I can ask for, right?"

I winced as I headed outside, because I ached everywhere. My head spun, and I grabbed the railing to steady myself. When that didn't work, I sat on the concrete steps and pressed my head against the cool metal of the handrail. Isa pawed at me, but I didn't respond. I was just trying to keep my dinner down at the moment.

I didn't know how long I sat there. Even after the world started to stabilize, I couldn't bring myself to drag my ass back to my car. I was just *so* tired after that spell, and I worried about driving home.

After a while, I heard footsteps from behind me. I lifted my head to see Priestess Stella leaving Octavia Hall. She slowed when she saw me.

"Nadine... you're still here," she said, sounding surprised.

I shrugged. "I'm not feeling the best."

"May I sit?" she asked.

I nodded.

She sat beside me, looking concerned. "I'm sorry about the way you were treated back there."

I eyed her curiously. "What do you mean?"

She glanced toward the doors, as if to make sure no one else was coming. "I noticed the way Margaret dismissed you when you said you had something to show us, and the way no one seemed concerned about your health. And then Margaret brought up curfew, like you're not to be respected as one of us."

I couldn't help the smile that touched my lips. I didn't particularly like the Imperium Council, but I suddenly liked Stella a whole lot more.

"Thanks," I told her. "I felt the same way. I mean, I'm going to be a priestess. I wish I was treated like one."

"I know the feeling," she admitted. "I was inducted shortly after graduation. I've been on the council nearly a decade, but because I'm the youngest, I still don't feel respected."

"It's like you constantly have to prove yourself," I said. "It can be exhausting."

"Yes!" she cried, chuckling.

I gazed down at my hands. "I get that I haven't proven myself yet. I wasn't hand-picked like the rest of you. I'm only here because I'm the council's only choice. But for them to treat you the same way... that's unfair."

She shrugged. "It is what it is. I'll serve the council until I die, so I'm sure there will be many other priestesses to work with in my lifetime."

"But you shouldn't have to wait," I argued. "You all hold the same power. You're on the council for a reason."

"Yes, that's true, but not everyone sees it the same way," she said kindly.

"Then challenge it," I suggested.

She shook her head. "The council must work in unison, Nadine. It's better to work in harmony than in disagreement."

"Disagreements aren't always bad, though," I told her. "Speaking up can lead to good changes."

"Sometimes, but you must pick your battles," she replied. "My power lies in seeing future catastrophes. I can tell when bad things are going to happen."

"Like when people are going to die?" I asked carefully.

She nodded. "Sometimes, yes, but my power is broader than that. Something big is coming. I know it. And we must be very careful about how we proceed. As a priestess, your greatest asset is respect. If you lose that, you lose your power. It's important that you remember that."

I let her words sink in a moment, then spoke carefully. "I wish to earn my respect from the coven, but I won't do that at the expense of my own voice. It is my voice that will earn me respect, or I'll have none at all."

Stella pondered my words. "I can see you're going to be a powerful priestess one day."

I smiled. It was the first encouraging thing any of the priestesses had ever said to me. Stella was officially my new favorite priestess. "Thank you."

"In the meantime, take it easy," she suggested. "This position can be very overwhelming at times, and I see it's already taking its toll on you."

"I can't slow down now," I told her. "We have to find the Crock of Death."

"You let *us* handle that," she offered kindly. "There's nothing more you have to do. You leave that up to us."

"But I want to help," I told her.

"You *have* helped," she reminded me. "The Imperium Council has resources. We will find the Crock of Death, and we'll retrieve the Alchemy Wand. The coven can't afford for you to get hurt right now, Nadine. You must consider your health."

I sighed. A piece of me was disappointed to be told to slow down. Another part of me felt a weight lift off my shoulders. I felt relieved to hand over this burden.

"Thank you, Priestess Stella," I said.

She smiled kindly. "Please, just Stella. Afterall, we're going to be priestesses together."

Stella walked off, and for the first time, I felt good about becoming a priestess. It appeared that I had an ally on the Imperium Council. Stella could help me with all of this, and I decided to trust her.

That was more than I could say about the rest of the priestesses.

A week later, my head was still reeling with the information Nadine had found. We knew what we were looking for, but we had no idea where to find it. It was driving me nuts.

"Lucas?" Dr. Mack said, snapping me out of my thoughts.

I lay on a couch in my therapist's office, staring up at the ornate designs on the tiled ceiling. I'd taken Helena's advice and finally started therapy. I'd had a few sessions already, and they seemed to be helping, though I had a lot of work ahead of me.

The room was dark, with tones of black and red surrounding me. I liked the small space. It reminded me of a cave, where I could hide away and not be bothered. I wondered if she'd decorated the room like that on purpose.

I turned my gaze toward her. She was a middle-aged witch, with short hair and cat-eye glasses. An eye tattoo was inked into the back of her hand, marking her as a Seer. She always wore long, flowing cardigans and a pin shaped like a cat. It looked strikingly similar to the orange tabby that slept next to her desk every session. A clipboard sat on her lap, where she took notes during our sessions.

"Linda?" I replied.

She insisted I call her by her first name, even though it felt more natural to call her Dr. Mack. I figured it was her way of trying to connect with me or something, but I didn't think it changed how much I opened up to her. It was hard, but I knew I wasn't going to get anywhere by bottling it all up inside. I knew I could trust Dr. Mack, and it'd gotten easier to open up after a few sessions, but I found myself still holding stuff back. I wasn't sure whether I was holding back from her—afraid she'd judge me—or if there were things I was too afraid to admit aloud to myself.

"You haven't said a word since you got here," Dr. Mack pointed out. "How are you feeling?"

I swallowed the lump in my throat. "I'm all right, I guess."

"That's good. How did things go with your parents?"

I shrugged. I tried talking to my mom, but it didn't go over well. "My parents found an apartment, and they've filed an insurance claim. They seem to be doing okay, but it's hard to tell. Mom barely said a word, and trying to talk to my dad… well, that's a useless cause. I don't really want to talk about my parents, though."

Dr. Mack nodded in understanding. "We don't have to talk about them. Last time we spoke, you said you wanted to talk about your hospital stay. Are you ready to discuss that, or do you want to save it for another time?"

I relaxed and looked back up at the ceiling. "I can talk about it. I guess the biggest thing is that I blacked out, and that was pretty scary."

"I can understand that," she said kindly. "How much of that day can you remember?"

"I remember the morning, and I remember hiking and riding my skateboard, but I can't recall anything after I saw the car," I told her. "It's like I got hit in the head or something, but the doctor said I didn't have a concussion. I guess I should consider myself lucky, but I can't help but think that maybe it wasn't the accident that made me forget. Maybe it was all in my head. And that terrifies me, because it means it could happen again. What if I forget something really important?"

"Sometimes our minds forget the details in very stressful situations," Dr. Mack explained. "It's our mind's way of protecting us. But it's a very real experience. Don't write it off as *all in your head*. What is any experience, if not in our minds?"

"Well, there are things that are real, and things that we make up," I said. "A concussion is a real, tangible thing you can see and diagnose.

My… amnesia, for lack of a better word… it's something I created because my mind is broken or something."

"Disassociation is just as real," Dr. Mack emphasized. "And you are not *broken*. You are wounded, and simply in the process of healing."

"What's the difference?" I asked.

"We're not looking to *fix* you," she said. "You're not something that needs to be glued back together. It's not about applying glue and a bit of paint to hide imperfections. We're bringing these wounded parts to the surface to be healed and released. Do you see the difference?"

I shrugged. I wasn't sure I did.

"Do you remember why you took your skateboard out that day?" Dr. Mack asked.

I drew a deep breath, trying to remember exactly what I'd been thinking that morning. "I guess I was trying to forget about things. Maybe *forget* isn't the right word. It wasn't even about the distraction, really. I just wanted to feel something again, you know? I thought if I started doing sports like I used to, it might make me feel better."

Dr. Mack looked thoughtful. "I think you had the right idea, but it sounds like you were looking to this as a cure, when sports are simply a tool."

"What's the difference?" I asked.

Dr. Mack paused before answering. "I have some concepts I want to share with you, Lucas. I think you're ready for them. But before I do, I want to remind you that I'm a coven therapist, which means that I speak first and foremost from the spiritual perspective of the Miriamic belief system. These beliefs were taught to us by Mother Miriam, and they don't necessarily translate to other cultures. I combine our belief system with psychology to assist you."

"I understand that," I told her, not quite understanding why she felt the need to remind me.

She must've picked up on that in my tone. "I mean to say that this spiritual perspective doesn't work for everyone—not even for all members of the coven. However, I ask that you open your mind to the ideas. Regardless of whether you choose to subscribe to them or not, it's safe to try on a new idea or two—like a new sweater."

She had me intrigued, and I wanted to hear more. "Lay it on me."

"Activities like sports can be helpful to inner healing, but deeper work must be done. Without it, these activities are simply temporary fixes, and do not address what's truly going on below the surface."

I eyed her curiously. "So, what *is* happening beneath the surface?"

She smiled slightly. "That's what I'm here to help you figure out. From what you've told me, I believe much of your anxiety and depression stems from a lack of purpose."

"Can't sports do that? Give me a sense of purpose?" I questioned. "I mean, I feel like they used to, but now the only thing that seems to give me purpose is Nadine, and I lost her."

I'd spoken to Dr. Mack about Nadine many times before. Nothing I said seemed to surprise her.

"Sports were never your purpose," Dr. Mack said. "They were a way for you and your brother to bond and escape your father."

"Maybe writing is my purpose," I suggested.

"Like sports, writing is a tool," she replied. "That doesn't mean it can't become your passion that drives your purpose. However, when we began these sessions, it sounded like you were using writing as a way to avoid Nadine, or take your mind off her. Now it seems that you are using it to reconnect with her. Writing can be a wonderful, effective tool, but the question is, who are you doing it for?"

I became more frustrated as Dr. Mack spoke. "If writing isn't my purpose, then I guess I don't have one."

She wasn't bothered by my harsh tone. "You are mistaking your passions and desires for your purpose."

"I fail to see a difference," I said. "If I'm passionate about writing, isn't that why I'm here?"

She shook her head. "You are not here to fit into a job, or a hobby, or labels. It's my belief, and the belief of many other coven members, that we incarnated here to learn and grow, and to become the best version of ourselves—our spiritual selves. Which makes your purpose, Lucas, to be yourself, whatever that may be."

I must've had a confused look on my face, because she continued to explain.

"I say writing is a tool because it can help you learn, grow, expand, and support who you truly are at a soul level," she said. "But you are not here to simply write. There are hundreds, even thousands of other things you could be doing to bring your spirit into the world and contribute, love, and shine. You are not here to produce for someone else. You're here to be you, and when you can do that, you touch everyone around you, and the whole world benefits simply because you exist in your natural, beautiful state."

I went speechless. No one had put it in words like that for me before. It made so much sense. It sounded like everything I ever wanted. "How do I reach this purpose? How do I become the best version of myself?"

Her eyes lit up, like she was happy to see I was getting it. "Don't you see, Lucas? You're already doing it! Your beautiful existence is not a destination. It is a journey—one full of many, many imperfections, and *endless* learning opportunities. Seeking growth does not make you more worthy of love and care. You have always been deserving of everything you desire. You care for yourself, because you are *already* worthy."

Worthy. It was such a strong word. I didn't realize how much I felt *unworthy* until now.

"Oh," I said in realization. "So, if I'm already living my purpose, why do I feel like shit?"

"From a spiritual perspective, your body and mind are out of alignment with your truth," she explained. "You are trying to create a reality that is one thing, but you don't see that in your environment, and so you are suppressing your true spiritual self. We can use this perspective to figure out what may have triggered—or what may be perpetuating—your depression. What is it about your external world that isn't aligning with your internal?"

The question was rhetorical. Dr. Mack and I had discussed such things in length in my previous sessions.

"I've become my own victim by losing touch with my reality," I thought aloud.

Dr. Mack nodded. "That is one way to see things."

"Are there other ways to see it?" I asked.

"There is the scientific approach, dealing with hormones and neurotransmitters," Dr. Mack said. "And we can always explore that side of things if you'd like. Many clients come to me seeking medication, and those who choose that route oftentimes truly benefit from it. But again, it is a tool. For some, spiritual healing is not enough, and they truly need medical intervention to help them. There are certain clients I will absolutely recommend medications to, and I always encourage listening to medical professionals first and foremost."

"Well, you're my doctor," I said. "Do you think I need meds?"

She didn't answer my question directly. Instead, she asked, "Are you asking me for them?"

I thought about it for a moment before answering. "I'm asking if that's the only way for me to get better. Not your other patients. *Me*."

"I think it's still too early in your journey to tell," Dr. Mack answered. "If medication is something you'd like to consider, I can make recommendations, but many of my patients choose to forgo medication altogether."

"I don't want meds if I don't need them," I told her.

"I'm glad to hear that, as I prefer to take a holistic approach to therapy myself," she said. "But I want to make sure you're choosing that route for the right reasons. There is absolutely no shame in taking medication."

"It's not about that," I assured her. "I just want to try other things first and see if they work. If I can make a lasting impact without meds, then I don't want them."

"Then that's what we'll do," she said kindly. "Just know that if you ever change your mind, we can revisit this conversation in the future."

"I appreciate that," I said honestly.

Silence stretched between us as I stared up at the ceiling.

"I sense you have more to add," Dr. Mack said kindly.

She was right, and that was probably why it was so easy to talk to her. Her empathetic powers made her perceptive to my feelings, and it felt like she actually cared.

I pushed myself to a sitting position and stared down at my feet while I spoke. "It's the thought of moving forward with all of this. All this inner work just seems... so heavy. I feel like I'm lying at the bottom of Lake Santos or something, with all this weight pressing down on me."

Dr. Mack nodded, like she understood. "That's very common. If you don't feel ready—"

"I'm ready," I interrupted. "At least, I want to be. It just scares me."

She tilted her head. "What about it frightens you?"

I shrugged. "I guess I'm scared to do all this work for nothing. How do I do it, Linda?"

She remained calm as she explained. "Your current identity is nothing more than a belief, and what is a belief but simply an idea with emotion behind it? You have power over your emotions, which means you have power over your beliefs. You can change who you believe yourself to be, and the rest will follow."

I considered her words. "I'm not sure I understand. How do I follow my purpose and become who I'm meant to be?"

"It's not about who you're meant to *become*. It's about who you already *are*, beneath all the layers. You are not your body. You are not your hobbies. You're not your religion or race or relationships."

"Well, no. I'm not just one thing," I said simply. "I'm all of it. Every little piece of my life comes together to make up who I am."

"That's a sense of self you've created," Dr. Mack explained. "Let me explain it better."

She flipped a page in her notepad and turned her clipboard around to show me. She drew a small circle in the middle of the blank page. "This is you," she said, pointing to the center circle. "This is the beautiful, glorious you before you incarnated into human form. When you were born, you formed an identity of *self* at a young age."

She wrote my name next to the circle, then drew two small stick figures. "Your identity included things like your name and who your parents were."

She drew a circle, encompassing all of the images, then started creating more doodles outside of the circle. When she finished those drawings, she drew another circle, creating layers that looked like a target. "As you grew, your identity expanded, adding more and more things to your identity. Your house, your pets, your brother. You didn't just see yourself as Lucas. You saw yourself as Eric's brother, a pet owner, a kid, a warlock, and many other things. Over the last year, you've added more and more things to your identity—Mortana, the Reaper's Apprentice, Nadine's boyfriend. For some, even depression becomes one of the markers of their identity."

I opened my mouth to protest, until I realized she was right. I *had* adopted depression as part of myself. "Is that why I've struggled with depression so much? Because I made it part of my identity?"

"It could be," she answered. "It isn't the case for everyone. As I said, many clients need medical intervention. But from what you've told me, I believe this may be one of the reasons you're having such a hard time. You see, we must create a sense of self in order for our limbic system to do its job. Our brain has to categorize what is *self* and what is not, to keep itself safe. When we encounter a lion in the wild, we need to know what we must protect and what we can abandon in order to get to safety. It's a survival mechanism."

I nodded along, absorbing her lesson.

"Perhaps I'm getting ahead of myself," she said, slowing down.

"No, keep going," I told her. "I'm ready to hear it."

She smiled, looking proud of me. "When your depression becomes your identity, overcoming it can become very difficult. Your ego resists help, because it sees it as an attack upon yourself."

I brushed my hair out of my eyes. "That makes so much sense."

"From this perspective, it's actually beneficial to categorize things like our loved ones into our sense of self," she continued. "If we protect our spouse and children, the human race survives."

"So I've gone into survival mode, even though there's no lion trying to attack me?" I questioned.

She nodded. "In some ways, yes. But this phenomenon is not unique to individuals with mental illness. It happens to all of us."

It was nice to know I wasn't alone.

"That's not to say that we shouldn't love other people and protect them," she continued. "The problem is that when we tie our identities to external things—like people or money or success—our experience becomes determined by those things. We lose our own sense of self, because everything we're feeling is dependent on how that other person feels about us, or what grades we're getting in school, or how much money we have in the bank. If we lose that person or that job, we feel like we've lost ourselves. Do you see where I'm going with this?"

I nodded. For once in my goddamn life, something actually made a bit of sense. "None of this is who I truly am."

"Precisely." Dr. Mack ripped the drawing from her notepad, then held it up. She tore the page at the edge, pulling off bits and pieces as she came closer to the center. "Your depression does not rule you, Lucas. Nor do any of these other things. It's in your power to peel away these layers."

Riiip.

"Some of them, we get to keep—not because they *are* us, but because we love and appreciate how they lift us up and expand us. Because they're *good* for our souls." She tore off the piece that said *Nadine*, then tucked it into her shirt pocket. She did the same with *writing*, *hiking*, and *Reaper's Apprentice*.

"Others, we can choose to abandon, because they no longer serve us." She tore off *depression* and placed it into the wastebasket beside her.

The weight that'd been resting on my shoulders all session seemed to lift slightly. I felt like I could breathe easier.

She continued tearing away the layers, until she held up the center circle she'd first drawn. "Eventually, what you're left with is *you*. The true you. The *soul* you."

She set the scrap of paper on the table beside herself, then took the other pieces back out of her pocket. She began sprinkling them around the tabletop. "Everything else is simply something which we choose to surround ourselves with. Our values, our beliefs, our people, our experiences—it's all there to support us."

I stared at the tabletop, absorbing the lesson. "So you're saying I have control over all that?"

She looked thoughtful. "To a degree. I do not want to confuse the power to choose with the power of control. For instance, you can choose to love Nadine, but you have no control over whether she loves you back."

Dr. Mack picked up the piece that read *Nadine* and pulled it out of the pile to illustrate before she continued on. "You can choose to write one of your articles and submit it for publication, but you cannot control whether the editors run your story. You can choose to skateboard down a mountain, but you can't control the wind, or whether someone else is driving on that road."

I chuckled lightly. "No. I guess you can't."

She rearranged the paper scraps as she spoke. "The beauty of separating your identity from these things is that should you take something away..." She swept up a few items, leaving half of them behind, including my soul in the center. "...You do not lose yourself. You are safe. Nothing on this earth can harm your soul unless you let it."

Warmth settled in my heart, and it was the first time in a long time I didn't feel ice cold. It was going to take some time to process her lesson, but I sensed that it'd already done more for me than she'd ever know.

I wrung my hands. "How do I do it? How do I separate myself from all this and start over?"

"You don't have to strip your old identity all at once," she promised.

"In fact, I encourage you to hold on to any identities that are serving you —anything you truly feel good about. There are many tools we can use in this process, though it will take time, repetition, and conscious effort. It's going to be difficult, but every other client I've had go through the process tells me that it's worth it."

"Okay, so we're not starting over." I made sure to choose my words carefully, to ensure I understood the message. "I'm just rearranging some things, healing others, and embracing who I truly am. If everything in my environment changed, what would I be left with?"

Dr. Mack beamed at the rhetorical question. "You're already on the right track, Lucas. I'm so proud of you."

Hell, I couldn't believe I was actually getting somewhere.

"The idea behind this is to essentially rewire the brain," Dr. Mack said. "We can use tools like journaling, meditation and hypnosis, deep breathing, dancing, music, prayer and rituals, affirmations—the list goes on—to help you overcome some of the beliefs and habits holding you back. I know it sounds like a lot, but we don't have to use all of these tools. There is no one-size-fits-all approach. For example, some of my clients really enjoy music and dance, because the activity keeps them grounded in their body and in touch with their reality. Other clients prefer the peace and quiet of meditation. The key is finding what works for you and to leverage it to your advantage."

I thought about it for a moment. "I like music. Maybe we can start there. Journaling has helped me before, so I could try that again. And maybe... affirmations? I'm not sure."

"Well, we can try it," Dr. Mack suggested. "If it doesn't work for you, we won't force it. I'm going to put together a playlist of songs I want you to listen to, and I'll send over some journal prompts that we can go over in your next session. I'm glad to see you taking this so seriously, Lucas."

I shrugged, like it wasn't a big deal, but I knew it was. "Something has to change. I hate that I've wasted so much time."

Dr. Mack's expression softened, like she really felt for me. "It's important that you forgive yourself for your past."

"Well, my past self was a bit of a whiny bitch," I joked.

Dr. Mack didn't seem to like the joke, because she frowned and stood. She walked over to her desk and opened a drawer. "There's a ritual I'd like you to try, if you're willing. I think you're ready."

My spine straightened. "What kind of ritual?"

She pulled out an old leather-bound book that looked like it must be a spellbook. "It's one of forgiveness and letting go of the past."

She flipped through the pages, then handed me the book. I scanned the open page to see it wasn't a spellbook at all. There was no magic involved. But I was willing to try anything.

I furrowed my brow. "Do you really think I'm ready for this?"

She smiled softly. "I do. You are open and ready to learn. I believe in you."

"Thanks. I think I'm ready to believe in myself, too."

I never thought I'd hear myself say that. The crazy thing was, it was actually true.

☽

IT DIDN'T FEEL right to rush into the ritual right away, so I spent the rest of the week preparing for it. Every moment I wasn't in class, I was writing in my journal, pouring my heart onto the page. By the time classes finished on Friday, I had half a notebook filled with confessions and fears. Once I started writing, I just couldn't stop.

I left after sunset on Friday night and hiked through the forest to a secluded edge of Lake Santos. By the time I reached the water, it was well past curfew. The small clearing I'd found housed nothing more than a rock just large enough for me to sit on. Trees surrounded me, and I felt cozy and alone, like no one else would bother me here. It was perfect.

It was the new moon, the perfect time to perform this ritual of new beginnings. The stars were the only light I had to see by. I stripped off my hoodie and tossed it beside me in the grass. The autumn night air was surprisingly comfortable, as if welcoming me to perform the ritual.

The ritual was going to be difficult—that much, I was certain. But for some reason, I felt totally calm. My hands didn't shake as I conjured my journal and the book of rituals. My feet felt steady in the grass, and I gazed out over Lake Santos with hope in my heart.

"I'm ready," I told myself. "Let's do this."

I climbed onto the boulder and sat upon it cross-legged. I placed my journal beside myself, then conjured an amazonite crystal to calm my mind. I situated five candles in a circle around the journal and lit them. I conjured a pair of scissors and set that beside the other items. My long hair tickled my eyelashes as I gazed down at the book of rituals to review it one last time. There was no incantation to speak, no magic to cast. This wasn't about using magic to heal my emotional turmoil. This was all me.

When I was ready, I subconjured the book of rituals and placed my hand over my heart. "Mother Miriam—" I prayed.

An innate sense of fear shocked my heart. I'd usually push it aside, but tonight, I welcomed it. The ritual wouldn't work unless I felt my emotions and let them pass through me. Bottling them up had done me no good in the past, and so I had to resolve to feel them.

I drew a deep breath, then started again. "Mother Miriam, I am ready. I ask for your strength and guidance as I embark on this journey of self-reflection and forgiveness."

A gust of wind rustled through the trees, and the fear in my heart began to melt away. It didn't disappear, but it became easier to bear.

"Tonight, I make a choice to let go," I said aloud. "I choose to set myself free of my past, and to open my heart to the future. No more will I hold myself back. I welcome the fear. I welcome the risks. I welcome the love, and the beauty, and the strength that I have within me. I know it all is here to guide me. And so I will no longer push it aside. I will listen."

I closed my eyes and soaked in the sounds of nature—the water against the shore, and the trees swaying around me. It was peaceful, but painful all at the same time. Part of me wanted to run away and hide, to say *fuck it* and forget about the ritual all together. It wasn't like saying this stuff out loud would magically change me, but that wasn't the point.

I focused on the rock beneath me to ground myself in the moment. "My fear does not rule me unless I let it. I am safe here," I told myself. "I am safe to let go of all that has been holding me back. I've been so afraid to let go because I thought it meant *forgetting*. I can't forget the things I've done, or the things that have been done to me. I hold on, in hopes of not repeating the same mistakes over again. But it's this holding on that has its power over me. I do not have to forget, but I can be okay moving on."

The wind brushed through my hair, and I breathed a long sigh. Just saying it out loud made a huge difference. Even if I didn't believe everything I'd said deep down inside, I knew that I could learn to believe it with time. The change started right now.

"I am ready to release this baggage," I spoke aloud. "I no longer wish to carry around the weight of my childhood memories. I do not have to acknowledge that my father's actions were okay, but I do not have to dwell on them anymore. I am free of him. The only chains that remain are those which I've created myself."

I lifted a strand of my hair, then grabbed the scissors in the other hand. "I am not my father, and I cannot control or change his actions. The experience taught me how to better treat people, and I will forever hold that lesson in my heart. But I choose to let go of this resentment. It will take time to fully heal, but I am ready to accept that the past cannot be changed, and that the future will be brighter. I am not a little kid anymore, and no one can abuse me like he did ever again."

I brought the handle of the scissors together, and the lock of hair fell to the rock. My heart swelled, and tears sprang to my eyes. I had no idea how powerful such a speech could be.

I took another strand of hair in my fingers and raised the scissors. "I choose to let go of the resentment I have for my mother. She never stepped in when my father lashed out, but I know she did the best with the resources she had. My mother loves me and always has. I cannot convince her to do anything she doesn't want to do. I cannot save her in the way I want, but I *can* choose to move on from this anger."

I cut another strand of hair, and it fell into a pile atop the first. A wavered breath left my chest, and a tear spilled from my eye.

"I choose to look back on Eric's memory with fondness, to accept that I cannot go back and change the past," I continued. "I loved my brother dearly, and I still do, but no amount of dwelling on it will bring him back."

I didn't realize until I said it that I still felt bitter about what had happened. I'd forgiven him for the choice he'd made. I no longer felt any resentment toward him, but there was something there—something deeper—that I hadn't realized still lingered.

"Life was hard before Eric died, but his death triggered something inside of me... something I realize now I've been unable to move on from," I realized for the first time. "It's like... like I clung to him for my worth, because Dad always told me I was never enough. Nothing I ever did was good enough for him—for anyone. But Eric made me feel like I was worth a damn, and when I lost him, I lost that sense of worth, too."

As the truth of it dawned on me, tears began streaming down my face. I paused to catch my breath, but the emotions twisting in my chest made it hard to breathe. I couldn't put a name to what I was feeling, because it was good and bad, all rolled into one—so complex there wasn't a name for it. But for the first time, I chose to *feel* it.

For a brief moment, I thought I was weak to do this. But I realized that was the voice inside of me that I'd formed to defend myself against my father. That voice was trying to protect me, convincing me of that weakness.

Men don't cry, my father would say. I'd done everything in my power to protect myself against him, that I had demonized the expression of my emotions.

But I wouldn't do that anymore.

It was safe to cry. It was safe to let this all go.

Something Nadine had said to me last year came to mind. It was the day I'd taken her to the abandoned mansion for the first time, when I'd opened my heart to her.

Crying doesn't make you weak. It's an opportunity to grow.

I didn't understand what she'd meant at the time. I thought she was just trying to make me feel better about crying in front of her. But I got it now.

It was a release. Everything that I'd bottled up until now came pouring out of me in one big, sobbing wave. I couldn't stop it even if I tried. Though it was difficult and painful, it was worse to keep it all inside.

I wasn't *weak*. I was strong, because I *could* face this. I could use my emotions as a tool, instead of a weapon. I had to tear myself open to do it, but I wouldn't run from it any longer.

I doubled over, pressing my forehead into the boulder. My shoulders shook, and my sobs filled the clearing, but I didn't give a shit. I needed this.

Tears streamed from my cheeks and formed tiny rivers along the boulder. For a long time, I didn't speak. I just let everything I'd bottled up inside flow out of me, until it felt like there was nothing left.

And then I cried some more. I punched the boulder with my fists, and I wailed. My chest twisted as if it was alight with the fires of the Abyss.

It was a beautiful moment.

"I broke when Nadine and I split up, because I thought it meant I'd failed," I said as my feelings bubbled to the surface. "I never believed I was good enough for Nadine, so I pushed her away. But in doing so, I pushed away everything I'd tied my worth to."

A sob broke from my chest, and another realization dawned on me. I gasped as I lifted my head, gazing out over Lake Santos through the tears. "Oh my Goddess. I keep doing that. I self-sabotage over and over. I pushed away my gift as the Reaper's Apprentice because I never felt worthy of such a gift and responsibility. I've never been able to understand why Mother Miriam chose *me*."

The realization hit me like a landslide. No amount of journaling or counseling I'd done had ever unearthed such a realization. Everything about myself suddenly seemed to make sense.

"I tried to change the wrong things," I realized. "I've been trying to *force* myself to feel better, by responding to my gift in new ways, or throwing out Nadine's stuff. But it's only helped on the surface. Deep down, I never felt worthy of anything."

Tears streamed down my face, but this time, my body didn't heave in sobs. This time, my emotions moved through me with ease. I felt so free, as if giving words to my deep-seeded feelings gave me power over them.

I grabbed my journal and held it over the candle flames. The pages lit, and all the fears I'd placed into the journal burned to ashes. I set the journal aside on the rock and watched it burn. An incredible spiritual feeling overcame me as my worries seemed to disappear.

A raindrop fell from the sky and hit the end of my nose. I turned my gaze to the sky and opened my arms wide, welcoming the storm.

"I choose to claim control over myself again," I announced to the sky overhead. "I have the power to work through my depression and anxiety. They do not control me."

Heavy raindrops splattered against my face, and the sound of them hitting the water seemed soothing. It seemed so symbolic, as if the rain had come to wash me clean.

I didn't really think about what I did next. It wasn't part of the ritual. I just felt like it *needed* to be done for me to truly move past all of this.

I stood and began stripping my clothes off. With every article of clothing I removed came another declaration.

"I am worthy," I claimed as I stripped off my shoes. "Not because Mother Miriam chose me. Not because Nadine wanted to be with me. Because *I* choose to be. Not someone else. *Me*."

I pulled off my socks, then tossed my wet hoodie onto the rock. "I am the Reaper's Apprentice because I chose to serve the Goddess. No one forced this upon me. I accepted. My gift is good, and I am worthy of it."

I yanked my t-shirt over my head, then kicked off my pants. "I am worthy!" I declared one last time, shouting it over the sound of the raindrops around me.

Then I stepped into Lake Santos. The chilly water made me shiver, but I was ready for this. I walked out into the lake, until I couldn't touch anymore. Raindrops ran down my face, but I didn't mind them. I took a deep breath, then allowed my body to dip below the surface.

I released my breath and sank to the bottom. I lay flat on my back, feeling oddly at peace beneath the weight of the water above me.

I am worthy. I am enough. Love surrounds me everywhere I go.

I repeated the affirmation over and over again in my mind. My chest began to feel as if it might implode, but I didn't stop just yet. I continued to repeat the phrase, until I actually started to believe it.

I am worthy. I am enough. Love surrounds me everywhere I go.

My aching chest told me to give up, to kick myself to the surface and take a breath. But I wanted to stay. It wasn't to torture myself. In fact, it was the exact opposite. There was something spiritual about laying here at the bottom of the lake, confessing my fears and welcoming a new perspective. I didn't want to leave until I had to.

I am worthy. I am enough. Love surrounds me everywhere I go, I repeated in my mind.

Then, the most amazing thing happened. I saw a light behind my eyes, as if the morning sun was coming out. But I knew that couldn't be. It was nighttime *and* storming.

I opened my eyes to see a white light floating above me in the water. Beyond it, I could see the ripples of the raindrops upon the surface of the lake. I thought I must be hallucinating. I'd gone too long without oxygen, and my mind had made up the white, glowing light.

Then came the voice. The white light spoke to me in a voice I'd heard once before. She was calm and supportive, like the voice of a mother.

"You are worthy. You are enough. Love surrounds you everywhere you go," the white light said to me. *"You are ready to show the world the light within you, Lucas."*

It was Mother Miriam.

A feeling of weightlessness overcame me, and even though I lay at the bottom of the lake, I felt like I was floating.

Thank you, I thought.

As if the light could hear me, it began to swirl around me. Then the light lowered, until it touched my head. A warm, comforting feeling swelled inside of me. The light seemed to enter me through the head, and it swept through me, permeating its beautiful energy into every cell in my body. I felt invincible.

I lost all sense of time when the light touched me. It was so spiritual and beautiful that my breath didn't even seem to matter at the moment.

I didn't know how I reached the surface of the water. I didn't remember kicking off the bottom or swimming to the top. But somehow, my head broke the surface, and the light that had touched me was gone. I sputtered and inhaled a deep breath, then glanced around.

Panic hit me when I realized how far away from shore I'd gone. I could barely make out the shadows of the shoreline. My arms and legs felt like noodles as I began to swim back to shore. My vision blurred as raindrops trailed into my eyes. It was so dark out; I wasn't even sure I was headed toward shore. Maybe I'd imagined the shoreline. For all I knew, I was headed out to the center of the lake.

Relief flooded my body when my toes hit sand. I stumbled toward shore and tripped on a rock. I gasped for breath as I crawled the rest of the way out. I'd expended all of my energy and collapsed into the grass. My wet boxers clung to my legs. My feet remained submerged in the water, and the side of my face became coated in mud as I sucked in deep breaths.

Something moved in front of me, but it was so dark that I couldn't make out what it was. Shaking, I lifted my head and squinted through the rain. I heard something like footsteps in the mud, and though any rational person would've made a run for it, I didn't move an inch. It felt safe, whatever it was. I reached out, and something soft nudged my fingers. A *meow* sounded.

It was a gray tabby cat.

My breath hitched as the world around me seemed to tilt from side to side. The scent of bergamot hit my nose. It instantly took me back to Saturday mornings as a kid, when Eric would brew a pot of Earl Grey tea for us to share. The taste of peanut butter cups filled my mouth, reminding me of mine and Eric's post-Halloween parties, where we stayed up all night trading candy and stuffing ourselves until we passed out. He always gave me all his peanut butter cups, because they were my favorite.

"Eric, you son of a bitch," I laughed. There was no doubt in my mind that this was him—my brother's soul reincarnated to guide me along my journey.

The cat nudged my hand again, and I scratched it behind the ears. He purred, like my touch was the most amazing thing in the world. My heart swelled with joy. I pushed myself up and reached out for the cat. The rain began to let up as I squeezed the creature to my chest. I buried my face into its fur, and it pressed its nose to my forehead.

"It's about time you showed up," I said as I wept into the cat's fur. "Just in time, too."

People always said your cat would arrive when you needed them most. I'd come here tonight a broken shell of a human being, but I'd emerged from the water a new man.

I was ready now—for whatever was ahead.

TWELVE

Several Hours Earlier

I felt like shit. I probably should've skipped class, but I didn't. I stroked Isa's fur and ignored my pain while I focused on my Moonology lecture.

"We've spent the last few weeks studying moon cycles," Professor Loren said. She paced in front of the room, her long black dress billowing around her ankles. "Today, we'll be discussing new moon rituals, before moving on to full moon rituals later this semester. This is important information to pay attention to, as various rituals are more powerful depending on what phase the moon is in when the ritual is performed."

She stopped beside her desk and stroked her cat's tail before continuing. "The new moon marks the beginning of a cycle. It is a time to focus on new beginnings, such as your goals and manifestations. The full moon, however, signifies completion. It is a time to celebrate your achievements, to let go, and forgive that which has come before. Both phases are important, and they can even work together. You will find that full moon rituals are just as important as new moon rituals for manifesting your desires. You must release the old in order to welcome in the new."

I raised my hand. "Is that why the full moon is so good for cleansing energy, and why we charge our crystals under the full moon? Because we're letting go of that old energy?"

"Precisely," Professor Loren said.

A few seats over, Stacey snickered under her breath. She leaned over to the girl beside her and whispered, "She's so clueless."

The other girl, Valerie, eyed me up and down. "What a freak."

I sank a little in my chair, and Amy leaned over to me. "I'll fry them with a battle orb if you want."

"Don't do that," I whispered back.

Professor Loren pursed her lips and shot a death glare at Stacey and Valerie. "We'll be focusing on new moon rituals first, so I want you to start thinking about something you'd like to create—a new beginning, if you will. You'll be required to perform a moon ritual during the semester and write a paper on your experience."

Professor Loren shared a brief overview of various new moon rituals, then gave us time to write out ideas for our projects. By the time she dismissed class, I hadn't come up with anything. I was so bothered by Stacey's and Valerie's comments that I couldn't think straight. I gathered my things, but I moved slowly.

"Do you want me to wait for you?" Amy asked.

"I'll be fine," I told her.

"Okay," she said, though she didn't look entirely convinced. "I'll meet up with you later."

Everyone had left the room by the time I stood. I felt horrible.

"Nadine," Professor Loren called before I reached the door.

I turned to her. "I'm sorry, Professor. I didn't mean to interrupt class with a stupid question."

"There are no stupid questions," she stated kindly.

"I think Stacey and Valerie would disagree." I tried to joke about it, but my words fell flat.

Professor Loren frowned. "And why should their opinions matter?"

I shrugged. "I don't know."

She waved her hand, and the door shut by itself. "Let's talk."

I took a curious step toward her. "About what?"

Professor Loren rounded her desk and sat, then gestured to the nearest chair. "First of all, I'm curious why you're in class today?"

I furrowed my brow as I sat. Isa jumped onto the desk in front of me, purring. "Why wouldn't I be?"

"It's come to my attention that your paperwork at the school's

Disability Services office has been approved," she said. "You're supposed to be taking it easy."

I grimaced. "I'm trying. I just have a bit of a cold."

It wasn't a lie. I'd definitely come down with some sort of infection.

Professor Loren shifted in her chair. "I know a flare-up when I see one."

My jaw dropped. I'd gotten so good at hiding my flare-ups that even Grammy couldn't always tell when I was feeling ill.

"You say that like you know first-hand," I pointed out.

She nodded. "I myself have Crohn's Disease. My symptoms are under control, but I spent many years with severe abdominal pain and fatigue."

"I'm so sorry," I told her. Goddess, was that all I could say? I hated when people said that to me. "It's nice to have someone who understands."

"I just want you to know that I'm here for you—whatever you need," she offered.

Her kindness was almost overwhelming. Even though she was legally obligated to provide accommodations for my disability, most professors did the bare minimum. They didn't actually understand. Professor Loren did—to some degree, at least.

She eyed me. Though she wasn't a Seer, she was quite perceptive. "Something's bothering you."

I frowned. "I know I shouldn't care, but I'm bothered by what Stacey and Valerie said in class. People keep saying stuff like that, like I don't belong in the coven and I should just leave. And sometimes I think... maybe I should."

"Do you truly believe that?" she asked, sounding a bit off guard.

I shrugged. "Sometimes."

"Mother Miriam wouldn't have gifted you your powers if she thought you didn't belong," she pointed out.

"That's one of the reasons keeping me here, I guess," I admitted. "So far, I've been too stubborn to let anyone drive me out of town, but I thought things would get better the longer I stood my ground, you know?"

Professor Loren pressed her lips together thoughtfully. "I'm not supposed to do this, but I have something that I think might help you."

My spine straightened. "You do?"

She conjured a small draw-string bag that fit in the palm of her hand. "These are Seer herbs," she explained. "They're a unique blend of herbs mixed by Alchemists. Traditionally, they're used by Seers to induce clearer visions, but they can be used by all Casts in prayer. These can help provide you with the clarity you seek."

I reached out for the baggie, intrigued. "How do I use them?"

"Tonight would be a good time, as it's the new moon—a time for new beginnings. You'll want to find a quiet spot, where you won't be disturbed. Meditate beforehand to clear your mind. When your mind has quieted, light the herbs and inhale the smoke as you pray to Mother Miriam."

I eyed the bag. "And this will provide me clarity?"

"It can *help*," she emphasized. "But you must be willing to confess your fears and open yourself to answers—whatever may come through."

"I can do that," I told her. "I'm ready for anything."

"Then I wish you the best," she said.

"Thank you." I left the room with Isa at my heels, feeling excited about my upcoming new moon ritual.

I was already on the edge of what I could handle for the day, so I had to be careful about where I put my energy. I decided to put off homework and take a nap to prepare for tonight. By the time I woke, the sun had already set. Talia had left a note telling me she'd be in the music room until curfew. I wrote back saying I'd be back as soon as I could, but to cover for me if I missed curfew. Something told me this was going to be a long night.

There was only one place I could think of where I could be alone. It wasn't ideal, because it reminded me so much of Lucas, but I knew I wouldn't be disturbed.

I walked through the forest, illuminating the trees ahead with a magical orb. Isa walked ahead of me, following the glowing orb and trying to catch it.

After fifteen minutes of walking, the clearing came into view. It was hard to see at first, because the forest was so dark and storm clouds were rolling in, but my orb floated overhead, illuminating the abandoned mansion.

I conjured the key Lucas had given me—the one he'd found inside the mansion. I unlocked the doors and stepped inside. The mansion was quiet, but in a peaceful way. To most people, this place would feel eerie and frightening, but for me, it felt like coming home.

Isa sniffed the dusty, broken staircase and sneezed.

"Isa," I cocked my head toward the living room. "This way."

The large room was a bit chilly, so I conjured a lighter and built a fire in the fireplace. Isa curled up beside it and closed her eyes. I conjured my yoga mat and sat upon it to begin my meditation.

Quieting my mind wasn't easy. A hundred questions raced through my thoughts.

Do I belong here?

Where do we find the Crock of Death?

How do we stop the Waning?

Did I give the priestesses enough information?

How do I fulfill the prophecy?

If I learned anything from my Meditation and Inner Magic class, it was to allow my thoughts to move through me without judgement. I tried to do that, but my mind jumped from one thought to another before I could really process any of it.

"Mother Miriam," I whispered to the empty room. "I am seeking guidance. Please, show me a sign."

I didn't truly know what I was asking for. It wasn't like Mother Miriam was going to light fireworks above the mansion or something. I was just so desperate for answers.

You have to be ready to receive them, I thought. I didn't know where the thought had come from, but I realized it was right.

There's no rush, I told myself. *You have all night.*

I didn't care about curfew. I had to remind myself that I was safe here, and that demanding answers from Mother Miriam would get me nowhere.

I shifted uncomfortably on my yoga mat. I hated just sitting here. I felt like I had to move.

I drew a deep breath and moved into various yoga poses. I stretched my muscles and focused on my breath. The minutes stretched into a half hour, then even longer. I fell into a trance, moving my body in whichever way felt good in the moment. I became so focused on my breath that the thoughts racing through my mind quieted.

Finally, when I felt my mind was clear, I sat back on the mat cross-legged. I conjured the baggie Professor Loren had given me, along with a bowl. I emptied the Seer herbs into the bowl and lit them. A sweet scent filled the room, and I lifted the bowl to my face, inhaling the smoke. I breathed a heavy sigh as my shoulders dropped.

As I continued to breathe in deep breaths, I placed the bowl in front of me, then put my hands over my heart. "Mother Miriam," I whispered to the empty room. "I pray to you tonight seeking guidance. I have so many unanswered questions. All I wish to do is help the coven, but I need your support. What must I do?"

I sat quietly, waiting. The seconds ticked by, until minutes had passed. I was met with nothing but silence.

My hands shook at my heart. "Please, Mother Miriam. I know that you can communicate with the coven. We have prayer and visions and intu-ition. I *must* know where to go next."

I wished I could say that it was as simple as listening to my heart, but my heart was as conflicted as my mind. I began to get frustrated, but I knew that would only delay the process. I tried to calm myself by taking deep breaths, but I couldn't help it when frustrated tears rose to my eyes.

"Goddess," I begged. "The coven is in danger. The Waning is threat-ening our magic, and there's a prophecy that says Lucas and I are chosen to save the coven. What must we do to fulfill this prophecy?"

The wind whistled through a broken window nearby, but that was the only response I received. Sobs broke out in my chest, and I doubled over, pressing my face into my hands. Why wasn't this working?

Professor Loren's words came back to me. *You must be willing to confess your fears and open yourself to answers.*

Perhaps I was trying to force the answers.

"I don't know if I can do this," I confessed. The truth twisted my gut. "I try to convince myself I'm so strong and resilient, but I can't be strong all the time. It's tearing me apart."

I wiped at my eyes, but the tears kept coming. The confessions felt like slicing my own stomach open, pouring everything out of me that I didn't even know was there. "I'm scared of this prophecy," I admitted aloud. "My illness is so unpredictable, and I'm so sick all the time. I fear that to save the coven, I'll have to lose myself. I don't think that's a decision I'm willing to make, especially when no one but my friends even want me here."

My whole body rocked in sobs, but I couldn't stop the confession once it started. "I don't understand why *I'm* responsible for saving the coven, when there are so many other people with more resources. Is it because I'm a Curse Breaker? Is that what the Waning is? A curse I need to break? Why me? Why am I the only witch of my kind? I don't understand."

I gasped for breath. It was all so overwhelming. "I just want the coven to live in peace. I feel that saving them will earn me my place here, but that feels so backwards. I don't want to save them just to prove myself. I want to save them because they're my people, because this is my home... at least, I want it to be."

My shoulders sagged as I released all desperation and surrendered. My voice quieted. "I just need to hear a message. What is it that you want me to know right now? What will help me through all this?"

A bright white light shone through my lids, and my eyes shot open. At first, I thought someone had discovered me here and was shining an orb through the window. But the light was different from a witch orb. It was brighter, more brilliant, and I could feel the love radiating off of it. I was so mesmerized by it. My tears ceased, and I wiped them from my cheeks.

The light floated toward me, and I reached out for it. I wanted to touch it, as if doing so would solve everything. It seemed like the kind of light that could wrap me in a hug and make everything better.

But before I could touch the light, it began to transform. The orb elongated, and the light became so intense that I had to shield my eyes from it. After a few moments, the light dimmed, and I lowered my hand to see the form of a woman standing in front of me. Her outline glowed, as if I was in the presence of an angel.

Only when my eyes focused on her face, I realized it was even more incredible than that. I'd seen her warm eyes and soft smile countless times before in the painting that hung above the mantle in the Main Foyer. I knew the gentle wave of her hair by heart.

It was Mother Miriam.

I was so starstruck that I couldn't find my lips. I gaped at her.

"M-Mother Miriam?" I stammered breathlessly.

She gazed down at me with a soft smile. I felt so welcome in her presence, but I didn't understand how she was here. I didn't think it was possible. I bowed my head to her.

"Nadine," she said kindly, reaching out her hand to me. "There is no need to bow to me."

My breath wavered as I lifted my gaze to hers. "I-I… I can't believe this."

"Believe it, my child. I am here," she assured me.

"I thought my Evoking Ceremony was the only time…" I trailed off. I could hardly find the words. It was like I needed to rationalize this, like maybe it was something in my mind.

"Traditionally, witches can only contact me on the night of their Evoking Ceremony," she explained. "Even the gods have a difficult time bending the rules of nature, and because of that, I'm often unable to appear outside of the ceremony. These are the ways of the spirit realm. But sometimes, when the planets and stars are aligned, and the energy of the witch summoning me is just right, I can appear. Walk with me, Nadine. I'm not sure how much time we'll have."

I didn't have to question it. I stood and followed Mother Miriam out of the mansion, leaving Isa sleeping by the fire.

"Is this real?" I asked her as we headed toward the trees. "Or is it a vision, like in my Evoking Ceremony?"

She smiled at me. "Are visions not real?"

I thought about it for a second. "I guess they are. Just not… physically."

"Well, why does something have to be physically present to be real?" she asked. "Can you see, touch, and smell *love*?"

"I guess not," I admitted.

"And yet it is one of the realest things in the universe," Mother Miriam pointed out. "Which makes me wonder, Nadine… what do you define as *real*?"

I gestured to the trees around us. "Well, the trees are real. They're solid. I can touch them and feel them."

"And those sensations are interpreted by your brain, yes?" she asked, pointing to her temple.

I wasn't sure where she was going with this.

She must've noticed my confused expression, because she explained further. "Everything you touch is interpreted as *solid* by your brain. Everything you see is light made into an image by your mind. Every taste you encounter is experienced by your brain. Your emotions are chemical reactions and interpretations of what is happening to your nervous system. *Everything* you experience is in your head, and you can't prove that something is *real* or otherwise. Reality is what we make it, Nadine."

Her words hit me harder than I thought they would. This wasn't just about the question I'd asked. It went much deeper. I didn't even realize I needed to hear the lesson until she gave it.

"I get what you're saying," I said. "Is that what you came here to tell me? Is that the answer I needed to all of this?"

She smirked lightly. "You tell me. You're the one who summoned me."

"I guess I didn't think you'd actually show up," I admitted. "I was expecting more of an intuitive answer, to be honest. I'm still learning how to listen to my intuition, though."

We wove through the trees, and she moved as if she was as solid as I was. Even her cloak billowed around her ankles in the breeze.

"Can I ask you anything?" I questioned.

She stopped and turned toward me. "Always, my child."

Anxiety buzzed in my chest. I had so many questions. I hadn't been sure I'd ever have a clear answer to them. I was both excited and scared to get those answers.

"I'm curious if I'm meant to be here—in the coven, I mean," I said. "I mean, I wasn't born here, and people don't seem to want me around."

"What do *you* want?" she asked.

I bit my lower lip. "Well, I love Octavia Falls. I love Grammy and Talia and all my friends. I feel like I could live here forever, if the coven wanted me."

"I'm not asking what others want," she pointed out. "What do *you* want?"

Her question struck me. I didn't think I'd ever asked myself that before. I was too worried about whether other people wanted me here, and if I belonged. What *did* I want?

I wanted to live a beautiful life here with my friends and family. I wanted to stay at Miriam College, where I could grow my powers. I was a witch, and no one could take that from me.

"I want to be here," I stated confidently.

"Then this is where you're supposed to be," Mother Miriam told me.

A weight seemed to lift from my shoulders. "That's my life path, then?" I asked. "To stay in Octavia Falls."

"That is up to you," she said kindly. "You're not supposed to be here because I said so, or because the coven demanded it. You are meant to be here because *you* want to be—because *you* chose to be. There is no other reason to consider."

I furrowed my brow as I considered her words. "That's comforting to know. I'm still wondering, though… why did you choose me as a Curse Breaker? What was it about me that made me worthy of this power, to be the only one of my kind?"

"Isn't it obvious, Nadine?" she asked. "I did not choose Curse Breaker for you."

"I don't understand."

She turned from me and kept walking. "*I* didn't choose this for you. *You* chose this."

I hurried to keep up with her. "Wait, what? But my Evoking Ceremony—"

"Is not a test," she finished for me. "I do not determine your worth, Nadine. *You* do. It's a common misconception that your Evoking Ceremony is a chance to prove yourself to me, but it isn't a test. It's a *demonstration*. It's a way for you to show me who you *choose* to be. I simply unlock that magic for you."

My knees shook as I walked. It was such a beautiful revelation that I didn't have words for it. But something didn't fit.

"In my Evoking Ceremony, you gave me the choice to trade my soul for Lucas's," I said. "I chose to go to the Abyss. Was that not a test? If we can choose, then why send one of us to the Abyss?"

"It was your final demonstration, the one that confirmed which Cast you truly belong to," Mother Miriam said. "But it was also a demonstration for Lucas, to show how badly he wanted to get rid of his gift."

"But people have gotten exiled because of their Evoking Ceremony, haven't they?" I asked. "They didn't pass."

"Only because the truth of their heart showed that they did not want to be here," she answered. "I have never rejected anyone. It is *they* who have rejected me."

She stepped around a tree before explaining further. "This is why people tend to end up in the same Cast as their family. It's because they grew up with similar ideas about the world as their parents, so they choose the Cast they resonate with. You can choose a Cast outside of your family because you always have the power of choice. That is your free will."

My eyes widened as she spoke. It was such a lovely concept. "So I'm the only Curse Breaker because… nobody else chose it?"

"Precisely."

"Why hasn't anyone taught me these things?" I asked.

"Misconceptions and misguided intentions," she said simply.

"But the coven worships you," I pointed out. "How could we have strayed so far from the truth?"

Mother Miriam didn't answer right away, as if considering my question. Finally, she spoke. "Why do you think there are no cathedrals in my name?" she asked rhetorically. "I do not wish to be worshiped as your savior, Nadine. I am your mother—your guide. I am always here for you and will lead you toward paths I believe will serve you best, but ultimately, the decision to walk them is your choice. The coven moves in whichever way it chooses due to free will. I will not step in the way of that. Your free will is your greatest gift."

That comforted me and confused me all at once.

"What about the prophecy?" I asked. "It says I was chosen to save the coven. Do I have free will over that?"

"You always have free will," she said gently. "Prophecies by members of the coven are not about writing your destiny for you. They're about *seeing* the road you're already on."

I stopped dead in my tracks, and my jaw dropped. "You didn't choose me, then?" I realized. "The prophecy is talking about *my* choice, isn't it? I can choose to save the coven."

Mother Miriam nodded.

"Is it a sure thing, though?" I practically begged. "If I choose to do this, will I win? And if I don't… will the coven be destroyed?"

Mother Miriam's features softened. "I'm afraid I do not have the answer. This is the nature of free will, my dear. But I can tell you this… you are stronger than you believe, Nadine. You have everything you need to save the coven."

"You mean my magic?" I questioned. "Then the Waning is a curse? Can you tell me who's responsible?"

She shook her head. "It is not your magic that I speak of. You are intelligent and determined, and you know how to make tough decisions."

"That means a lot," I said honestly. "But I don't know if I'm ready for this."

"Then why are you asking me where to go next?" she questioned.

I opened my mouth, but the answer hit me so hard it practically knocked the wind out of me. "I've already made my decision," I realized.

She nodded. "The prophecy wouldn't have been made otherwise."

"Then I'm going to do everything to stop this," I stated confidently.

She smiled, looking proud. "You are a true member of the coven, Nadine. Don't let anyone tell you differently."

"If I'm to stop this, I need to know more," I insisted. "You must know who's behind the Waning and where the Oaken Wands are. Can you tell me?"

It was at that moment that the storm began to pick up. Wind swirled around me, and heavy raindrops splattered the top of my head. Mother Miriam began to fade. Her cloak became translucent, and her hair fell neatly to her shoulders, no longer affected by the wind.

"Wait, you can't go!" I insisted. "Please tell me who's behind this. Where do I find the Wands? How do I stop this?"

She began talking quickly, like she knew our time was up. "The first Wand lies inside the cursed cauldron, as you predicted. You, Nadine, must be the one to pursue the Alchemy Wand."

"But the priestesses—"

"Won't retrieve it without you," she interrupted. "The Oaken Wands can stop this dark magic, but you must—"

Before she could finish speaking, she vanished. I swore something inside of my chest left with her.

"I must *what*?" I cried to the empty forest. "What do I do?"

There was no answer but the howling wind. I became so unsteady that I dropped to my knees. The rain picked up, soaking me from head to toe, but I couldn't seem to move as I processed everything Mother Miriam had said.

I didn't know how long I sat in the rain, staring at the empty space in the forest where Mother Miriam had vanished. I shivered in the cold and wrapped my arms around my legs, as if holding myself together.

Eventually, the sound of a *meow* broke through the forest, and I squinted into the dark rain to see a shadow moving toward me.

"She's gone, Isa," I whispered.

Isa nudged her head against my arm, until I let go of my legs and pulled her onto my lap. I was half surprised I didn't fall into a million pieces right then and there. The fact that I didn't sent a wave of calm washing over me.

I recalled something Mother Miriam had said to me—not tonight, but the night of my Evoking Ceremony.

You are not defined by what happens to you. You are defined by how you react to it.

The coven could not break me unless I let it. Everything I was dealing with lately—the Waning, the Oaken Wands, the mystery of nightshade, breaking up with Lucas, and my disability—they were all just things that happened to me. They did not define me.

I defined who I wanted to be—and I was an unbreakable, unstoppable witch.

That hole that had opened up inside of me closed. Rock-solid resolve took over, and I rose to my feet, cradling Isa to my chest.

"Mother Miriam believes in me, and it's time I start believing in myself," I told Isa. "I have a destiny to fulfill."

The coven had gone too long without a Curse Breaker. I was going to be the best damn Curse Breaker there had ever been.

I would find the cauldron. I would retrieve the Wand.

And I *would* save the coven. No matter the price I had to pay.

THIRTEEN

The week following my spiritual awakening was odd. I found myself sleeping all the way through the night, and colors seemed more vibrant during the day. I hadn't felt this alive in ages. What was even more strange was that I wasn't unsettled by it at all. I was more optimistic than ever.

Halloween was approaching. It was always the best time of year in the coven—a time to celebrate our magic, to perform rituals while the veil was thin, and even talk to our loved ones on the other side. This year was particularly special, because Halloween fell on a full moon—a *blue moon*—which meant any rituals performed that night would have extra power behind them.

I heard the conversations in the hallway. Everyone seemed to be preparing for their ritual—whatever it may be. Professor Warren asked me about it in my advisor meeting on Wednesday.

I sat in his office. Oliver curled up in my lap, purring softly. I'd struggled to come up with a name for him at first. I just wanted to call him Eric, but it was customary to give your cat a new name, to separate their experience in this life from their last. I remembered how Nadine had named Isa after her mother's middle name, and it seemed so perfect. I started calling him Oliver after Eric's middle name, and it stuck.

"This Halloween is very special," Professor Warren remarked, leaning back in his chair. "Have you thought of performing any rituals during the full moon?"

"Not really," I admitted. "You?"

Professor Warren frowned. "This meeting isn't about me, Lucas. I'm worried about you."

"I'm doing better," I told him honestly. "Dr. Mack is really helping me. And it's nice to have Oliver here."

Professor Warren's shoulders relaxed. "I'm glad to hear that. Perhaps you and Dr. Mack could discuss rituals that might help you this Halloween. The full moon is a good time for letting go and forgiving old wounds."

"I know," I said simply. "Dr. Mack already gave me a ritual to try… and well, I did. It helped. I mean, it's no cure. Things aren't perfect. But I just need time to process this first before I start shedding new layers, you know?"

Professor Warren's eyebrows shot up. "That's a very… insightful perspective. I'm proud of you."

I shrugged, though it meant a lot to hear him say that. "Thanks, I guess."

Professor Warren sat up straighter. "This is all good news. I know you've confided in me in the past, but I'm not a licensed therapist. It's good to see you talking to someone who can help in ways that I can't."

"Oh, come on," I jabbed. "You're not completely useless."

He smirked. "I like to think I've taught you something."

"Sure you have. I know now that necromancers shouldn't try to reanimate dead tortoises, or they might spontaneously combust," I joked.

"That was one time," he sighed. "Will I ever live that down?"

"Not as long as I'm alive," I chuckled.

He laughed, and the corners of his eyes crinkled. "It's good to see you laugh, Lucas. Sometimes I worry you take life too seriously."

I shrugged. "I guess we have that in common."

He sighed and fiddled with the watch on his wrist, probably so he didn't have to look me in the eye. "Unfortunately, when you've been through what I have, it's hard not to take everything so seriously."

"You mean… because of what happened to your wife?" I asked carefully. The atmosphere in the room suddenly shifted. I knew his wife had died years ago from terminal cancer, but I'd never heard him speak about it.

He nodded solemnly. "That, and other things that ended in disaster…"

He stared off into the distance, and his brow furrowed at the painful memories. I wondered what he was talking about, but I didn't get a chance to ask.

He straightened. "Those are stories for another day. We're here to talk about you. Your classes sound like they're going well. I think your attendance rate can be salvaged if you don't skip any more classes this semester. Is there anything else I can help with?"

I thought about it for a moment. "There is, actually. It's not about my classes, but you might have some insight. I'm curious about summoning rituals. Specifically regarding Mother Miriam."

The memory of the bright white light I'd seen in the water during my new moon ritual came back to me. It'd been so peaceful and welcoming—like Mother Miriam had come to me herself.

"Can she appear outside of an Evoking Ceremony?" I asked.

Professor Warren nodded. "At times, though it's rare. Do you intend to contact her about something?"

"Maybe if we could contact her, we could learn how to end the Waning," I pointed out.

He shook his head. "I'm afraid it's not that simple. The gods have their own rules about interfering here on earth. If she were to appear outside an Evoking Ceremony, it'd have to be during specific astronomical alignments, and she wouldn't necessarily appear in full form."

"What do you mean?" I asked, intrigued.

"There are stories of Mother Miriam appearing as a bright white light —more of an energetic form than a spirit," he explained. "She chooses which form to appear in, based on what the summoner needs at the time. As legend goes, that form is not always what you'd expect. Most of the time, she doesn't show up at all."

I pressed my lips together. That light I'd seen *must* have been Mother Miriam's energy. It soothed me to know she was with me that night. I only wished I could've spoken to her.

"Anything else?" Professor Warren asked. "I sense there's something on your mind."

"Have you ever heard of the Crock of Death?" I blurted. I'd been trying to learn more about it, to see if the stories gave us any clues, but I hadn't gotten anywhere.

He furrowed his brow. "I'm afraid I haven't. What is it?"

"It's nothing," I told him. If I was honest about it, he'd warn me to leave this mystery alone, and I couldn't do that. "Just something I heard in passing."

He eyed me, like he suspected something. "Well, if that's all, we'll meet again in a few weeks. I don't want to have to lecture you about your attendance again."

"I think we can both agree to that," I said before leaving the room. Oliver jumped out of my arms and walked beside me.

My shoulders slumped as I headed down the hall. I'd been hoping Professor Warren might know something about the Crock of Death. The fact that we'd gotten nowhere with the legend left me feeling let down. I had class in an hour, so I had time to kill.

I made my way to the pool. No one was in here this time of day, except for my friends. Grant swam laps, and Talia and Mandy lay on pool chairs, chatting.

I waited at the end of Grant's lane. He moved through the water with ease, cutting through it like a blade through warm butter. I'd seen him swim plenty of times, but he kept getting better and faster. His swim times had gotten quite impressive, and I noticed his form had improved since last season.

Oliver sniffed at a puddle on the floor, then hid behind my leg. He didn't like the water.

Grant noticed me when he reached the end of his lane. He held the edge of the pool and pulled up his goggles. "Hey, Lucas. What's up?"

"I had my advisor meeting," I said. "Professor Warren doesn't know anything about the Crock of Death."

"Dammit," Grant muttered as he hoisted himself out of the pool. Water dripped into a puddle around his feet. He placed his hands on his hips, as if deliberately drawing attention to his shimmery purple Speedo. "That's not our only problem."

"Yeah, I see the problem," I cracked. "You need to put some pants on."

Grant glanced down to his Speedo. "What? You don't like it? You know the *point* is to draw the eye, right? I've gotta keep things interesting.

That's why I'm thinking of picking up juggling for the talent show. I've already started practicing."

Grant walked over to a cart full of pool toys and grabbed a few diving rings. He started juggling them and caught one before promptly fumbling with the others. Oliver chased after them, but he backed off when they rolled into the pool.

I winced. Mandy chuckled under her breath a few pool chairs away from us, but Talia couldn't seem to take her eyes off Grant's chest. The Tarantulas were going to have a field day tormenting Grant about his new *talent*.

"It's… a good start," I said.

Grant's shoulders slumped. "I've been mostly practicing with balls."

"I'll bet you have," Mandy snickered under her breath.

Grant whirled toward her, narrowing his eyes. "You're one to talk."

Mandy smirked. "Let's not make this dirty."

Talia laughed. "Too late."

Mandy shrugged and sat up straight in her pool chair. She waved her hand nonchalantly. "Fine. Balls, butts, boobs… they're all great. Moving on. Did I hear you mention the Crock of Death?"

"Nadine filled you in?" I guessed.

Mandy held her head up proudly. "Yes, and I've been tasked with eavesdropping on any and all gossip regarding nightshade."

"Is that why you're hanging out at the pool between classes?" I asked.

"Actually, Talia and I are here as Grant's moral support," Mandy replied. "It's better than—"

She cut off, and I eyed her curiously. "Better than what?" I questioned.

"It's nothing," she said. "Girl drama."

Talia finally tore her gaze off Grant's naked torso. "What's this problem you mentioned, Grant?"

He stared at the floor. "Well, you see, Amy and I have been working on figuring out what's in nightshade. We have a list of ingredients, but it's incomplete. We almost finished when…"

I felt the blood drain from my face. "Tell me you didn't."

Grant winced. "I'm sorry, man. I fucked it up. One wrong move and *poof*! It's all gone."

I groaned. "Where are we going to get more? After all our encounters with the Tarantulas, James, and Gregory, I'm certain we've ruined any chances we have of getting our hands on more. Everyone knows not to sell to us."

"I know," Grant sighed. "I've tried finding dealers, but no one will talk. I'm having a hell of a time."

Mandy held her head high. "I think I might know someone who's dealing."

"Really?" Talia asked. "Who?"

Mandy grimaced. "It's best if I don't say, to protect you all. Give me a couple of days to feel them out, and I'll get you your nightshade."

"Thanks for the help," I said. "It means a lot."

She brushed her dark hair out of her eyes. "Hey, I want to catch these creeps as much as you do. Anything you need, I'm here to help."

I blinked a few times. "You could help by finding me some eye drops. My eyes are burning at the sight of Grant's Speedo."

Mandy doubled over in laughter, and I chuckled loudly. Talia tried not to laugh, but she couldn't help it.

Meanwhile, Grant drew himself up proudly. "It's called confidence. You should try it sometime."

I was laughing so hard that I threw my hand over my mouth. "I didn't mean anything by it. Honestly."

Grant smirked, like he was having a good time but wouldn't admit it. "You think you're such a funny guy. I'll give you something to laugh about."

He shoved me playfully, and I lost my footing. My heart lurched as I tumbled over the edge of the pool and splashed into the water. At any other time, I would've been pissed, but when my head surfaced, I was still laughing. Oliver's head had been drenched in the splash, and he glared at me in displeasure. He shook his head, spraying water droplets everywhere.

"Very creative," I said, my tone dripping in sarcasm.

Grant beamed proudly. "That's what you get for—"

I grabbed his ankle and yanked him into the water. He squealed, but it was silenced as his head dipped under water. He came up for air a second later.

"I'm not even bothered," he said. "I was already wet."

"Saved by the Speedo," Mandy snickered.

"Hey, they're not just for speed," he said. "They're pretty comfy, too."

I pulled myself out of the water. "Well, you're going to have to put pants on before Protection Magic. Class starts soon."

Grant glanced up to the clock on the wall. "Shit, you're right. I'm going to hit the locker room."

"Here's a towel," Talia offered me.

"Thanks." I patted my face dry, but the towel became soaked pretty quickly. "I've gotta change. I'll catch up with you in class. Let us know what you find, Mandy."

"I will." She saluted me as I left the pool.

By the time Protection Magic started, I was in dry clothes and Grant had changed. We stood outside on the lawn, where Professor Ward was holding class today. It was a beautiful autumn day. Shades of orange and red painted the forest nearby, and leaves drifted slowly across the lawn. Oliver played with a leaf at my feet. He caught it, chewed on it for a moment, and then let it go in the wind so he could catch it again.

"Today, we'll be pushing the limits of our shield magic," Professor Ward announced. She was a middle-aged witch with a Seer tattoo below her ear. Her hair was tied into a loose knot at the base of her neck, and she'd been wearing a pointed witch hat all month in honor of Halloween. She was a knowledgeable professor, but quite difficult to please. "We're outside today so we have enough room to practice. I want each of you to see how big of a shield you can make. The more you push the limits of your shield magic, the better you'll be at fine-tuning smaller shields. Eventually, you'll be able to create shields around others at a distance, rather than just around yourself."

I furrowed my brow. I'd created a shield around Ryan during our warlock's duel. It'd been easy, but Professor Ward spoke as if it was advanced magic.

She must've noticed the confused look on my face. "Mister Taylor, did you have a question?"

"Is that supposed to be... hard?" I asked, unsure how to word the question.

"I haven't seen any student perform it before their final year at Miriam College," she said.

Grant exchanged a glance with me. He looked a bit confused, too. He'd seen me form that shield around Ryan during our duel. "Really?" Grant asked her. "Nobody?"

She shook her head. "Not a soul."

Grant nudged me in the side and chuckled, "Guess you don't have a soul, buddy."

Professor Ward narrowed her eyes. "Are you suggesting you can perform such magic, Mister Bryant?"

Grant's eyebrows shot up. "Me? No. Lucas can, though."

He shoved me forward, and I stumbled to the front of the class. All eyes were on me. I shrank a little under my classmates' gazes.

Professor Ward eyed me. "You can create a shield separate from yourself?"

"Uh, I guess," I admitted.

She lifted her nose, like she didn't believe me. "When was your Evoking Ceremony, Mister Taylor?"

"November twenty-ninth, two years ago. Why?"

She ignored my question and asked, "So you'll be twenty-one in November?"

"Yes," I said, glancing around at my classmates. I wasn't sure why she was grilling me on my birthday.

She shook her head. "There's no way you can create such a shield. You don't have enough experience."

I shrugged. "I didn't think it was that hard to do. I have friends who created shields and battle orbs in their first semester."

"But to what degree?" she challenged.

"Uh, I don't know..."

"Show me," she demanded, like she still wasn't buying it.

I furrowed my brow. "Is this going to be graded?"

"I'll give you extra credit if you can complete the task," she offered.

I shrugged. Sounded like a good deal to me. I could use the extra credit.

I lifted my hands and created a shield around Professor Ward with ease. I barely had to think about it. A transparent dome surrounded her. I could see the corners of the shield shimmering in the sunlight.

She reached out and skimmed her hand along the edge of the shield. The skin on her palm flattened, like she was pressing her hand to a pane of glass. She spun in a circle, testing each side of the dome to see if the shield was complete. I noticed her lips twitched slightly, like she was impressed.

Professor Ward was impossible to impress. I could fart butterflies out my ass, and she'd complain that the butterflies weren't colorful enough. To bewilder her even slightly was a great feat.

She stopped with her back to me. I barely saw the battle orb form in her hand before it shot from her palm and slammed into my shield. I felt the magic ricochet through me, vibrating up my arms, but I kept my palms up, and my shield held.

The high-powered orb bounced off my shield and flew back toward Professor Ward. She caught it, and it fizzled out in her hand before she turned back toward me. I dropped my shield.

"Very well done, Mister Taylor," she praised. "The extra credit is yours."

"Do we all get extra credit?" a guy named Leroy Benson asked, as if it was unfair.

Professor Ward cocked an eyebrow at him. "If you can perform the same magic as Mister Taylor, I'll award you *double* extra credit."

Leroy chuckled. "That's easy."

He lifted his hands, but his shield magic was weak. All he managed to do was create a shield the size of a dinner plate in front of him. Professor Ward threw an orb at him to test the shield, and he yelped and jumped out of the way. The orb exploded like a firecracker and rained sparks down on Leroy's head. He practically curled into a ball, even though the orb wouldn't hurt him.

"Confidence goes a long way, Mister Benson," Professor Ward said before turning to the rest of the class. "Get into groups of four—one member of each Cast per group."

"I'm not working with other Casts!" Leroy protested.

Professor Ward didn't even look at him when she spoke coolly. "Then you shall fail this assignment. You will be joining your magic with that of your groupmates. The object of the exercise is to see how large of a shield you can create together. Since Mister Benson seems so desperate for extra credit points, I'll award five points to each member of the team who can create the biggest shield."

She shot a glare at Leroy, like she was challenging him. "You may begin."

The two girls closest to Grant and me turned to us. "You want to team up?" the one with the Seer tattoo on her arm asked. Her name was Ashley

Blake, and though we'd hardly spoken before, she'd always seemed really nice.

"Better you than Leroy." I shrugged.

The other girl, Christine Nelson, giggled. Her tattoo wasn't visible, but I was certain she was a Mentalist. A white cat with black ears prowled at her side. It looked much older than Oliver. The cat sniffed Oliver's nose, and the two must've decided they liked each other, because Christine's cat started licking Oliver's ears.

Grant eyed the girls as we formed a circle. "You're different Casts, right?"

Christine leaned down and raised the hem of her pants to show off the tree tattoo on her ankle. "I'm a Mentalist. You sound surprised."

"Everyone else seems to have clanned up with their own Cast," Grant pointed out. "I swear Lucas and I were the odd ones out."

"We're all odd," Ashley joked.

"And proudly, too," Christine added.

"If you ask me, all this division of the Casts is stupid," Ashley said. "It's going to cause nothing but problems."

"Yeah," Christine agreed. "Ashley and I have been best friends since the first grade. Not even the Waning can change that. I've heard people are breaking up over it."

"People are just scared," I pointed out. "But dividing isn't the answer. Why do you think Professor Ward made it a point to practice this spell today? She knows we're stronger together, and she's trying to prove it to us."

"You're right," Ashley said. "We're not supposed to cover this until after Halloween. It's in the syllabus. She's trying to make a point."

I smirked. "Then let's show them what the Casts can do together."

I joined hands with Grant on one side and Ashley on the other. "Let's start with a shield around ourselves," I suggested.

The three of them nodded, and we got to work. I pushed my protection magic outward. At the same time, I felt their magic flowing toward me, like a current passing through me and growing stronger and stronger. As our magic combined together, it swelled exponentially. A shield formed around us easily. Oliver noticed the dome edges shimmering and batted his paw at the colors.

"That looks good," I said. "Do you think we can make it bigger and encompass that maple at the edge of the forest?"

"I think we can do it," Christine said confidently.

I closed my eyes and concentrated. Our magic swelled, but it hit a limit. Soon, our magic pulsed at a constant rate, but the growth stopped. I opened my eyes to see that we'd created a large shield, but the maple tree was only half-encompassed inside.

"It feels like something is resisting us," Grant remarked. "I can't push anymore."

"Me either," Christine said. "I'm giving it all I've got."

I focused on the magic for a moment. I felt the resistance, but I knew we could do better. Magic resisted when you didn't believe in yourself—when you reeled it in and stopped it from flowing.

"It's not about pushing our magic," I said thoughtfully. "It's about synchronizing it. Don't try to force it. Open yourself up to everyone else's magic, and let it flow through you."

"We should use an incantation," Ashley suggested. "It will help us synchronize our energies."

I nodded. "Good idea. How about, *Sunlight's touch and love's embrace; bless our hearts and protect this place?*"

Grant eyed me for a beat before saying, "That's really good. You just came up with that?"

I shrugged. "It's a talent."

"I like it," Christine complimented. "*Sunlight's touch and love's embrace; bless our hearts and protect this place.*"

We all began repeating the incantation, our voices ringing out in unison. As we did so, our magic seemed to match frequency, and I witnessed our shield grow larger until it encompassed all four of us, our two cats, and the maple tree. Christine's eyes widened in wonder, and Grant smiled proudly.

I glanced around at my group members. "Everyone good?"

Ashley and Christine nodded.

"Getting tired, but I can keep going," Grant admitted.

"Should we try separating the shield from ourselves and encompassing the school?" I suggested.

Christine shot me a skeptical glance. "Do you think we can?"

I smirked. "We won't know unless we try, will we?"

Ashley wore a cunning smile. "Let's give it a shot."

Grant's grip tightened on my hand, and we continued chanting the incantation. As we focused on the shield together, it began to move across the lawn, passing over us until we were no longer inside its protective barrier. The magic swelled several stories high, until it covered the entire mansion.

Grant blew a breath of disbelief. "Holy Goddess, we did it!"

My breath caught as I witnessed the shimmering shield cover the entire building. I'd never performed such a large spell before.

"This is crazy!" Ashley cried.

"They must be cheating!" Leroy accused from across the lawn.

I glanced over to him and noticed for the first time that everyone had stopped to watch us. Students stared up at our massive shield in wonder. Professor Ward's gaze darted to Leroy, and I read hesitation in her eyes. She looked to be considering that we might actually be cheating.

"That's enough for today," she announced, though her tone was flat. "A job well done."

My team and I dropped our hands, and our shield vanished. My shoulders felt heavy, like I'd just carried my own weight up a mountain. It was difficult magic for sure, but we'd done it. I was proud.

"Check them for crystals!" Leroy demanded. "They're cheats!"

"Shut up, Leroy," I snapped. "Everyone knows carrying magically-charged crystals in this class will earn you an automatic F."

Professor Ward narrowed her eyes. "Yes, Mister Taylor. I *will* fail anyone using crystals in my class. Empty your pockets."

My face paled. I wasn't sure I'd heard her right. "What? You can't seriously be accusing me of cheating."

She crossed her arms. "Empty. Your. Pockets. Now."

I gaped at her. Everyone was staring.

"Prove her wrong," Grant muttered between gritted teeth. He was obviously as angry as I was that I was being asked to prove myself. It was bullshit. I was a talented warlock, and that apparently made me a criminal.

"Fine," I growled. I turned my pockets inside out, but there was nothing inside of them.

"And your stash," Professor Ward demanded.

"What, my *whole* stash?" I gaped. "Even if there *was* a crystal in my stash, I couldn't use it while it's subconjured."

"How do I know you didn't just subconjure it when you reached inside your pocket?" she challenged.

My nostrils flared. "I'm not a cheat."

She tilted her chin upward. "Then prove it."

I didn't know what she was trying to prove. If I *did* have a crystal somewhere in my stash, she'd never know. I could conjure everything but leave that behind. But it wasn't like I actually had anything to hide.

I scoffed. "Fine."

It was embarrassing as hell to have your personal stash searched in front of the school. It was like going directly into my dorm room and emptying all my drawers into the hall.

I conjured everything I had. Belongings spilled out of nowhere and scattered across the lawn. Journals and notebooks landed in a pile with my textbooks. My phone and wallet tumbled onto the grass. A few odds and ends scattered—pens, a water bottle, and a jacket. The beads on my enchanted bracelet that unlocked my dorm room clinked together as it landed.

Professor Ward crossed her arms and stared down at the pile. When I finished, she cocked an eyebrow. "Is that all?"

"Yes, that's all," I practically snapped. "What were you expecting? A pile of condoms?"

She scoffed. "Well, it *would* be appropriate for a college boy, wouldn't it?"

"Not for the Reaper's Apprentice, who curses any woman he fucks," I growled.

Her features paled, and whispers traveled around the group. I was *pissed* that my personal space had been invaded.

Professor Ward was mortified, and that made it worth it. The whole ordeal had embarrassed her big time. She abruptly turned on her heel and announced, "Class dismissed."

I opened my mouth to assure my group that I hadn't cheated, but before I could, Christine scooped up her cat and ran after Professor Ward.

"Wait, professor!" she called.

Ashley took off behind her. "Professor Ward, are we still on for our meeting?"

I turned toward Grant. "I'm sorry. I wasn't trying to show off and get our team in trouble."

Grant scowled at Professor Ward. "It's no problem. I know you wouldn't cheat. Professor Ward's just mad you don't fit into the pretty little box of expectations she has for her students."

"So it's bad to exceed them—?" I cut off when I heard Ashley say something.

"But you said you'd help us research the Oaken Wands!" she insisted.

Grant and I exchanged a quick glance.

"Did they just say—?" he started.

"Yeah," I replied in a quick tone. "Come on!"

We raced behind the girls, but they'd already entered the school behind Professor Ward. I burst through the doors to a back hallway, but Ashley and Christine were already gone.

"Fuck," I growled under my breath. "Where'd they go?"

"Maybe back to Professor Ward's office?" Grant suggested.

I started in that direction, my heart pounding in anticipation of answers. If Ashley and Christine knew anything about the Oaken Wands, we had to find out what information they had.

We checked Professor Ward's office, but the lights were off. Oliver growled, like he was displeased.

"They couldn't have gone far," Grant remarked. "We'll find them."

"Better sooner than later," I replied, turning down the hall. "The more we know, the faster we can fix whatever the hell is happening around here—"

I cut off when I spotted a girl coming down the hall. She walked beside a black cat and talked quietly to it. Oliver stopped dead, watching the other cat prowl toward him. I didn't realize I'd stopped walking until Nadine lifted her gaze and caught my eye.

Her eyebrows furrowed as she approached me. "Is everything okay? You two look... troubled."

"We might've found someone who knows more about the Oaken Wands," I said.

Her eyes lit up. "Really? Who?"

"We overheard Ashley Blake and Christine Nelson say they were researching them with Professor Ward," I explained.

"We need to ask them about it, then," Nadine stated. "I just saw them headed toward the Lounge when I left class."

I nodded firmly. "Then let's go."

When we arrived at the Lounge, we found Ashley and Christine sitting alone on one of the big couches, looking defeated. They whispered lowly to one another, but stopped abruptly when they noticed our approach.

Ashley's shoulders fell. "Lucas... I'm so sorry about how Professor Ward treated you in class. It was unfair."

"I'm not here about that," I said, gesturing to the couch opposite her. "We heard you mention the Oaken Wands. Mind if we sit?"

Ashley shrugged. "Go ahead."

Nadine sank into the couch, and Isa jumped on her lap. Grant claimed the chair next to her, which left me only one place to sit—right next to Nadine. I hesitated, but she didn't say anything, so I sat. Oliver curled up at my feet. I was so eager for answers that I could hardly sit still.

Christine leaned forward. "I take it you're as curious about the Oaken Wands as we are. What do you know about them?"

"We know they were created as a fail-safe against stolen magic," I said. "And that they were lost several decades ago."

Ashley and Christine exchanged a glance. "That's about as far as we've gotten, too," Ashley said. "We ran across the legend when we were researching for our Wand Theory class last semester. We think finding the Wands could stop the Waning."

"We do, too," Nadine agreed. "Are you looking for them?"

"We're more or less looking for information that we can pass along to our professors," Christine admitted. "We figure they can actually do something with the information—maybe take it to the priestesses or something."

Ashley eyed Nadine curiously. "You're going to be a priestess. Maybe you can help."

Nadine stroked Isa's fur. "Believe me, I want to."

Ashley knotted her hands in her lap. "It's just... I've encountered the Waning half a dozen times now. I'm afraid at some point, my magic won't return. The last thing I want is for *anyone* to lose their magic."

"Same," Grant said with a nod.

"Has Professor Ward been helpful?" I asked.

"Not yet," Christine replied. "We've been asking all our professors, and Ward offered to help us."

"Except we were supposed to meet about it today, and she blew us off," Ashley added.

"She's just in a pissy mood because Lucas showed her up." Grant laughed.

Christine smirked. "She can be harsh, but she cares about the coven."

"We all do," Nadine assured her. "Have you run across any clues of where the Wands might be?"

The girls exchanged a glance, but it was Ashley who spoke. "There's a rumor, but we're not sure how true it is."

I leaned forward curiously. "What rumor?"

Ashley gestured to her Seer tattoo. "I'm a Seer. I don't see ghosts, but I can hear them. It's complicated, because I can't control it. Anyway, I've heard whispers that one of the Wands is here in the school."

Nadine's wide-eyed gaze shot to mine for a brief second before turning to Ashley. "Any idea where? Which Wand?"

Ashley shook her head. "I have no idea. That's all I know. I've tried to listen for clues, but they don't talk about it much."

Grant frowned. "There has to be a way to contact the ghosts and learn more."

"We've tried," Christine said, chewing her lower lip. "We don't know who Ashley heard it from. A lot of the ghosts seem clueless, which is why we're not sure it's actually here."

"But it's a start," Nadine said confidently. "I don't think we can discount the information."

"I agree, but the school is so big," Ashley said. "I wouldn't even know where to start looking. It could be in someone's stash for all we know."

I pressed my lips together. "It sucks for sure, but it's more information than we had before. Thanks for your help."

"Anytime," Christine offered. "We'll let you know if we learn anything else."

"That would be a big help," Nadine said, sounding relieved. "Thank you."

"We should be thanking *you*," Ashley replied. "You're going to be a priestess in a week. If anyone can help us fix this, it's you."

Nadine went rigid, and her eyes glistened. After a beat, she composed herself. "That means a lot. More than you know, actually."

It was at that moment that Christine's cat began yowling loudly. Christine rolled her eyes and stood. "She does this every time she's hungry. I should probably take her back to our room. We'll see you guys later."

"See you," I said, waving to them.

As soon as they were gone, Grant, Nadine, and I turned to each other. Grant spoke immediately. "We need to get in contact with these ghosts Ashley mentioned—"

"Did someone mention talking to ghosts?"

I turned to see Miles and Talia entering the Lounge. Their cats followed closely behind. Miles plopped down onto the couch opposite us, and Talia sat on the arm rest.

"Who's contacting ghosts?" she asked.

Grant smirked. "Miles, if he's up for it."

Miles rubbed his hands together. "I sense trouble."

"That shouldn't be a problem," Grant teased. "You're used to trouble."

Miles shrugged. "It's a gift."

I shot a quick glance at Grant. "What are you guys talking about?"

"Oh, you didn't hear?" Grant chuckled.

"Stop it," Miles insisted. "It's not funny."

"Yeah, it is," Grant argued. "You literally said this morning it was hilarious."

Miles blushed. "Okay, it's kind of funny. I *may* have been caught out after curfew last night, and I *may* have spent the night in a jail cell."

Nadine's eyebrows shot up. "You spent the night in jail because you missed curfew? Did you try to fight back or something?"

Miles sat up straighter. "No, which is what made it so ridiculous! Kiki and I made a detour through the woods on our way back from town. I didn't realize how late it was, and the cops picked me up in the park. I got slapped with a huge fine, and they said something about putting this on my permanent record."

"That's crazy!" Nadine protested.

"They're overstepping their power, if you ask me," Talia agreed.

"Yeah, but what am I going to do to fight it?" Miles asked in defeat.

I shook my head. "There's nothing you really *can* do. I mean, they're the cops."

Miles frowned. "There's no use in worrying about it. I paid the fine, and it's over. I just have to be careful not to break the curfew again. Anyway, what are you guys up to?"

I shot a glance around the room, but the closest people were over at the restaurant. I kept my voice low anyway. "We've learned that one of the Oaken Wands might be here at the school."

"The Oaken Wands?" Miles questioned.

"They could help us end the Waning," Grant said.

"Yeah, but we have to find the Crock first," Talia pointed out.

"The Crock?" Miles questioned.

The four of us exchanged a glance. I gave a subtle nod, indicating that we could trust Miles. Grant shifted in his chair and explained everything we knew in a hushed whisper.

"Whoa," Miles breathed when Grant finished. "That's a lot to take in, but I'll help in any way I can."

"Any chance you've seen a fae cauldron lying around?" Nadine joked.

"Unfortunately, no," Miles answered, sounding disappointed.

"I'm glad Ashley and Christine didn't ask what we know," Grant mumbled. "I don't know how many people we should tell about the Crock."

"Nobody else, if we can help it," I said. "We really don't know who we can trust."

My friends nodded in agreement.

I turned to Nadine. "Did you learn anything from the priestesses?"

She glanced around, then lowered her voice. "Only that the Waning is being caused by demon magic. The priestesses don't think the Waning and nightshade are connected."

I pressed my lips together. "Either way, we have to find that Wand. Do they know nothing about the Crock?"

She shook her head. "They promised me they'd find it, but I don't think they know anything more than we do. Either way, I'm going after this thing with or without them. What did you learn?"

I frowned. "Nothing. And Grant hasn't been able to crack the formula for nightshade yet."

Nadine turned to Talia. "Did you get any visions from my grandpa's stuff?"

"Nothing about the Crock, unfortunately." Talia sounded disappointed. "But I've started working on a suspect list."

She conjured a stack of papers and began shuffling through them. "I'm certain the person—or people—behind this are Alchemists, but they must be older in order to have the power to pull this off. I started by listing people who've graduated, but the list was so long. I figured whoever's brewing nightshade has to have some real-world experience on top of their degree, right? So I'm looking for anyone over thirty who works in an Alchemy-specialized career."

"That could be anyone," Grant pointed out. "There are so many culinary and pharmaceutical Alchemists in the coven."

Talia frowned. "I know. I'm still working on narrowing it down."

"What about professors?" I asked.

Nadine looked thoughtful. "You don't think we have another Professor Carlisle on our hands, do you?"

I shrugged. "I think we need to keep our options open. We know Professor Daymond was working for someone. He was funneling drugs into the school, but it didn't stop once he died. Someone else was either working alongside him, or they took on his role once he died."

"That's a good point," Talia said. "If there's a Wand here at the school, do you think it could be the Alchemy Wand?"

"It's possible," Nadine replied. "Which means the cauldron could be here. Where would that be, though? In a dorm room? A professor's office? An alchemy lab?"

"If someone's using it, it wouldn't be out in the open like in an alchemy lab," Grant pointed out. "And I doubt a professor would risk keeping it in their office."

"And we're ruling out students for now," I added. "So it's probably not in anyone's dorm. What about an abandoned storage room or something like that?"

"I don't know of any storage rooms that aren't protected by magic," Grant pointed out.

I drew a sharp breath. "Hold on. Last year, I caught Daymond sneaking into one of the alchemy storage rooms. I assumed he was stealing ingredients, but what if that was their headquarters? The room *was* protected by a ward."

"Then we need to figure out which professor is in charge of that room," Nadine suggested.

"Professor Richards," Grant said automatically.

Nadine looked skeptical. "No. Professor Richards *can't* be behind this. He's too gentle."

I gave her a look. "We thought the same thing about Professor Carlisle."

She dropped her gaze. "Damn it. You're right."

"I can follow Professor Richards," I offered. "I'll see what dirt I can dig up. If he goes into that storage room, I'll be there to see what's inside."

"Let's add Professor Blackbird to the suspect list," Nadine said. "He's the wand professor and *should* know something about the Oaken Wands. When I asked him about it, though, he claimed they were just stories."

"To throw you off the trail, you think?" Grant asked.

Nadine looked thoughtful. "I'm not sure, but it's worth considering."

Talia scribbled names down on her suspect list. "I have more suspects than bristles on a broom. Seriously, it could take us months to investigate all these people."

"Do we know anyone else on the list?" Nadine asked curiously.

Talia shuffled through her papers. "Literally every alchemy professor, a ton of parents, even Headmistress Verla and Nadine's rheumatologist."

Nadine looked skeptical. "Verla? Dr. Yonker? That's a stretch."

Talia sighed. "I know, but I was going for any Alchemists with the skills to do this. I even have Krista and Keith Thomas on the list, but they're the last people I'd suspect, after what they went through with their son going missing."

"Unless it's some sort of revenge on the coven," Grant pointed out.

Talia scrunched up her nose. "I doubt it, but we have to keep our options open. Let's see… who else? Amy's parents, but they're so sweet. You guys know Darcy? Her mom's on the list. I've got William Connor and Hector Lawson, too."

"Who are they?" Nadine asked curiously.

"William Connor's the new owner of The Gingerbread House," Grant said.

Miles titled his head. "Isn't Hector Lawson the cook at the Cat-fé?"

"Yeah." Talia sounded hopeless. "I've listed every brewery owner and chef in the coven. Even the lunch ladies are on here! I seriously don't know how useful this list is. It's basically just a list of every Alchemist in town. I've been trying to narrow it down, but it will take time. I've been looking into the *Miriamic Messenger* archives. I'm willing to bet whoever is running this thing has stepped into a lot of money in the last few years. I'll keep an eye out for any Alchemists who have made the news recently —big business purchases and things like that."

Grant nodded along, looking thoughtful. "While Talia works on that, I'll keep working on the nightshade ingredient list. In the meantime, we have ghosts to talk to."

Miles sat up straighter. "Tell me more. I've been *dying* to use my gift for good."

Nadine eyed Miles curiously. "What exactly *is* your gift?"

He smirked. "I can speak to ghosts."

"Not just speak to them," Grant clarified. "He can… how do I put it? Pull spirits onto the physical plane so that *anyone* can speak to them."

Nadine's jaw dropped, but Miles was quick to explain. "I can't do it with *any* spirits. So far, it's only worked with uncrossed spirits. Once they cross over to Alora, I can't speak to them anymore. And they have to *want* to be seen. I can't see just anyone."

Grant chuckled. "He freaked me out last week when I saw him talking to the Lady of the Tower."

"Who's the Lady of the Tower?" Nadine asked.

"She's the ghost who haunts the astrology tower," Miles said. "A nice lady, really. She used to teach astrology here. She never really moved on from the position."

A silent beat passed before Talia said, "Lucas, you look like you have an idea."

I hadn't realized I was leaning against the armrest of the couch, staring off into space. I sighed heavily. "I know someone who will have answers. Whether he wants to speak to us or not is another matter entirely."

"We won't know until we try," Miles stated, sounding confident.

"Who were you thinking?" Nadine asked.

I turned my gaze to her, frowning. "We need to talk to Professor Daymond."

☽

THE DARK SKY WAS OVERCAST, and the air was cold when we left the school that night. Nadine shivered, even though she was wrapped in a warm jacket.

"Are you okay?" I asked her.

She pulled her hood around her face, and I noticed her fingernails had turned purple. "I will be. The extreme temperatures have been making me feel awful lately. Every time it gets too cold, my hands swell up."

"Here." I conjured a pair of gloves and handed them to her.

"Oh, I don't need—" she started, but I cut her off.

"You do." I pushed them toward her as we followed behind our friends.

"Really, it's not that cold," she protested.

"It is to you," I pointed out. "Take them."

Nadine hesitated, but she grabbed the gloves and slipped them on. "Thank you," she said softly.

The five of us—along with our four cats—piled into Talia's car and parked on the edge of town. We snuck through the darkness of the trees, until we reached the back of a quiet neighborhood. Gothic turrets stretched high above the trees.

"Are you sure he'll be here?" Miles asked.

"No," I admitted. "But it's my best guess."

Ghosts either haunted the places they died—or the places they'd *lived*. Professor Daymond had died in prison, but we couldn't go there, so we had to try his home. We had no way of knowing if he'd moved on yet, but if his last thought was any indication, I suspected he'd stuck around.

I could still hear the thought as if he was standing next to me. *Forgive me, Mother. I have sinned against my people. I wish for more time to right those wrongs.*

This was our best shot.

Miles smirked. "Let's go get ourselves a ghost."

We stopped in the tree line behind Daymond's old house. The lights were on inside, and we could see the new family who'd moved in walking by the window. We were technically trespassing, so we remained hidden in the trees.

"How does this work?" Talia asked.

Miles turned to her, rubbing his cold hands together. "So far, I've only spoken to ghosts who want to be seen. I'll have to coax this guy out."

"Like a séance?" Nadine asked, sounding intrigued.

Miles smirked. "You like séances, Nadine?"

Was he *flirting* with her? *Hell no.*

Nadine opened her mouth to say something, but I pushed my way between them. "Yeah, yeah. We all like séances. Let's get this over with."

Miles scowled at me, but he gestured to the mossy ground. "Let's all relax and take a seat."

We sat in a circle, while Miles conjured candles and lit them. Talia bounced a little, looking excited. "I haven't done a séance in forever."

"If only we were contacting someone other than Professor Grump-ass," Grant cracked.

Miles frowned. "If you want him to talk, you might want to show a little respect."

I chuckled lightly. "Believe me, Grant's giving him more credit than he deserves, but we'll behave ourselves."

"Who knew him best?" Miles asked. "They should lead the séance."

We all exchanged a wary glance, but I was the one who spoke. "It might be better if you do it. I don't know if he'll want to talk to us."

Miles gave me a skeptical look. "Okay. It might help to know a bit more about him."

"Professor Archibald Daymond," Nadine said thoughtfully. "What can we say about him? Well, he was a Mentalist who taught Defensive Magic. Should we mention his abusive tactics, or no?"

Miles sighed. "Guys, this isn't going to work if you're harboring these harsh feelings against him. Regardless of how he treated you, he needs to feel welcome in this space, or he won't come."

We all went silent. I dropped my gaze, thinking hard about it. "Well, I guess he *did* care about his students, in his own way."

"Yeah," Talia agreed. "I mean, I won't say I agree with his teaching methods, but he was just trying to challenge his students."

"People *did* walk out of his class knowing something," Grant added. "I don't think he would've stuck at the college for so long if he didn't care."

All eyes turned to Nadine. She chewed on her lower lip, like she was thinking. After a few silent moments, she finally spoke. "He *was* tough on me, but maybe he was just doing what he thought was right by the coven. And if he cares that much about the coven, then I have to trust that he'll help us save it."

"I think he was harder on himself than anyone else," I said thoughtfully. The forest fell silent as we all let it sink in.

"There we go," Miles said softly. "I think we're ready."

Miles reached out for me on one side and Nadine on the other. I joined hands with him and Talia, and Grant completed the circle across from me. Oliver settled into my lap, like he was perfectly content. I began to relax as he started purring.

"Professor Archibald Daymond," Miles said aloud, calling out into the dark forest. "Are you there?"

A breeze rustled the trees overhead, but no response came.

Miles tried again. "Archibald... Archie? Your students want to talk to you."

I heard nothing but the purr of cats around us and the rustling of leaves drifting across the forest floor.

"Professor Daymond?" Miles repeated. "It's safe to come out. We just want to talk to you."

Several long minutes passed like this. I was starting to wonder if Daymond would show up at all. I knew he had answers, but I wasn't holding my breath that he would want to give them to us. What Daymond truly wanted was—

It hit me, and I interrupted Miles to blurt out, "You want forgiveness."

Miles abruptly cut off. I peeked my eyes open to see him nod his head in my direction. He was giving me the go-ahead to take over.

I knew Daymond's last thought. I understood what he truly wanted. Daymond had been a total asshole, and I couldn't excuse his behavior, but maybe I could forgive it.

"Professor Daymond," I said, because it was weird to call him by his first name. "I know you're stuck here because you fear Mother Miriam won't accept you into the afterlife. But if you were truly damned to the Abyss, you'd be there already. You have more work to do."

A strong breeze swept through the trees. My hair rustled, and the candles in front of us blew out. Oliver's ears perked, and his hair stood on end. I glanced around, but I saw nothing.

"He's here, isn't he?" I asked Miles.

Miles's eyes were locked on something behind me. He nodded. "Professor?"

Several moments passed, and Miles's gaze followed something I couldn't see.

"What's he saying?" Nadine whispered.

"He doesn't want to talk to any of you," Miles said. "He claims you caused him nothing but trouble."

I turned my gaze toward where Miles was looking, knowing Daymond was standing right there, even though I couldn't see him. "I know we had our differences, but this is bigger than us. The coven is losing more and more magic by the day. Whoever is brewing nightshade is in possession of a cauldron, which contains a wand that could help us stop this. We need to find it. Please help us."

Several moments passed before Miles said, "He claims he doesn't know anything."

My stomach twisted, but I wasn't leaving here without answers.

"I know why you're stuck here," I said gently. "Let me help you."

Silence settled over the forest, then Miles said, "He wants to talk, but he seems *really* pissed. Are you sure about this?"

I nodded confidently. "I'm sure."

Miles took a deep breath. The outline of Professor Daymond formed in front of my eyes until he appeared solid in the forest. He scowled down at me, and I jumped to my feet. Oliver meowed.

"What do *you* want?" Professor Daymond sneered.

I stood tall, not bothered by his tone. I didn't blame him, considering the last encounter we had. I'd left him knocked out in his house. At least I'd called the cops, but I suppose he blamed me for that, too. He'd died in his jail cell after he'd made his confession. It'd been ruled a heart attack, but we all knew better. Someone had cursed him.

"I want to help," I told him.

"No, you don't," he snapped. "You're nothing but a selfish little child."

I cocked an eyebrow. If I wanted to help Daymond—and for him to help me—I had to speak his language. "So we have that in common?"

Daymond narrowed his eyes. "You think you're so clever. Thought you could just turn me in and all your little problems would be solved?"

"This isn't about me," I said.

Nadine stood beside me, and everyone else followed suit. "Please, Professor—"

"You don't get to speak, half-blood," he snarled so loudly that Nadine and I both took a step back. I wanted to punch the guy for calling her that, but he wasn't exactly solid, and violence would get us nowhere.

"I know you're mad," I said gently. "And you have every right to be. I went poking in places I didn't belong, and it got you killed."

"So you take responsibility?" he accused.

"I didn't kill you, if that's what you're asking," I told him.

"Of course I know you didn't kill me!" he cried. "Someone cursed me, and I daresay a student of your ability would not have the power to do so. The dark magic that entered me that night…"

He shivered at the memory. I didn't know ghosts *could* shiver.

"I heard your last thought," I blurted, thinking that might get us somewhere.

His lips curled into a sneer. "It's intrusive! You should not have such power."

"If Mother Miriam didn't want him to have the gift, the gift wouldn't exist," Nadine shot at him. Her hand curled into a fist beside me, but I placed a gentle hand on hers. Electricity sizzled between us, and she looked up at me with sad eyes.

"It's okay," I whispered to her.

She stared at me for several long seconds, her lips trembling in worry. I remained calm. Finally, she stepped back. "Okay. I trust you."

I turned back to Daymond. "I'm here to take the burden off your back of the greatest regrets you held on to. I know you don't remember and you're probably confused, because you handed those thoughts off to me. And that's okay. That's how it's designed, so that you can move on from those regrets."

Daymond shook his head. "You cannot have my thoughts!"

"It's okay," I assured him. "You can move on now. As the Reaper's Apprentice, I will carry your regrets. By the time you get them back in Alora, they'll mean nothing to you."

Daymond trembled. I'd never seen him look so weary. His tone softened, shocking me. "I want to know."

"You want to know—?" I started.

"My last thought," he said quickly. His eyes glistened, and though he was a ghost, he never appeared more human. "What was it that I feared? What did I regret?"

I drew a heavy breath. "You asked Mother Miriam to forgive you. *Forgive me, Mother. I have sinned against my people. I wish for more time to right those wrongs.*"

Daymond's lips trembled, and he threw his hands over his mouth. "I thought I had more time."

Nadine stepped forward. "You do. Your time is now, Professor. Mother Miriam will always forgive you, but you must forgive yourself first."

Daymond shook his head, like he didn't believe her.

"We want the same thing," I assured him.

"Oh, and what's that?" he asked harshly.

"To protect the coven," I replied. "You only got in on the drug trade to secure your future. You told me you needed the money for your retirement. You care about the coven more than you admit, even if you had to bend some of your morals for your people."

Daymond hesitated, and I continued. "You cared about your students. We all know that. You pushed us to the point of breaking, because you never wanted to see anyone stand there unable to defend themselves."

Daymond frowned. "Well, I didn't take this teaching job for the salary."

"Exactly," I emphasized. "But the coven is losing their magic. We're losing our ability to defend ourselves—from both internal and external threats. If we can catch who's behind this, we can stop it. You may not be able to teach us defensive magic anymore, but you *must* be able to help us defend ourselves in this fight."

Daymond glanced around at my friends, as if considering my words. "You overestimate my role in this. I was not privy to many of the drug ring's secrets. Very few are. I had my job, and I didn't ask questions."

"You must know *something*," I insisted.

Daymond nodded. "I know one thing. I saw the man who killed me. He visited my jail cell that night. Unofficially, I believe, or he would've been caught by now. He threatened me about the confession I'd made and told me that I must rescind it. I told him it was already done and there was nothing I could do. He's the only person involved with nightshade who could've carried out the curse that took my life."

I held my breath, awaiting the answer. My voice shook when I asked, "Who?"

"Magnus Knight."

The wind whooshed out of my chest, and my friends gasped in unison. None of us should've been surprised. Gwen's father fit the bill to a T—an Alchemist with a thirst for power. He was talented, too—certainly strong enough to brew nightshade.

But the confirmation chilled me.

Professor Daymond looked out into the forest. I shot a glance behind my shoulder, and my jaw dropped when I saw a portal appear.

"What is it?" Nadine asked.

"You don't see it?" I questioned. A beautiful white light emanated from the portal, yet my friends seemed oblivious.

"See what?" Talia asked.

"It's a portal," I breathed. "Daymond got his chance to help the coven. I think he's ready to move on, but… where's his reaper?"

Nadine nudged me. "Lucas, *you're* a reaper."

I went speechless. I was only the Reaper's Apprentice. I wouldn't join the Reaper Order until I died. But if I could see this portal, then that meant Professor Daymond was *my* assignment.

"Um, Professor? I think I'm supposed to help you to the other side," I said.

Daymond's features softened when he looked at me. "I'm ready."

"Wait, he has to know more," Nadine insisted.

"He doesn't belong here," I reminded her. "He belongs on the other side. We got more out of him than we should've. It's time for him to rest."

I reached out, and Daymond placed his hand on my arm. He appeared solid, which must've had something to do with my reaper power. I led him forward, until we reached the portal. He couldn't take his eyes off of it, and I saw true wonder in his features.

Daymond turned to me. "Thank you for carrying that last thought for me."

"It's no problem," I told him. "I think you're ready for that forgiveness. Rest in peace, Archie."

Daymond stepped into the portal, and then he faded away. In an instant, the light vanished. A gust of wind swept through the trees, and our candles suddenly lit again. Everything went still. It was both eerie and comforting at the same time. I turned back to my friends.

Nadine smiled, though tears dotted her eyes. "I'm proud of you, Lucas."

I furrowed my brow. "For what?"

"You've been searching for the good in your gift for two years," she reminded me. "I think you just found it."

I hadn't realized it until she said it. I *had* used my power for good. I'd helped Daymond cross over. My heart swelled with pride. If I never helped another person, at least it was worth it to help one lost soul.

"I guess I did," I said, letting it sink in.

"We make a good team," Miles said proudly.

I smiled. "We do. But we have bigger things to worry about. Gwen's *dad* was the one who killed Daymond?"

"I can't say I'm surprised," Talia said thoughtfully. She didn't sound bitter—more like she was making an observation.

"He's gotta be on your suspect list," Grant said to Talia.

"Yeah, of course he is, but so are a bunch of other people," she stated. "I mean, I knew Magnus Knight was a dick, but he has enough businesses generating him money. I didn't think he'd *need* nightshade."

"Well, he already threatened me on move-in day," Nadine said. "If it's not money he's after, then it's the Alchemy Wand."

"Or both," Miles said. "Even if he's already rich, this is another investment option for him. I mean, how many billionaires do you know who just *stop* making money?"

The five of us looked between each other.

"Regardless of his motives, we have to go to the priestesses," I said. "We have to turn Magnus in."

Nadine held her head high. "I agree. He can't walk free. Plus, if we get him off the streets, nightshade will disappear, too."

"He's a murderer," Grant sneered. "He deserves a life in prison."

"Where will we find the priestesses this time of night?" Talia asked.

Nadine checked her phone. "It's not quite curfew yet. They're probably still at Octavia Hall. They've been pulling long nights trying to solve this thing. Some of my meetings have gone later than this."

"Then let's go," I decided.

We returned to the car and drove to the center of town. A security guard stopped us before we entered the building.

"I can't let you through," he stated firmly. "This building is secure."

Nadine was at the back of the group. She pushed through us and held her head high. "Excuse me, Lincoln? Are you refusing entry to a future priestess?"

The guard narrowed his eyes. He didn't acknowledge her as a priestess yet, and he didn't have to—not until her ceremony next week.

"What are you all doing out of bed anyway?" he demanded. "You best get back to the dorms before curfew."

Nadine wasn't taking any of his shit. She faced him and growled, "Next week, I will be a priestess. Let's see the curfew apply to me then, since I'm the one who will be making the laws. If I remember right, I'll also be responsible for hiring and firing employees of the city."

The threat of losing his job got the guard moving quickly. "Yes, of course. I can let *you* through, Miss Evers. As for your friends—"

"Lucas is coming with me," she stated bluntly.

Nadine grabbed my hand as the guard opened the door for her. She dragged me through before he could protest. Our cats slipped in behind us, but our friends were locked out.

My heart fluttered as we headed down the hall. Her hand was still on mine, and even though she wore gloves, it felt amazing. "Why'd you drag me along?"

She stopped at the bottom of the stairs and gazed up at them hopelessly. "Because this building was constructed before elevators were invented and I can't make it up two flights of stairs by myself."

Shit. I knew Nadine was sick all the time, but I didn't know how truly awful she'd been feeling lately. Truth be told, I didn't think I'd ever understand it.

"I'm here for you," I told her gently.

She wrapped an arm around my waist and gazed up at me. It wasn't romantic like I wanted it to be. Nothing about this night was *romantic*. But it felt good to hold her again.

"Thank you," she said with a soft smile.

Nadine leaned against me as we climbed the stairs. Her lavender and rose scent surrounded me. I was surprised to find that it didn't hurt so much anymore. If anything, it was comforting rather than painful.

I didn't know how much I was helping, but I must've done something, because she seemed to relax when we reached the top of the stairs. Nadine knocked on the door to the Imperium headquarters.

It swung open. Priestess Lilian stood behind the door, and she scowled when she saw Nadine. "Miss Evers. I wasn't aware we had a meeting scheduled."

"We don't," Nadine said. "We have information."

Priestess Margaret stepped forward. "Come in, both of you."

She pulled two chairs over to the table the priestesses sat around. A fire crackled in the attic's fireplace, and Isa and Oliver took cautious steps inside. Nadine and I sat beside each other, so close that we were nearly touching.

"You've found a Wand," Priestess Lilian assumed. Her robes billowed as she sat across from us.

"Not yet," Nadine said. "We have information regarding nightshade, which could lead us to the Crock."

Priestess Stella sat straighter in her chair, like she was very intrigued to find out what Nadine knew. "What kind of information?"

"Magnus Knight killed Professor Daymond," I said. "He's distributing nightshade."

Priestess Lilian frowned skeptically. "Mister Knight is a highly distinguished businessman. The coven adores him."

"He wouldn't be the first coven member to surprise us," Nadine pointed out.

Priestess Stella eyed Nadine curiously. "Where exactly did you come across this information?"

"Professor Daymond told us himself," I said. "We contacted his ghost."

Priestess Stella's face paled, as if she was starting to believe us. I'd be worried too if I knew a murderer was roaming free on the streets of Octavia Falls. Hell, I *was* worried.

"Where is his ghost now?" Priestess Margaret asked. "We should contact him and confirm this."

I hesitated and exchanged a glance with Nadine. "He crossed over."

"Well, then I'm afraid this is not sufficient evidence," Priestess Stella said.

"What?" Nadine balked. "We're witnesses to his confession. All our friends heard it, too!"

Lilian frowned. "And how do we know you didn't make that up?"

"Why would I do that?" Nadine demanded.

"Revenge on Gwen, perhaps," Lilian suggested. "I can't keep up with the *drama* of college girls these days."

It was obvious she only saw Nadine as a child. Regardless of her induction next week, the priestesses were never going to see Nadine as a competent priestess. They were only inducting her because it was the law.

"I would never go after Gwen's father just to get to her," Nadine insisted. "This is what Professor Daymond told us."

"Even if he did, we can't use a dead man's testimony," Priestess Stella pointed out. "Ghosts can be very confused—"

"He wasn't confused," I practically spat, losing my patience. "He knew exactly who killed him. He told us in no uncertain terms that Magnus Knight was involved in the production of nightshade."

Lilian sighed, like she didn't have the time for this. "Look, I know you're a *reporter*, but you need to step back from this. You're going to get yourself hurt."

She was mocking me. I didn't appreciate it much.

Priestess Margaret spoke kindly. "I think what my colleagues are trying to say is that regardless of who believes you, this confession will not stand in a court of law, as there is no way to definitely confirm it. A judge would throw this case out within minutes, and you two would be hanged for accusing Magnus of such crimes with no evidence."

"Yes," Priestess Charlotte agreed. "Please understand that we say this to protect you. What we *can* do is question Magnus Knight, but we need his confession or something similar to try him."

"Then put me on the witness stand!" Nadine shouted as she shot out of her chair. "Put *all* of us on the witness stand! My friends and I heard what Professor Daymond said. He was *certain* Magnus Knight cursed him."

"And where is *his* evidence?" Lilian questioned.

"This isn't about the evidence," Nadine snarled. "You insist on shutting me down every chance you get. The reality is *you don't trust me*. Decide now if you want me to be a priestess, and if you want my help finding the Oaken Wands, because by next week, there's no turning back. I'm going to be sitting on this council. I will *not* be treated like a child when I'm placed in a position to do everything in my power to serve this coven in the same capacity as each and every one of you."

Holy hell, Nadine was hot when she stood up for herself. My pants tightened a little at her speech.

The priestesses gaped. Lilian opened her mouth to shoot something back, but Nadine wasn't done.

"You've made it *very* clear that you need me to find the Oaken Wands," Nadine snapped. "While you sit here wondering if I'm right or not about Magnus Knight, people are losing their magic, more and more every day. You can hole up here in your cozy little headquarters, but I'll be out there looking for some damn answers that you're all too cowardly to go get yourselves!"

At that, Nadine whirled toward the door and stomped out. I was so shocked that I just sat there for a second.

Priestess Lilian leapt out of her chair and slammed her palms on the table. "Miss Evers, you cannot speak to us like that!"

Nadine was already in the hall, and she didn't turn back. I scrambled out of my seat and hurried behind her. Our cats ran to follow.

Though she had trouble climbing stairs, Nadine had no issues going down them. She was outside of the building before I could catch up with her. The car was parked around the corner, and I was certain our friends were waiting for us there.

"Nadine!" I called.

She whirled toward me on the sidewalk. "I don't need a lecture, Lucas. I know no one else is willing to talk to the priestesses like that, but screw it. The priestesses don't take me seriously, and until they do, I don't know how much help I can truly be."

She pressed her hand to the side of her face. "Goddess, I don't even know if we should be doing this."

"We have to," I stated. "If we don't, who will? You're going to be a priestess soon. If it's not your job now, it will be next week."

She sighed heavily. "I know, and there's the prophecy and everything. I just… I just—"

I silenced her by pulling her into a hug. I'd been wanting to do that all night, and it was so much more comforting than I ever could've imagined. Holding her again was like waking to the sun after a century of darkness. She was warm and bright, and tingles spread all across my skin. It was different from what I expected, because that desperation I'd felt twisting in my chest the last few months wasn't there anymore. I was overcome with a soft, warm sensation. It didn't seem to matter if we were together or not. Right now, I was a friend—a rock for her to lean on. And if that's all I could ever be for her, I was okay with that.

Nadine relaxed into my embrace. She laid her head on my chest and drew a deep breath. I thought she might pull away, but she didn't. She sighed, like the hug was everything she needed right now.

"We'll figure this out," I promised her.

"I hope so," she breathed. "Because if we don't and Magnus goes free for his crimes, the coven is doomed."

FOURTEEN

The day of my induction ceremony had arrived, and my nerves were in overdrive. I wasn't sure whether to feel excited or anxious. It was definitely a mix of both.

I woke on Halloween to find three shadows standing above my bed. I startled, until my eyes adjusted to the light. I'd slept in late to prepare for a long night tonight, so it was already late morning. Talia, Amy, and Mandy smiled down at me. Isa stirred from where she slept at my feet.

"Goddess!" I gasped. "What are you guys doing?"

Talia bounced on her toes, and I noticed she held a small box wrapped in pink foil. "We couldn't wait."

"Wait for what?" I asked.

"Your presents!" Mandy cried in excitement.

I furrowed my brow. "It's not my birthday."

"But it's your induction day," Amy reminded me. "This is *better* than your birthday."

My heart melted. "You guys didn't have to."

"But we did," Talia stated with a smile. "Open mine first."

My body ached as I shifted to prop myself up higher on my pillow. I'd made sure to take it easy over the last week so that I'd have the energy to make it through my priestess induction, but it still took some time to wake up.

I took the pink box from Talia and tore off the paper. Isa startled awake at the sound, but she relaxed when she spotted Gus and Stormy playing with a ball of yarn across the room. She yawned, then jumped off the bed to go play with them.

I opened the box and smiled. Inside sat six miniature muffins. "Barry's Enchanted Muffins?" I asked.

Talia beamed. "Only your favorite."

"You know me too well." I unwrapped a chocolate chip muffin and popped it in my mouth. A serene calmness swept over me, and it felt as if I was melting into the bed. "It feels… good."

"Relaxing, right?" Talia asked.

"Mm… I could sit here for hours," I replied, enjoying the calmness. It lasted a minute before my body seemed to solidify again.

"Open mine next!" Mandy handed me a small box wrapped in black paper. I tore the paper off and opened the lid. Inside sat a crescent-shaped rainbow moonstone necklace.

My chest warmed. "You made this?"

She smiled proudly. "I sure did. I told you your tattoo was an inspiration. I thought you could wear it for your ceremony—unless you had something else in mind."

"No, this is perfect," I told her. "Thank you so much."

"And finally…" Amy lifted a basket, showing it off from various angles. It hadn't been wrapped, but it was filled with all types of pampering products, like bath bombs, Epsom salts, and lotion. "We thought you could use a nice long bath before your ceremony."

Tears sprang to my eyes, and I pressed my hand to my mouth. The three of them looked between each other, but they had no idea how much this meant to me. Sometimes, all I wanted was for people to treat me like I was normal. I didn't want people to think I was incapable because of my lupus. But I wanted my needs and limits to be respected, too. For my friends to acknowledge my lupus—and how I managed with Epsom salt baths every morning—meant the world.

If I had any reservations about becoming a priestess before, they all melted away. I knew then that I'd made the right choice staying in Octavia Falls—if not for anyone else, then for my three best friends.

"What's wrong?" Talia asked gently.

"I can't believe you did this for me," I sniffled.

"It wasn't a big deal," Mandy said.

"But you cared enough to do it," I pointed out. "Thank you so much."

I reached out, and each of them leaned in for a hug in turn. None of us rushed to get ready, because we had plenty of time. My friends played with our cats, and Talia tinkered on the piano, until I finally dragged myself out of bed and ran myself a bath. I melted into the hot tub, enjoying the lavender-scented bath bombs and salts Amy had gifted me.

By the time I finished, I was feeling *really* good. My friends' gifts this morning had made me feel like I could tackle anything today. I took my meds and threw on some sweatpants and a t-shirt before returning to the room.

Mandy looked up from the mirror where she was applying her Halloween makeup. Her face was pale, with dark shadows all over it made to look like a skeleton. It was incredibly intricate and realistic. Talia had changed into a green and blue dress that shimmered in the light. Her costume came complete with peacock tail feathers. Amy wore a black dress with a layer of fabric attached to her arms in the shape of bat wings.

"You guys look *so* good," I told them. "I haven't decided what I'm going to wear yet. I was thinking the Cheshire Cat, but I don't want to wear makeup for my ceremony. I thought Sherlock Holmes would be neat, but I don't have everything for the costume."

"Don't worry," Talia said. "We have the perfect thing for you."

I eyed her curiously. "You do?"

"It should be here any minute—" she started to say, but she was cut off by a knock at the door. The girls shared a knowing glance.

I narrowed my eyes suspiciously. "What do you have up your sleeve?"

"Nothing," Amy said innocently.

Mandy smirked. "You'll just have to open the door and find out."

My curiosity piqued. I turned to the door and was shocked to find Grammy standing behind it. She held a white box in her hands, and Cornelius followed beside her.

"Grammy!" I exclaimed, excited to see her. "I thought I wouldn't see you until tonight."

"Nonsense," she said, waving her hand. "I had to drop this off."

She handed me the box. "What is it?"

She winked. "You'll have to open it and find out."

I gestured Grammy into the room, and she walked over to sit on the couch. Cornelius immediately ran to play with the other cats.

I stared down at the box, thinking about what Talia had said. "Did you get me a costume?"

Grammy smirked. "Nope."

They were all being cryptic, and this was a puzzle I couldn't quite figure out. I set the box on the bed and opened it. My friends all stood and gathered next to each other, eyeing me eagerly.

Inside sat a thick piece of fabric with crescent moon shapes subtly embroidered all over it. Curiously, I lifted the fabric, and my breath caught as it unfurled. In my hands, I held a long black cloak, with cutouts for my arms and a hood to keep me warm. I laid the cloak out on the bed and fingered the designs. Each crescent moon was connected by a string of stars. The threads matched the fabric, so it was hard to see the design unless you looked closely.

I turned to Grammy with tears in my eyes. "This looks like the cloaks the priestesses wear."

She nodded, her eyes glimmering. "It's tradition for a priestess's Cast to design her cloak and gift it to her the morning of her induction."

Talia stepped forward sheepishly. "But you don't have any Cast members, so we thought..."

She looked to Amy, who smiled. "Who better to gift you your cloak than your family?" Amy finished.

If I thought their gifts this morning meant something, it was nothing compared to this. I couldn't help it when my voice cracked. "You... you all made this for me?"

They exchanged a glance, but it was Mandy who spoke. "I designed it, but Talia picked out the fabric, and Amy treated it with a blessing wash she brewed herself. Your grandma embroidered the moons and stars, and I sewed the layers together."

My shoulders began to shake as tears welled in my eyes.

"Nadine, it's all right," Grammy said gently. She stood and pulled me into a hug.

I broke into sobs, shaking against her as I held her in my arms. "I know. It's perfect! Thank you all so much!"

I could hardly see past the tears, but I gestured my friends forward, and they wrapped me into a group hug. I didn't know how long we stood there like that, but I didn't want to pull away. This moment was so beautifully perfect. It was everything I could ask for the morning of my induction.

Finally, we all drew away from each other, and I wiped my nose. "Becoming a priestess has been so nerve-racking and stressful, and this just makes me feel like... like it's something I can actually *do*. Your support means everything."

Mandy beamed. "Do you want to try it on?"

"Yes!" I cried.

Mandy draped the cloak over my shoulders and tied it shut. When I turned to the mirror, my breath caught. The cloak was the perfect length, and the black looked really good on me. I thought for certain I'd feel like a fraud wearing one of these, but certainty settled in my heart when I saw myself in it. It didn't just feel like this cloak was made for me—it was as if the position of priestess was *meant* for me. Maybe I didn't fit in with the other priestesses—I wasn't as wise or experienced as they were—but one thing was for certain.

I belonged in this cloak.

At that moment, I didn't think about the other priestesses. I didn't worry about how they would treat me, or if I'd fit in. All I knew was that this felt right. No matter who else was serving on the council, I belonged there, too.

Shock riveted through me as I stared at myself in the mirror. I never thought I'd go into my induction ceremony *wanting* this. I thought for sure I'd be dragged into it by obligation alone. But when I put on that cloak, everything changed. I didn't just *look* like a priestess; I embodied one.

Grammy admired me in the mirror. "I'm *so* proud of you, Nadine."

"Thank you all," I said. "I don't know if I could do this without you."

Grammy took my hand. "You don't have to."

"Check out the inside of the cloak," Mandy whispered.

I got excited when she said that, so I quickly opened the cloak and peeked inside. There were all kinds of zippers and pockets.

"I designed the cloak with inside pockets, in case you don't want to conjure things," Mandy said. "Look, you can keep your wand right here."

She pointed to a long, skinny pocket that was just the right size. Excited, I conjured my wand and slipped it inside. It was perfect.

"I love it," I told her.

"Well, I need to get going," Grammy announced. "I'm helping with a pumpkin painting booth down at the festival. You girls have lots of fun today. I'll see you at your ceremony tonight, Nadine."

I smiled brightly. "I'll save you a front-row seat."

Grammy placed a kiss on my head, then left with Cornelius. I was still running my fingers over the soft fabric of my cloak long after she left. I changed into a long black dress and comfortable shoes, though no one would notice what I was wearing under my cloak. I just wanted to look nice for my ceremony. Mandy twisted my hair into a pretty bun.

While Mandy worked on my hair, Amy announced, "Tate said she wanted to hang out today. I'm going to see if she's ready."

Amy left the room, leaving the door open behind her. Mandy scowled, and I caught it in the mirror.

"You don't like Tate?" I asked.

Mandy relaxed her features quickly, like she realized she'd been caught. "It's not that. It's just... they've been spending so much time together."

"Amy's all my sister can talk about," Talia confirmed. "I get it. You miss her."

Mandy dropped her gaze. "Yeah, I... miss her."

"I'm surprised they aren't dating yet," I added. "They obviously like each other."

Mandy frowned. "Tate wants to *keep her options open*. She's stringing Amy along, and it's unfair, if you ask me."

We heard Amy and Tate's exchange from next door.

"Tate, are you okay?" Amy asked, sounding worried.

"I'm fine," she replied, though her voice sounded groggy, like she'd just woken up.

"You don't look fine," Amy pointed out. "I thought you'd be dressed and ready by now."

"I'm not coming," Tate sighed. "I'm sorry. I'm just not feeling well."

"Is it the Waning?" Amy asked.

"No, it's..." Tate trailed off. She didn't sound anything like her upbeat self. "It's something else. I just need to sleep it off. You have fun."

Amy sounded disappointed. "I'm sorry you won't be able to make it. Let me bring you soup or something."

"I'm not hungry," Tate said. "Really, it's fine."

"Okay. If you need anything, call me. I'll come back as soon as I can."

Mandy made a face in the mirror and muttered something under her breath.

I heard the rustle of fabric, like Amy and Tate had hugged. The two had gotten really close over the last few months.

Amy returned a few moments later. "She's not feeling well."

Talia started for the door. "I'll go check on her."

Mandy continued doing my hair, and the three of us sat in silence, waiting. Talia had gone into Tate's room, so we couldn't hear them, even though we tried.

After several minutes, Talia returned. "That was… weird."

"She's okay, though?" Amy asked hopefully.

"She will be," Talia responded. "She's not acting like herself. It's like she's… depressed. She says nothing's wrong, though."

"I wish there was something we could do to help," Mandy said. Even though she seemed to have a problem with Tate, she seemed worried for her.

"We just have to give her space," Talia said.

"Maybe she'll feel better by tonight," I suggested.

Mandy applied a light layer of makeup so I didn't have to expend any of my magic. It wasn't long before we were ready to go.

I was practically bouncing in my seat as we left the school. It was a beautiful day out—a little chilly, but the perfect temperature beneath my thick cloak. The sky was overcast, so I didn't have to worry too much about hiding from the sun. Curfew was waived tonight, so we could stay out as long as we wanted. My ceremony would take place under the full moon, so we had all day to enjoy the festivities.

We walked to the edge of campus and past the main gate, where a line had formed at the edge of the forest. A horse-drawn wagon stood there, and over a dozen students piled on for the hayride. We figured parking near the festival would be packed already, so we might as well hitch a ride into town.

"Your costume is wicked," Talia told Mandy, eyeing the bones printed onto her black shirt.

"Just wait until tonight," Mandy replied. "They glow in the dark."

I stopped in my tracks as we came to the back of the line. Ahead of us stood three guys. I didn't recognize them at first, until the one dressed in a red and white striped shirt turned to us. My breath caught at the sight of Lucas. He wore a matching red and white hat, with round glasses.

Beside him, Grant wore a white mask that only covered half of his face —the Phantom of the Opera. Miles was dressed as a police officer, but he wore shorts instead of long slacks. He looked more like a stripper than anything. Isa stopped playing with Gus, and her eyes locked on Oliver. The two cats had turned to statues.

"Hey, *chicas*!" Grant exclaimed. "Perfect timing. You want to share a ride?"

"Sure!" Mandy said brightly, before anyone else could object.

And why would they? We were all friends… but the sight of Lucas standing there turned my insides to mush.

"Awesome costume," Talia told Grant.

"You too," he said, eyeing her peacock feathers.

Lucas looked at me. "Your cloak looks nice."

"Thanks. Grammy made it with the girls." I gestured to them. "It's not really a costume, though."

"It's better than mine," he chuckled. "I'm—"

"Waldo," I finished for him. My cheeks flushed. "I loved the *Where's Waldo?* books as a kid."

Lucas yanked the beanie off his head and fiddled with the loose strands. "Yeah, uh, Eric and I used to spend hours looking at those books."

"It, um, looks good on you," I said.

Talia must've noticed the awkwardness in the air, because she quickly cut in. "Hey, Lucas. How'd it go with Professor Richards and Professor Blackbird?"

Lucas sighed and situated his beanie back on his head. "It was a bust. I followed Professor Richards, but I didn't find anything. He left the supply closet open when he was in there, and I took as many photos as I could. Even looking at them afterward, I didn't find anything out of the ordinary."

"No cauldrons?" Amy asked.

Lucas shook his head. "Not even unicorn hair."

"Dammit," Talia muttered under her breath.

Grant straightened. "I'm happy to report that Mandy is as resourceful as she claims. She got me the supplies we needed, and Amy and I are back on track."

Mandy smiled proudly. Grant couldn't say *nightshade* out loud, because there were a few other students ahead of us in line.

"At least we're making progress there," I said.

"Progress is good, so let's not worry about it right now," Mandy suggested. "It's Halloween! Let's have some fun."

"Plus, it's Nadine's induction," Lucas added. "That's reason enough to celebrate. No point in worrying about things we can't change today."

There was something in his voice that suggested he was worried. I could tell. But he was right. There *wasn't* anything we could do right now —not until the priestesses found out more or Grant broke down the nightshade formula. This was one of the biggest days of my life. I *should* enjoy it.

Another wagon arrived, and we piled in. Somehow, I ended up seated next to Lucas. We were so crammed onto the long benches lining the perimeter of the wagon that his knee touched mine.

"What should we do first?" Mandy asked, bouncing in her seat. "Tour the apple orchard? Visit a haunted house? Pumpkin bowling? Cider tasting?"

"The apple orchard sounds fun," Lucas said.

"We can start there," I agreed.

"I was thinking we could go to the festival first," Grant suggested.

Miles nudged him. "Gotta be the first to get all the candy?"

Grant blushed. "That's not the *only* reason…"

"We don't all have to go together to everything," Amy added.

"True," Talia said. "I was hoping to go shopping before all the clearance items are sold out."

Everyone kept suggesting things to do that I couldn't keep track of the plan—if there was one. I thought we had decided to tour the orchards and go from there, but when the wagon stopped at a haunted mansion, Amy and Miles hopped off. Several strangers joined us on the wagon, until I was squished so close to Lucas I could hardly move. My head spun at his proximity, but I avoided his gaze and kept my eyes on the beautiful orange tones of the landscape.

The wagon stopped in the heart of town. Talia gasped and pointed at a shop window. "Mandy, look at that dress on clearance!"

Mandy squealed. "You *have* to get it! Screw the orchards!"

A huge group of people shuffled off the hayride, and another group piled on. It wasn't until we were drawing away that I realized my friends had disappeared into the crowd. Grant must've followed the girls, because Lucas and I were the last ones left.

I glanced around the wagon. "Um, did they just ditch us?"

"I think they did." Lucas shrugged. "But hey, if they want to miss out on the best apples in the world, that's their problem."

We sat in silence for a few minutes, until I saw the apple orchard ahead of us. "Are the apples infused with magic, like the coven's cider and maple syrup?" I asked.

Lucas nodded. "The fertilizer is made by Alchemists. You've never had the coven's apples in season, have you?"

"Not yet," I admitted.

He clicked his tongue. "You've been missing out."

"No kidding," I said. "I've been here over a year, and I haven't been to the apple orchards yet."

Lucas smirked as the wagon came to a stop. He held out his hand. "Allow me to be your guide."

I stared at his hand for a moment, unsure if I should take it. But when I looked up into his inviting green eyes, I couldn't refuse. I took his hand, and we hopped off the wagon. Our cats followed closely behind.

The orchard was packed with people. Children bobbed for apples and ate caramel squares, while adults stood in long lines to purchase freshly picked apples and large pumpkins.

Lucas walked over to a stack of baskets and grabbed one. "How many do you want?"

"All of them," I teased with a smile.

"I can grab more baskets," he said, playing along. "But I suggest starting with one."

"One is perfect. Where do we start?"

Lucas guided me behind the building, where a tractor pulling a wagon was driving up to take people to the far corner of the orchards. We climbed on. Lucas pointed out the apple varieties as the wagon wove through the trees.

"See the difference between the bright red ones and those apples over there?" he asked.

I nodded.

"You might think those bright red ones are the best, but I'll beg to differ," he said. "The *best* apples are the honeycrisp. They're smaller and not quite as bright, but they taste like heaven."

"Then I want to try the honeycrisp," I replied.

The tractor dropped us off, and Lucas led me to a row of trees growing yellowish-red apples. Isa sniffed at the apples on the ground, and Oliver tried to eat one. Most of the low-hanging fruit had been picked, but Lucas reached up and plucked one off the branches that I couldn't reach.

He handed it to me. "Try this."

My heart fluttered when our fingers touched. I bit into the apple, and sweet juice filled my mouth. The apple was crisp, with the perfect amount of crunch. "Mm… that is *so* good."

"I told you." Lucas crunched into his own apple. "How many do you want to pick?"

"Let's fill the whole basket," I replied enthusiastically.

Lucas started picking apples. I stood on my toes, but they were all just out of reach.

"Try this," Lucas offered.

I turned to see him holding a long stick with a small wire basket twisted onto the end. I took it, then lifted it into the tree. The wire cupped an apple, and I tugged. The apple fell perfectly into the picker.

"That's handy," I said. "Thanks."

We continued until our basket was full, then hitched a ride back to the main building on the tractor. We paid for our apples and subconjured them.

"What's next?" I asked eagerly. The apples had been so good that I was excited to try more things.

Lucas smirked, like he had *so* much more up his sleeve. "I hope you like apple cider."

I drew a deep breath, and the scent of cinnamon and nutmeg filled my nose. "I can already smell it."

"Follow me," he invited.

Lucas led me inside the building. We entered a dining room with endless rows of cider lined along tables.

My jaw dropped. "There are so many! I don't even know where to start."

"Start here and work your way down," he suggested.

I grabbed a tiny disposable cup and poured myself the smallest bit of cider. The label read *Honey Cider*. I downed it in one gulp, the warmth permeating my bones. It was so sweet that my taste buds sang.

"Mm… I don't know if I need to try the others. That one might be my favorite," I said.

Lucas smirked, like he knew something I didn't. "You're going to want to try them all. Trust me."

I went down the row, and each favor was better than the last. There was lemon cider, pumpkin spice, lavender, ginger, rose, pear, and even pineapple. The only one I didn't like was the cinnamon, which was too spicy.

"What do you think?" Lucas asked as we neared the end.

"It's a tough call," I replied thoughtfully. "I'm leaning toward the pumpkin spice or pear."

"Nah, the lavender is the best," he argued.

"No way. Your taste buds are broken."

"Try it again," he insisted, shoving a cup my way.

I sipped it slowly, letting the cider sit on my tongue. "You might be right. We'll have to try them all twice, just to be sure."

Lucas and I argued for at least half an hour about which cider was the best. We narrowed it down through the process of elimination, until we decided that the pumpkin spice won.

My phone buzzed, and I checked it to see I had a message from Talia.

Where'd you end up?

I'm with Lucas at Blossom Orchards, I texted back.

Do you need us to rescue you? We're still shopping, but we can head over.

I hesitated. Normally, I would be begging her to get me out of this, but I hadn't realized until then that I didn't want to leave. I was actually having a really good time with Lucas, and I didn't mind hanging out with him.

It's fine. We'll meet up when you're done.

I put my phone away and turned to Lucas. "What's the next best thing in town?"

He pressed his lips together. "How do you feel about mazes?"

A smile instantly touched my lips. "I love them."

"Come on." Lucas led me across the road, to a cornfield that had trails cut through it. We paid the admission and entered into the maze.

"What's our strategy?" he asked as we wound around the cornfield.

"Let's explore a bit, and we can—" My heart leapt into my throat when we turned a corner and came face-to-face with a real human skeleton. It reached out for me, and I screamed.

Lucas instinctually grabbed me and yanked me backward, but he tripped, and I toppled to the ground on top of him. He landed on Oliver, and the cat hissed. I looked up to see the skeleton lowering its hand.

I couldn't help it when I burst into laughter. The skeleton was harmless—just a prank set up by a necromancer.

Lucas clutched his stomach while he laughed. "Did I forget to tell you it's a *haunted* corn maze?"

"Yes, you jerk!" I cried, punching him lightly in the shoulder. I dusted myself off as I stood. "Your warning came a little too late."

"Looks like this is a dead end, so we should try that way." Lucas pointed.

I followed him. My pulse was still working on slowing even long after the skeleton disappeared from view.

We turned another corner. Even though I was prepared this time, I jumped when someone dressed in zombie makeup lunged at us. I reacted without thinking, and a battle orb shot out of my palms. Luckily, Lucas grabbed my wrist at that exact moment, and the orb went spinning off into the cornfield, knocking down stalks along the way. The zombie guy didn't seem to care, as if he'd been dodging battle orbs all day. He reached out for me again and groaned.

"This way!" Lucas yanked me along behind him.

We started running, but the zombie picked up speed. My heart hammered in exhilaration. Even though I knew the maze was harmless, I was having fun.

"I thought zombies were supposed to be slow!" I cried.

"Only the real ones!" Lucas replied.

"I don't run fast," I protested.

Lucas yanked me around a corner. "Get on my back."

I didn't have to think about it. I just jumped on his back, and he sprinted through the maze faster than I could run on my own. Our cats raced beside us. People dressed as ghosts and ghouls jumped out at us, and I buried my face into Lucas's shoulder. I laughed out loud—this was so much fun!

When we finally came to an empty trail, he set me down. "It should be safe now."

I peeked around the corner, but the zombie guy had abandoned us. "I really thought he was going to get us."

"Nah, I threw up a shield back there," Lucas chuckled. "He wasn't coming close."

I placed a hand on my hip and wrinkled my nose. "I think that's cheating."

"I wasn't aware there were rules," he stated. "Sometimes you have to think outside the box."

I pointed to the end of the trail, which opened into a wide parking lot. "Apparently, it pays off, because we're already at the end."

Lucas frowned. "That was too easy. Want to go again?"

I smiled brightly. "Absolutely."

Lucas and I went through the maze two more times, exploring every trail until we had the whole thing mapped out in our heads and could get to the exit with ease. Every actor that jumped out at us made my heartbeat pound faster and faster.

"If you like the haunted corn maze, wait until you tour the haunted houses," Lucas said.

I bounced on my toes. "Yes, please! I would like the scariest one in town."

Lucas smiled. "I know the perfect one."

We rode one of the wagons through the forest and to a house on the edge of town. Out front, fake tombstones stood crooked in the yard, and cobwebs hung from trees. Spiders crawled around, along with animal skeletons that moved with necromancer magic. Someone had stuffed a pair of trousers into some boots and half buried them, so it looked like a dead body was being uncovered. An alchemist must've brewed fog potion, because a light layer of fog drifted across the lawn. Paint peeled off the siding of the house, and the windows appeared crooked. To anyone else, this might give them the chills, but I was more excited than I'd been in a long time.

"Welcome, welcome!" a woman in a nurse's costume greeted us when we entered. She had fake blood all over her face and hair. "You must be here about the murder. Please help us find who did this to Mister Floyd!"

I knew instantly that Lucas had brought me to the right haunted house. The actress led us into the living room, which was set up like a crime scene, with tape outlining the shape of a man and everything. She gave us a sob story about how her client had been murdered just earlier today.

"I was upstairs organizing Mister Floyd's medication when I heard him scream," she said. "I came down to find him lying here with his neck slashed. I did everything I could to save him. That's how I got the blood all over my uniform. You must go to each room. Interview *everybody*. Find out who did this. The head detective will be waiting for you on the back porch."

Lucas and I exchanged a confident smirk. "We'll have your murderer arrested before dinner," I told her.

She looked skeptical. "Many detectives have tried to solve this murder. Good luck."

She handed us a clipboard, which listed all the suspects we were supposed to talk to. We headed down the hall and passed by someone dressed in ghostly makeup. She had a vacant look in her eyes and muttered something incomprehensible under her breath.

We made our way through the rooms, playing along with the actors as we interviewed them. There was a butler, a cook, a maid, and the daughter of the deceased. Each of them had their own sob story to tell, and they all pointed at one another as the culprit. Lucas and I looked down at our notes after we interviewed them all.

"Who has motive?" Lucas thought aloud. "The daughter said she thought the maid had been stealing things. Maybe he caught her, and she killed him before he could call the authorities."

"Possible, but look at the daughter," I said. "She stands to gain quite the inheritance."

Lucas pressed his lips together. "The butler and the cook were having an affair, so maybe he walked in on them."

"It's possible," I said thoughtfully. "But I'm almost certain it wasn't them."

"Why not?"

"Well, the maid saw them heading to the kitchen together right before they heard the screams," I pointed out.

"And the butler said he'd just taken tea up to the daughter's room," Lucas added.

"The daughter saw the nurse upstairs right before that, but…" I narrowed my eyes at the paper. "We need to talk to the ghost we saw downstairs."

Lucas eyed the clipboard. "She's not on the list."

I stabbed the list with my pen. "This is the box. Remember, we need to think outside of it."

He smirked proudly. "You're on to something, aren't you?"

I didn't say anything—just gave him a knowing smile. We made our way down the hall, until we found the actress in ghostly makeup pacing.

"Excuse me?" I said, approaching her.

She didn't look at me, but her muttering got louder.

"We have a few questions," I said. "Did you happen to see anyone come through here earlier today?"

Again, she didn't respond. It must've been part of her script. She was only allowed to say one thing to us, so I listened closely.

"Go back to your room, Minerva," the actress muttered. "I'll take care of this. Go back to your room, Minerva. I'll take care of this."

I smirked proudly, then circled two names on my clipboard. That was the plot twist. Everyone was looking for *one* culprit, but there'd been two.

Lucas eyed my choices curiously. "Why them?"

"You'll see."

We headed to the back porch, where we were supposed to turn in our suspect list with an actor dressed as a detective.

"Case closed," I said proudly, handing my clipboard over to him.

He looked down at it with a raised eyebrow. "Interesting choices, junior detective. How did you decide that the daughter *and* the nurse were to blame?"

"The first thing I noticed was the blood pattern on the nurse's uniform," I said. "She said she got blood on her uniform from trying to save Mister Floyd, but the splatter pattern wasn't right. I thought it was just bad makeup, but then I saw that the pill organizer in the bathroom was empty. She was lying about being upstairs organizing her pills. But the thing that didn't add up was that the daughter—Minerva—said she saw the nurse upstairs just before Mister Floyd screamed. Then the butler heard the footsteps on the stairs. It's implied that that was the nurse running downstairs to be the first on the scene, but the ghost gave it away. It was Minerva running *upstairs*. She was covering for the nurse."

"But the butler said he'd just taken Minerva her tea," Lucas pointed out.

"Didn't you notice, though? Her teacup was full. She hadn't touched it."

Realization dawned on Lucas's face. "So she had time to go downstairs, kill her father, and return upstairs?"

I nodded. "The nurse was there, too. The maid said Mister Floyd was sick, and she worried the cook was poisoning him. And the cook said she witnessed Minerva give the nurse a lot of money. The cook wasn't poisoning him. The *nurse* was. Minerva was paying her to kill her father, and she was sharing the inheritance money. But she must've gotten impatient with the poison and killed him herself."

The detective looked impressed. "Very well done. We worried we'd made the mystery too difficult this year. You're the first to figure it out."

I smiled proudly. "I kind of have a thing for murder mysteries."

"Congratulations. Enjoy your prize." The man handed us a gift certificate to one of six different restaurants downtown.

I waved the paper at Lucas. "I hope you're hungry."

"What are our options?" he asked, eyeing the gift certificate.

I spotted Wasabi Lounge on the list of logos. "We could do sushi. You said you've never had it."

"Sushi?" Lucas balked. "Nad, we *have* to go to The Pie Shack. It's a Halloween tradition."

"But sushi's delicious!" I argued.

"So is pie," he pointed out. "I said I'd be your guide for the day, and it wouldn't be Halloween without The Pie Shack. Come on."

Lucas grabbed my hand, and I got hot all over. I couldn't even protest, because it was fucking *hot* when Lucas took the lead.

We rode back into town. The Pie Shack was packed, but we managed to get the last open table. Isa curled up at my feet, and we ordered right away.

Lucas adjusted his thick-rimmed glasses, and I heard something clink onto the table. "Crap," he mumbled. He set the glasses on the table, and I noticed that the hinge had broken on one side. "I lost a screw."

"I knew you had a few loose screws," I teased.

He chuckled as he struggled to put the tiny screw back into the hinge. "More than a couple, I'm sure."

I watched him a few moments longer. "Do you need help with that?"

He frowned. "This screw is so small."

"Hold on. I know this one." I pulled my wand from my cloak and pointed it at the glasses. I muttered a fake incantation.

Nothing happened, and Lucas pressed his palm to his forehead.

I shrugged. "It was worth a try."

"It's useless," he laughed.

"It did what I intended," I argued.

He eyed the glasses, which were still broken. "No, it didn't."

"Sure it did. It made you laugh," I pointed out.

Lucas tried to hide his laugh, but he smiled and shook his head. "You're ridiculous."

"It's a natural talent." I reached across the table and took his glasses, then worked the screw back into the hinge before handing them back.

"Thanks," he said, placing them back on his nose.

Our pie arrived. Lucas and I cut our pieces in half and traded, so we could each get a taste of the different flavors. The apple pie was incredible, and the pumpkin melted in my mouth. The seasonings changed with every bite, and I never knew what I was going to get.

We sat in silence a while longer, savoring our food. As we reached the end, Lucas broke the silence. "The murder mystery was impressive, by the way. You looked so… in your element."

"I *love* murder mysteries," I said, but my stomach twisted. "I mean, the fake ones. Real murders are…"

"Sad," Lucas finished, dropping his gaze. "But you still want to be a homicide detective."

I nodded. "It is sad, but what's worse is never catching the murderer. I want to give the deceased and their families some sort of closure, you know? No one deserves to die that way."

It hurt to say that out loud, after what I'd done to those witches. I didn't think I'd ever get over the guilt, even though I'd done the right thing by saving my friends. I felt like I'd be spending the rest of my life making up for it.

Lucas fiddled with his straw. "You're going to be really good at it."

His words caught me off guard. "You think I can do it?"

"Of course. Why wouldn't I?"

I thought about what Grant had said the night of our date. He didn't think I could possibly be a detective because I had to be a priestess instead. "Well, I'm going to be a priestess."

"You can be both," Lucas said. "I believe in you."

Everything I had thought about Lucas over the last several months seemed to vanish in that moment. All the anger and betrayal I felt didn't seem to matter. When he said he believed in me, my head began to spin, and I forgot why I'd broken up with him in the first place.

Shock must've shown on my face, because Lucas asked, "Are you okay?"

I cleared my throat. "Yeah, I just…"

Slowly, all the reasons we'd broken up came back to me, but they didn't seem quite as intense as before. I nudged them aside, because I didn't want to think about the past right now. I just wanted to be in the moment.

"I had a really good time with you today," I admitted.

"I had a good time with you, too."

Silence stretched between us then, because neither of us knew what to say. The air felt thick, and emotions shifted through me so quickly that I couldn't place them. It terrified me a little.

"We should probably find everyone else," I suggested.

"Yeah, probably," Lucas agreed. I couldn't read his tone.

We didn't have to go far to find our friends. As we left The Pie Shack, we spotted them entering a candy shop across the street.

Lucas shook his head. "Of course they're at the candy shop. Grant's going to end up sick."

"We better rescue him, then," I joked.

We caught up with our friends in the candy shop, where Grant already had his shopping basket half full. Miles had popped a piece of prank taffy in his mouth from one of the samples nearby. It was so sticky that he couldn't get it off his teeth. Amy tried a cleansing spell, but the taffy didn't budge.

"There you are!" Talia cried. "You missed the dress sale at Winifred's. They sold out!"

"Only because we practically bought the whole store," Mandy added.

I shrugged. "I can shop anytime. How was the haunted house, Amy?"

"Wicked," she said, her eyes lighting up. "Miles screamed like a little girl. I think he almost wet his pants."

"I did not!" he protested, but his cheeks flamed. "Okay, I might've just a little bit."

"We went to the murder mystery house," Lucas said, sounding proud. "Nadine was the first junior detective of the day to crack the case."

"Really?" Grant asked. "I hear those mysteries get harder every year."

"It wasn't *that* hard," I said. "Did you make it to the park yet?"

"Not yet," Talia replied. "We were headed there next."

We browsed the candy shop for a while, until Miles ate a gummy bear, and green goo oozed out of his nose. He got sick of the prank candy and insisted we leave.

We made it to the park, where all kinds of vendors had been set up in rows. We spent the rest of the day playing games like pumpkin bowling, giant chess, and a ring toss that used tiny, pointed witch hats instead of bottles. I ate skull-shaped cookies and biscuits made to look like mummies. We stopped at a palm-reading booth, then had a Seer predict our final grades. I was going to get a solid B-average, according to the Seer. He must've been nuts, because I didn't know how I was going to manage that with how much class I'd missed.

I laughed with my friends more than I had in ages. I wished every day could be Halloween.

When night fell, we danced around the bonfire, waving our stems of yarrow and St. John's Wort to ward off the faeries. I couldn't help but notice that Lucas was twirling along with us. Last year, he sat out of the ritual, because he said he didn't like to dance. I didn't think he noticed what a difference it was to see him dancing around the bonfire, smiling and laughing with everyone else. I had a hard time taking my eyes off him all night.

The full moon climbed higher in the sky, and I knew the time was coming for my induction ceremony.

"Are you ready for this?" Talia asked.

I sat on a bench near the bonfire, sipping another cup of hot cider. Isa purred beside me. "I am, honestly. I thought I'd be scared, but I'm not. It helps being with all of you today. I feel like this is where I'm meant to be. I don't question that anymore."

"Good," Talia said. "Because I think you're meant to be here, too. I'm really excited to see you become a priestess. You're going to be really good at it."

"That means a lot. Thank you." I leaned over to give her a hug.

"Nadine!" I turned to see Grammy waving at me. She wore a black dress with cat ears, which matched Cornelius perfectly. "The priestesses are ready for you."

I stood. "Thanks for letting me know."

I finished my cider and tossed the cup in the trash. Grammy walked with me to the main stage, where a band played a beautiful tune in a minor key. The priestesses were waiting for me behind the stage.

"Nadine," Priestess Margaret greeted. "Your ceremony will begin in half an hour. I wanted to go over the procedure before we start."

"Your cloak looks beautiful," Priestess Stella remarked.

"Thanks," I told her.

I didn't miss Lilian crinkle up her nose, like she didn't think it was anything special. But it was to me, so screw her.

"We've discussed the ceremony, but there's one part I want to make sure we don't get wrong," Priestess Margaret said. "Traditionally, the members of a Cast will be asked to accept the priestess as their governor. Seeing as you are the only member of your Cast, you will have to stand up and accept yourself. Can you do that?"

The priestesses eyed me intently, like they weren't quite sure I was cut out for this. I glanced to Grammy, who offered a kind smile.

I straightened my shoulders. "Yes. I can do that."

Margaret nodded. "Very well. We will begin shortly."

Grammy squeezed my hand. "I'll be in the front row. I love you, and I'm *so* proud of you."

"Thank you, Grammy. Your support means everything." I hugged her, but she was gone far too soon. My nerves returned momentarily, but Isa was with me, and that was enough support for now.

I could hear the crowd gathering on the other side of the stage. It wasn't the whole coven. There simply wasn't enough room in the park for that many people. But judging by the sound of voices carrying across the park, there were *a lot* of people who had come to watch my ceremony. I stole a glance past the stage and saw my friends sitting in the front row next to Grammy. My heart swelled.

"Nadine, it's time," Priestess Stella said.

I drew a deep breath and dropped my shoulders as she guided me up the steps and onto the stage. The band had finished playing and moved their equipment. The only item on the stage was a single chair. The crowd had gone so quiet that I heard nothing but the sound of my own footsteps as I crossed the stage. Isa followed me, and the priestesses came on stage after us.

"Boo!" someone shouted. My heart lurched, and my confidence faltered. The priestesses had promised the ceremony would be safe, but it was clear some of the coven members objected.

"She's no priestess—" someone started to say.

"*Silentium,*" the priestesses muttered. Their voices were so low that no one in the crowd could hear them, but all objections ceased in that moment. The priestesses weren't going to stand for interruptions.

My knees shook, and I suddenly felt like running off the stage. Then I saw Lucas in the front row. He smiled brightly and shot me an encouraging thumbs-up. All my remaining anxiety melted away. My pulse remained calm and steady as I sat in the chair and gazed over the audience. The crowd was huge, lit only by the silvery light from the moon.

The four priestesses surrounded me. In unison, they each conjured a candle in their hands and lit it. A shiver traveled down my spine when the candles ignited, but in a good way. I felt powerful—like anything was possible.

The priestesses began to circle me. I closed my eyes, taking in every sound, every sensation. This was where I was meant to be. This was *who* I was meant to be.

This was who I *wanted* to be.

The priestesses spoke an incantation. "*Tonight we call this priestess, to serve her Cast and all the coven—to uphold our Miriamic laws, to protect our people and to govern. Through good and bad, through light and dark, through peacefulness and strife, Mother Miriam's blessing will be laid upon her, and she'll serve as priestess all her life.*"

The priestesses came to a stop. I opened my eyes and stared out at the crowd. My eyes connected with Grammy's, then Talia's, before moving over all of my friends.

"Nadine Evers," Priestess Margaret said, her voice projecting over the crowd. "You have been selected by the Miriamic people to preside over and protect the coven from now until your death as a high priestess. The priestesses confirm you a fit as the Curse Breaker high priestess. May we offer you our wisdom and blessings to guide you along the journey you embark on tonight."

I bowed my head to her, and Margaret placed her hand upon it. "Nadine," she said. "I bless you with the gift of bravery, to face your responsibilities with courage. As a priestess, it is not the power over your people that makes you strong. It is your willingness to fulfill your duties and responsibilities. The coven is relying on you, and you must exercise the courage to protect them at all costs—even when you face the most difficult of choices."

"I will be brave, priestess," I told her, as was my part of the ritual. "So shall it be."

"So shall it be," she repeated.

The priestesses shifted in a circle again, until Priestess Charlotte stood in front of me. She placed her hand on my head. "Nadine, I bless you with the gift of cooperation, that you may work with the members of the council as one unit, and listen to the people whom you serve. It is our duty to celebrate with the coven when times are good, and to serve and protect them when times are bad."

I nodded. "I will listen, priestess. So shall it be."

"So shall it be," she replied.

They circled me again, until Priestess Lilian placed her hand on my head. "Nadine, I bless you with confidence, that even in the midst of difficult decisions, you may stand certain and strong in your choices. The moment a priestess loses confidence in herself, she loses confidence in her people."

"I will be confident, priestess," I stated. "So shall it be."

"So shall it be."

Finally, Priestess Stella touched my head. "Nadine, I bless you with the gift of wisdom and intelligence, that you may seek to learn and understand your people. May you uncover creative solutions to all problems that arise in your position. As leaders, we must explore all possibilities to make the best decisions for the coven."

"I will embrace my wisdom and intelligence, priestess," I said. "So shall it be."

"So shall it be."

Priestess Margaret stepped in front of me again. "Becoming a priestess is a life-long commitment. Once you are named a priestess, your communication channel to Mother Miriam will be opened. Your intuition will grow. You will become more susceptible to signs, so that you may gain a better understanding of what is best for the coven. Are you prepared to take on this role, from now until the day you die?"

"I am," I stated firmly.

Priestess Margaret turned to the crowd, who watched the ceremony eagerly. Grammy wiped her eyes from the front row.

"The Curse Breakers of the coven may now stand and accept Nadine Evers as their priestess," Priestess Margaret announced. "Should any member of the Curse Breaker Cast object to this ceremony, they may speak now."

She turned and gave me a subtle nod. There were no other Curse Breakers to speak for me. I had to be the one to accept myself. I stood from my chair and gazed over the crowd—the people I would govern for the rest of my life.

For a moment, I hesitated, but Mother Miriam's words came back to me. *You are not supposed to be here because I said so, or because the coven demanded it. You are meant to be here because you want to be—because you chose to be.*

Now was the time to make my final decision. I opened my mouth, unsure of what would come out, but when Isa brushed her tail against my leg, confidence swelled within me.

"By the name of Mother Miriam, I accept myself as the Curse Breaker priestess," I said.

Nobody in the crowd spoke, but it wouldn't matter if they did. I accepted myself, and that was the only validation I needed to embark on this journey.

Priestess Margaret conjured a large vial filled with a clear liquid. "Take these blessings with you into your priesthood. Solidify them now in your soul by drinking the herb of the heart."

I didn't know what the *herb of the heart* was exactly, but Margaret had explained it to me as the extract of a magical plant grown only by the Miriamic Coven. It was used in the coven's most sacred ceremonies.

I pulled the cork off the vial and drank the liquid inside. It was sweet and slid over my tongue with ease. Warmth settled into my belly. Tingles spread through my extremities, like the light of Mother Miriam herself was permeating every single cell in my body. I felt courageous, powerful, and confident.

A light began to glow from on stage. I looked down to see that it was coming from somewhere beneath my cloak. I gasped when I pulled back the fabric to see that the bright light shone through my dress in the shape of a crescent moon. My tattoo was glowing!

The priestesses had told me this would happen. It was a sign from Mother Miriam that the ceremony was complete. I was a priestess now!

But knowing what was going to happen and actually witnessing it were two very different things. When my tattoo glowed a bright white, all I could do was stare. Tears pricked at my eyes. It was so beautiful.

"Come," Priestess Margaret said, taking my hand. "There is one final part of the ritual. You must complete your first act as a priestess and help us reinforce the protection spell around Octavia Falls. You will gain control over the spell alongside us, as a literal and symbolic protector of the coven."

We stood in the center of the stage in a circle. Margaret held her hand out, and Lilian placed hers on top. We all joined in, until our hands were stacked atop one another.

Margaret began the protection incantation. *"Magic in our hearts and all around, go forth tonight and protect this town."*

We repeated the incantation in unison. Energy swelled within me as our magic came together. The magic built, until we couldn't contain it anymore. A bright ball of light shot out of our hands, straight up to the sky like a firework. The crowd gasped, and my eyes followed the magic upward. It slammed into an invisible barrier high above our heads and exploded. White light as bright as the full moon shone down on us from the area of impact. For several seconds, the protection spell around the town became visible, appearing as a shimmering dome around our entire population. The light spread over the dome, until it reached the horizon and faded.

Priestess Margaret dropped her hand and turned to me. She took my hand and led me back to the front of the stage, facing the crowd. Her voice was strong as she announced, "I present to you Priestess Nadine!"

People in the crowd began to cheer. It wasn't everyone. In fact, most of the crowd looked less than pleased. Surely the rumors about me going around school had spread around town. But all I could seem to notice was my friends in the front row, cheering and hollering for me. Grammy sobbed, and Talia and Mandy leapt out of their chairs to give me a standing ovation. Lucas beamed up at me, and my heart swelled with joy.

I may not have the entire coven's approval just yet, but I would prove myself to them one way or another. I was their priestess now.

And it was my duty to protect the coven, for now and forever.

Halloween used to be my favorite day of the year when I was a kid. Eric and I would dress in the creepiest costumes we could find and stay up all night pigging out on Halloween candy. But I didn't think I'd ever had as much fun on Halloween than I had with Nadine. Laughing with her was like being with a whole different person. Hell, I felt like a different person myself. And watching her priestess ceremony made my heart full. I was so proud of her.

I was feeling pretty good after my session with Dr. Mack on Monday, which I'd scheduled between classes. We talked about Halloween, and she pointed out how much progress I'd made.

I must've been beaming by the time I made it to Intercast Magic, because Grant noticed. He was already sitting in the back next to an empty seat, waiting for me. Oliver jumped onto our table when I sat. I scratched him behind the ears, and he lay down.

"You look happy today," Grant remarked.

I shrugged. "I'm feeling good."

"Excellent, because rumor has it there's a pop quiz today," Grant said. "The spell will work better if you're in a good mood."

"What kind of spell?" I asked.

Grant didn't have a chance to respond before Professor Perez entered the room. He was a middle-aged Mortana who always seemed a bit disorganized. His hair was a mess, and he carried a stack of papers that slipped from his hands when he walked. He fumbled with the papers before giving up and subconjuring them. He straightened his suit and stood at the front of the room.

"Welcome back, students," he said. "I trust you all had a wonderful Halloween. If you'll get into groups of three—separate Casts, please— we'll be placing a ward on these locks today."

He conjured a small box shaped like a treasure chest. He pointed to the lock on it. "You and your teammates will be securing the lock, so that it can't be unlocked with a simple spell. With at least three Casts together, your power should be strong enough to secure what's inside. You'll find the spell on page seventy-two of your spellbooks. I'll come around at the end of class and test your ward. You'll be graded on the strength of your spell. You may begin."

Professor Perez began walking around the room, handing out the small boxes. Grant looked to the Seer next to us, a girl named Kenna Farlane. "Want to join us?" he offered.

She looked nervous. Kenna was shy, and she seemed even more reluctant to talk in class ever since the Casts started dividing. In fact, everyone in this class seemed a bit on edge.

"Um, I guess," she said timidly, before moving her chair over to join us.

Kenna ducked her head and buried her face into her spellbook. It sucked that everyone was acting like the other Casts were their enemies. This wasn't right.

I also knew the spell wouldn't take if we didn't work together, and Kenna seemed apprehensive. I wanted to talk to her, but I didn't know what to say. My eyes caught sight of a charm bracelet on her wrist. I noticed the cupcake charm first.

"Do you like to cook?" I asked her.

She eyed me curiously, but didn't say anything.

I gestured to her bracelet. "I saw your cupcake charm. I thought you might like to cook. Grant's crazy about the cupcakes at the Cat-fé. He's tried every flavor."

A light sparked in Kenna's eyes. "Really? I'm working an internship at the Cat-fé. I decorate the cupcakes."

"No way," Grant said. "That's wicked! How do you get the frosting so fluffy?"

Kenna smirked. It was good to see her loosening up. "It's a secret recipe. I'll actually be presenting it at a baking competition in Paris next semester."

"That's incredible!" Grant exclaimed. "You must be really good."

She blushed. "My parents are Alchemists, and they own a bakery. They taught me everything I know."

Grant's eyebrows shot up. "And you get that flavor *without* Alchemy magic. I'm impressed."

She smiled. "I feel like cupcake decorating is an artform. That's part of my power. I *see* it in my mind before it's finished."

Grant asked her a bunch of questions about cake decorating, before Professor Perez finally reached our table and handed us our box. Kenna had loosened up by then, and I felt like we might actually ace this assignment.

"Here's the spell," she said, turning her spellbook toward us.

It was a little more complicated than normal, but that was the point of intercast magic. To perform the spell, we had to meditate together, then confess one secret to each other before the spell could be cast. It was symbolic of locking our secrets inside or something. I wasn't really sure.

"I don't want to share a secret," Grant said.

"It doesn't have to be your *deepest* secret," I told him.

Grant blushed. "Yeah, but there's nothing you don't know."

"There has to be *something*," I pressed.

Grant bit his lower lip. "Okay. Sometimes… I pee in the shower."

I scowled. "That's a groundbreaking secret," I said sarcastically. "But it'll work. My secret is that when I was in kindergarten, I used to sneak gum into class and stick it to the bottom of Miss Leanne's desk."

Kenna chuckled. "I remember when she found that! I thought for sure it was Gregory."

I smirked. "She never caught me."

Kenna smiled. "My secret is buttermilk."

I tilted my head. "Buttermilk?"

"The secret ingredient in the frosting. It's buttermilk," she said. "I think we can do the incantation now."

We joined hands, surrounding the box on our table. *"Our secrets have been shared, and we've set aside our pride. Fasten this lock, and secure what we've put inside."*

Magic swept through us, and the lock clicked shut. We dropped our hands, and Grant picked up the box to inspect it. He muttered a quick unlocking incantation, but the box remained locked.

"I think we did it," he announced.

"All finished?" Professor Perez asked. He came over to our table and tried to unlock the box, but nothing happened. "Very well done. You've all passed. You should be proud of yourselves."

Kenna sank in her seat a little. "Thank you."

Perez excused us from class early. Grant and I were passing through the Main Foyer when we caught sight of Talia and Nadine. Talia stood next to a short, plump professor, chatting enthusiastically with him. She clutched a stack of papers to her chest.

"Thank you so much, Professor Warbright," she said. "I can't wait to start practicing."

Professor Warbright smiled. "It was no problem, really. Whenever you need sheet music, all you have to do is ask. I can't wait to hear what you come up with for the talent show."

Nadine lifted her gaze and caught sight of us passing through the foyer. She waved us down. "Grant!"

We made our way over to them. Professor Warbright gave us a kind nod, then left.

"What's up?" Grant asked.

"I got the supplies," Nadine said. "You can stop by my dorm whenever you're ready."

"Supplies?" I asked, glancing between them.

Grant smirked. "Nadine offered to help me with my act for the talent show."

My eyebrows shot up. "And?"

"And it's a surprise," he replied.

"It's going to be great. I promise," Nadine said.

"I'm really excited to see it," Talia added. "I'm working on something myself. Professor Warbright is helping me with the arrangement."

Nadine winced, though she tried to hide it.

"You okay?" I asked her.

She forced a smile. "It's nothing—just a bad flare-up. My back is killing me, but I'll be fine."

"Get your hands off of me!" someone shouted.

The Main Foyer went silent as everyone turned to look. My stomach twisted. Two Miriamic police officers dragged Professor Daniels down the hall. Three others followed, their hands on their wands like they expected they might have to use them. Professor Daniels struggled against their hold, but they were a lot bigger and stronger than she was. Her brown hair flew in all directions, and her bangle cat yowled wildly as it followed behind her. Tears streamed down Professor Daniels's face.

"I'm telling you I didn't do anything!" she cried. "Why are you—ow!"

Talia's voice shook. "What's going on?"

Nadine's face had gone paper white. "I have no idea."

"Let's find out," I said. I walked straight up to the police officers and stepped in front of them. They both frowned when they noticed my approach. "This is unnecessary. Can't you see you're hurting her?"

"Out of the way, kid," the one with a dark beard growled. I noticed his uniform said *Officer Baker*. "This doesn't concern you."

I crossed my arms. "She's my journalism professor. I think her students deserve to know what's happening."

"Lucas, please, stay out of this," Professor Daniels begged.

"I said it's none of your business," Officer Baker snapped. "Get out of the way, or you'll be arrested next."

Nadine stepped up beside me. "I demand to know what's going on."

Officer Baker smirked. "You'll want to bring that up with the priestesses then, my dear."

"Don't call me that," Nadine snapped. "I *am* a priestess. Tell me what's going on."

"You want to know what's going on, sweetheart?" Officer Baker taunted. "Leila Daniels here has been found guilty of murder. She'll be hanged tonight in the square at dusk."

All the blood in my body drained to my toes, and a gasp traveled around the Main Foyer. This wasn't possible.

"Murder?" I gaped. "Who did she supposedly murder?"

"Her own colleague," Officer Baker sneered. "She *killed* Archibald Daymond, and she'll be rightfully hanged for her treason."

Professor Daniels began to wail. How could they possibly think she had anything to do with this?

"*She* didn't kill Professor Daymond!" Nadine protested. "Who on earth would find her guilty of that? As a priestess, I demand you let her go!"

"No can do," Officer Baker said. "We have orders from the Imperium Council to bring her in immediately."

"I'm *on* the Imperium Council!" Nadine shouted.

"Then you'll have to take this up with the other Imperium members," he said. "Step aside, before she gets hurt for real."

It was a threat. He'd do whatever he had to do to arrest Professor Daniels—and we couldn't stand in his way. The officers began dragging her away.

"It's okay, Lucas. You have to let me go," Professor Daniels said. "Don't worry about your assignment. It's in my desk—top right-hand drawer. Your substitute teacher will help you finish it."

All we could do was stare as the officers dragged her out of the school. After a full minute, whispers began to rise within the Main Foyer.

Grant turned to us. "What are we going to do? Professor Daniels is innocent."

Nadine's hands curled into fists. "I'm going to talk to the Imperium Council. *Now.*"

"I need to go to Professor Daniels's office," I said in a hushed whisper. "I didn't hand in any assignment. There's something in there she wants me to find."

"Any idea what?" Talia asked.

"She told me she was writing a piece on nightshade," I said. "It might be her research."

Grant's face paled. "You think someone could've targeted her because she was asking too many questions?"

"We're gonna find out," I promised. "There must be something there that will prove her innocence. Otherwise, why would she want me to have it? We don't have much time."

While Nadine took off toward Octavia Hall to talk to the priestesses, I made my way to Professor Daniels's office. People whispered in the hall. News had already spread about what happened.

When I reached her classroom, the lights were still on, but her office at the back was shut. I tried the door, but it was locked. I muttered an incantation, but that didn't work. Whatever she was hiding in there must be important.

I checked the table at the front of the room and found some paper clips, then used those to pick the lock the way Nadine had taught me. The door swung open, and I hurried inside. I yanked open the top right-hand drawer. On top sat a voice recorder, and beneath that a thick file. It wasn't marked, but when I flipped it open, I saw that it was filled with endless notes, interviews, news clippings, and more—all tying back to nightshade.

I subconjured the recorder and the file, then left the room, locking the door behind me. I just barely shut the door when I heard the sound of footsteps approaching. I quickly ducked behind one of the tables in the back of the room. Heels clicked on the floor, and I peeked beneath the chairs to see three pairs of feet.

"I don't know what you think you'll find," Headmistress Verla said. "Leila Daniels was one of our best professors. Surely she can't be involved."

"We're unable to discuss specifics," a deep voice replied. "All we can tell you is that we have a warrant to confiscate all her belongings."

I dared to peek over the table. Headmistress Verla led two officers across the room. They were different from the ones who'd dragged Professor Daniels away, but they had the same bulky build. Verla conjured a set of keys and unlocked the door.

"Very well," Verla said, though she didn't sound happy about it. "Let me know if there's anything else I can do to help your investigation."

The three of them entered the office, and I scurried out of the classroom as fast as I could. I returned to my dorm room, my heart racing. I immediately conjured the file and began shuffling through her notes. I pored over them the rest of the afternoon, looking for anything that could prove her innocence.

Professor Daniels had learned a lot about nightshade, but there wasn't much here I didn't already know. I listened to her interviews, and it became clear that she was close to exposing Magnus Knight, though I didn't think she'd figured out the depth of his involvement. None of her notes pointed to him as the man behind Professor Daymond's murder. If they had, I could present the evidence to the council and exonerate her.

My phone buzzed. I hadn't realized how much time had passed. I was so engrossed in finding answers that when I looked up, I noticed the sun was already dipping toward the trees. When I saw the name on the screen, my heart leapt.

"Nadine?" I answered.

"The priestesses have outvoted me on *everything*," she fumed. "They're refusing her a trial. They won't even let me see her."

"There has to be *something* we can do!" I cried.

"There's nothing! Grant and Talia are trying to plead for more time with the judge, but the priestesses are above him. They've already made the call. We need to talk. In person."

"Where do you want to meet?" I asked.

"I don't know. Somewhere *outside* of Octavia Falls, please. I can't stand to be here right now."

"There's a scenic outlook not far outside the town's perimeter, but it's outside the protection spell," I said. "It's called Perry's Point."

"That's perfect," she said. "I'll meet you there."

I left Oliver sleeping in my dorm room and took Grant's car to Perry's Point. Nadine was already waiting for me. She leaned against her car with her arms crossed, holding her thick cardigan closed to keep herself warm. I slammed on the brakes as I sped into the parking spot beside her. I leapt out of the car and rushed over to her.

"What happened?" I demanded.

Nadine's eyes were puffy and blood-shot. She looked like she was barely holding herself together. "They found evidence at her house— everything you'd need to cast the curse that killed Professor Daymond."

I gaped. "How's that possible? She couldn't have done this."

Nadine swallowed. "That's not all they found. Lucas, they've tied her to nightshade production."

"Someone planted it," I insisted. "Professor Daniels was *researching* nightshade. She couldn't be behind this."

Nadine gritted her teeth. "I know. That's not even the worst part."

My blood turned to ice. "What is it?"

"Magnus Knight is gone," she growled.

"What!?" I shouted. "I thought the Imperium Council was questioning him!"

"They did, and they found nothing!" she said.

My hands curled into fists. "So they question him, he takes off on— what—a business trip? And they just so happen to find another suspect two days later? They have to see this is a cover-up."

She shook her head. "They won't listen."

"They must be working with him to frame Professor Daniels," I stated firmly. "It's too suspicious."

"I don't know, Lucas. They seem pretty damn upset about nightshade. I think they're too afraid of it to think rationally. Magnus must've framed Professor Daniels, and the Imperium is jumping on their first opportunity to convict. They've gone too long without taking action. It's a political move to placate the coven."

"What about a trial?" I demanded.

"They say the evidence is too substantial. They've voted to hang her, and there's nothing I can do, even as a priestess. I'm the odd man out."

"So they'll hang Professor Daniels without a trial, but not Magnus Knight, who we *know* is the real killer?" I demanded. "We heard Professor Daymond's testimony!"

"It doesn't matter to them!" Nadine raged. "I thought the coven believed in forgiveness and second chances. Santos got a second chance when he married Mother Miriam. But that doesn't matter now! The Imperium doesn't care about the truth. All they can see is the story that's been manipulated for them."

"By Magnus," I snarled. "He could've taken the Crock with him when he left. Our chances of ending nightshade *and* finding the Alchemy Wand could be ruined."

"Magnus had other people working for him," Nadine reminded me. "I'm not sure he'd give up the operation unless he got caught. There's too much money in nightshade. He must've left someone in charge, and we can't prove Magnus is involved until we uncover his entire operation. In the meantime, please tell me you found something."

I shook my head. "Nothing to prove Professor Daniels's innocence. I'm starting to wonder if that's not why she sent me to her office. It's like she knew nothing could be done. Remember, she told me to stay out of it? It's more like she wanted me to finish her work."

Nadine sighed. "Professor Daniels knew there was too much evidence against her and not enough time. Goddess, this is so wrong. If anyone else called for a hanging like this, *they'd* be the ones headed for the gallows, but because it's the priestesses, they can do anything. And I'm sitting here completely powerless!"

"There must be something we can do to stop this," I said.

Nadine's hands trembled. "We can't, Lucas! The sun is setting. She'll be hanged any minute. All I know is that the priestesses have gone too far, all in the name of protecting the coven. They couldn't find solid evidence on Magnus Knight, so they want someone else to blame. I can't work for people who will go to these lengths."

"You want to stop working for them?" I asked.

"I have to! If this is what they're willing to do to their own people, we have to find the Wands before they do. My grandpa took them from the council for a reason. Grammy said the council was corrupt back then. There may be new priestesses on the council, but nothing's changed. They're still bad. If this is what they'll do to exercise their power, I don't want to know what will happen when they possess all five of the Oaken Wands."

"You're right," I agreed. I reached out for her trembling hands. "And I will be beside you every step of the way."

"Thank you." Nadine gazed out toward the setting sun. "I can't be there when it happens, knowing there was nothing I could do to stop it."

"We'll stay here," I offered. "All night, if we have to."

She gazed up at me. "Is there anywhere to sit down? I'm not feeling well."

She was downplaying it; I could tell. She looked like hell, and her hands felt swollen when I touched them. I could only imagine what her joints felt like during today's flare-up.

I pointed. "There's a patch of rocks just through those trees."

"Thanks." Nadine leaned against me as I led her through the woods.

The rocks were further than I remembered, but we eventually found them. Twilight fell over the forest, and my stomach twisted. The thought of what was going on in the town below made my knees quake. I bet everyone in town was there, watching Professor Daniels hang.

I sat beside Nadine. On instinct, I wrapped my arm around her shoulder. I expected her to draw away, but she sagged into me.

Nadine sighed. "I thought being a priestess would change things. I thought it would give me a stronger voice. But I've never felt so powerless before."

I rubbed her arm. "I'm so sorry. I wish there was more I could do."

"Like what?" she asked.

"I wish I could at least make you feel better."

"It's not your responsibility to make me feel better," she said.

"I still want to," I replied. "With everything. You're so independent. You never let people help you when you're not feeling well."

"I feel like shit now," she admitted. "And I let you help me over to these rocks."

"It's a start," I said. "But I don't have to be your boyfriend to care."

Nadine sat up straighter to look me in the eyes. "You know why we're not together."

"I didn't mean it like that," I said quickly. Her eyes searched mine, and I found myself breaking down, confessing all my feelings to her. "I screwed up, and it may not mean much to you now, but I'm sorry for how I treated you. All I ever wanted was to protect you, and it felt like driving you away from me was the only way to save you from the Reaper's Shadow curse. The things I said to you when we broke up, though… there's no excuse for it."

Nadine dropped her gaze. "It wasn't all your fault. I said things that I regret, too."

"That may be the case, but I need to take responsibility for my part in it," I said gently. "I'm not going to lie, Nad. I want to be with you."

I was shocked to hear the words come out of my mouth. I never intended to admit that to her, as much as it tore me to pieces. I didn't want to cause her any more pain. "I know you've already made your decision, and I will always respect that," I promised. "No matter how I feel, all I want is what's best for you. Please just know that I'm not trying to beg for you back. I know you don't want that."

Nadine's gaze shifted over my features. I couldn't quite read her, but something in her eyes caught my heartstrings.

"Or do you?" I asked carefully.

She hesitated, and her voice came out as a whisper. "I don't know. Sometimes I wish you would get on your knees and beg, but I know how things would turn out if you did. It's like I'm protecting myself. If *you* begged for me back, then I could blame you when we broke up again. It's stupid and immature, and I know that, but that's how I feel deep down."

"You don't have to feel ashamed of how you feel," I said gently. "I'm glad you felt like you could share that with me."

Nadine shook her head. "You're making this really hard, you know?"

"I thought I was trying to make this easier on you."

"*That's* the hard part," she replied. "You're so sweet and understanding.

Everything in my heart tells me to run back into your arms, but if I lost you again… I don't know if either of us could go through that."

"You're scared. I get that. I am, too. If we got back together, I'd want it to be for good. I couldn't stand around waiting for the other shoe to drop."

"I can't do that, either," she said. "Which is why I think we might be better off as friends. At least then we know what the future holds."

My heart became heavy in my chest, as if it'd been replaced by a cinder block. I knew Nadine was right, but hearing her say it made me want to hurl. "You're right," I said, mostly to convince myself. "A relationship would just be a distraction. We can't have any distractions while we're trying to help the coven. This is too important."

"Or maybe…" Nadine hesitated. "Maybe *this* is the distraction—trying to convince ourselves we're something we're not."

I furrowed my brow. "You're saying things would be easier if we got back together?"

She pressed her hand to her forehead. "I don't know what I'm saying. Even if we got back together, the Reaper's Shadow curse still stands. That's always going to be an issue. Ugh… I don't know what I want, Lucas. With what's going on in the square right now, maybe we *need* the distraction. I'm making no sense."

I gently guided her face back toward mine so that I could look into her eyes. "Hey, you're not alone here. I don't get any of this, either."

Her eyes glistened as she stared up at me. "Lucas, I'm so scared—of everything. The council, these Wands, nightshade… us."

I shook my head. "You don't have to be afraid of us. Whatever happens, we'll make the decision together."

Her voice cracked. "I don't want to make any decisions right now."

"Then we won't," I said gently. All I needed right now was *her*—even if I didn't know what the future held for us.

Nadine reached up, and her fingers caressed the side of my face. She was so warm, so welcome, and so familiar. I could melt right into her.

"Lucas," she whispered, like she was about to say something. But she never got the chance. Nadine leaned into me, and my breath caught when she paused halfway. It was an invitation—one that my brain didn't even process before I was saying yes to it.

I closed the distance between us, and my lips connected with hers. I didn't know how it happened. One moment we were talking, and the next, Nadine and I were making out. It never should've happened, and yet it felt like this moment was always meant to end this way. Warmth swelled in my chest, and a spark ignited in my heart. Desire for her burned through me unlike ever before. Regardless of what happened in the future, Nadine was mine in this moment—for as long as she let me have her.

My hand came up to cradle the back of her neck, and I looped the other around her waist. Nadine sagged against me, and her tongue slid into my mouth. My pants tightened as her lips roamed over mine and passion surged between us.

Nadine shifted, and I guided her onto my lap, until she was straddling me. Her hands ran through my hair, and I moaned as mine cupped her ass. She came up for air, but she pressed her body against mine. I began trailing kisses down her neck, and she gasped.

"How's this for a distraction?" I asked as I buried my face into her collar bone. Goddess, she smelled *so* good.

"It's definitely working," she said through ragged breaths.

"Nad, I—" I started, but she silenced me with a kiss.

"Shh…" she said. "Let's not talk about this."

Nadine was vulnerable, and I knew it wasn't right to take advantage of her. I forced myself to draw away, and I took her hands in mine. "Nad, we shouldn't."

"Don't try to save me from this, Lucas," she begged. "I need to be sure of how I feel. I want this… if you do."

"I do," I said. Hell, I was *desperate* for it. I'd be an idiot to refuse her invitation.

My lips connected with hers again, and we continued making out. Nadine rolled her hips, and I gasped as my dick hardened. Neither of us said another word. We didn't need to, because our hands did all the talking. Nadine's cardigan sagged from her shoulders, and I trailed kisses all over her exposed shoulders, over the top of her breasts, and back to her lips. Her hands roamed up my shirt and across my back. Goddess, I'd forgotten how fucking good it felt to feel her hands on me. It was a miracle that we'd spent any time apart, because the mere contact was enough to make my head spin.

Nadine's fingers trailed down to my waistband, then I felt them on the button of my jeans. I drew away from her to look down and saw that she'd already unzipped my jeans. My breaths came in shallow heaves in anticipation. I watched her curiously, unsure exactly what she was going to do. She shot me a smile, as if asking my permission. I leaned back on the rock, supporting my weight with my hands and inviting her in.

We weren't getting back together, but damn it all if this wasn't the best distraction ever.

Nadine set me free, then ducked her head. My pulse spiked as her lips connected with my dick. I gasped as she pulled my tip into her mouth and rolled her tongue over me.

Holy fuck.

Of all the ways this night could end, I hadn't anticipated *this*. I couldn't help it when I tilted my hips upward. She grabbed the base of my dick and slid it deeper into her mouth. She was so wet and warm, and it drove me crazy. The thrill I got from her lips on me was unlike anything I'd ever felt before. Speeding down the mountainside on a skateboard didn't even compare.

As her tongue rolled over me, I couldn't help but plunge my fingers into her hair. Her head moved up and down, and it was *so* hot. My heart hammered so hard that I thought it might explode in my chest. I couldn't tear my gaze off of her as I watched my cock move in and out of her mouth. She was so fucking…

I didn't finish the thought before passion built inside of me. My breath caught as I reached my peak. My fingers tightened in her hair as I emptied into her. She noticed me tense, and she increased her speed, using her hand to pleasure me further.

I sagged against the rock, and my head spun so much that I saw stars where the trees should be. When my head finally cleared, Nadine was kneeling beneath me, beaming. She swallowed, and I smiled wide.

"If you were trying to convince me we shouldn't be together, you're kind of doing a shitty job of it," I teased as I buttoned my pants.

"Let's not question my motives," she joked back.

"Motives?" I smirked. "What motives—?"

Footsteps rustled in the distance. I jumped to my feet and grabbed Nadine's hand.

Her features paled. "No one knows we're out here."

"It might just be hikers," I said, hoping that's all it was, but dread twisted in my gut. "Stay behind me."

We walked toward the footsteps, my heart hammering. As we stepped out from behind the bushes, my pulse came to a full stop. A group of eight people stood before us—four boys and four girls around our age. A frizzy-haired girl walked beside a nervous-looking boy, and a blonde with huge glasses clung to the arm of a tall man with pale hair.

At the head of the group was a redhead. She looked completely panicked, as if she was in a great hurry to save someone's life.

One of the guys looked like he'd been beaten. A hugely muscular man dragged him along the ground. His face was covered in bruises, and his body appeared starving. The guy looked to be withering away against some kind of magical bonds he was bound by.

I didn't know *how* I knew what they were, but I could sense it immediately. It must've been something magical inside of me that I didn't even know was there. I could practically smell the wet dog on the wolven shifter and the reptilian scent of the dragon. Something rebelled inside of me, like I knew these individuals were my worst enemy.

A battle orb formed in my hand. "Get back, Nad! It's a group of fucking fae!"

The group came to an abrupt halt, and several of them stared at me like a deer in the headlights. The girls threw their hands up in surrender.

I didn't trust them. Fae, in Octavia Falls? They should know better than to come here.

"We're not here to harm you," the frizzy-haired girl said quickly. "We need help."

"Yeah?" I challenged. "Then what did you do to that guy?"

The one who looked beaten convulsed. He frothed at the mouth, seething to escape. Something was dreadfully wrong with him. I felt it in my gut.

"He's been possessed," she replied desperately. "We've been told there's a witch who can save him."

I narrowed my eyes. "Why should we believe you're not invading? There's eight of you!"

The biggest, burliest guy spoke. He had to be the dragon shifter. "Yeah, we might've been able to do this without *everyone* coming along."

The fiery redhead took charge. Her accent was soothing to me—she had to be American, like us. Strange for a fae. "What are your names?"

I opened my mouth, but Nadine spoke first. "Nadine and Lucas."

I scowled at her. She didn't know how dangerous the fae could be. She shouldn't be giving them our names.

"Nadine. Lucas," the redhead repeated. "My name is Emma. This is my mate, Ethan. He's been possessed by a forest demon." She gestured to the agonized man writhing against the ground in pain.

Something in my chest twinged. Demons were *not* to be messed with. Every witch knew that. If she was telling the truth, this guy could be hours away from death.

Emma pleaded with us. "He's in the final stages of possession. The demon's totally taken over his body. The demon's being held by a binding spell, but it won't keep him contained forever."

This was dangerous—way too dangerous to get involved in. I wanted no part in it. "If he's that far gone, nobody can help him," I said.

Tears pricked at Emma's eyes. "There's a witch there that might be able to save him. But she lives in town, and as fae, we can't cross the ward. If you can take it down for us, just for a second, we might be able to save his life."

My stomach sank. The way her voice shook… nobody could fake that. This girl was about to lose her mate, and faerie or not, she needed our help. But letting them through the barrier would put our whole town in jeopardy. I glanced to Nadine, and she shot me a worried expression.

"Who do you want to see?" Nadine asked.

"Hattie," Emma replied.

I tried not to let my emotions show, but I was sure she noticed that I recognized the name.

We couldn't risk this. "You're a fae. You're obviously lying. This has to be a trap."

Nadine grabbed my arm. "Lucas, if this man's dying, we have to help."

She obviously didn't know what we were dealing with. I turned to her. "Do you know how many witches have died because of fae? We don't have to do anything."

Emma's voice cracked. "Please. I don't care that you're a witch, only if you can do something to save my mate. The coven is our only hope. Wouldn't you do anything to save the person you love?"

Nadine looked at me. It wasn't hard to read the look in her eyes. She was pleading with me, begging me to let her help them. She couldn't stand there and watch someone suffer if she could do something about it —and she *could* help. Nadine could control the protection spell and let them through, since she was a priestess now. Had the fae run into anyone else tonight, there was nothing any witch or warlock could do to help. This guy didn't look like he had enough time left for us to run and get Hattie and bring her back to Perry's Point. He'd be long gone by that point.

But they hadn't run into just any witch. The fae had found Nadine. It was almost like fate had led us here tonight. Maybe this was our way to help someone, when we couldn't help Professor Daniels.

"Fine," I finally agreed. "But if this is a trap, don't blame us when all hell comes down on you."

"Trust us," the dragon shifter said. "We don't want to be here any longer than you do. We wouldn't be asking witches for help if we hadn't exhausted every other option."

"Follow me," Nadine said.

She went on ahead, but I hung back, following the group from behind. I had to keep an eye on every single one of them. No matter how much I wanted to help this guy, I didn't trust the fae. This could still be a trick.

We reached the edge of the boundary. Though we couldn't see the ward, Nadine must've been able to feel it. She lifted her palms, and a small area around the ward began to glow. It appeared as a shimmering tear, as if she'd pulled back a curtain to let them inside.

"Here," Nadine said. "This will get you inside."

"Can we get out once we leave?" the frizzy-haired girl asked timidly.

I cleared my throat. There was only one way we could help them with that. "The hole in the ward will last until morning. Once that happens, you're on your own."

The dragon shifter stepped past the ward. "Trust me, the last thing we want to be is trapped inside a witch village. We'll be gone long before sunrise."

Emma followed him. "You guys want money or something?"

Nadine shook her head. "We're just trying to help. Pay us back later."

I grumbled internally. Nadine should know better than to make a deal with the fae, but she didn't—she hadn't been taught a thing about them. I really had to sit her down and instruct her on these things.

Emma nodded, like we had a deal. "Where can we find Hattie?"

I lowered my voice. "She lives in an apartment above her shop. The place is called The Jolly Pumpkin. It should be pretty deserted—everyone's at some big event on the other side of town."

I didn't tell them what was really happening. How could I admit what our own people were doing—that witches were hanging each other? "If you're lucky, you should get in and out unseen. Good luck."

Just looking at their possessed friend made my skin crawl. Fae or not, I really hoped Hattie could help them, or this guy was going to be dead before morning.

The fae took off toward town, and Nadine turned to me. She pulled her cardigan around herself and shivered. "I did the right thing, didn't I?"

I watched the fae go, until they disappeared into the trees. "I don't know," I admitted. "I've been taught my whole life not to trust the fae, but right now, I don't even trust our *own* people. I guess we'll find out. That whole thing was… weird."

"At least if Hattie can help them, we saved one person tonight," Nadine whispered. She took a step forward, then winced. I reached out to catch her, and she steadied herself against me.

"Your flare-up's getting worse, isn't it?" I asked.

She nodded. "Can you take me back to my dorm? I don't know if I can drive."

"Yeah, of course." I helped Nadine back to the parking lot and into the passenger seat of Grant's car. We would come back another day and pick up her car.

When we got back to the school, it was practically abandoned. Everyone was either at the square to watch the hanging, or hiding from it in their rooms. Grant and Talia weren't back yet, and I knew they must've gone to watch. It was horrifying to even think of being there right now.

Isa gave a happy meow when we returned. I helped Nadine into bed, then stripped off her shoes. "Can I get you anything? Water or your meds?"

"I can manage my meds," she said. "I need to use the bathroom anyway."

I helped her stand. As soon as she shut the door to the bathroom, I sank into the couch. This night had been wild—in more ways than one. But the brief high we'd experienced couldn't make up for the rest of it. None of it felt quite real. Isa must've noticed my unease, because she jumped onto the couch beside me and nudged me until I scratched her behind the ears. That didn't satisfy her, though. She kept pawing at me and meowing, like she was trying to get my attention.

After several long minutes of silence, the door to the bathroom opened. Nadine gingerly stepped into the room. When I caught sight of her, my stomach plummeted from my abdomen. The worry in her eyes was horrifying.

"What's wrong, Nad?" I demanded, shooting to my feet.

Her bottom lip quivered. "Something's wrong, Lucas. I think this is more than just a flare-up."

I immediately conjured my phone. "I'll call the infirmary and let them know we're coming."

She shook her head, and my stomach bottomed out. "I need to go to the emergency room. Now."

Anxiety tangled in my gut. When I saw the foam in my urine, I knew something was seriously wrong. I'd been stupid enough to write my pain off as a bad flare-up. This was so much worse.

I felt like I was dreaming when we entered the hospital. Lucas tried to talk to me, but I had no idea what he was saying. He must've called Grammy, because she showed up shortly after and helped fill out my paperwork. Isa curled up on my feet when I was admitted into a room. She looked really worried.

"We're going to get you an answer as soon as possible," the doctor promised. "I'll call your rheumatologist right away."

I barely processed what he said over the ringing in my ears. I couldn't remember much of what happened before Dr. Yonker arrived. He was dressed in street clothes with a lab coat thrown over them. He must've already been finished for the day and rushed back to the hospital to care for me.

"We're going to run a few tests," Dr. Yonker told me.

Grammy stood at my bedside. "Do you have any idea what's going on?"

Dr. Yonker frowned. I noticed something in his eyes that worried me to my very core. He suspected something, but he wasn't ready to say it out loud. This was *bad*. "We're going to get you an answer as soon as possible."

Hours passed while we waited for my test results. I fell asleep and didn't wake until after sunrise.

Lucas gently shook me awake the next morning. "Dr. Yonker has your results."

I feared the worst. Grammy must've too, because she knotted her hands in her lap. Dr. Yonker approached my bedside with another doctor in tow.

"Do you know what's wrong with me?" I asked him.

He drew a deep breath. "We're going to have to run some more tests to know for sure. Right now, all we know is that your kidneys aren't functioning properly. This is Dr. Anna Tracey. She's a nephrologist, and she's here to help."

My swollen hands trembled. "A nephrologist? You're a kidney disease specialist. Is that what's wrong with me? I have kidney disease?"

I knew the statistics. They'd frightened me for years. Around half of lupus patients developed kidney problems, due to the disease attacking our kidney cells.

Goddess, let it be anything else. I wasn't ready for another life-altering diagnosis.

"We'll need to take a kidney biopsy to be sure of anything," Dr. Tracey said gently.

I glanced between Grammy and Lucas, as if they could provide me with something—anything—to explain what was going on. They tried to hide it, but I saw the worry in their eyes.

"When can we do the biopsy?" I asked.

"I'd like to do it immediately," Dr. Tracey said. "Given your condition, we'll want to expedite the test results. I hope to have an answer for you in the next twenty-four hours."

It felt like too long, yet not nearly long enough to process what was happening. I'd had lupus for years, and my symptoms had been progressively getting worse, but this felt like it came out of nowhere.

"Okay. Let's do the biopsy," I said.

Dr. Tracey nodded. "We'll get prepped right away."

"You're going to be okay, Nadine," Dr. Yonker promised. "I've worked with lupus patients before, and they've always pulled through."

What if I don't? I wanted to ask, but I couldn't. As hard as it was right now, I wanted to believe him.

I reached for Lucas's hand when the doctors left the room. "You should go home," I said. "It's going to be a while before they have my results back."

Lucas shook his head. He wore a mask of strength, but I could see through it. "You shouldn't be alone right now. I'm not going anywhere."

As much as there was a part of me that just wanted to be alone to process this, a bigger part of me was grateful to have him here.

I turned toward Grammy. "You've been here all night. You should get some sleep."

"I want to help," Grammy protested.

Goddess, all I wanted to do was cry, and for some reason, I couldn't do it in front of her. I could only fall apart in front of Lucas.

"I could use some help with Isa," I admitted. "She hasn't eaten since last night, and she should probably use a litter box."

Grammy seemed thrilled to help. Isa, on the other hand, didn't want to leave my side. After a while, Grammy managed to drag Isa out of the room. The door clicked shut, and silence settled between Lucas and me.

A lump rose in my throat. I could hardly breathe as I stared at him. "I'm scared, Lucas."

"I know, Nad," he said gently. "But you have *good* doctors. They're going to help you fix this."

"What if they can't?" My voice cracked.

"They're going to," he insisted.

I shook my head. "You can't know that. I'm terrified that my kidneys are shutting down and I'm going to die. And I feel so... *guilty* even being afraid of that. I mean, we know there's life after death, so why am I so afraid of dying?"

Lucas placed his hand on mine. "You're not afraid of death, Nadine. You're afraid to leave this earth before you finish everything you came here to do."

"I don't even know what that is. I thought my purpose was to protect the coven, but I'm already failing at that."

"Hey, Nad," Lucas said firmly, shaking my hand a little until I looked at him. His gaze was so comforting. "I will never be able to say I understand what you're going through right now, but I know fear better than any other emotion. I know what it's like for the corners of your vision to blur. I know the taste of copper in your mouth, and how your hands and feet can turn ice cold. I know, and I can help you. I will be here for you every step of the way, if you'll let me."

A sob broke from my chest, and tears streamed down my face. My whole body shook as I cried. Lucas leaned over me and pulled me into an embrace. I clung to him like he was my very life. He didn't say anything—just held me as I let my emotions pour out. I never thought I'd need Lucas the way I needed him right now.

Finally, I caught my breath, and I drew away. "You have no idea how much I needed to hear that right now. Thank you for being here for me."

He nodded, his eyes glistening. "I'll always be here."

It wasn't long after that before the doctors came in to explain the procedure. They would sedate me and insert a long needle into my back so they could grab a tissue sample of my kidney.

"It's going to be okay," Lucas promised me, but I was scared to death.

Grammy returned with Isa, but I told her to go home and that I'd call her when I had the test results. Lucas refused to leave, though the doctors wouldn't let him stay in the room for the biopsy.

I passed out the moment the sedative hit. I didn't know how much time had passed before I came to, but Lucas told me I'd only been gone an hour.

"I got you something," he said, conjuring a gift bag.

"You went down to the gift shop?" I asked. "You didn't have to."

He shrugged. "We need to kill some time while we wait for the test results."

I opened the bag and smiled when I pulled out a gorgeous puzzle. The artwork was of a black cat with green eyes and the moon shining behind her. It was the first time I'd smiled in over twenty-four hours. Isa eyed the artwork curiously.

I turned the puzzle toward her. "It kind of looks like you, doesn't it, girl? Thank you, Lucas."

"It was no big deal," he said, but he was a liar. It meant everything right now.

The doctors said I could go home while I waited, but I insisted I wasn't going anywhere until I had answers. I was too much of a nervous wreck, anyway. Lucas and I put together the puzzle, chatting about our classes.

"Did I ever tell you about the time Samantha accidentally conjured a dildo in my first semester conjuring class?" Lucas asked.

I chuckled as I fitted two pieces of the puzzle together. "No, but I want to hear about it."

"That's basically the whole story," he laughed. "She was practicing conjuring, and everything spilled out of her stash. You should've seen our professor's face when he saw it. It's like he didn't know what it was at first. You could see the second it hit him. He dismissed class early."

I smirked. "Maybe he thought it was a... *wand.*"

Lucas chuckled at my joke. "Oh, speaking of which, have I shown you mine? I found one for Wand Theory."

He conjured his wand and handed it to me.

I turned it over in my hands. It was simple but elegant—a light wooden wand with a twisted handle. When I looked closer, I noticed intricate swirling designs in the blade that I didn't see at first. "It suits you."

He shrugged as he took it back. "It works."

"You know you're missing Wand Theory right now to do this puzzle," I pointed out.

Lucas shook his head. "I'm not missing class for this puzzle. I'm missing class for you."

My face heated.

A silent beat passed between us, and Lucas eyed me curiously. "What is it?"

I drew a deep breath. "It's strange. My health is nothing but shit, and I haven't felt this normal in a long time. Thank you for staying and taking my mind off things. This is... nice."

Lucas offered me a kind smile. He looked like he was about to say something, but he must've stopped himself. He glanced down to the puzzle and grabbed for the last piece before fitting it into the center of the puzzle. "There," he said, admiring our work.

Isa stood on my lap and stared down at the puzzle. She batted at it with her paw and meowed, like she feared the cat was trapped inside the painting.

I snickered. "I don't think Isa's pleased."

"No, I—" Lucas started, but he cut off when a knock came at the door.

We both turned to see Dr. Yonker and Dr. Tracey enter the room. My heart immediately began hammering.

"Well, Nadine," Dr. Tracey said gently. "We have good news and bad news."

My stomach twisted. "Please just tell me what's wrong."

Dr. Yonker drew a deep breath. "The good news is that we have a diagnosis, and it's treatable."

I should've felt relieved to hear that, but I didn't. I knotted my hands in my lap. "What's the bad news?"

A silent beat passed, and every inch of my body began to tremble. It was the same life-altering silence I experienced when I was diagnosed with lupus.

"It's lupus nephritis," Dr. Yonker said, shattering my world with those three simple words. "It's a condition—"

"I know what lupus nephritis is," I said, my voice cracking. Tears beaded in my eyes, and I clutched the star necklace I wore. I'd come so far since my lupus diagnosis, and it seemed like none of it mattered anymore.

"What's lupus nephritis?" Lucas asked, his tone hollow. He could tell this was bad.

"It's kidney failure in lupus patients," Dr. Yonker explained. "It's caused by Nadine's immune system attacking her kidney tissue."

"How bad is it?" I rasped.

Dr. Tracey shot a glance at Dr. Yonker, and I knew it was worse than I imagined. "Nadine, you have class five lupus nephritis."

I gasped for breath, because it felt like I'd just been punched in the stomach.

"That sounds bad." Lucas's voice wavered. "What's class five?"

"There are six classes or stages," Dr. Yonker explained. "Class five is characterized by immune deposits in the kidneys. Essentially, Nadine's kidneys are damaged, and they're unable to filter her blood properly."

"H-how come we didn't catch it sooner?" I stammered.

"It can develop very quickly..." Dr. Yonker started, but I didn't hear the rest of what he said. All I could hear was *class five*, repeating over and over in my head.

"You said it can be treated," I blurted. "How?"

"We're going to start you on dialysis immediately, and you'll be placed on the transplant list," Dr. Tracey said.

Lucas gaped. "She'll get better, right? Her kidneys can heal. She'll recover."

Dr. Tracey's features turned sad. "Unfortunately, with the damage her lupus has already done to her kidneys, Nadine's condition can only be reversed through a kidney transplant. In the meantime, she'll attend dialysis three times per week. Even patients who have been on dialysis for years lead normal lives."

I couldn't move or speak. All I could do was sit and stare at the wall, absorbing the news.

"This is an opportunity, Nadine," Dr. Yonker insisted. "A transplant will likely clear up *all* your lupus symptoms."

"How likely?" Lucas demanded.

"There's a three to five percent chance her lupus would return following a transplant," Dr. Yonker said.

"But I have to literally swap out my organs!" I cried. I couldn't wrap my head around the idea of this surgery.

Lucas shot to his feet. "I'll do it!"

I furrowed my brow at him. "You'll do what?"

"I'll get tested," he said firmly, as if his mind was already made up. "If I'm a match, I'll do it. I'll give you my kidney."

I grabbed his hand. "Lucas, no!"

He yanked his hand from my grasp. "Why not? I only need one kidney."

"You're probably not even a match," I insisted.

"What if I am?" he asked. "I want to at least get tested. Nad, this could be life-changing for you."

"I know." My voice cracked. "But to ask you to do this for me—"

"You didn't ask. I offered." He looked to Dr. Tracey. "How soon can we know?"

"The process usually takes several months," she said.

"You expedited Nadine's biopsy results," Lucas pointed out. "Can't you expedite these tests?"

"We want to be certain that everything will work out before undergoing such a large procedure," Dr. Tracey stated gently. "You'll have to undergo blood tests, a psych evaluation—"

"It's okay," Lucas cut in. "I'll do anything. Whatever it takes."

A smile touched Dr. Tracey's lips. "Very well. You're a very lucky girl, Nadine. If you two are a match, you might have a new kidney in just a few short months."

"I hope so," Lucas said. As soon as the doctors left the room, he turned to me.

"Lucas," I started to say, but I was at a loss for words. I didn't know whether to thank him, or try to convince him this wasn't going to work out. I couldn't stand for us to get our hopes up if he wasn't a match.

He squeezed my hand. "It's going to be okay. I know this is really scary right now, but I'm not going to let anything bad happen to you. Understand?"

I hesitated. "Yes," I finally said.

I had to believe him, because I couldn't bear to accept the alternative.

NEARLY A WEEK PASSED, and I was still trying to process my diagnosis. Lucas and I hadn't spoken about our relationship all week, and neither of us mentioned the moment we'd shared at Perry's Point. All conversation had halted, unless it involved my health. I wasn't sure I could handle anything else right now anyway.

Talia came with me to the hospital that weekend. "I want to see what your dialysis is like," she said.

"It's boring," I insisted. "I have to sit in a room attached to a machine for four hours at a time, three times per week."

"So let me keep you company," she offered.

It was nice of her to care so much, so I brought her along. Isa and Gus stayed back in our dorm room, because Isa got uneasy when she had to sit here for hours.

"So this is your artificial kidney," Talia said thoughtfully as she eyed the machine that filtered my blood.

"That's it. It's nothing fancy," I told her while the nurse hooked the tubes up to my arm.

"Nothing fancy?" she teased. "Nadine, one of your organs is a machine. You're part robot!"

I chuckled. "I'm bionic?"

"A bionic werewolf!" she laughed. "You know, because *lupus* is Latin for *werewolf*. It was a dumb joke."

"No, it's cool," I told her. "I can be a werewolf. I'm just glad the dialysis is helping. I'm feeling so much better."

Talia eyed me curiously, but she waited until the nurse left the room to speak up. "Are you sure you're doing better? I know you won't admit it, but I can tell that you're scared."

I dropped my gaze. "I feel better physically, but I *am* scared. I know I can live a normal life on dialysis, but people die all the time waiting to reach the top of the transplant list. It's just… what if dialysis isn't enough?"

"It will be enough," Talia insisted. "It has to be. We're all here for you, and we're going to fight to get you whatever care you need."

I shot her a smile. "Thanks, Tal. It means a lot."

She eyed the machine. "So, how does this all work?"

I pointed to one of the tubes in my arm. "This is the arterial line. My blood leaves through this tube and gets filtered by the dialysis machine. Once it's clean, it goes back into my veins through the venous line here."

"What does it feel like?" she asked.

I shrugged. "Not much, really. The worst part is the needles. Oh, and my diet. I can't eat whatever I want to anymore. I'm supposed to eat more protein and less salt."

"What do you normally do during your dialysis?"

"I've had plenty of time to learn my Rubik's Cube, and I can solve it pretty quickly. Sometimes I do puzzles and—ugh—homework. Usually it's no fun, but maybe you can help. There's one full moon before the end of the semester. I'm supposed to perform a ritual for my Moonology class, but I don't know what to do."

She pressed her lips together. "Well, tonight is the last quarter moon. That's a good time for releasing energy and letting go. Is there anything you need to let go of?"

I dropped my gaze. "Maybe…"

"Like what?" she asked.

I hated to admit it, but I knew I could confide in Talia. "I've been holding on to all this resentment, and it's done nothing but hurt me."

"Resentment towards who?"

"Myself," I admitted. "When the doctors told me I needed a transplant, I couldn't help but resent myself—resent my choices. Like maybe if I ate healthier or didn't push myself so hard, I could've done something to prevent this."

"You did nothing wrong," Talia assured me.

I sighed. "I know that logically, but I can't convince myself of it. I just feel like I'm to blame for what's happening to me."

"It's no one's fault."

"I know. But it's not just that, either," I continued. "Lucas wants to give me his kidney—if we're a match. Part of me hopes that we aren't, because I don't know if I could take it."

Talia furrowed her brow. "What do you mean?"

I knotted my hands in my lap, because I didn't know how to explain it. "Ever since we broke up, I think I've resented him. On some level, I blamed him, even though I knew the breakup was mutual. I can't help but think that I'm drinking poison and hoping it will punish *him*."

"You're still hurt," Talia stated.

"Yes," I admitted. "We talked a little about our relationship, but then I was in the hospital, and we haven't talked about it since. We agreed not to make any decisions yet, but we need to decide eventually. The thing is, I can't seem to find a reason to be apart anymore, so why am I not running into the arms of the man I love?"

I froze. I hadn't meant for that last part to slip out.

"It's been almost six months," Talia pointed out. "If you still love him—"

"Oh, Goddess," I sighed. "I didn't realize *how much* I still love him until I said that out loud."

A smile spread across Talia's face. "I think you have your answer for your ceremony. It sounds like you have a lot of reflecting to do."

"You're right," I said, feeling as if the answer was clearer than ever. "Thanks for letting me talk it out with you."

"Anytime."

The sun had set by the time I finished dialysis. I stopped by the school library to check out a spellbook. I nervously flipped through the book until I found a spell that was marked as one of the strongest releasing ceremonies in the coven.

The problem? I needed Lucas to perform it.

I started flipping through other pages. To hell with that. I'd find a simpler spell and—

I stopped dead. This wasn't just about my class assignment. This was about my life. If Lucas and I were a match, I wasn't going to be able to accept his kidney with this resentment hanging over me. If I truly wanted to let go, I couldn't take the easy route. I had to use the most powerful spell in the book.

I clutched the spellbook tight to my chest and navigated the halls. Isa followed alongside me. She noticed Oliver and ran ahead of me down the hall. Oliver looked delighted to see her and tackled her to the ground.

Lucas smirked as he stepped around the cats. "Hey, Nad. How are you feeling?"

"Pretty good," I said. "I had dialysis today."

"That's great," he replied, shoving his hands into his jeans pockets. "I'm glad it's helping."

Tension filled the air. I couldn't bring myself to ask him to help me with the ceremony, but I sensed he had something to say, too. "What is it?" I asked.

Lucas sighed. "I know the doctors said it could take months, but I hope we get an answer soon about the transplant."

I fidgeted with the pages of the spellbook. "I actually wanted to talk to you about that."

Worry filled his eyes. "Did they tell you something?"

"No," I said quickly. "Besides, they'd call you first if they knew anything, since you're the donor. It's just... can we go somewhere to talk?"

"Yeah, anywhere," Lucas said.

I glanced to Isa and Oliver, who were wrestling in the middle of the hall. Isa was winning.

"Let's leave the cats," I suggested. "I want to be alone."

"Sure, but Nadine... you're scaring me."

"Don't be scared," I reassured him. "It's not like that."

"Can you at least tell me what's going on?" he asked.

I glanced around the hall, and several people were passing through. "I need help with some homework," I told him vaguely.

He eyed me curiously, but he followed. I conjured a coat and slipped it on, before we left the school and snuck into the forest. It was chilly out, and snow dusted the ground, but when Lucas and I wanted to be alone, there was only one place to go.

After several minutes of walking, we emerged into a clearing. The abandoned mansion we'd visited so many times before stood in front of us. I shivered.

"You okay?" Lucas asked.

"I'm just cold," I said. "Let's get inside and start a fire."

I felt better once we were inside, but my stomach dropped when I saw all the wood beside the fireplace was gone.

"I must've used it all up the last time I was here," I said.

Lucas eyed me curiously. "Do you come here often?"

I shrugged. *More than I'll ever admit.* "I've come a few times."

Lucas cocked his head. "I think there's a pile of wood in the master bedroom. Let's go check."

For as many times as I'd been inside this mansion, I hadn't really explored it. It was falling apart, and I feared one wrong move would bring the whole room down on us. I'd never been upstairs, because the staircase didn't look safe.

But when I stepped into that master bedroom, I felt a sense of relief wash over me. The room had long been abandoned, but there was happiness and warmth here. A large four-poster bed was set against one wall, with a chaise at the foot of it. Long black curtains covered the ornate windows, but the fabric had been torn through the years. A rusted chandelier that looked like it'd been gorgeous in its prime hung above us.

"Here we go," Lucas said, hurrying over to the fireplace. We found a small stack of wood there, and he lit it. He performed a quick cleansing spell on the area, and the dust swept out of the room.

"Thank you," I told him, picking at the worn corner of the spellbook.

"So, what's your homework?" He gestured to the book in my arms, but he looked skeptical, like he knew it was more than just a homework assignment.

"I'm supposed to perform a ritual for my Moonology class, but I can't do it myself."

He tilted his head. "You need my help… why?"

I swallowed the lump in my throat. "Because the ritual is for you. Well, not *for you*, exactly. About you, maybe? For both of us?"

I was rambling, and Lucas noticed.

"Can I see?" He reached for the spellbook and gently took it from my hands.

"It's a type of forgiveness spell."

He flipped to the page that I'd bookmarked. His eyebrows knitted as he read over the spell, and I bit my lower lip. Finally, he lifted his gaze. "You're sure you want to do this?"

"Yes," I said confidently. "There's a lot I haven't said—a lot I haven't even admitted to myself—and I think we both deserve to hear it said out loud."

Lucas handed the spellbook back. "Okay, I'll help you, but I want to do it, too. I want to share how I feel about you."

I smiled up at him. "I'll listen."

"Then let's get started." Lucas gestured to the area in front of the fireplace, and we sat on the floor facing each other. The fire was warm and cozy… so why did I feel so cold?

I conjured a short pillar candle. "The spellbook says we have to light it together."

Lucas placed his hands over mine, so that we were both cupping the candle. "Okay. Together."

We tilted the candle, until the wick pointed toward the flames in the fireplace. The wick lit, and I set the candle between us. Next, I conjured a knife and pressed the blade to the end of my pointer finger, holding it above the flickering flame.

"Woah!" Lucas stopped me. "What are you doing, Nad?"

I glanced at the spellbook. "It's part of the spell. *Pour your heart out over the flame.* I have to bleed onto the wick while I confess my feelings, until the flame goes out."

"No, that's blood magic," Lucas explained. "This spell is using a metaphor. *Pour your heart out* means to express your feelings—don't hold anything back. You're supposed to do that until the candle burns out."

I set the knife aside. "Oh, so the candle is just giving me a time limit?"

"Yes," Lucas said.

I breathed a sigh of relief. "Okay, that makes things a little easier… or not."

"Sharing your feelings is never easy, Nad," Lucas said gently. "But that doesn't mean it isn't good for you. If I've learned anything over these last few months, it's that this shit is powerful."

I chuckled nervously. "Well, it's a spell. All magic is powerful."

"So are your words and your emotions," Lucas said. "Sometimes, that's even more powerful than magic."

"You say that like you've been through something like this before," I remarked.

He nodded. "I did a ritual last month, a lot like this one. I didn't use magic, but it was the most powerful thing I'd ever done."

My breath quivered as I stared into his eyes. They were so gentle and honest. I couldn't help but feel safe in his presence. "Then show me how," I begged.

"I can do that," he offered. Lucas leaned over to take my hands in his. They warmed my fingers more than the fire possibly could. "Nadine, I've spent so much time stuck in the past, wondering how things would've turned out differently if I'd just changed one tiny thing. If I'd gotten to Eric sooner, would he still be alive? If I heard the Imperium Council follow us into the trees, would your secret still be safe? If I'd bottled up my feelings that night on the Catwalk, would we have broken up? I can never go back and change what I said to you or how I treated you. But I can choose to accept that the past cannot be changed. No amount of worrying can possibly take me back in time. I'm done living there. I'm ready to look toward the future."

"You say it so elegantly, I don't even know where to go from there," I admitted. "I spent the summer blaming you, when I deserved the blame. But maybe that's the problem—thinking there's someone to blame. Maybe none of this is *anyone's* fault. Maybe it's not good or bad, but it just *is*. I thought there was no way to fix what we'd broken, and that relationships should be easier than this. But I didn't even try. I thought that you couldn't accept me—darkness and all—but you've done nothing but love me. Part of me couldn't handle the way that you showed it."

"Because I worshiped you," Lucas stated. "That's a problem. Loving you in that way was intense and unfair. You wanted a partner, and I didn't know how to be that for you back then."

"But you know now?" I asked, my heart fluttering.

"I'm trying," Lucas said. "I understand it better now, and I'll do my best to keep learning. I'm seeing a therapist."

That shocked me. "I didn't know that."

"Well, I didn't tell you," Lucas said. "I've been going to therapy ever since I got out of the hospital."

"I'm really proud of you." I didn't think I'd ever uttered a truer statement. "I have a lot to learn, too—about myself, and about being in a relationship. I'm not perfect by any means, and I know I never will be, but I can at least try to be a better person every day."

Lucas chuckled under his breath.

"What is it?" I asked.

He smirked in a way that made me swoon. "You're so perfectly imperfect, Nad. All your imperfections and flaws make you human. That's why I must accept you—darkness and all. I love that you want to be a better person."

"I love that about you, too," I told him. "I can see how much you've changed, and it's like night and day. I thought I came here tonight to forgive you, but I don't even know anymore what I have to forgive you for. I think I came here to forgive myself, and I can't think of anyone better to pour my heart out to than to you."

Lucas squeezed my hand. "Me, either. Thank you for trusting me so much."

"Of course," I said. "Everyone should trust their partner."

Lucas went rigid, and I realized what I said.

"I-I didn't mean," I stammered. "I don't know what I meant by that."

Lucas's features turned thoughtful. "You said it, though, so it must mean something. Nad... do you still think of me as your boyfriend?"

"No..." I furrowed my brow, because I had thoroughly confused myself. "Maybe... I do? I wonder if a part of me expects us to get back together someday—like our breakup was nothing more than a break... a tiny little blip on the map. It makes no sense, because a few months ago, I was certain we would never get back together. But every time I see you..."

Lucas eyed me curiously. "Yes?"

I drew a deep breath, but it didn't stop the tears from rising to my eyes. "Lucas, you offered to give me your kidney. You love me more than I can ever fully comprehend, and as much as I've told myself I can't be with you, my heart refuses to believe that I don't love you. I have been asking myself every day why we can't get back together, and I have yet to come up with a single reason."

"A month ago, we had all kinds of reasons," Lucas pointed out.

"Yeah, we had all these reasons to stay apart, but what about all the reasons to be together?" I asked.

His breath wavered. "Like what?"

"Like the way that you support me in anything I go through," I said. "You believe in me in a way that nobody else does. When I told Grant I was going to be a detective *and* a priestess, he didn't think I could be both.

When I told *you* that, you didn't even question it. You've never questioned how I'm going to achieve things. Your only question is to ask what you can do to help. Hell, did you ever wonder why Grant and I only had one date?"

"A bit, yeah," Lucas admitted.

"Grant is one of my best friends. He's a total freaking sweetheart, but I'm not," I said. "Grant wants to sit in the background and avoid conflict, which is fine. He's helping us decipher the nightshade formula. But I'm out there following drug dealers and asking questions, and I need someone by my side to do that with me, someone who's willing to get involved in things that are dangerous. If I could choose anyone, I'd want it to be *you*, because you support me, and you challenge me. Right now, I can be totally open to you in ways that I never have with anyone else. You help me make sense of the world."

Lucas's hands trembled. "I agree. You have been patient with me in my own growth, and you never judged me for my depression. You broke me out of my shell, and I can never thank you enough for that. I think it's great that we reflect our issues back on each other so that we can grow. But the last time it got too hard, we broke up instead of working through our shit together."

"I was scared," I said. "Being with you terrifies me. But nothing can compare to when I was sitting in that hospital room waiting for my kidney disease diagnosis. As scared as I am that I might lose you again, I'm even more afraid that I could die without you. I realize now that no matter what I'm going through, I want you there by my side. I want to be with you. And I want you back."

Tears spilled from Lucas's lids, and I thought for certain he was going to tell me he couldn't be there for me—not in the way I hoped. Instead, Lucas's voice cracked as he said, "I thought I'd never hear you say that."

His hands immediately left mine, and he grabbed my face. We rose to our knees as our lips connected in a passionate kiss. His fingers warmed my cheeks, and his cinnamon scent surrounded me. The whole room seemed to tilt around us, spinning unevenly as something more powerful than magic itself surged between us.

The candle we'd lit continued to flicker. I carefully climbed over it and into his lap. Lucas grabbed my hips and rolled me onto a soft rug at the foot of the bed. I moaned as he hovered above me, planting passionate kisses on my lips over and over again. I wrapped my legs around his hips and yanked him closer. His body pressed against mine, and I felt his hardness against me. I moaned in pleasure as I tangled my fingers into his hair.

"Goddess, Nad," he groaned. "I've missed you so much."

"I missed you, too," I replied, desperately clinging to him like I thought he might vanish at any moment. "I love you. I'm sorry I let you go—"

Lucas's lips connected with mine again, silencing my apology. "Shh," he whispered. "None of that matters anymore."

I tilted my head back as he trailed kisses down my neck. My shoulders seemed to melt into the floor as tingles spread all throughout my body. Lucas's hands roamed over me, trailing up my shirt and across the fabric of my bra. I couldn't stand these clothes between us, and I yanked on his shirt. He got to his knees so that I could pull the fabric over his head. My breath caught as I admired his bare chest. Firelight flickered across his skin, creating deep shadows across his muscled abdomen. Heat pooled between my thighs as I drank him in.

He leaned over me again, kissing me like his life depended on it. I never felt more alive than I did when I was cradled in his arms, his tongue rolling over mine. My hands explored every inch of his exposed skin, until they connected with the button of his jeans. He moaned and rolled his hips toward me. Taking his invitation, I unbuttoned his jeans and freed him. My heart hammered as I took his length in my hand, pumping up and down as we made out. My other hand slid beneath his waistband, and I grabbed his ass. He gasped.

Goddess, these clothes were useless! I guided him off of me, until he lay on his back. I wore a greedy smile as I climbed on top of him and pulled his shoes off. He quickly kicked off his pants, until he was lying naked in front of me. All I could do was sit there and stare. Lucas eyed me curiously, like he was trying to figure out what I was thinking.

"You're so amazing," I breathed, trailing my fingers up his legs.

Lucas shivered, and he grabbed my hand to stop me. "I've never done this before."

I tilted my head. "Done what?"

"You're the first person I've ever been totally naked in front of," he admitted. "Feel."

Lucas guided my hand to his chest, and I splayed my palm over it. His heart beat furiously, like a heavy drumbeat against his rib cage.

"I've never done that, either," I told him. Slowly, I reached for the hem of my shirt and pulled it over my head. Lucas couldn't take his eyes off of me as I began stripping down in front of him. The desire in his eyes drove me crazy. I wanted to ride him into the morning.

My fingers trembled as I pulled my jeans off and tossed them aside. I knelt in front of him, in nothing but my bra and panties, before slowly unclasping my bra and letting it fall from my shoulders. Lucas inhaled a sharp breath at the sight of my naked breasts. He reached out, and his fingers wrapped around the waistband of my panties. Neither of us spoke, but we moved in sync as I rolled onto my back, and he pulled them off of me. My chest rose and fell rapidly. My heart felt as if it was trying to break free of my chest.

"You're gorgeous," Lucas whispered, his eyes roaming every inch of my body.

I reached out to take his hand. "You, too. I wish I could make love to you."

"Nad, the curse…"

"I know our limits," I said. "I would never ask you to step past them. I just love you so much, and I wish you could feel what I do."

"I already do," Lucas whispered. His gaze dropped to the apex of my thighs. "Besides, we don't have to cross any lines to make love."

Lucas's fingers grazed my most sensitive area. Tingles spread through my entire body, and I gasped. His fingers slid inside of me, and I went totally breathless. I squeezed my eyes shut and relished in the pleasurable sensations as his fingers worked inside of me and his thumb circled my clit.

I moaned. Lucas dipped his head, and his lips brushed over my breasts. I arched my back, begging for more. And holy hell, did he deliver. Lucas's lips curled around my nipple, and he sucked it into his mouth. Pleasure shot downward, to where he was working me with his fingers. My fingers dove into his hair, yanking on the strands to ground me to reality. A magical sensation built up inside of me, making my head spin.

"Oh my—" I gasped as I reached my peak, tumbling over into an earth-shattering orgasm. His lips collided with mine, and he pressed his fingers into me deeper as I contracted around him. I clutched him closely to my body, never wanting to let him go.

I drew a deep breath as I came down from the orgasm. Goddess, I'd never felt so good in my life. Lucas drew away from me, and I stared up at his gorgeous features.

He rolled over, and I climbed on top of him, straddling him. I was a mere inch away from pressing myself against his cock. Lucas noticed, and his whole body shuttered. I wrapped my hand around him and began pumping as we made out. Lucas's tongue slid into my mouth. One hand tangled in my hair, while the other caressed my breast. He moaned as I pumped him harder and harder, until he reached his peak.

We collapsed onto the floor, breathing heavily. Lucas conjured a towel to clean up with, then a blanket to cover us both. My pulse finally began to slow as I curled into him. I rested my head on his chest, enjoying the sound of his breath and his heartbeat against my ear. He wrapped his arms around me, sighing heavily. Even on this cold winter night, Lucas was so warm, and his skin was soft against mine. I never wanted to draw away from him. I stared at his arm, tracing his veins with my finger and replaying everything that had just happened in my mind. Goddess, it was glorious.

"This is perfect," Lucas said breathlessly.

I pressed my naked body even closer to his. "It is."

He stroked my shoulder with his thumb. "Nad, if we're going to get back together, we need to agree on a few things."

"Anything," I said.

Lucas stalled with a long breath. "I need you to understand that even though I'm doing better, I'm still struggling with depression. Some days, it hits me worse than others. I don't want us to run away again when things get hard. If we do this, I'm in it for good. That means that you need to be okay with me being sad… and I need to be okay with *you* being sad some-times, too."

I drew away to look him in the eyes. "That's fair. We're both sick in different ways, but we're going to be here for each other. We'll have to trade off."

Lucas smirked. "I get Mondays and Wednesdays. You can be sick the rest of the week."

I sucked a breath between my teeth, trying not to laugh. "Ooh, that's not going to work for me. I need Wednesdays, but you can have Thursdays."

Lucas laughed, then pressed a kiss to the top of my head. "Thursdays it is."

We fell silent for a beat before I asked, "Can I make a request?"

"Of course," he replied gently.

I paused, because I wasn't sure exactly how to word it. Finally, I said, "I want to be able to rely on you for anything, but I don't think either of us can rely on each other for how we feel."

"You're right, Nad. I can't expect you to make me feel a certain way." Lucas squeezed me tighter to his chest. "I feel amazing when I'm with you, but that's not your responsibility—it's my choice. All we can really do for each other is to support each other."

"And I will," I promised. "I'll support you in anything."

"And I need to do the same. I need to support you in breaking the Reaper's Shadow curse, if that's what you want."

I furrowed my brow. "But you've always been so against me even trying. You said it was too dangerous."

"That's my problem, not yours," he said. "I just wanted to protect you, but holding you back isn't going to do you any good. I have to trust you with this. You're powerful, and I have to be okay with that."

"You think we can learn how to break it?" I asked.

"The least we can do is try," he replied. "I don't want you to have to sacrifice a thing for me. If we're going to get back together, I want you to have it all. Hell, *I* want it all—marriage, kids, all of it, even if that scares me."

I placed my hand on the side of his face. "It scares me, too, but with you by my side, I feel like I can do anything. You have no idea how much it means to have your support."

Lucas hugged me closer to his chest. "Always, Nad."

I glanced at the candle to see that it had completely burned out. I snuggled closer to Lucas, and euphoria settled in my chest. Somehow, Lucas and I had managed to steal this perfect moment. We'd never stop stealing them. Even though everything else had gone wrong lately, *this* was right.

We were together again, and nothing could ever break us apart.

After that night at the abandoned mansion, everything changed. I walked Nadine to class every day, and kept her company during dialysis. Weeks passed, and it seemed that life couldn't get any better.

We'd been researching the Reaper's Shadow curse, but we wanted to get everything right before we tried breaking the curse. I was still gathering information. Our friends were thrilled to see us back together, and I didn't think we'd ever been happier. Nadine gifted me a hand-made blanket for my birthday, and I wrote her a poem once a week and slid it under her door.

But life couldn't stay perfect for long. Finals week was quickly approaching, and Octavia Falls looked different than ever before. Ever since the hanging, people had divided even further. The cafeteria seemed to be split by invisible lines that appeared out of nowhere. Nobody sat in groups outside of their Cast. My friends and I hadn't hung out in public in weeks, because people stared and whispered every time we did, like we were to blame for what was happening. We'd all started getting takeout and hanging out in Nadine and Talia's room during our lunch hour.

Thanks to my new Journalism professor—who'd replaced Professor Daniels—I was now failing Journalism Ethics. He had a serious prejudice against anyone who wasn't a Seer, and he definitely didn't like anyone from Mortana.

I was passing through the Main Foyer after Protection Magic when I spotted my friends gathered in a corner. Oliver followed at my heels. Grant caught my eye and waved me over. He stood beside Talia, who was fidgeting. She bit her lower lip and glanced around. Mandy and Amy whispered lowly to one another. Miles stood with his arms crossed, glaring across the foyer like he was ready to start a fight with anyone who approached. Tate sat in one of the chairs, studying an open newspaper. She seemed so hyper-focused on it that she didn't even look up when I approached.

"What's up?" I asked.

"Where's Nadine?" Talia questioned immediately.

"Not with me. Last I saw her, she was headed back to her dorm room," I said. "We were going to meet up in the library to study for Wand Theory, but to be honest, it sounded like she was having a hard day. Is everything okay?"

"Nadine should be fine," Talia said. "We should let her rest. We can tell her later."

"Tell her what?" I asked.

Talia shot Grant a worried look, then gazed back down to her hands. "Something happened during my Seer exam."

"What kind of something?" I asked carefully.

"The Miriamic Police Department was there when I got there," Talia explained. "My professor said they were helping monitor the exam. They must've thought people were cheating, because in the middle of the exam, they stopped us and started searching people's stashes."

"They *what*?" I demanded.

Talia's voice shook. "They lined us up against the wall and did some sort of spell. I've never seen it before. I didn't even know such a thing existed."

"A *spell*?" I gaped. "They *forced* a search on your stash?"

Talia nodded. "Everything just came spilling out. I couldn't stop it."

"That's a huge violation of privacy!" I growled.

"They're the police," she said. "They have the right."

"Nothing about this is *right*," Grant said with a frown.

"Who's going to stop them?" Talia challenged. "It's not like any of us know a counter-spell."

Miles's features hardened as he listened. He turned toward Tate. "Did you find anything yet?"

Tate chewed on her cheek as her eyes darted across the newspaper. It was like she was in a totally different world. She hadn't heard him.

Mandy leaned over and snapped her fingers in front of Tate's face. "Earth to Tate! What'd you find?"

Tate snapped out of it and shook her head. "Sorry, I was in the zone. I can't find anything that would explain why they're doing this. There are no notices, no mandates, nothing."

"Shouldn't they have to tell us the police are coming in for our exams?" Amy asked. "I mean, how many of us are going to pass if we're nervous the police are watching?"

I pressed my lips together. "What are they scared of? The Imperium wouldn't be ordering the police to attend our exams if they weren't looking for something."

"Please. We already know they're frightened about the Waning," Mandy pointed out. "Everyone is."

"Why target students?" I asked.

"Why not?" Grant scoffed. "They already put a curfew on us."

"There isn't a single student strong enough to cause the Waning," I said.

"What about a group of them?" Miles asked. "If someone's caught cheating, could that make them a suspect in the Waning? It means they're willing to turn to forbidden magic."

"Or maybe it's not about the students," Amy added. "Maybe they're watching our professors."

"Then why target *us*?" Talia asked.

Grant narrowed his eyes. "Maybe they want to see how the professors react."

Mandy chewed on the end of her fingernail. "You think they're trying to see who will comply and who will fight against them?"

Grant shrugged. "Maybe."

"Or maybe they're trying to scare the coven," I thought aloud. "If you wanted to exercise your power and show off a new spell like this, where would you start?"

"With the students," Talia said, sounding disgusted. "We're still learning our magic, so we won't be able to fight against their spell. And they *know* we're going to be pissed about it. We're going to take this home to our parents, and *everyone's* going to hear about it."

"It's a publicity stunt," Tate sneered. "Those bastards are—"

Tate cut off, and my friends' eyes all went wide. I turned around to see four police officers step into the Main Foyer. I recognized Officer Baker, one of the assholes who'd arrested Professor Daniels. He was partially responsible for her death. I half wished he would hang for it himself.

My hands curled into fists, and my nostrils flared. Talia grabbed my wrist and tugged on my arm. "Don't do it, Lucas. We don't need to draw any attention to ourselves."

Grant cleared his throat. "I think we already have."

The four police officers had spotted us and were making their way toward us.

"Act natural," Miles said under his breath.

But the whole foyer had gone silent. All eyes watched as the officers approached us. Their heavy footsteps sounded like ominous drumbeats.

"Can we help you, officers?" I asked when they stopped in front of us.

Officer Baker narrowed his eyes at us. "Mind telling us what's going on here?"

"A study session," I stated flatly.

"It's a bit unusual for so many different Casts to study together, isn't it?" he sneered.

"Not really," I replied, but my tone was less than friendly.

Officer Baker narrowed his eyes. "Are you back talking me, kid?"

I shook my head, but I already wanted to throw a battle orb in this guy's face. "No, sir."

"I don't like your sass, and I certainly don't like seeing all these different Casts *studying* together. Something's not right," Baker sneered.

I glanced between the officers and noticed various tattoos. "But sir… you and your colleagues are all different Casts."

"That's it!" Officer Baker grabbed me and yanked my arm behind my back. I gasped as pain shot through my shoulder, and my friends jumped back in shock. Officer Baker shoved me against the wall, and Oliver hissed. "I'm sick of your attitude. Search him!"

"I didn't do anything!" I shouted. He drove his elbow into my back, pinning me to the wall. My friends stared in shock. Out of the corner of my eye, I saw the other officers twist their hands in a complicated manner. Their spell hit me like a punch to the gut. The air knocked out of my lungs, and belongings began to spill out of my stash, falling into a heap from out of nowhere.

Panic swept through me. I had nothing incriminating on me—a jacket, blanket, my wallet, textbooks, my journal, and some other odd items—but this was a gross overreaction, and it had happened so fast. I couldn't wrap my head around what was happening. What if they had targeted me? What if they were planning to plant something in my things?

I was *pissed*. This was far worse than when Professor Ward had forced me to conjure my belongings in class. That was ridiculous and uncalled for, but *this*? This was dehumanizing. A warlock's stash was his one piece of privacy that no one else could ever touch... or so we thought.

There was nothing I could do to stop this. Even when I pulled back, I couldn't overpower their spell.

"Look what I found," one of the officers said, like he'd just hit the jackpot.

"What are you—?" I turned my head as far as I could, but Officer Baker still had me pinned to the wall. I saw the other officer lift my poetry journal. My stomach dropped as he opened the leather-bound book and began flipping through the pages so fast that they tore.

"That looks like a spellbook," Officer Baker growled. "Someone's been writing incantations between classes."

"So what if I was?" I spat. "We're encouraged to write our own incantations."

"Not if those spells are designed to hurt somebody," Officer Baker said, as if accusing me of something.

"They're not incantations," I insisted honestly. "It's just poetry."

Officer Baker scoffed. "*Poetry*."

"I swear—" I started, but I cut off when I heard the sickening sound of tearing paper. The officer flipping through my book had been careless. He tore a page out completely, and my heart lurched.

"Please don't," I begged. My poems had helped me so much through my depression. They helped me make sense of my feelings—make sense of the *world*. I couldn't imagine something so intimate being taken from me.

"*We'll* be the judge of the incantations you've been writing," Officer Baker sneered.

My blood boiled when the other officer subconjured my poetry book. It vanished from sight, and all I wanted to do was punch these fuckers in the face. Fighting back was a good way to earn myself a criminal record, though.

"How many times has the Waning hit you?" Officer Baker demanded.

"I don't know," I spat. "A few?"

He scoffed. "Like I thought. You're a weak warlock."

"How do you figure?" I asked.

"The weakest in the coven lose their magic first," Baker shot back.

"Yeah? When'd you lose yours?" I questioned.

He dug his elbow into my back harder, making me wince. "All the students here are weak. No wonder the Waning is hitting the school the hardest."

"Well, we *are* still learning. You figure that one out on your own?"

"I don't like your attitude," he growled. "I suggest you shut your mouth before I book you. I've already got your spellbook. You want to spend the night in jail with it?"

I had a million comebacks on my tongue, but I kept my mouth shut and gritted my teeth. I knew this asshole wasn't messing around. Hell, he was probably the officer who'd booked Miles for missing curfew.

Officer Baker laughed lightly. "That wasn't so hard, was it? You best learn how to comply, son, or you'll be hanging from the gallows next."

He shoved me one last time, and I fell to the floor. He walked off with the other officers, heads held high as they breezed past onlookers and headed out of the school. I turned around, my knees shaking. The Main Foyer was so silent, not even a cat meowed. Everyone stood frozen, and my friends stared at me in shock. Oliver was the first to move, rubbing against my leg like he was sorry about what just happened.

Whispers began to spread around the room, and people started moving again. I shook in rage.

"What the hell was that?" Miles asked.

"It was a demonstration," I growled. "Just like the one they put on during Talia's exam."

I knelt down and began subconjuring my belongings. Talia rushed over and helped me organize my things.

"It'll be okay," she said kindly. "You can write more poems."

I frowned. "I don't remember them all, though. I'll never get those ones back."

Her eyes glistened. "Lucas, I'm so sorry. If I lost my songs…"

I shrugged, though it bothered the fuck out of me. I just wouldn't admit it. "They're just poems."

I noticed my poetry book wasn't the only thing missing. They'd also swiped my Journalism Ethics notebook, which had all my notes for the semester in it. Assholes.

"What does he mean about people being weak?" Grant wondered.

I picked up a stack of textbooks. "It means their prejudice runs deeper than Cast lines. Still think this is about our professors?"

Grant looked shaky on his feet, and he grabbed the arm of a chair to steady himself. "The cops, the council… they're trying to show us who's in control."

I eyed him. He didn't look so well. "Grant, you should sit down. When's the last time you ate?"

"I-I don't know," he admitted.

Miles groaned. "Grant, you know better than that. Come here."

Mandy jumped up from one of the chairs so Grant could sit. Miles grabbed his brother's shoulders and guided him into the seat. He conjured a candy bar and handed it to Grant. "Eat. I can tell when your blood sugar is dropping."

Grant took a bite. "I've been anxious all day. I forgot."

"Well, the cops left, so I doubt they'll be searching anyone else's stash today," Talia offered.

Grant shook his head. "It's not that, though this doesn't help."

I finished cleaning up my stuff and stood. "What else has you on edge?"

Grant shot a glance around the Main Foyer, but everyone else had returned to their own conversations. He lowered his voice anyway. "It's the nightshade. Amy and I are *so* close to cracking the recipe. We expect it to be ready today. It needs just a few more tweaks, and we should have some answers."

My heart jumped. We'd been waiting so long for this.

Amy glanced at the big clock that hung next to the stairs. "It actually might be ready by now."

"Let's check it out," I said immediately. I needed something to distract me from what had just happened.

Amy glanced around the foyer, then lowered her voice. "Meet us in my dorm in five minutes. We'll go separately, so we don't draw any more attention than we already have."

I nodded. By the time I finished organizing my stuff, my friends had dispersed. Miles and Tate had gone in a different direction. It'd look too suspicious if we all went to Amy's room. No one was watching me, but I kept throwing glances over my shoulder as I headed to Amy and Mandy's room. I knocked lightly, and the door swung open. I quickly slipped inside, and Mandy gestured me over to where Grant and Amy were working. Talia watched on with intrigue.

I hadn't seen their setup yet, but it was impressive. Amy's desk had been entirely taken over by cauldrons and vials of various sizes, with different colors of liquid inside. I assumed they were all filled with night-shade at different stages of the breakdown process. Grant organized the vials like he knew his way around with ease. It was safer to keep the supplies with Amy, considering the run-ins I'd had with the druggies.

Amy stirred a cauldron, and Grant poured a clear liquid into the smallest cauldron. It turned to a deep shade of purple. The two shared the same bright look.

"What is it?" I asked. "You learned something."

Amy turned to me, beaming. "We just confirmed the final ingredient—the one thing we've been missing all this time!"

My pulse quickened. Finally, we were getting somewhere.

"What does it mean?" Talia asked. "What's the ingredient?"

Grant pointed to an open book on the desk. "The potion indicates that nightshade contains high levels of a magical plant called *tortus vitis*—also known as *twisted vine*. The plant is used in potions to help improve focus and concentration. It was supposedly really effective, but Alchemists stopped using it years ago due to its side effects."

"What kind of side effects?" I asked.

"Irritability, mostly," Grant said. "But it had killer withdrawal symp-toms, too."

"That explains the nightshade symptoms we've heard about," I pointed out. "This is good news, right?"

"It's a step in the right direction," Amy said, but her features turned worried. "But we don't know much more about twisted vine. That's all our textbook tells us, and we don't use it in any of our classes."

"Which *is* good news," Grant added. "Because it's rare."

"How is that good news?" Talia asked. "Won't it make it harder to find?"

I thought about it for a moment. "It might, but this also narrows things down for us a *lot*. Once we know where this twisted vine grows, we can find out where the dealers are getting it. We're one step closer to exposing Magnus."

"Exactly," Grant agreed. "But I'm not even sure what environment it grows in."

I pressed my lips together. "It sounds like we might have to pay a visit to Professor Lewis."

Amy glanced between Grant and me. "You two should go. Professor Lewis doesn't like me ever since I spilled a potion in my Alchemy 101 lab and lit one of the tables on fire."

"We'll see what we can find out," I said.

Grant and I left the room. We caught Professor Lewis just as she was leaving her office.

"Professor Lewis!" I called.

She turned to us. "Lucas? Grant? What can I help you with?"

Grant and I weren't in the same class, but we both had her this semester.

"We're trying to settle a debate," Grant lied.

She looked intrigued. "Oh? A debate about what?"

I played along. "We ran across this plant in one of our textbooks —*tortus vitis*."

"Twisted vine?" Professor Lewis said thoughtfully. "It's quite rare, and the school hasn't been able to get its hand on samples for years. We stopped studying it over a decade ago. What questions do you have about it?"

"We're wondering where it grows," Grant said. "See, I'm convinced it grows like grape vines—in full sun with lots of heat, whereas Lucas is *convinced* it's a swamp plant."

She shook her head. "It's neither, I'm afraid. The conditions needed to grow *tortus vitis* are precise. It's why the plant is so rare. It requires a dark, damp environment. Even the slightest bit of sunlight will cause the plant to die."

"No sunlight?" I wondered aloud. "That's strange."

"Well, aren't all magical plants?" Professor Lewis pointed out. "If you look into the history of *tortus vitis* deep enough, you'll know that it was first discovered in a cave. But there are few caves that can grow it properly. If the cave is too far underground, the plant won't grow. And if you're too close to the surface where sunlight touches the leaves, it will suffer."

I furrowed my brow. We didn't have much for caves in this area. All our caves were more like crevices in the rock. The sunlight would surely touch anything inside. Where could the dealers be growing this?

Unless they weren't growing it themselves... they could be trading it with other supernatural races, just like they were doing with the unicorn hair.

"So if someone wanted to grow it, they'd have to find the perfect cave?" Grant questioned.

"Oh, no," Professor Lewis said. "It was *discovered* in a cave, but it can grow in similar environments."

"Like a basement?" I asked.

"Yes and no," she explained. "Most modern basements are too dry to grow the vine. It requires a damp environment. Think more like... a dungeon."

Grant and I shared a wide-eyed gaze.

"Of course, there's nothing like that in Octavia Falls," Professor Lewis added quickly. "But this was all hypothetical, wasn't it?"

I quickly cleared my throat. "Yes, of course."

"Very well," she said, like she was happy to help. "Perhaps you can move on from hypotheticals and study for your finals."

Grant straightened his spine. "I'm studying hard. I promise."

"I'll see you both in class," she said, before striding off down the hall.

I turned to Grant the second she disappeared from view. "The Dungeon."

His eyes went wide. "Do you think she knows about the club?"

"I don't know," I admitted. "But either way, that club would be the perfect place to grow twisted vine. I mean, it's in the basement of the school, so no sunlight, and the entrance changes all the time, so anyone searching for it without an invite couldn't find it."

"But Professor Lewis said the plant grows in damp places," Grant pointed out. "I don't remember The Dungeon being damp."

"How do we know that club is all there is to it?" I asked. "There could be other rooms down there that we didn't see the last time. Goddess, I can't believe we didn't think of this before. Think of the people who frequent that place. They're the *perfect* kids to rope into buying or dealing drugs."

Grant bit his lower lip.

"You know something?" I asked.

He shook his head. "Not exactly. But I remember *seeing* drugs down there when we went last semester. I didn't realize they were nightshade at the time."

I felt the blood drain from my face. I recalled seeing Gregory surrounded by a group of girls, who were dropping liquid under their tongue. I thought it was just some potion that would help them loosen up. I didn't think it was a hard drug like nightshade.

"We need to get back in there," I pressed. "Whether twisted vine is being grown there or not, someone down there knows something."

"I agree, but how are we going to get in?" Grant asked. "No one's going to extend an invite, and we'll be kicked out the second we walk in. All the druggies know not to mess with us."

"Mandy got her hands on nightshade for us. Maybe she can get us some tickets," I suggested. "As for being recognized, we're going to need disguises."

Grant looked thoughtful. "I might have an idea, but it's going to be tricky to get my hands on ingredients, and it will take over a week to brew."

"Then let's get started on it right away," I said. "We have until the end of finals week to get into The Dungeon before school shuts down for break. We need to get answers before then."

"Agreed," Grant said.

We returned to Amy's dorm to share what we learned. Mandy promised she'd get us tickets to The Dungeon, and Talia agreed to help Grant gather ingredients for his brew.

After I left my friends, I paced the halls nervously, not really sure where I was going. Nadine had heard from Talia that I was busy hunting down answers on nightshade and left for dialysis without me. That left me too much time to think. I wanted answers, but I knew we wouldn't find anything until we got into the club undetected.

Instead, I focused on what I felt I could control—hunting down answers about the Reaper's Shadow curse. Nadine and I had looked into it before and never found anything, but I was determined to learn how to break it now more than ever. I'd been researching for weeks, but I'd hit a dead end. It was time to finally ask for help.

I headed to Professor Warren's office. He was hunched over his desk grading papers when I arrived. His features brightened when he saw me in the doorway. "Lucas. To what do I owe the pleasure?"

"I have some questions, if you have some time," I said.

He gestured to the seat across from him. "Sure. Come on in."

I closed the door and sat. Oliver prowled around the room, eyeing the collection of animal skeletons on Professor Warren's shelves. "Before you shut me down, please hear me out. It's about the Reaper's Shadow curse."

Professor Warren leaned back in his chair, looking thoughtful. "I was wondering when you'd come to me about this."

I furrowed my brow. "What do you mean?"

"Given that your girlfriend is a Curse Breaker, I assume you believe there's a chance to break the curse."

I frowned. "Of course you heard."

"Given the current political climate, intercast relationships are high profile right now," he pointed out.

I crossed my arms. "That's bullshit."

"I didn't say it was okay," he replied. "I disagree with the division of the Casts as well. People are scared, and they'll go through extreme measures to mitigate their fear."

His gaze bore into me, and I sensed he meant more than he was saying.

"You think I'm coming to you about the Reaper's Shadow because I'm scared?" I questioned.

He shrugged. "Are you?"

I pondered it for a moment. "No, not really."

"Then why do you wish to break the curse?" he asked curiously.

"It's not about fear… it's about love," I admitted. "I love Nadine, and she wants to be with me. I can't avoid her when I feel this way about her, but I can't let her live with the threat of this curse hanging over her, either. The only way to save her is to let her break this curse."

He nodded along, like he understood. "The curse begins at marriage and physical intimacy. Why do you think those are parts of the curse?"

"I'm not sure, exactly."

"Okay. Why do you want to get physical with your girlfriend?"

My stomach twisted. I was mortified we were having this conversation, but I needed Professor Warren's help, so I had to be honest with him. "It's not something I can put into words. It's something I just *feel*. It's not about sex or a wedding. It's about how I can show her how much I love her. It sounds shallow, I know. I can't explain it. It's like… that time together is ours. The experience is *just ours*. I don't get to share that with anyone else—just her. And getting married, it's so much more than a piece of paper. Nadine's disabled, and I love her so much that I want to provide for her when she can't help herself. Everything the curse targets —sex, marriage, kids—it's a deep soul contract that I never get to fulfill as long as this curse stands."

Professor Warren smiled. "There you go, Lucas," he said proudly. "That's your answer. *That's* why intimacy is part of the curse. The man who cast it was jealous of his parents' affection toward one another. This curse isn't specifically about the act of sex. It's about what it represents— the love, trust, and vulnerability that manifests in physical form, which was something your curse caster could never have."

I felt all the blood in my body drain to my toes. "Physical intimacy? So I could've already cursed her."

"Hold on, let's back up," Professor Warren said quickly. "That's not what I said."

"But if it's true, then I…" I trailed off. Nadine and I were no strangers to physical intimacy, but we thought there was a strict line. If what Professor Warren said was true, then I'd already cursed her.

Fuck. Nadine's kidney disease!

I stood from the chair and began pacing around the room. "Goddess, I've made Nadine sick. Her kidneys are failing, and I-I-I…"

"Lucas, sit down," Professor Warren insisted, but I barely heard him.

I clutched my chest, sure I was on the verge of hyperventilating. Oliver spun around at my feet, meowing in worry. "No, no, no, no… why would you—?"

"Lucas, let's talk about this." Professor Warren rose from his chair, but he sounded frantic, like his mind was racing a million miles per hour trying to fix this. "You shouldn't be ashamed of anything."

"I'm not ashamed!" I cried. "But I'm sure as hell scared! I thought there were pretty damn clear lines."

"What lines, exactly?" Professor Warren asked. "Virginity is a social construct. Many would argue where the line is drawn."

"I THOUGHT THERE WERE LOOPHOLES!" I trembled as I screamed. Goddess, what had I done?

"Lucas, please," Professor Warren pleaded. "There's no judgement here."

"*I'm* judging myself!"

He reached for me and guided me back to my seat. "I think we can use this to our advantage."

I clutched the armrest of the chair. "How?"

He returned to his seat. "Curse Breakers work by drawing the magic from a curse and reworking it, right?"

I nodded.

"So, if Nadine's already cursed, maybe she can pull the magic out of herself." He spoke quickly, like he was grasping at straws. He obviously hadn't known where this conversation was headed when he started asking questions.

I drew a deep breath and started to calm down. "She's broken a curse on herself before, but…"

But she and Chloe had to work together to break it. Nadine wouldn't be the first Reaper's Shadow in history. What about those other women?

"If she can break the curse on herself—"

I stood abruptly, cutting him off. "Thanks for your help, but I need to talk to Nadine."

I fled from the room. I couldn't wait to talk to her, so I hurried to the hospital. Her jaw dropped when I entered the dialysis room. There was a chair next to her machine for visitors, but I couldn't sit.

"Lucas, what's wrong?" she asked.

I paced back and forth. Oliver and Isa both watched me. "I wish I could put it into words, but I…"

I caved and sat in the chair next to her. The coven's dialysis center was small, with only three machines since it was all our town needed. No one else was around, but I lowered my voice anyway.

"I just spoke with Professor Warren about the Reaper's Shadow," I blurted. "I-I didn't realize what it—Nadine, I'm so sorry."

She tilted her head. "What do you mean? Sorry about what?"

I drew a deep breath to calm myself. "Professor Warren said the curse isn't specifically about sex, marriage, and kids. He seems to think it's about the physical manifestation of intimacy—about what it all represents."

Nadine looked thoughtful. "You know, I've never been able to put into words *why* I'm so desperate to be with you in those ways, but I like the way you just put it—*the physical manifestation of intimacy.*"

"Nad, you don't get what I'm saying," I pressed. "If the curse is about the abstract, about what it all represents, then maybe we've already crossed the line."

Her features fell, and she glanced at her dialysis machine. "No. You don't think…?"

"Nad, I'm so sorry." My voice broke. "I think I already cursed you."

"No," Nadine stated firmly. She grabbed my hand and squeezed it tightly. "No, Lucas. You can't blame yourself."

"If this is about how much I love you, then it's already done," I argued. "You've been cursed. You're sick because of me."

"Don't say that," she insisted. "I was sick long before you and I ever met. I'm hooked to this machine because my lupus has been out of control for over a year. My magic made it even worse. I was going to end up here one way or another."

She didn't deny that she'd been cursed, and there wasn't any way to know for sure.

"I'm going to get better," she promised. "The dialysis is already helping, and once I get a transplant, there's a good chance I'll go into remission for good. Whether I'm cursed or not, I can still break the curse. I'm strong enough to do this."

I relaxed a little, but I was still worried to death. "You're right."

Just then, my phone started ringing. My heart leapt when I saw the number on the screen.

Nadine paled. "Is that—?"

"Dr. Tracey," I finished for her. I punched the screen to answer, then stood and began pacing around the room. My stomach twisted into knots. "Hello?"

"Hello, Lucas Taylor?" Dr. Tracey asked.

"Yes, it's me. You have my test results?"

"I do, but I'm afraid it's not good news."

My ears started to ring, and I turned my back to Nadine. The rest of the world seemed to fade to black as I listened to Dr. Tracey. The phone shook in my hand, and my knees trembled. I could barely respond when she asked if I was still there. Her voice was static, and so far away.

"Yes. Um, thank you for calling," I said flatly.

She started to reassure me, but I couldn't process it. I hung up and slowly turned back to Nadine. Her wide eyes met mine, and her face had gone pale.

"You're not a match," she guessed.

I swallowed the massive lump in my throat and grabbed for the chair beside her before I collapsed into it. "I am," I replied breathlessly.

She gasped. "You're a match? So, I'm getting your kidney?"

Goddess, she sounded so excited. It killed me to be the one to tell her. Tears pricked in my eyes, and my bottom lip trembled.

She blinked a few times, her eyes turning red. "I'm… *not* getting your kidney?"

"Nad, I'm so sorry," I said through shallow breaths. "I'm a match, but they won't do the surgery. I… I didn't pass the psychological exam."

"What!?" Nadine cried. She threw a trembling hand over her mouth. "How could they deny you?"

"I don't know," I said desperately. "They know I'm being treated for depression. Dr. Mack's not recommending me. The doctors must think I won't be able to handle giving up my kidney."

"What are they afraid of!?" she demanded. "You're not suicidal!"

"It's bullshit," I agreed. "I'll fix this, Nad. I'll redo the interview. I'll convince my therapist. If we have to, we'll leave Octavia Falls and find someone else to do the transplant."

"How long will that take, though? Lucas, do you know how long the transplant list is? It could take me *years* to get a kidney."

Tears welled in her eyes, and guilt racked my entire body. Nadine wasn't getting a kidney, and it was my fault.

I couldn't accept this.

"You don't need that list," I insisted. "You're going to get mine. I'm a match."

"That doesn't matter if the doctors won't help," she said.

Shit. *One* of us had to be strong right now, and I didn't expect it to be her. I leaned over and wrapped my arm around her. Nadine curled into me, and her tears soaked into my shirt. Seeing her break down like that was enough to crush my spirit. I felt myself begin to unravel, and there was nothing I could do but hold her.

I had to do more. I had to save her. There was no other option.

I gently stroked her arm. "We're going to do whatever it takes. One way or another, I'm giving you my kidney. I promise."

Goddess, I hoped I didn't just tell the biggest lie of my life.

EIGHTEEN

To say I was devastated was an understatement. I had been holding on to the hope that Lucas and I were a match. The joy and hope that swelled in my heart when I heard we were was unlike anything I'd felt before. It only made the following disappointment worse—such polarizing emotions that nearly tore me to pieces. I couldn't believe the doctors would do this. It was obvious Lucas was really torn up about it, but it wasn't his fault.

I didn't really know what to do with myself, because I couldn't think straight the rest of the week, and it wasn't lupus fog like normal. This was a pure broken heart.

My magic wasn't working quite right, either. At first, I thought it was because of how I felt, but when I failed to conjure my meds, I realized it was the Waning. I freaked. I'd been subconjuring my medication ever since Lena had poisoned me last semester by planting fake pills in my room. I called Dr. Yonker immediately, and he ordered an emergency prescription to cover me until my magic returned.

I tried talking to him about the transplant, but he told me there was nothing he could do. I was just going to have to wait for another kidney.

It terrified me.

Lucas kept me company when he could, to take my mind off things. He surprised me with a date jar for my birthday. It was filled with endless date ideas that he'd folded into the shape of hearts, so that I could pick a date whenever I wanted. I loved it.

Finals week arrived, and my first exam was Wand Theory. The promise of sitting next to Lucas through the test was the only thing that made me want to go. His knee brushed against mine the whole way through the written text, which was enough to relax me enough that I was pretty sure I passed with a decent grade.

After the written part of the exam, we were called into Professor Blackbird's office individually, to demonstrate our practical use of Wand Theory. It was a simple test, and all I had to do was cast three different spells using my wand. I performed a cleansing spell, a locking spell on his door, and a glowing enchantment on a paperweight that sat on his desk. It glowed for a solid minute before fading back to normal.

He frowned as he stared down at the paperweight. "Are you experiencing the Waning, Miss Evers?"

I shook my head. "I was last week, but my magic is back now."

He sighed. "The Waning isn't making these final grades easy. I'm glad to hear your magic is doing well, but that last enchantment just saved your grade. I'm afraid your first two spells were elementary, though you've impressed me with the enchantment. You infused orb magic into the paperweight, correct?"

I nodded. "It's all I could think of."

He marked something down on a piece of paper. "It was a creative choice. You can expect to have your grade back by the end of the week. Take care."

That was all he said before he dismissed me.

"How'd it go?" Lucas asked when I stopped at our table. He was still waiting to take the practical portion of his exam, and he had another exam later that day.

I shrugged. "I'm pretty sure I passed."

"That's good," he replied. "I'm going to fail, thanks to the Waning. My magic's totally useless today."

"I think Professor Blackbird will be sympathetic," I said.

"I hope so," he replied. "I'll catch up with you at dinner?"

"That sounds great. I'll see you then."

I leaned over and gave him a kiss. Screw anyone who was watching.

They may not agree with intercast relationships, but half of their parents were from different Casts. It was hypocritical, at best.

I tried to study in my dorm, but I couldn't focus. Isa kept walking all over my books and shoving her butt in my face, so that didn't help, either.

To take my mind off it, I pulled out my craft supplies. Ever since I made Lucas a blanket for his birthday, I'd started really getting into it. It was really easy and therapeutic. All it took was two pieces of fleece and a pair of scissors. I cut the ends into strips and tied them together. I made a pink blanket for Talia, with cats on one side and flowers on the other. I left it on her bed, then took the others to the nursing home.

"Thank you so much for your donation," the receptionist told me. "Our residents will love these."

From the front desk, I could see several of the residents in the community room. Some played cards, and others watched TV.

"Would you mind if I stayed for a while?" I asked.

"No, not at all," the receptionist said kindly. I didn't think she knew who I was, because most people around here weren't that nice to me. "The residents would love to meet you."

I entered the community room. A nurse greeted me and asked who I was there to see. I told her I was there to keep the residents company. The nurse gestured to a lady in a wheelchair. "I'm sure Rose would love a visitor."

Rose was working on a puzzle. She looked a bit confused as she tried fitting one of the pieces into another. It didn't fit, but she was persistent and tried another piece. She didn't look up when she spoke. "You must be lost, my dear."

I smiled. "Not anymore. I found you."

Finally, she lifted her gaze, and a smile touched her lips. "I'm Rose."

"Nadine," I introduced.

Rose invited me to help her with her puzzle. The whole time, she told me stories about herself. Her husband was long gone, and her son didn't live in Octavia Falls anymore, ever since he left for grad school and got married. She used to visit her grandkids all the time, but she couldn't anymore with her health.

"My health isn't the best these days, either," I admitted.

"Oh, dear," she said, looking worried. "It's treatable, yes?"

"Yes. It's my kidneys," I told her. "I'm on dialysis, and that's really helping me feel better, but I'm on the transplant list, and—" I choked up a little and couldn't finish.

"My dear," Rose said kindly. She reached out and placed her hand on mine. "You'll get your transplant. Mother Miriam will make sure of it."

"But we have free will," I argued. "And the doctors are the ones who get to make this decision."

"Free will or not, Mother Miriam is always there to support you," Rose reminded me. "Have faith in her. She will not abandon you."

I relaxed a little after Rose said that. We finished our puzzle in under an hour.

Eventually, the nurses told me it was time for Rose's meds, so I left. I was feeling so much better after visiting the nursing home and vowed to visit again. Maybe I'd make it a point to swing by before dialysis once a week. After all, the best way to feel better when you were in a crappy mood was to help someone else.

The traffic back to school was insane. It was so congested that I came to a full stop on Main Street. Cars honked, and I craned my neck, trying to see what was going on.

I caught sight of a group of people crowded in front of Octavia Hall. The crowd was so thick that people stood on the street. They looked angry, shoving each other and shouting things. Lincoln, the poor guard stationed in front of Octavia Hall, tried to keep the crowd back, but he couldn't control them. The police hadn't arrived yet.

I had to do something, or Lincoln was going to get trampled. I shoved my car into park and jumped out. The car behind me blared their horn, but it wasn't like traffic was moving anytime soon.

Snow dusted the sidewalk. I pulled my cloak's hood up and hurried over to the crowd. I didn't recognize anyone in particular, but they all looked my age. Someone at the school must've organized this protest. I shoved my way past them. I got a few elbows in the side in return, but I managed to force my way to the front.

"What's going on here?" I asked Lincoln.

He had his hands up, creating a shield to keep the crowd away from the doors. "They just showed up!"

"We demand an audience with the Imperium Council!" someone shouted.

"We're losing more and more magic by the day!" another screamed. "The council needs to be doing more to stop this!"

"They're doing everything they can!" Lincoln boomed in a deep voice.

Glass shattered, and I flinched. Someone had thrown a battle orb into the window, and glass rained over the sidewalk.

Lincoln thrust his arms apart, spreading his shield so wide that it shoved people into one another. Several people stumbled and fell into a heap, close to where the window had been shattered. "I suggest you back up *right now*. The police are on their way."

These people were *pissed*, but something told me most of them were all experiencing the Waning right now. Otherwise, there'd be a lot more damage to Octavia Hall than a broken window.

A girl shoved me aside, until she was right up next to Lincoln's shield. She pounded on it with her fist, like it was a window. "The Imperium Council has a duty to hear us out!" she screamed.

My jaw dropped when I looked over to see it was Tate. "What are you doing here?"

She turned to me, but her features were hard. She looked like she wanted to punch someone in the face. "I'm sick of the Waning! We all are!" she seethed.

"You don't even have your magic yet," I pointed out.

"I'll have it soon enough," she countered. "That is, if the Waning doesn't steal it from me first. The Imperium Council is sitting back and doing *nothing*!"

"Tell me this protest isn't getting out of hand, Tate," I said. "The Imperium Council will see this as a threat—trying to break into their headquarters."

"Fuck off," she growled. "This is a peaceful protest. We have every right."

"Someone just broke a window!" I yelled. "Somebody could get hurt. Who organized this?"

Tate scoffed. "Like I'll tell you. You're one of them."

I gaped at her. Of course I expected Tate to be involved in something like this. I didn't blame her. We were all angry about what was happening in the coven. But I thought we were *friends*.

"Tate, I—"

"Don't," she snapped.

"I want to listen! Maybe I can help," I pressed. "I've been affected by the Waning, too. Believe me, the priestesses don't want this to happen."

"Then do something!" Tate shouted. She grabbed my hood and yanked it down. Around me, people gasped.

"It's her! One of the priestesses!" a girl shouted. The crowd looked ready to eat me alive.

"Priestess! Priestess Nadine!"

I turned to Lincoln, who was shouting my name. He cocked his head, as if inviting me past the shield. I quickly jumped toward him and passed through his shield like it was nothing but air. No one else could get past, though, as he'd opened it only for me.

I faced the crowd. "I am Priestess Nadine, and I'm here to listen—"

I cut off when someone grabbed me by the back of my cloak and yanked me backward. Suddenly, I was inside the building, being dragged by my collar. I stumbled backward but finally found my footing inside the main lobby. I turned around to see Priestess Lilian had been the one to pull me inside. The three other priestesses stared at me.

"*What* in the name of the Goddess is this?" Priestess Lilian barked.

"I don't know," I answered. "I was driving by and—"

"If anyone is to address these people, we do it together," Priestess Lilian demanded.

"I was just trying to help," I defended myself.

"And we will," Priestess Margaret said. "But these people are angry. They're not ready to listen. We are doing everything we can to get to the bottom of this."

"They don't know that!" I shouted. "For all they know, we're behind it."

"How *dare* you even suggest that!" Priestess Lilian gasped.

"I'm *not* suggesting it," I replied. "But like you said, these people are angry. Without answers, they'll come to their own conclusions. *I* know you're trying to stop this. *They* don't."

"What are you suggesting?" Priestess Charlotte asked. "That we divulge all our plans and secrets? If anyone learns of the Wands, it could compromise us finding them."

"I'm not saying we should tell them about the Wands," I said. "While we're looking for the Wands, we're also trying to figure out what's causing the Waning. The coven at least deserves to know what we're doing to help."

"A public relations campaign?" Priestess Lilian sneered, like she despised the idea.

"It may be the only thing to keep the coven from dividing further," I argued. "They've already divided themselves by Casts. People are losing their jobs over it, and families are being torn apart. Do you want it to be the Imperium Council against the coven next?"

I was met with stunned silence.

Stella stepped forward. "Priestess Nadine makes a good point. It may be time to address the coven formally."

Lilian glared down at me. Her voice was strained, like it was difficult to admit I was right. "We'll need some time to prepare a statement. It's nice to see you actually *contribute* to your position."

"You know why I'm not here full-time like the rest of you. I have class and dialysis."

I swore I caught Priestess Lilian roll her eyes, but I couldn't be sure. I'd had to tell the priestesses about my kidney disease, but I didn't understand how they felt about it until now. It was obvious Priestess Lilian didn't care. My illness was nothing more than a burden to her. Hell, *I* was a burden to this woman.

Priestess Margaret at least looked sympathetic. "Nadine's classes are crucial to her position on the council. She will continue to attend college with a full course load. Once she graduates, her schedule will be wide-open to assist the council full-time. I assume by then, she will have a new kidney and be off dialysis."

"Actually… I may not," I told them. "It could take years for me to reach the top of the transplant list."

"I thought you had a donor lined up," Priestess Stella said.

I shook my head. "He was only in the testing stage."

Stella frowned. "And he's not a match."

"He is," I countered. "But the doctors won't let him go through with it. Something about his psych evaluation. I don't have all the details."

Something hit me just then. "Could the Imperium Council persuade the doctors?" I asked. "I mean, we *are* the greatest governing power in the coven."

Priestess Margaret pursed her lips, looking doubtful. "None of us are medical professionals. Something like this should be left up to your doctors."

"But we *are* a match!" I argued. "Lucas is being treated for depression, but he's not on meds or anything. His treatment has nothing to do with the transplant. Please, you must have the power to convince them. This may be my only chance."

The priestesses all looked at one another, but I couldn't read their gazes. I held my breath.

Finally, Margaret turned to me. "Bring us a Wand, and we'll see what we can do."

All the blood in my body drained to my toes. I'd expect that kind of response from Lilian, but for the other priestesses to agree? It horrified me to my very core. They didn't care about me—only about what I could offer.

They had the power to convince my doctors to go ahead with the transplant. I *knew* it. But they chose to hold my kidney hostage in exchange for the Wands. Nausea rolled around in my gut. I didn't know how they could be so heartless.

"But I've helped you in other ways," I insisted. "I got you the information about the Crock of Death—"

"And we have yet to find it," Priestess Lilian snapped.

I solved Professor Daymond's murder, too, but you wouldn't listen! I wanted to yell.

But the priestesses weren't on my side, and I already knew that.

"Bring us a Wand, and we'll get you your kidney," Priestess Lilian said. "Otherwise, I suggest you prepare for the worst."

That's all she said before the priestesses turned and swept off, leaving me alone. They were manipulating me in the worst way possible. I was a fool to even request their help.

But it may be the only thing that could save me.

"THIS IS BULLSHIT," Lucas growled when I told him what the priestesses had said.

I sat on his bed, running my hands over the fleece blanket I'd made him. He paced around the room. The notebook he'd been studying when I arrived flopped around in his hand as he became enraged. Isa and Oliver watched him curiously.

"It *is* bullshit," I agreed. "But there's nothing I can do about it."

"They can't do this to one of their own priestesses," he protested.

I cocked an eyebrow. "They *are* doing it. The council runs on a majority rules system. I literally have no power unless the other priestesses agree with me."

Lucas stopped pacing. He set his notebook on the nightstand, then sat beside me. "Nad, I'm *so* sorry this is happening. There must be something we can do."

He draped an arm around me and pulled me close. I laid my head on his shoulder. My heart calmed at his touch.

"I think the only thing we *can* do is find one of the Wands and hand it over," I said, feeling the defeat sink in my belly. "Problem is, I don't trust the council with the Wands—not after what they did to Professor Daniels."

Lucas stroked my arm. "We'll think of something."

I sat up straighter, though my voice cracked. "I really don't think I'm in a place to come up with solutions right now. Right now, I just really want—"

I cut off when my eyes landed on his notebook. Slowly, I reached out to grab it so I could get a better look. At the top, he'd scrawled the words *Reaper's Shadow*. Below that was a long list of names and dates.

"I thought you were studying for finals," I remarked, my eyes scanning the page. "You've been researching the curse?"

Lucas nodded, and a proud smile twitched at the corners of his lips. "I figured out how to break it."

My jaw dropped, and I jumped to my feet. "Are you for real right now? You did?"

His smile grew so wide, he was beaming. "I did."

I squealed and threw my arms around him. We tumbled onto the bed together, and Lucas laughed as his arms came around me.

"You're really excited," he remarked.

I planted a kiss on his lips. "Of course I am. This is huge!"

His smile disappeared. "This could still be dangerous, Nad. Are you a hundred percent sure you want to do this?"

"Yes," I stated confidently. "I've been practicing my magic with Verla all semester. I know my limits. I want to try."

I climbed off Lucas and sat up. "How do we do it?"

He took the notebook from me. "When you broke your family curse, you and Chloe had to work *together* to break it, right?"

"Yes, but I'm wondering… if I'm already cursed, could I just break it on myself and be done with it?" I asked.

"If we don't break the curse completely, it will return," Lucas pointed out. "It wouldn't do anything but delay the consequences."

"That makes sense."

"For this to work, we need to gather together all the women who have ever become the Reaper's Shadow."

"They're all dead now, though," I said thoughtfully. "Are you suggesting we grave rob?"

"Sort of." He bit his lower lip, before quickly adding, "I'm pretty sure it will work without actually uncovering their bodies. Once we're in the cemetery, you should be able to sense the magic, right?"

"I would think so," I said. "So, you found all these women?"

Lucas flipped the page, where there were even more notes. "There actually weren't that many. I've been researching the coven's records, and I've been able to track the timeline from when the curse was cast until now."

"What'd you find?" I asked.

"We know the origin of the curse," he explained. "Roughly two hundred years ago, a guy named Samael Davis killed his mother."

I nodded. "I recall. He was the son of a Reaper's Apprentice. The event caused the curse to be cast."

"Right," Lucas said. "Samael fled the coven afterward and was presumed dead. His father, Jasper Davis, remarried. His second wife, Sarah Davis, was the first Reaper's Shadow."

I eyed his notes, but there was so much information to absorb. "What happened to her?"

"After they married, she lost her sister to a drowning accident," Lucas said. "Shortly after, she became very ill. The records don't say what she had—probably something they couldn't diagnose back then. I never found any mention of kids in their obituaries, but I did learn that she and Jasper died around the same time."

"So she never reached the final stage of the curse?" I said thoughtfully.

"No, and I don't think anyone even *knew* about the curse back then." Lucas flipped through his notes. "After Samael's father died, two other Reaper's Apprentices took wives and had children. The women both died at the hands of their firstborn. It wasn't until the second woman was killed that the coven drew the connection. The thing is, curses leave trace magic behind. The coven was able to go back and confirm that the murder caused this curse. They were able to work out the details based on the similarities between the cases. Every woman experienced trauma, illness, and death in conjunction with marriage, intimacy, and kids. Journal entries confirmed the dates."

"That's three women for sure," I said. "Were there more after the coven confirmed the curse?"

Lucas shook his head. "Four other Reaper's Apprentices followed, until I was handed the job. But by then, they all knew about the curse, and none of them ever married. I can't find a single mention of any woman in their lives in newspapers, photographs, or journal entries."

"That's it?" I asked, relief flooding through me. "We only have to find three graves?"

"I'd be looking for four," Lucas said. "We don't know if the magic touched Samael's mother when she died, but we should check her grave, just to be sure."

I got to my feet. "What are we waiting for? Let's go!"

Lucas grabbed my wrist. "We don't want to rush this."

"Well, I don't want to wait," I told him. "If it's true that I'm already cursed—"

"Then you can wait one more day," he offered. "I want to make sure you're ready to perform this magic. I'd feel a lot better about it if you had a good night's rest. Tell me honestly; how are you feeling right now?"

My shoulders sagged. "Wiped out. I'll feel better after my dialysis tomorrow."

Lucas took my hand. "Then we'll wait until then. What finals do you have tomorrow?"

"None," I said. "I have the day off."

Lucas smirked. "Consider your day booked, then."

"Lucas, I—"

"Please," he begged. "I know you're eager to get this over with, but I want to do this right."

I narrowed my eyes. "What do you have in mind?"

He smirked. "Would you be opposed to a surprise?"

"Yes." I laughed. "You know me better than to ask."

He chuckled. "I just need the night to come up with a plan, okay? We're going to do this, Nadine."

"One night," I told him, holding up a finger. "I'll agree to one night. But by tomorrow evening, we're breaking this curse."

Lucas took my face in his hands, then pulled me into a passionate kiss. "Tomorrow night, Nad. This curse doesn't stand a chance against you."

My heart lifted at his encouragement. I felt untouchable as I pulled him into another passionate kiss.

By the time I woke in my own bed the next morning, I felt fantastic. I'd slept really well, and I had this hope stirring in my chest. It seemed as if nothing could get me down. The priestesses may have refused to help me, but it didn't seem to matter right now. I was going to break the Reaper's Shadow curse tonight, and Lucas and I could finally be together with no restrictions.

The scent of pumpkin spice hit my nose, and I rolled over to see a plate of eggs and toast on my nightstand. Next to that sat a cup from the Cat-fé. I knew instantly that it was pumpkin spice cocoa—my favorite.

Talia stood at her dresser, applying makeup.

"What's this?" I asked her.

She turned, looking happy to see I was up. "It's breakfast in bed! Lucas stopped by. He said it's a *very special day* for you."

My heart melted at the gesture. "Aw, that's so sweet of him."

Talia picked up her mascara, but she kept her eyes on me and wiggled her eyebrows.

I bit into my toast, but I couldn't hide my smile. "So, he told you what we're up to?"

"That, and more," she smirked.

My jaw dropped. "He told you his surprise! Tell me."

She shook her head. "I can't, but trust me—you're going to love it. He said he'll be there to pick you up after his exam this morning. You have plenty of time for breakfast and a nice, long bath."

"You expect me to relax when I know there's a surprise coming?" I teased.

"You can try." She chuckled before turning back to her mirror.

I finished my breakfast and sat in bed for a while, sipping on my pumpkin spice cocoa. It was *so* good. Isa lay on my lap purring, which helped me relax.

When I finished my drink, I got up and went to the bathroom. I stopped in the doorway when I saw what was inside. Rose petals trailed from the door to the tub. A basket full of Epsom salts, bath bombs, lotion, and chocolate balanced on the edge of the bath. There was a mix of my two favorite scents—lavender and rose. Gingerly, I stepped into the bathroom, and my gaze locked on the mirror above the sink. Over a dozen sticky notes had been stuck to the mirror, all in Lucas's handwriting.

You're amazing.

You make me smile.

I love you.

My jaw dropped as I read over each one, my heart warming more and more with each word. "Lucas," I breathed. "You shouldn't have."

Except it felt *so good* that he had. For the first time, I could actually say I *loved* the surprise. I drew myself a hot bath and used the lavender Epsom salts Lucas had given me. Isa sat on the edge of the tub, batting at the water and splashing me in the face. I splashed her back, and she lost her balance and face-planted into the water. She squealed as she jumped out of the tub and ran behind the toilet, growling at me. I couldn't stop laughing.

Just as I finished getting dressed, a knock came at my door. I opened it to see Lucas standing there with Oliver at his heels. He pulled his hand from behind his back to reveal a single red rose.

"Lucas," I breathed as I reached for it. "You didn't have to do this."

He shrugged. "I wanted to."

I smiled, then gave him a peck on the lips. "This is all really nice."

He smirked. "I'm glad to see you're enjoying the surprise."

I wrinkled my nose. "Perhaps just a little."

"Good. There's more." He took my hand.

"More surprises?" I asked as we walked down the hall. Our cats followed close behind.

He eyed me with a playful expression. "You want me to stop surprising you?"

"Um… I'll allow surprises for one day only. Deal?"

He nodded firmly. "Deal."

Lucas took my keys and put a blindfold over my eyes as he drove me through town. I wasn't allowed to take it off until we came to a stop. It killed me not to steal a peek, but I had agreed to a surprise.

I was shocked when I opened my eyes and saw we were parked in the strip mall, in front of the spa. "Are you serious?" I squeaked.

He smiled brightly. "But you don't like surprises, right?"

"How are we going to afford this?"

"Don't worry about it," he said.

We spent the morning being pampered with a couple's massage. I didn't think I could relax any further, until Lucas took me to The Cozy Cat café, and we ordered delicious cherry pie infused with calming magic. He let me choose our afternoon activity, so we went to the movie theatre to see the latest mystery based on Sherlock Holmes. It was a matinee showing, and we were the only ones there, so we took free reign of yelling at the characters and throwing our popcorn at the screen.

After my dialysis, Lucas took me to a new place for dinner at one of the breweries in town. We shared a plate of sweet potato fries, which were *amazing*. The sun was starting to set by the time we left.

I held his hand on our way back to the car. "I had a really good time today."

"That was my goal," he said with a smile.

"It was all so thoughtful. I felt like I could forget everything and just enjoy myself with you," I said. "You may be warming me up to surprises."

He chuckled. "That's something I never thought I'd hear you say."

"I can be unpredictable," I teased as we turned a corner to a secluded street. "You're the one with a stick up your ass."

I poked him in the side, and he laughed.

"Oh, *I'm* predictable?" he challenged. He didn't give me a chance to respond before he scooped me up in his arms and started carrying me down the sidewalk.

I threw my arms around his neck, laughing. "What are you doing?"

"Being unpredictable." Lucas kicked open the back door to my car and tossed me onto the backseat. He climbed in behind me, and his lips connected with mine before I heard the door close. Isa and Oliver must've slipped in behind us, because I heard them jump into the front seat. I moaned as I leaned back, lying across the back seat. Lucas climbed on top of me, laying passionate kisses on my lips.

I ran my hands through his hair. "Very unpredictable."

He smirked. "You like that? There's more where that came from."

Lucas kissed me again, and our hands began roaming each other. Heat pooled deep in my belly as his fingers slid beneath my shirt. As his kisses trailed down my neck, I finally got a chance to breathe.

"Your day of pampering was a success," I told him breathlessly. "I'm feeling *very* good about tonight."

Lucas drew away, biting his lip. Goddess, when he looked down at me like that, I didn't want to wait to break the curse. I wanted him to take me right here, right now.

"Are we ready for this?" he asked.

I nodded. "I'm feeling really good. I can do this."

He ran his thumb over my cheek, staring down at me with a soft expression. "I know you can."

"Then let's do it," I told him.

Lucas and I drove to the cemetery. By now, the sun had set, and the stars twinkled above us. The cemetery gates were locked, but all it took was one simple spell to sneak inside. Snow covered the gravestones and crunched beneath my feet. The further we walked, the more my heart hammered.

"Are you okay?" Lucas asked, noticing the look on my face.

"I'm nervous," I admitted, twisting my hands beneath my cloak. "But not enough to stop me from going through with this."

Lucas stopped in front of me and grabbed me by the shoulders. "If at any point you want to stop, you don't have to do this."

"I know, but thank you." I drew a deep breath. "I'm ready. Where do we find these graves?"

Lucas pointed. "The west side of the cemetery is the oldest. I'll bet you anything we'll find them all there."

I can do this, I told myself. "Come on, then. We have a curse to break."

Lucas and I walked between the tombstones, but I didn't see any of the names he'd mentioned.

"Could we be wrong?" I wondered aloud. "Maybe their graves are gone. It's been over a hundred years. They could've been moved. How old is that mausoleum? What if they'd been placed to rest there?"

Lucas shook his head. "No, I checked. The coven records say they were all buried in the cemetery."

"This place is huge," I pointed out. "But we'll stay here all night if we have to—"

Isa meowed, and I turned to see her sitting in front of a nearby gravestone. It was so old that it was tilted and chipped. Lucas and I exchanged a glance, then hurried over to the grave. A light dusting of snow covered the name. My fingers trembled as I reached out and wiped the snow away. When I touched the gravestone, something dark twisted inside my belly. Hair rose on the back of my neck, and my knees buckled. I fell to the ground at the edge of her grave.

Marianne Davis.

A shiver ran down my spine. "This must be her… Samael's mother."

Lucas came to an abrupt halt beside me, and Oliver meowed. "It is," Lucas said, his voice sounding hollow.

I drew a wavered breath. "We found her. Goddess, she's waited so long for this."

"You don't think she could carry the curse with her to the afterlife?" Lucas asked.

I shook my head. "No, but I wouldn't want to wait two-hundred years for my remains to be laid to rest properly. There's something here… Marianne never got her closure. She's not at peace."

"How can you tell?" Lucas asked.

"I can feel the curse in her bones," I whispered. The magic was so strong and tragic that tears rose to my eyes just being near her.

"How can I help?" Lucas asked.

"I don't know if you can," I admitted. I dashed the tears from my cheeks. Isa gazed up at me with worry in her eyes, and I scratched her behind the ears to let her know that I was going to be okay. "Just be here for me, okay?"

Lucas nodded firmly. "I'm here for whatever you need."

I hesitated. I knew how to break a curse, but that didn't feel like enough. Marianne had been in love with the Reaper's Apprentice. Her son had been born from the darkness his father carried with him every day. She died because she'd been in love with a reaper.

I felt a deep connection to Marianne, though I couldn't explain it. It went deeper than my emotions, as if the curse brought us together magically. I shook the nerves from my body, then focused on her grave. Something about this didn't feel right.

"Do you have a candle?" I asked Lucas.

"Yeah, here." He conjured a candle and lighter and placed them in my hands.

I turned back to the grave and set the candle at the base of it. The moment I lit it, a cold breeze swept through the cemetery, blowing snow past our faces. Isa pressed closer to me, and I pulled my hood around my face. The wind died down, though the candle flame continued to flicker.

"Marianne," I said aloud. "I don't know if you can hear me, but I am *so sorry* about what happened to you. Nobody deserves that kind of ending, and I pray that you found your happiness in the afterlife. Even though you've passed on, it's not right to let this curse live in your bones. I will break this curse, and end this cycle that your son started, and I pray that it will provide you the closure that you didn't get when you were alive. Goddess bless you, Marianne."

I pressed my hand to her gravestone and closed my eyes. I sensed the darkness swirling in the earth beneath me—the curse that I had to break. It was frightening and intimidating, because I didn't even have to reach out with my magic to feel it. Lucas had been right. This curse was strong and insanely dangerous. But I had to do this—not just for me, but for all the other women who had come before me, and all the others who would come after.

I barely reached outward with my magic before the darkness of the curse slammed into me. My stomach clenched, and I gasped.

"Nadine!" Lucas reached for me.

I held a hand up to stop him. "I can do this."

Lucas gingerly took a step back. I could see the pain in his eyes, like he couldn't watch me do this but didn't want to leave.

"No matter what it looks like, you have to let me finish, okay?" I told him.

"O-okay," he stammered.

"Promise me?"

Lucas hesitated, but I held his gaze. "I promise," he told me.

I knew his promise was genuine. I turned back to Marianne's grave and took a deep breath. My magic dove into the earth and traveled over Marianne's decaying bones. I could feel them with my magic, as if I'd grabbed her body with my hands. My head spun, and the cemetery blurred in front of me.

Pain stabbed through my gut so hard and fast that I doubled over, clutching my stomach. The magic that cast this curse had permeated the memory of the murder into her body. It was as if Samael was standing in front of me, stabbing me through the stomach in real-time. Marianne's heart-wrenching pain from the betrayal rippled through my body. The energy signature from this curse was unlike anything I'd ever experienced before—worse even than the dark magic I'd encountered when I'd killed a demonic monster last semester. No darkness could compare to the betrayal Marianne experienced when the one person she would always love unconditionally turned on her. I felt it in the magic—in the memory. Even as Samael drove that blade through her gut, she still loved him. Her only regret was that she couldn't save him.

"Samael!" I screamed as my fingers curled around the edge of the gravestone. I shrieked the name in my own voice, but something about it didn't sound like me, either.

My voice... the pain... it was all so heart-breaking.

I knew from my practice in Curse Breaking that the only way to break a curse was to transform the magic into something comparable. The only thing that came even remotely close was complete and utter destruction...

Boom!

The gravestone exploded, sending a blast across the cemetery. I was launched off my feet over top of the gravestone behind me. I landed flat on my back in the snow so hard that the air left my lungs. Isa yowled as she landed on top of me. Tiny pieces of rock rained down on us. The magic had reduced the gravestone to nothing but sand.

Lucas groaned from nearby, but my vision blurred so badly that I couldn't make out the stars above. The stabbing pain in my gut intensified, and I knew it was because I hadn't broken the curse yet. That was a mere piece of it, but there was far more to face.

"Nadine!" Lucas cried as he and Oliver rushed toward me.

"I'll be okay," I groaned as he helped me up. I must've winced, because Lucas didn't look convinced.

"This isn't worth it," he insisted. "You're hurt, and it's only going to get worse."

"No," I protested. "I want to keep going. Show me the other graves."

Lucas froze for a moment before finally giving in. "Let's keep moving."

We found Sarah Davis's grave next, as it wasn't far from Marianne's. She'd never had kids, so the curse wasn't as intense in her bones. Still, drawing it out was like eating glass. Lucas had told me Sarah had suffered an undiagnosed illness as part of the curse. When I touched the magic inside of her, it felt as if her ailment was transferring to me. Pain landed deep in my abdomen, and fatigue swept through my body. Every joint seemed to swell. My best guess was that Sarah had suffered from some sort of uterine cancer. Add that on top of the stabbing pain from Marianne's death, and I thought I was going to hurl. Goddess, I wanted it to stop right then, but I was almost halfway through. I had to finish this.

I funneled the magic into Sarah's grave. A crack like the sound of thunder filled the cemetery, so loud that Isa jumped. I yanked my hand back and saw that Sarah's grave was cracked completely in half.

"Are you okay?" Lucas asked.

I nodded, though I wouldn't admit how much pain I was truly in. "Two down. Two to go," I said in a strained voice.

I leaned against Lucas as we followed Isa and Oliver. Oliver stopped in front of a grave several rows down. "Adeline Grey," I said as I read the name. "She was the wife of the next Reaper's Apprentice?"

"Yes," Lucas said. "She had some sort of muscular disorder, lost her leg in an accident, and then finally…"

"Died at the hands of her child," I whispered, my mouth going dry. "How'd it happen?"

"Blunt force trauma to the back of the head." Lucas's voice was hollow.

I didn't tell him that I was experiencing the physical pain of each of the victims, or he'd never let me finish this.

I knelt at Adeline's grave, running my hands over the top of the stone. "Adeline," I whispered. "I hope this helps you rest in peace."

As I drew the curse from her bones, pain twisted through my muscles, as if my flesh was being ripped apart piece by piece. I winced as her illness permeated my body. Then came the loss of sensation in my leg, and finally the ungodly pain throbbing in my head.

"Goddess!" I gasped. My entire body trembled.

Lucas knelt beside me and held me. "I'm here."

It was obvious in his tone that he meant more than he was saying. *Just say the word, and we'll stop.*

Fuck it. I had years of experience in unending pain. I could handle this, too.

I gritted my teeth as the magic filled my body. The cemetery spun around me, and I reached for the grave but couldn't find it. I felt Lucas's hands on mine, and he pressed my palm to the stone. Magic shot from my hands, and the gravestone shattered into dozens of pieces. One of them slammed into my shoulder, and I gasped, but it was nothing like the pain pounding in my head or twisting in my gut.

"Nad…" Lucas started.

"It's fine," I rasped. I was sure Isa was nearby, but the cemetery seemed to shake like an earthquake, though I knew *I* was the one shaking. I couldn't find my cat. "One left."

I heard a meow. By now, I could barely stand. Lucas wrapped an arm around my waist. I tried to walk, but I'd lost all feeling in my left leg. I sagged against him. I wasn't sure what it looked like, but I felt on the verge of collapse.

"Nadine—"

"You promised," I cut Lucas off. "We're almost there. I can do this."

Lucas must've picked me up to cradle me, because the next thing I knew, my feet were off the ground. I could barely keep my head up as he walked us to the final grave. I could make out Isa's and Oliver's shadows, but I couldn't read the name on the stone.

"Clara Samson," Lucas said as he set me down in the snow. "She was the last Reaper's Shadow… before you."

"Clara," I whispered, though I wasn't sure I actually made a sound. I wanted to say more, but I couldn't find my voice.

My whole body shivered, and I lost control when I reached for the gravestone. I fell into it face-first, catching my cheek on the edge. Everything went black for a moment, but Lucas had just barely touched me when I became conscious again. The cold wet snow stuck to the side of my face. Lucas hoisted me into his arms, and I sagged against him like a ragdoll. I noticed several drops of blood in the snow, but the cut on my cheek was the least of my worries.

"I… we're so close," I said.

"We need to stop," Lucas demanded. "I'm not willing to do this if it's going to kill you. It's not worth your life."

I shook my head, though it was the smallest of movements. "No, but it's worth *their* peace."

Tears spilled from my eyes, and sobs racked my body. I shook in Lucas's arms, but I couldn't find the strength to lift my hands and touch Clara's gravestone. My trembling hand fell limp at my side, landing in the freezing snow.

"Nadine, they're already gone…" Lucas was saying, but his words disappeared as I began pulling Clara's curse from her grave.

Lucas didn't have to tell the details of her curse, because I felt them. Clara had lost six babies to miscarriages before birthing her first child. I experienced the trauma in my heart. It felt as if someone had reached in my chest and squeezed my heart with their hand, because I swore it was no longer beating. Pins and needles entered my joints. Whatever illness she'd encountered had affected her joints.

But Clara's death… dear Goddess, her death. I felt the fire consuming me, peeling apart my skin layer after layer. I tried to scream, but nothing came out. I couldn't imagine a death more horrifying than burning alive.

I kept my gaze on the stars as I transformed the curse with my magic, but they faded above me, as if they were burning out one by one. The gravestone beside me shattered, but that seemed like an afterthought as the cemetery faded around me.

"Nadine! Nadine!" Lucas's voice cut through as I began slipping away. I thought he shook me, but I couldn't be sure.

I'm not done, I wanted to say. I'd broken the curse on all the other women, but I'd taken it on myself. Lucas and I had crossed a line we didn't know had been drawn. I was his Reaper's Shadow, and I carried the burden of this curse alone.

I had to break the curse on myself.

The magic within me was difficult to find past all the pain. I searched for it in my belly, as I had done with my family curse before, but it didn't seem to reside there. Goddess, the pain was everywhere…

That's when I realized, the curse was *way* stronger than the family curse I'd grown up with. This magic wasn't localized in one place. It swirled through my entire body, making it feel as if it was tearing me apart from the inside out.

That's what this curse did.

Emotional trauma, illness, and betrayal from those you love most… it destroyed you from the inside out—until it broke you completely.

Pain stabbed through my back and through my kidneys. I swore I heard myself scream, but I didn't remember opening my mouth. A deafening *snap* sounded, and I felt my body lurch as the ground shifted.

That was all I remembered before everything went dark.

NINETEEN

I paced outside Nadine's hospital room. I hadn't been able to sit still since I brought her here hours ago. I still couldn't wrap my head around what had happened—how Nadine had split the earth in two with the power of the curse. The crack in the earth must've been a full foot wide and covered at least an acre. Gravestones had been upturned, and I'd caught sight of caskets deep within the crack. To be honest, I hadn't even been sure she was still breathing when I rushed into the hospital with her in my arms.

I stopped abruptly as Isa stepped in front of me. I swore to the goddess the cat frowned at me. "Don't look at me like that. I fucked up. I shouldn't have let her go through with it. I knew it was dangerous, but I wanted to believe she was stronger… I didn't want to be the one to stand in her way and doubt her. I should've protected her."

I had no idea what Isa was thinking—or if the cat could even understand what I was saying—because she turned from me and hopped onto a chair beside Oliver. The hospital was empty because it was late—well past curfew. Nerves twisted in my gut, and it felt like I'd been waiting forever.

Someone cleared their throat, and I turned to see a doctor standing behind me. "You're with Nadine Evers?"

"Yes. Is she okay?" I asked desperately.

"She's stable and awake," the doctor replied. "She's asking for you."

"Thank the goddess!" I cried. I rushed into the room, the cats following close behind. My stomach dropped when I saw Nadine. All the color had drained from her face, and her lips were dry and cracked. Her hair stuck up, and she had an IV hooked to her arm.

I grabbed her hand. "How do you feel? Are you okay? I'm so sorry. I never should've—"

"I did it," she breathed.

My eyes searched hers, but my emotions ran so high that I couldn't read her. "You mean…?"

Nadine swallowed. "I broke the curse."

"You… finished it?" I asked, unsure if I believed it. I thought for certain the curse had been too much.

Tears beaded at the corners of her eyes. "The whole time, the curse made me feel what they felt," she admitted in a raspy tone. "I don't know if it was the connection that we shared, or if it was part of being a Curse Breaker, but I felt their ailments and trauma and…"

"Their deaths?" I asked in a wooden tone. To think of what she'd been through tonight terrified me. If I'd known what she'd go through to break the curse, I never would've asked her to do it.

"It's okay," she assured me. "It's gone. The pain is gone. The curse is broken."

Relief flooded through me. "You have no idea how incredible that is to hear. I'm glad you're all right."

"I really am." Nadine closed her eyes, sinking deeper into the pillow. She looked totally at peace, and that eased all my nerves.

I pushed her hair out of her eyes and pressed a kiss to her forehead. "I'll let you rest. Sleep well, my miracle."

Nadine smiled. "I will."

☾

NADINE WAS RELEASED from the hospital the following day, but between our exams, we didn't get a chance to talk. She messaged me after lunch. *I have my final with Headmistress Verla today. I'll see you at the talent show.*

I'd almost forgotten about the talent show. I hadn't signed up, but all our friends would be there.

My Protection Magic final ran late into the afternoon. I barely had half an hour to grab dinner before I stopped at Nadine's room. She answered the door wearing a short black dress. It revealed quite a bit of leg, but I wasn't complaining. She carried a sparkly black bag over her shoulder.

I eyed the bag curiously. "The Waning?"

She frowned. "Unfortunately. My magic worked through my final earlier. I had no problem charging up the rainbow moonstone in my wand with Curse Breaker magic. Verla seemed impressed. I only felt the Waning around dinnertime."

"That's not good." I sighed.

"Hopefully my magic will be back soon," she said. "At least I don't need it for the talent show."

"I didn't know you'd signed up," I remarked.

Nadine shrugged. "It was a last-minute thing."

"Ready to go?" I asked.

She tossed her hair over her shoulder. "Almost. Talia's just getting her music together."

"I'm ready!" Talia called. She hurried over to us, carrying a stack of papers.

Oliver spotted Gus and immediately rushed over to him. They tackled each other in a playful game. Isa jumped in and held Oliver to the ground.

Nadine laughed and shook her head. "Behave yourselves," she scolded. "Save your energy for the show."

I tilted my head. "Isa's going to be in the show? What exactly *is* your talent?"

Nadine winked as we started down the hall. "You're not the only one who gets to keep secrets. It's a surprise."

"Are you trying to kill me with anticipation?" I teased.

She pressed her lips together. I couldn't take my eyes off her as we descended the grand staircase.

Talia leaned toward us and lowered her voice. "Speaking of secrets, you wouldn't happen to know who vandalized the cemetery last night?"

Nadine and I exchanged a shocked expression. "Vandalized?" I asked.

Nadine smirked, but her voice came out innocent. "I have no idea who would do that."

Talia snickered, like the two were speaking in code. "I'm glad you guys figured it out."

Oh, that. I squeezed Nadine's hand. "It was all Nadine."

"Hold up. No," Nadine protested. "You're the one who found the names. We did it together."

"I guess we did," I said.

We reached the ballroom, where a stage had been set up for the talent show. Chatter filled the room, and performers in all different costumes came and went from a door behind the stage.

"We have to check in," Nadine said. "Do you want to find us a spot?"

"Sure." I scooped up Oliver, then caught sight of Mandy and Amy, who were sitting in a row near the front. Several chairs sat empty beside them. Nadine and Talia disappeared backstage, and I made my way over to the other girls.

"So, Lucas. Did you sign up?" Mandy asked, bouncing a little in her chair.

I set Oliver on my lap and stroked his head. "Yes, because I'm *so* talented on stage," I said dryly.

Mandy frowned. "Everyone has a bit of a performer in them. You just need to harness it."

"She even convinced me," Amy said.

"Well, I'm excited to see what you came up with," I encouraged, before glancing around the room. I saw the Tarantulas gathered near the stage. I was shocked, because they had no talent other than getting into trouble. I'd bet my wand it was going to suck. I continued to scan the room and noticed someone was missing. "Has anyone heard from Grant?"

"He's getting set up," Nadine said as she returned.

I eyed her curiously. "What exactly *is* his talent? Tell me it's not juggling."

"Oh, *Goddess*," Mandy scoffed. "He gave that up weeks ago."

"It's cool. I promise," Nadine said. She sat beside me, and Isa jumped onto her lap.

Talia and Gus sat on her opposite side. "Shh..." Talia hissed. "They're about to start."

The lights dimmed, and people quickly took their seats and quieted. A girl walked onto stage, though I didn't see who it was until she stepped into the spotlight. Ashley Blake, a girl from my Protection Magic class, stepped in front of the microphone.

"Welcome to the Miriam College Drama Club's first annual Winter Talent Show!" Ashley said. "I hope you're ready to loosen up during finals week, because we have an amazing lineup for you tonight—singers, dancers, skits, and more. So to all my guys, gals, and no-binary pals, hold on to your wands! It's going to be an amazing night. Put your hands together for our first act, the Treacherous Tarantulas!"

The crowd cheered, but I leaned over to Nadine to whisper, "They actually had her call them that? Like they're some sort of boy band or something?"

Nadine snickered. "The winning act gets five-hundred dollars. It's the only reason they entered. The runners-up get gift certificates to the Lounge, but it's the grand prize everyone wants."

My eyebrows shot up. "Five-hundred dollars? I have to see this."

Ryan took the microphone from Ashley, and she rushed off stage. "Hey, hey, hey!" he shouted, throwing his fist into the air. He sounded like a frat boy. "How are we doing tonight?"

A few people in the crowd cheered, but Ryan yelled into the microphone, "I can't hear you!"

The crowd cheered louder, but my friends and I exchanged glances. This was more comical than anything.

"Let's go!" Ryan snapped his fingers, and music started playing over the speakers. The Tarantulas formed a line. The beat dropped, and they burst into song and dance. Ryan began rapping, and the other four Tarantulas danced *exactly* as if they were a boy band.

To say I was surprised was an understatement. All the years Ryan and I hung out in high school, and not *once* had I heard him rap. I would've bet my magic he didn't have it in him. I mean, the performance wasn't *great*, but it wasn't a train wreck, either.

Nadine's jaw dropped. "Who gave them a talent-enchanting potion?" she teased.

"I think it's legit," Talia whispered. "I saw them coming out of the music room the other day. I think they were practicing."

"Damn, they really want that five-hundred dollars," I said. Their movements were a bit uncoordinated, and Ryan stumbled over his words a few times, but I was actually impressed.

The crowd cheered when they finished. It must've stroked Ryan's ego a bit too much, because he ripped off his shirt and tossed it into the crowd. A group of girls fought over it, until it ripped completely in half.

"Wow! What a performance!" Ashely said when she reached the

microphone again. She introduced the next act, and my friends and I calmed our laughter enough to watch.

Kenna Farlane, a girl from my Intercast Magic class, came on stage next. She played a pretty tune on the flute, but she must've been really nervous, because she fumbled with the notes a few times.

"Come on, Kenna. You can do this." Talia sighed. "I've heard her in the music room. She's really good."

Kenna looked about ready to puke, but she bowed at the end of her act, then rushed off stage.

Onyx appeared on stage next. She was Nadine's lab partner last semester, but I didn't know much about her. She always seemed really quiet and kept to herself. Her cat followed behind her. I expected her to say something as she stepped up to the microphone. Her gaze shot around the room, and she ran her fingers through her purple hair. She opened her mouth, but she quickly snapped it shut. She didn't say a word. Instead, she grabbed the stand and moved it out of the way. The audience seemed to hold their breath in anticipation as she sat cross-legged center stage. Her nerves seemed to ease as she closed her eyes, like she forgot she was in front of an audience. I had no idea what to expect.

Music came over the speakers—a fast classical tune. Onyx raised her hands, and light orbs blasted out of them. The crowd gasped as the orbs shot toward our faces like fireworks. My heart lurched, but the orb flying toward my face never reached me. It stopped right in front of my nose and hovered there a second before shooting up toward the ceiling.

The crowd gasped as the orbs split apart, then came back together in beautiful shapes. The starry patterns spun above our heads to the music, creating unique images like flowers and diamonds. The lights pulsed with the intensity of the song. It must've taken a lot of magical control to create such intricate shapes. It was like art in motion.

As the music slowed, Onyx drew back on her magic, until the orbs came together on stage and touched her heart, disappearing completely.

The crowd went dead silent when the music ended, then erupted into cheers. Talia whistled and shot out of her chair. The rest of us quickly followed, giving Onyx a standing ovation.

"She's going to win!" Nadine said.

"She has to. That was impressive," I agreed.

A few people I didn't know followed. Their performances weren't as good as Onyx's, but they weren't bad, either. One girl sang, and a boy played the violin.

"We're up soon," Mandy whispered, before she and Amy hurried backstage.

The dance team came on stage next. They weren't horrible, but the whole performance left a bad taste in my mouth—probably because Lena was front and center, and I couldn't stand her. At least she didn't seem to notice me in the crowd.

As the dance team was walking offstage, another dancer emerged from backstage. I couldn't tell who it was in the shadows, but I saw Lena slam her shoulder against the other girl. There was clearly some rivalry going on there.

When she reached the spotlight, I saw that it was Chloe. The music began, and Chloe began twirling and leaping across the stage. The precision in which she moved looked like it belonged on Broadway. I hated to admit it, but it was pretty obvious that Chloe had been carrying the dance team on her back last semester. She had more talent in her pinky toe than the whole dance team combined. Chloe finished her dance in the splits, and the crowd erupted into cheers.

Nadine beamed as she clapped for her. "If Onyx doesn't win, I hope Chloe does. That was amazing."

"You *want* Chloe to win?" I asked.

Nadine shrugged. "We're on better terms now. I mean, she's not my best friend, but I do wish the best for her."

I smiled at that, but my attention was stolen by the next act on stage. Music started playing, and Mandy started across the stage, swaying her hips like she was on a runway. She wore a long black evening dress that complimented her curves well. A voice came over the speakers, but I didn't see anyone. It sounded like Ashley reading from a script.

"Ladies looking for their next Midnight Formal fashion, look no further than our very own resident fashion designer, Mandy Lane! She's sporting an original gown made from satin. Notice the rhinestone details on the bodice!"

Ashley went on, using a bunch of fashion terms I didn't know. Mandy stopped at the end of the stage, then spun to show off her dress. As she was walking back, Amy stepped on stage. She wore a dark blue dress with a crescent moon embellishment around the waist.

Mandy appeared moments later in another dress, showing off for the crowd, all while Ashley read from her script. The girls showed off one more dress each, before Ashley announced that the dresses would be for sale after the show.

Fashion wasn't really my thing, but all the girls in the crowd seemed starstruck. I was mostly impressed that Mandy had managed to design and make all those dresses in one semester.

"We're up soon," Talia whispered to Nadine.

Nadine nudged me. "You want to come? So you're not alone?"

I glanced at the empty chairs beside me. "Sure."

We hurried backstage between acts. The room was cramped with performers, racks of costumes, mirrors, and a countertop full of makeup.

Talia rushed up to Mandy. "That was amazing!" she gushed. "Your dresses are gorgeous."

"I had no idea you had so many designs!" Nadine said. "And Amy, you were such an awesome model."

"She was *so hot!*" Tate rushed up and draped an arm around Amy's shoulder.

Amy blushed. "You really think so?"

"I *know* so," Tate said, tickling Amy's side. The two giggled, and their noses got so close I thought they were going to kiss.

Nadine leaned over to Talia. "Did I miss something?"

Talia didn't get a chance to respond before Mandy answered. "They're *unofficial.*" Mandy made air quotes, and she didn't sound pleased about it. She crossed her arms and shot daggers at Tate.

Tate stepped back, and I finally got a look at what she was wearing. She wore an all-black bodysuit with glow sticks taped to her body in the shape of a skeleton. I noticed Miles across the room, wearing the same thing.

"When are you up?" Talia asked her sister.

"Soon! I had to hide out so no one saw my costume," Tate said.

Mandy narrowed her eyes. "And the glow sticks are for...?"

"Dancing!" Tate said. "No spotlight! It's going to look really neat."

"Tate Murphy and Miles Bryant!" someone called. I turned to see it was Christine, another one of the girls from my Protection Magic class. "You're on deck."

"I gotta go," Tate said in a rush, before hurrying off to join Miles near the door.

"I want to go watch her," Talia told us.

We snuck out of the room and watched from the side of the stage. The room went completely dark when the duo climbed on stage, and the music began. Their act was way cooler than I expected, since you couldn't see them at all. Their black clothes blended in with the curtains, and all you could see was the dancing skeletons on stage.

The crowd cheered when they finished. We remained on the sidelines to watch the next few acts. Alex and Shane performed a magic trick that was supposed to look like teleportation, but we all knew it was just two identical twins playing one guy. Nobody was surprised.

Soon, Nadine was up. She winked at me before stepping on stage. She sat on a chair that'd been placed in the center of the stage. My eyebrows shot up when she pulled a Rubik's cube from her bag and asked a few of the audience members to come on stage and mix it up. A timer projected onto the curtains behind her, and the crowd cheered her on as they watched in anticipation.

Nadine shot out of her chair and shouted, "Done!"

The timer buzzed, and the projector stopped at three minutes and twelve seconds.

"No way!" someone in the front row shouted.

"That was amazing!" another person cried.

Nadine beamed as she left the stage. I grabbed her around the waist when she came over to me. "That was incredible," I whispered to her, before brushing my lips across her cheek.

She shrugged. "I've had a lot of time to practice at dialysis."

"Don't downplay it," I told her. "It's a real talent."

She looked down to her solved Rubik's Cube. "I guess it is pretty impressive."

"*I* enjoyed the performance," I told her.

Music began to play, and Nadine swatted at me. "Talia's up."

Talia's fingers moved over the keyboard without missing a single note. She played an upbeat tune and sang into the microphone. It was a beautiful song, but the lyrics were kind of sad. It was all about her feelings going unnoticed by the guy she loved.

You hear the thought I think out loud
My secrets are a sacred vow
But there's just one thing I can't admit
And you don't seem to hear it

"She's *so* good," Nadine gushed.

"She really is," I agreed. "I can't believe she wrote that."

Talia bowed to the crowd, then rushed off the stage. "I did it! I hit the high note at the end. I wasn't sure about it."

"You did amazing," Nadine told her.

Oliver bumped against my leg, and I looked down at him. I suddenly noticed that Isa and Gus were gone.

"Uh, your cats are missing," I told them.

Nadine smirked. "Don't worry about it."

I narrowed my eyes at them. "What do you have planned? I still haven't seen Grant. He wasn't backstage."

Nadine patted my chest. "Trust me, okay?"

A few other acts came on stage, but none of them were as good as my friends had been. Gregory tried his hand at stand-up comedy, but it came off as highly offensive toward women. The only people laughing were the Tarantulas. Everyone else seemed pretty uncomfortable, and Gregory cut his act short.

The drama club did a skit, but Felicia Green had been cast as the main character, and her performance was a bit stale. After a juggling act and a guy who could beatbox really well, Ashley returned to the stage to announce the final act.

Nadine grabbed my arm. "This is it!"

I watched the side of the stage curiously, but Grant never appeared. Instead, the lights faded, until the room was cast in complete darkness. The curtains at the back of the stage parted, and I could barely make out the shape of a tall shadow.

The sound of an organ blared over the speakers. In sync with the chord, a blast of blue magic exploded on stage. The magic lit up, billowing like smoke out of a large cauldron. I was finally able to make out the scene on stage. Grant stood in front of an elaborate laboratory setup, with endless cauldrons set up at various levels—almost like a drum set, but with cauldrons instead. He was dressed in his *Phantom of the Opera* costume from Halloween, complete with the white mask. He held a potion vial high above his head like he was showing it off to the crowd.

The music notes shifted, and I recognized the tune as the theme from *The Phantom of the Opera*. With every note, Grant placed a drop of potion into another cauldron. Colors exploded in perfect time to the music, creating flashing lights of all different colors on stage. As a long chord sounded, he placed another drop into a large cauldron and swirled his hand as the bright magic swelled upward. It looked as if he was controlling it, though I knew that was only part of the act.

Grant moved from one cauldron to the next on the beat, creating a light show unlike I'd ever seen. He really got into it, too, bending his knees and moving his hands like a conductor lost in the music.

And that's what he was—a conductor to the magic show on stage. Everyone's eyes locked on the flashing lights emitting from the cauldrons, but it was Grant who was the true star. The potions he'd brewed for the show were incredible, and it was amazing how in sync it was with the music. Some of the magic sparkled and was gone within moments. Others glowed bright and lingered.

Isa and Gus appeared from behind Grant. They each wore a small bowtie, and they held tiny potion bottles in their mouths. The cats jumped onto the cauldrons, one on either side of Grant. They balanced on the edges. I thought for sure one of the cats would fall into one of the pots, but they didn't. As the music intensified, the cats dropped some of their potion into different cauldrons, while Grant poured potion into others. It created an incredible light show that he never would've been able to pull off with only two hands working.

My jaw dropped, and I leaned over to Nadine. "How did you train them to do that...?"

"Isa's *very* smart," she snickered.

I was so mesmerized by Grant's performance that I was shocked to hear a group of people laughing in the front row. My gaze darted to the Tarantulas. Ryan was doubled over laughing, like Grant's light show was hilarious.

"It's just potions!" I heard Ryan laugh. "Any Alchemist can do that."

My hands curled into fists. This show was incredible. It wasn't something just *any Alchemist* could do. It was obvious Grant put a lot of time and energy into coordinating his potions. I had half a mind to go over there and kick their asses, but the last thing I wanted to do was interrupt Grant's performance. It wasn't fair to him that they were being so loud in the first place.

I noticed Grant's eyes darted toward the crowd, and his hand faltered. He fumbled, and the potion he held dropped out of his hands. Isa squealed in shock and fell off the cauldron she stood on. She rolled across the stage. The music continued, but the stage went black.

Nadine gasped, and I went as still as a statue.

"Fuck, is he going to finish?" I asked.

Grant bailed. All I saw was his shadow racing off stage, then he darted into the room backstage.

"Come on." I tugged Nadine's hand.

We hurried after Grant and were the first ones backstage. Talia followed behind us. We walked in to find Grant pacing nervously.

"That was bullshit!" I cried.

Grant chewed his thumbnail. "I screwed up. It wasn't supposed to end like that."

"No shit!" I raged. "You should get a redo. The Tarantulas interrupted your performance."

The door opened behind us, and I turned to see Ashely and Christine enter the room. Christine held her clipboard to her chest, and she shot a nervous glance to Grant.

"Is everything all right?" Christine asked.

"I'll be fine—" Grant started.

"That wasn't fair!" Talia cut him off.

"I agree," Ashley said, "but we can't give anyone a redo."

Grant's shoulders sagged. He looked devastated. "I guess I can try again next year."

"No," I protested. "This needs to end."

"How?" Nadine asked. "You could've killed Ryan in your warlock's duel, and he knows it, yet he's still tormenting Grant."

I hesitated a second, but then it hit me like a stunning spell. "You know what? Fuck the Tarantulas. Fuck *anyone* who has something to say about Grant. They want someone to make fun of? I'll give them something to talk about."

Nadine's brow furrowed. "What are you thinking?"

I didn't *think.* I just reacted, because nothing seemed to matter right now but showing the Tarantulas just what my friends and I were made of. I turned to Ashley and Christine. "You have music set up?"

Ashley's mouth bobbed, but she quickly composed herself and answered. "We can play anything you want."

"Then you have one more performance tonight," I stated firmly. "Nadine, give me your dress."

Talia's eyebrows shot up so high that it was comical.

"Lucas, you don't have to do this," Grant said, but I didn't listen.

Nadine smirked. "In front of everyone, Lucas?"

I leaned toward her and ran my fingers under the strap of her dress. She shivered beneath my touch. I got so close that my lips grazed her cheek as I whispered, "I dare you."

Nadine's jaw dropped. "Lucas Taylor."

"Don't tease me, or I'll back down," I warned her.

Her lips curled into a wide smile. She grabbed my hand and yanked me behind a rack of costumes. She quickly stripped off her dress and tossed it at me. I didn't even have a moment to take in her exposed skin, before I was stripping off my own clothes and pulling on her dress. It was tight across my chest and so short it nearly showed my underwear, but it was stretchy and worked. She quickly yanked on my clothes.

"Thanks," I told her in a rush.

I turned, but Nadine grabbed my arm. "Wait! You need these!"

She grabbed a top hat and a cane from the costume rack and shoved them in my hands. As I emerged from behind the rack, Christine poked her head into the room. I hadn't realized she'd left.

"Ashley just announced you as a bonus act!" she said. "I've got three songs ready for you. Which one do you want?"

She rattled off a few pop songs, and I picked the one at the top of her list, because it was the one I'd heard the most. It'd even been on Dr. Mack's playlist she put together for me.

"Perfect," Christine said. "You're up!"

"Good luck!" Nadine cried, squeezing my hand.

I took the stairs on stage two at a time. I should've been nervous as hell, but I didn't give myself a moment to question it. I took center stage and struck a pose in the darkness. I faced the back curtains, with my hip stuck out to the side.

The music started, and the spotlight flicked on. I spun around, twirling my cane and moving my lips in sync with the lyrics. I strutted across the stage in large, dramatic motions, drawing inspiration from Mandy's fashion show from earlier.

A mixture of gasps and laughter came from the crowd, stroking my spiteful ego. I could just barely make out Ryan's features from the front row. His jaw dropped, like he couldn't believe it was *me* on stage. Hell, I could hardly believe it.

But I was doing it. And it made Ryan speechless. I was fucking pleased.

I twirled around, then dropped my ass to the floor, placing the cane upright between my legs like it was a stripper pole. I spread my knees and smacked my ass as I stood. The crowd cheered louder. As the beat dropped on the chorus, I grabbed my top hat and threw it into the crowd. A group of girls leapt to their feet, all trying to catch it at once. They argued over it, but I was already moving on, dancing across the stage.

I made large hand gestures as the music intensified, as if I was singing the song myself and not just lip syncing. As the final beats of the chorus sounded, I slammed the bottom of the cane against the stage, then thrust my hips toward it in a highly suggestive manner.

The crowd went fucking nuts. People screamed, and a few girls even stood on their chairs and cupped their hands around their mouths to yell louder.

The song continued, and I got *really* into it. Who ever would've thought that I—*Lucas Taylor*—would find such freedom in dancing like a stripper in front of the whole school? And in a dress, no less? Hell, I'd never felt such a high in all my life. Just the mere satisfaction of Ryan's shocked expression was enough to keep me going. Fuck him!

I did a few more suggestive motions, even putting the cane between my legs and rolling my hips over it. The crowd seemed to like that one. I became so lost in the music that I stopped paying attention to the crowd's reaction. By the end, I was on my hands and knees, spinning my head around and around, my hair flying in all directions. The song ended, and I panted as sweat dripped down the side of my face.

My gaze went out toward the crowd, and they went fucking wild!

Someone whistled loudly from the side of the stage. I looked over to see Grant jumping up and down, whooping and hollering. As my racing heart settled, it hit me what I'd just done. I could hardly believe I'd had the courage. Ashley stepped onto the stage, and I hurried offstage toward my friends.

"That was incredible!" Nadine exclaimed.

I took her hands in mine. "You really thought so? I can't believe I did that."

"Did you see Ryan's face?" Talia laughed.

I smirked. "They won't be making fun of Grant anymore, that's for sure."

Grant stepped toward me. "Thanks for that, man. I don't know what to say."

"You don't have to say anything," I assured him.

"Shh…" Talia said. "They're announcing the winner."

I draped an arm around Nadine's shoulder and turned my attention toward the stage. She leaned into me and whispered, "That was *really* hot."

The corners of my lips twitched, and I lifted the hem of the dress. "You like this?"

She wiggled her eyebrows. "I like your dancing. That's for sure."

"Maybe I'll have to dance for you sometime." I leaned down and kissed her.

"The judges have made their decision," Ashley announced. She said it like it was a big deal, but we all knew the judges were just a few kids from the drama club. "In third place, Chloe Olson, with a solo dance routine!"

The crowd applauded for her, and Chloe came on stage to claim her prize. Ashley handed her an envelope.

"In second place, Onyx Foxe, with a lights show!" Ashley announced.

Onyx hurried on stage as the crowd cheered.

"And finally, our grand prize winner… Talia Murphy, with an original song!"

A loud round of applause filled the room, but Talia didn't move. Mandy nudged her. "Girl, you won! Go get your prize."

Talia's jaw dropped. "I *won!*"

"Hell yeah, you won!" Nadine told her. "You were amazing."

"Congratulations!" Grant said, sounding happier to see Talia win than if he'd won himself.

Talia scrambled forward and claimed her prize on stage. She was beaming by the time she returned. "I can't believe it. There were so many good acts."

"*You* were a great act," I assured her.

She smiled brightly, clutching her envelope to her chest.

"Let's go celebrate," Grant offered. "We have almost an hour before curfew. We could grab something in the Lounge."

"That sounds great," Talia agreed. "Drinks on me."

Nadine and I slipped backstage to change into our own clothes, then joined our friends as the crowd funneled out of the ballroom. We ordered our drinks at the Lounge restaurant, then claimed the couches near the TVs. Everyone was here, including Miles and Tate, who were still wearing their glowstick costumes. Amy sat next to Tate and leaned her head on her shoulder. Nadine had ordered warm milk for the cats, and they gathered around a bowl and licked it up.

"I'm sad we didn't get to see the end of your performance, Grant," Talia said. "It was really cool. Did you brew all those potions yourself?"

"Yeah," he replied as he sipped hot cocoa. "But I can't take all the credit. Nadine helped with the choreography, and it was her idea to use the cats."

"Good job to both of you," Amy praised. "It was badass—"

She cut off as a loud group of guys entered the Lounge, laughing their asses off. I turned to see the Tarantulas staring at me. "He's an embarrassment to warlocks everywhere," Ryan quipped, as if I couldn't hear him. "What a stupid performance."

I wasn't going to say anything—screw what Ryan thought—but Grant slammed his drink onto the coffee table and leapt to his feet before I could. "*What* is your fucking problem!?" he yelled. All the chatter in the Lounge died, and all eyes turned toward us.

Ryan's lips curled into a sneer. "My problem is people like *you* ruining shit for the rest of us."

"What does that even mean?" Grant demanded. His hands curled into fists at his sides. "You can't handle that Lucas ditched you and found someone else to hang out with? Or are you bothered by half-bloods with power greater than anything you can imagine? Maybe our illnesses and disabilities have you uncomfortable, or is it lesbians that trip you up? Maybe you can't stand to see your ex-girlfriend happy. You expect every woman to fall at your feet, and when they don't, something must be wrong with *them*. But nooo, it can't be your shit-ass personality. Or maybe it's the fact that the prettiest girl on campus can show you up at anytime and win the talent show. You're nothing but a pathetic little child with a jealousy issue who expects the world to bow to your demands and fit into a nice little box, because your fragile little ego can't handle it—"

"SHUT UP!!!" Ryan shouted so loudly that his voice echoed off the walls. His hands shook in rage as he lifted them, but Grant was faster.

Grant flicked his fingers, and a powerful defensive spell sliced through the air. Ryan's shirt ripped open, as if an invisible blade had sliced his abdomen. A string of blood appeared. It wasn't very deep, but it was enough for Ryan to jump back, looking scared as shit. Grant lifted his palm, and a high-powered battle orb shot outward. It whizzed through the air so fast that Ryan didn't have time to throw up a shield. The orb slammed straight into Ryan's chest, throwing him off his feet. Ryan knocked into his buddies, and they all went tumbling to the ground like bowling pins. Ryan went limp. I was certain Grant had knocked him out.

Grant stepped forward and placed his foot on Ryan's chest. The Tarantulas started for him, but Miles threw up a shield, and they slammed straight into it. I rushed to Grant's side, cracking my knuckles in warning.

Nolan hesitated a moment, but the second I conjured my scythe, he backed the fuck off. My fingers curled around the handle.

Ryan shook his head as he came to. Grant leaned down, putting more weight on Ryan's chest. "You want to fuck with us? Fine. But don't be surprised when we fight back."

Grant stepped back, his chest heaving. He stared down at Ryan like he was curious to see what he'd do.

Ryan jumped to his feet, his nostrils flaring. His eyes darted behind us. I glanced over my shoulder to see the girls standing with their arms crossed or their hands on their hips. Each shared the same death glare, looking ready to spill blood.

"Fuck you," Ryan growled. "You said it yourself; you're nothing but freaks. You're not even worth it."

He whirled around and stomped out of the Lounge. The other Tarantulas hesitated, then scampered after him like lost puppies. The room remained silent for several beats, then slowly filled with whispers. Ryan wanted to act tough, but he was nothing but a coward.

I turned to Grant. "That was bold."

"It felt *so* good." He sighed in relief. "But there's one more thing I have to do before the adrenaline wears off."

Grant stepped past me and stopped in front of Talia. "If I can stand up to Ryan, I can do this."

Her jaw dropped as he took her hand in his.

"Talia," Grant said. "I have been in love with you since the moment I laid eyes on you. I admire everything about you—your talent, your beauty, your magic. I have so much fun when I'm around you, and you just seem to *get* me in ways that no one else does. When you're playing music, it's like you're speaking to my soul. You hold yourself with this incredible confidence that I can help but be drawn to. After the song you sang today, I think you feel the same way, and I can't keep hiding how I feel. I love you, Tal."

Talia's eyes watered, but she was beaming. "I know, Grant."

"So, uh…" Grant stammered. "Do you want to go out with me?"

"I thought you'd never ask!" she cried. Talia threw her arms around Grant, and he lifted her up, twirling her around. Their lips connected, and I'd never seen either of them look happier.

About fucking time.

My friends and I cheered, and even a few onlookers rooted for them. Finally, Grant set Talia down, and the two of them blushed bright red.

"Oh, get a room!" Miles laughed.

"For once you have a good idea," Grant quipped.

Nadine leaned into me and whispered, "Looks like love is in the air. I'm happy for them."

"So, if they take *my* room tonight, does that mean I get to stay in yours?" I teased.

She entwined her fingers in mine. "I like that idea… but Grant and Talia could walk in on us in *either* room."

"Then we'll have to go somewhere else," I suggested. "I've wanted to get you out of that dress since the moment I saw you in it."

She bit her lower lip. "It's almost curfew. If we're gonna go somewhere, we'd better make it quick."

I'd never turned around so fast. "Uh, we're going to call it a night. Catch up with you guys later!"

Nadine and I waved to our friends. We hurried out of the Lounge so fast that Isa and Oliver didn't even see us. It was fine, because we knew they'd get back to our dorms safely tonight. Our friends would make sure of it.

"Where are we going?" Nadine asked.

I squeezed her hand and winked. "Come on."

Nadine giggled as she raced behind me. We ran through the halls, and a few people shot us odd glances. Eventually, we reached a deserted hallway and slowed down.

"Where are you taking me?" she asked.

I smiled. "Somewhere no one will find us."

I opened a door, revealing an ascending, twisted staircase. "You haven't taken Astrology yet, have you?"

She shook her head. "Not yet."

"Then allow me to show you around the astrology tower," I offered.

I dragged Nadine up the staircase and muttered a quick incantation to secure the door behind us. It wouldn't be hard for a professor to break the spell, but it'd give us a heads up if anyone tried to follow.

We stepped into a room at the top of the stairs. The room was circular, set on the highest level of one of the school's turrets. With the spell that made the school larger on the inside, the tower was far bigger than anyone would guess from the outside. Dark wood flooring spanned across the room, and shelves had been built into the outer walls. They were filled with spell books and candles. The room housed a section with tables and a projector, and another with telescopes. There was even a sitting area next to a fireplace.

The most amazing part of the room, however, was the domed glass ceiling. Light from the waxing crescent moon filled the room, and the stars twinkled above us. Snow dusted the bottom edge of the glass dome. Something about it seemed magical.

Nadine tilted her head back, taking in the massive dome. "This is amazing."

She looked so happy, and it warmed my heart to the very core. "You think that's cool? There's more."

Her eyes brightened as I headed over to the projector and turned it on. I clicked a few buttons on the remote the professor had left there, and suddenly, the night sky was all around us. Constellations projected onto the dark walls, spinning and dancing in a beautiful display. Soft music played in sync with the visuals. The program was used for teaching purposes, but Nadine took it in like it was a work of art.

She spun around, eyeing the twinkling stars on the walls. "Lucas, I love it."

I couldn't take my eyes off her. "I love *you.*"

Her breath caught as she looked up at me. "I love you, too."

I reached for her dress, and my fingers grazed over the strap. For all the stars in the room, she was the most gorgeous thing here. "Am I wrong for thinking that this is perfect?"

She shook her head. "Tonight has been so much fun. I haven't felt this comfortable in ages. I mean, watching you dance on stage…"

I chuckled. "Maybe we shouldn't talk about it."

"No," she said with a smile. "Let's talk about it. I thought it was sexy as hell."

My eyebrows shot up. "Me? In your dress? Was… sexy?"

"I've never seen you look so confident. And that thing you did with your hips…" She bit her lower lip, and her gaze dropped to my jeans. "The whole time you were on stage, all I could think about was how I wanted you to do that to *me.*"

I chuckled. "You were jealous of the cane?"

"Hell yeah, I was jealous," she said.

I moved my hand, and the strap of her dress slid down her shoulder. She didn't move to lift it back into place. Heat flared through my body, and my heart hammered. Holy shit, could this be it?

My mouth went dry in anticipation. "I already got you out of that dress once tonight. Think I can do it again?"

Nadine placed her hand on the side of my face and leaned in. Her lips brushed across my cheek, then whispered the words I'd been dying to hear. "I dare you to."

I had no idea what it would feel like to finally succumb to the desire. Nadine's invitation made me move faster than I had in my entire life. I swept her up in my arms and carried her over to the couch nearby. She laughed as I laid her down, and she tossed her purse to the side.

"What's so funny?" I asked as I stripped her shoes off.

Her chest heaved as she stared up at me. "Nothing at all. I'm enjoying myself."

"Oh, you are?" I teased. "You like this?"

I ran my hands up her leg, stopping just before I hit the apex of her thighs. She shivered beneath my touch.

"I do," she said breathlessly.

"You like this?" I wrapped my fingers around the bottom of her panties, grazing her wet areas.

She moaned. "I do."

"You like… this?" I drew back and began spinning to the music that filled the room.

Nadine sat up straighter, eyeing me with hungry eyes. "Keep going…"

"And this?" I thrust my hips forward, like I had when I was on stage.

Her jaw dropped, and I realized for the first time how serious she'd been about finding my act sexy. I thought she'd meant it was entertaining, not that it actually *turned her on*.

"What do you think of this?" I teased as I pulled my shirt over my head.

Nadine took in shallow breaths as her eyes roamed over my naked torso. "You're such a tease!"

I leaned over the couch, closing the distance between us in a second. My lips hovered an inch away from hers. My breath wavered, but I kept my voice calm. "You want to be teased? Because I can tease you."

Her lips curled into a smile. "For how long?"

It was a challenge. She wanted to see which one of us would crack first. It sure as hell wasn't going to be *her*.

My lips swooped down to meet hers, and she flung her arms around my neck. Nadine leaned back, and I lay on top of her. Her lips moved over mine with such fervor that my head spun.

"Make love to me, Lucas," she said breathlessly.

She didn't have to ask me twice. I yanked on her panties, but I was apparently too eager to get them off, because they ripped in half on one side. I paused for a moment, but she grabbed them out of my hand and tossed them aside.

"Don't worry about it," she said, before her lips were on mine again.

Nadine yanked my belt off, then unbuttoned my pants. All the blood in my body seemed to go to one place. I couldn't think of anything but her—of taking her right here, right now, and showing her just how much I loved her.

I kicked my pants off, then my underwear. Nadine's hand curled around my cock, and I gasped.

"Are you sure about this?" I asked between kisses.

"I've never been... surer about... anything," she gasped between breaths.

My hands moved up her dress, running along her curves, until I pulled the dress off. Nadine undid the clasp of her strapless bra and tossed that on top of our other clothes. We were both completely naked, and my entire body trembled in anticipation. Our naked bodies collided as we kissed. Her skin was so soft and warm. It was amazing. I positioned myself on top of her, my dick landing between her legs.

"Wait!" Nadine said, pushing at my chest.

My whole body gave a start. "Is something wrong?"

She leaned over, fumbling for her purse. A moment later, she held up a foil packet. "We forgot protection."

My shoulders sagged in relief. "Thank the Goddess you remembered."

Nadine smiled as she opened the packet and rolled the condom over my length. I shivered under her touch. She lay back down, and I couldn't help but stare at her naked form. The swell of her breasts, the curve of her tummy, and the sight of her most sexual areas had me going wild. But it was the look in her eyes that did me in—the passionate desire reserved just for me.

"I'm ready," she whispered.

I kissed her like I'd never kissed her before, then slid inside of her. Nadine gasped, then began moaning in pleasure. She wrapped her arms around me, then yanked me closer with her legs. I thrust my hips into her, and we moved in a rhythm that I didn't think was possible for our first time together. But we knew each other better than anyone else. Whatever she thought, I swore I *felt*. Tiny little moans escaped her lips, and I lived for them. I thrust harder and faster, and I explored every inch of her body with my hands, then trailed kisses to every body part I could reach.

Nadine pressed her heels into the couch, lifting her hips so I could go deeper. I grabbed her ass and increased my speed.

I didn't think she'd meant to, but she lifted her hips even further, and we went spiraling to the ground. I caught us in the midst of the fall and slowed our momentum. I landed on my back, and Nadine bit her lip.

"Whoops. I'm sorry!" she said. "I was just really getting into it."

"Don't worry about it," I told her, eyeing her up and down. "I think I like you on top."

A blissful smile spread across her face. "I can be top."

Nadine eased down onto me again, so slowly that it sent shivers up and down my body. She began rolling her hips over me, and her breasts bounced. I grabbed them, and she gasped in pleasure. My hands explored her, until they settled on her hips. Feeling her move over top of me in that way was so fucking sexy—it was my undoing.

I gasped as I reached my peak. She rolled her hips faster, and I thrust my dick deeper into her. If she didn't know how I felt by now, she never would, because I'd never felt so in love as I did in that moment.

Nadine and I settled as I came down from my high. All I could do was lie there limply, enjoying the tingles spreading across my skin. I closed my eyes and let my breath slow.

She leaned down and placed a soft kiss on my cheek. "How was that?"

"Amazing," I breathed.

"You look so happy," she whispered.

"That's because I am," I said.

"Perfect."

I finally opened my eyes and saw that Nadine was beaming. I clicked my tongue. "Not perfect yet," I told her.

She raised an eyebrow. "Oh?"

"Your turn."

I grabbed her around the waist, then lifted her back onto the couch. Nadine chuckled as I spread her legs and ducked my head. The moment my lips grazed her bud, her laughter died. It was immediately replaced by one gasp after another. My fingers slid inside of her, and I massaged her in the way I knew she liked.

One final moan left her lips, before she was contracting around my fingers. She grabbed my hair and writhed beneath me, and I buried my face into her soft skin, inhaling her sexual scent.

"Oh, my..." Nadine breathed as she sagged against the couch. "That was..."

"Perfect?" I finished for her. I stripped off my condom and tossed it on top of my clothes, before I climbed onto the couch beside her. I lifted her until she was cradled in my arms.

Nadine tilted her head back and closed her eyes. A blissful smile spread across her face, and I pushed her hair back to admire her incredible features. To know that *I* made her feel like that was the greatest feeling in the world.

She breathed a sigh. "Yeah… it was perfect."

TWENTY

I remained curled in Lucas's arms the rest of the night. When I told him it was perfect, I meant it in every sense of the word. I never wanted the moment to end.

Our first time together was unlike anything. The stars dancing around the room from the projector were like a metaphor to the unraveling of the cosmos occurring around us. When we made love, it was like we were the only two people in existence.

The prophecy was right. Lucas and I were bound together, our souls entwined. Last night had proven that in the best way possible.

But perfection couldn't last forever. When I returned to my dorm room the next morning, a sense of dread settled in my gut. Isa purred at my feet, which usually comforted me, but didn't today. It was Friday, the last day of the semester, which meant tonight was our last chance to visit The Dungeon before winter break, and find out the truth about the nightshade dealers.

"Are we ready for The Dungeon?" I asked Talia when she woke up. She and Grant had obviously had a long night, but I suspected they'd only stayed up talking, because she was alone when I returned to our room.

"It's all covered. Our disguises are ready. We'll meet here in our room tonight." Talia must've noticed the worried look on my face, because she added, "Are you okay?"

"My magic doesn't feel right yet, because of the Waning. What if we need it tonight?"

"It should be back soon," Talia said, though I thought she was just trying to reassure me. It was obvious the Waning worried her. "And we'll all be there. It's going to be okay."

I hoped, but deep down inside, I feared what sort of answers we might find about nightshade—and what we wouldn't.

Luckily, my Miriamic Law final was a written test. I was pretty confident I passed, but at this point I didn't really care what grade I got. I was just ready for this semester to be over.

The sun had already set by the time my friends and I gathered in my room. Mandy and Amy wore matching dresses, though Mandy's was black and Amy's was white. Talia had ditched her pink wardrobe for a navy-blue dress, as to not draw extra attention to herself, and Grant had taken extra time gelling his hair.

Lucas looked hot in an open button-down shirt that he'd rolled up to his elbows. His forearms were so damn distracting. I got hot just looking at them. All I could think of was what he looked like with his clothes off.

I had to distract myself. "How will this work?" I asked.

Mandy held up a stack of tarot cards. "I have enough tickets for everyone."

"I meant the disguises," I said.

"I came up with something that I think is going to work really well." Grant stepped forward with a proud smirk on his face. He conjured four small potions vials. "It's a potion I created. Well, Talia helped."

"I only got you the ingredients," she said. "You did the hard part."

"You stole the ingredients?" Lucas asked.

"We had no other option," Talia stated. "But my gift paid off. When Professor Lewis wasn't looking, I snuck into her office. My powers showed me which ingredients were used for different potions."

"How'd you steal them, though?" I asked. "Aren't there wards all around the school to prevent that?"

Talia shrugged. "It must be the Waning, because nothing happened. I snuck out faeshrooms."

"Faeshrooms?" Lucas asked.

"Mushrooms from Malovia," Grant said. "They're super rare in the coven, because the fae don't like to trade with us unless they have to, which is why I only got four vials out of it."

"What do the mushrooms do?" I asked.

"They contain trace amounts of fae magic," Grant explained. "Specifically, illusion magic. The potion won't change the way you look, but people won't recognize you when they look at you, either. It's like we're tricking their subconscious."

"This is perfect," Lucas said. "But who's going to take them? There's not enough for all of us."

"Amy and I will go in as ourselves," Mandy offered. "People know we hang out with you, but I talk to everyone. People still trust me, and Amy… well, she has connections, too."

Talia tilted her head. "You do?"

"I may know someone who's going to be there," Amy admitted, but she sounded eager to change the topic. "What exactly are we looking for at The Dungeon?"

"Anything we can learn about nightshade," Lucas said. "Our goal is to track down where twisted vine is growing, so we can expose the truth. It's possible the operation is headquartered in The Dungeon, but if it's not, we need to find out where it is. Nightshade didn't dry up when Magnus left town, so we have to find out who else is involved. Someone took over, and we have to stop them. We'll talk to people and search The Dungeon for clues."

"The priestesses won't do anything without proof, though," I added. "We need to be taking a record of everything we find. Pictures, voice recordings—anything."

Lucas held up his voice recorder that he used in his journalism class. "I'll be recording audio all night."

"Then let's go," I stated. I quickly changed into a cute crop top and tight jeans.

After I changed, Grant passed around the potion, and we drank it. I knew who my friends were based on what they were wearing, but when I looked at them, it was like seeing them out of the corner of my eye.

"That is *wicked*," Mandy raved.

"It will only last a few hours, though," Grant said. "It's just past sundown, so we have until curfew to get our answers."

We hurried out of the room and to the basement of the school. We didn't take the cats, because we didn't want to be recognized. We followed the map on the back of the tarot cards, until we found the spot marked with a white dot. It was in a different place than last time, but the same door materialized from out of the bricks.

Music pulsed down a long hallway lined with red curtains. At the end of the hall, we entered a room full of flashing lights and dancing students. Talia covered her ears and said something, but I couldn't hear her; the music was too loud.

I leaned over and shouted, "What?"

"Exactly!" she screamed back. "I can hardly hear myself think!"

I gazed over the club from where we stood on the balcony. There wasn't a band on stage like last time—just music pulsing from the speakers overhead. A few girls had climbed on stage to dance. The dance floor was packed so tightly that it looked impossible to wade through. Students lounged around on couches, chatting and laughing, and the bar was packed. It didn't look like the bartenders could keep up with their orders.

"Nad and I will take the bar!" Lucas shouted to the others. "We'll see who will talk."

"Amy and I will talk to people on those couches," Mandy replied. "See what you can get out of the twins. They're the ones I got the nightshade from, along with The Dungeon tickets. I think they know more than they'll tell me."

Lucas nodded firmly. "We'll see what we can find out."

Talia and Grant were left with the dance floor. "We'll survey the room for possible exits," Grant said. "If nightshade is being brewed down here, the room could be hidden."

We all split up. Lucas held tight to my hand as we waded through the crowd. When we reached the bar, another couple was leaving, and we pushed through everyone else to grab a seat. I spotted Christine and Ashley on the other side of the bar, laughing and clinking their glasses together. They were obviously thrilled that finals were over, but they looked a bit out of their element. I didn't think they came here a lot.

We waited a while before the bartender finally came over to us. When he turned, I realized that it was Alex—or Shane. I still couldn't tell the difference between them.

"Alex! Another!" someone from down the bar shouted, confirming which twin it was.

"I'll be right there!" Alex called back. He set a coaster in front of each of us. "What can I get you two?"

Lucas leaned over the bar. "Could you pour us some… nightshade?"

Alex's eyes flashed. "I'm not familiar with that drink."

"Then perhaps you can point us in the direction of someone who is," Lucas said.

Alex frowned. "Sorry, friend, but I don't know what you're talking about."

He was a bad liar. I tugged my shirt down a little, showing off my cleavage, and I leaned over the bar. "Alex, was it?" I practically sang. The voice I used made me want to gag, but it was part of the ruse. "Surely my best friend didn't lie about you. She said you'd show us a good time."

Alex narrowed his eyes. "Who exactly is your friend?"

I hesitated a moment. I couldn't out Mandy, so I said the first name I thought he'd recognize. "Tate Murphy."

Alex chuckled and shook his head, like it was typical of Tate. "She ran out? Of course she did. I warned her it wouldn't last if she was going to share."

I was shocked, but I didn't let it show. Alex couldn't be serious. *Tate* was using nightshade?

It actually made a lot of sense, now that I thought about it. There were times when Tate seemed extra bubbly, and times when she was downright depressed or laser-focused on a task. She could get irritable in an instant. I always thought maybe she had some undiagnosed personality disorder, but these were all classic signs of nightshade use. I couldn't believe we hadn't seen it. There was no way Talia knew about this.

"Look, I'll be straight with you," Alex said, lowering his voice. "All I've got behind the bar is alcohol. If Tate needs something else, she knows where to find it. So, can I pour you a drink?"

"Sex on the beach," I said, because it was the only drink I knew. "For both of us."

Alex poured our drinks, and Lucas left him a tip. We turned from the bar to look out at the crowd. I only pretended to sip my drink, because I didn't drink alcohol.

"Can you believe Tate's dealing?" I asked.

"Maybe she's just using," Lucas pointed out.

I shook my head and sighed. "Ugh. She seems so innocent."

Lucas cocked an eyebrow. "Does she?"

I pressed my lips together. "You may have a point. But she can't know anything, right? I mean, Gregory didn't."

Lucas shrugged. "We won't know until we ask."

I looked around the room. The longer I studied the crowd, the more I saw it—nightshade was *everywhere*. All around the club, people opened their mouths and dropped liquid under their tongue. They tried to be discreet about it, but it was obvious if you paid attention. If they weren't actively taking nightshade, they were certainly high on it. Dilated pupils stared back from everywhere I looked.

"Holy shit, it's everywhere," Lucas said as he glanced around.

My eyes continued to scan the crowd, and I noticed dark hair spilling over the back of one of the couches. Tate threw her head back and laughed. Shane sat next to her and draped his arm around her shoulder. He lifted his hand above her head, and I saw the small drop of liquid fall through the air. She caught it in her mouth and continued laughing, like she was having the time of her life. She was already getting high.

I nudged Lucas. "I found her."

He set his drink down. "Looks like Tate has some questions to answer."

We stood and started toward the couches.

"What's our play?" Lucas asked.

I smirked. "I think I know just how to speak Tate's language. How good are you at acting?"

"I can try," he offered.

I looped my arm through his elbow. "Just go with it."

I threw my head back and laughed loudly, stumbling into Lucas like I was drunk. As we made our way past Tate, I pretended to trip, landing right in her lap. Tate looked surprised for a moment, until her eyes darted down to my breasts.

"I'm *so* clumsy," I giggled, before throwing my arm around her. "Heeeey, girl! Hope you don't mind."

"Not at all," she said, pulling me closer.

That must've made Shane uncomfortable, because he took his arm off the back of the couch and leaned away from Tate.

"Unless your boyfriend minds," she added, shooting a glance toward Lucas.

"Oh, no!" I said, wiggling my eyebrows. "In fact, I'm sure he'd love to join us."

Shane scowled and turned to Tate. "Want another drink?"

"Absolutely!" she answered. "Oh, and grab one for my new friends!"

Shane obviously had a major crush on Tate, because he couldn't handle our fake flirting. He got up, and Lucas quickly took his spot.

"You're so pretty!" Tate said, before turning to Lucas. Her gaze roamed over his exposed forearms. "And you, sir, are handsome as hell. What are your names?"

"My name?" I chuckled, coming up with a blank. I spat out the first thing I could think of. "Faith."

"I haven't seen you around," Tate said.

"We're seniors," I lied, showing her the fake alchemy tattoo on my arm.

"Ooh, that's hot," she practically sang, but she couldn't take her eyes off my boobs.

"You look like you're having a good time," I remarked.

"Finals are done, and this club is the best place in this school." Tate laughed.

I plastered on a fake smile. "Well, my boyfriend and I are looking for a good time. Think you can help us?"

Tate's eyes brightened. "I would *love* to."

I giggled like a drunk girl and leaned close to Tate to whisper in her ear. "We heard this is a good place for nightshade."

Tate snickered. "You heard right."

She lifted her palm, and a vial of nightshade appeared out of nowhere. "The first hit's on me," she offered.

Lucas and I exchanged a wary glance. "You first," I practically sang to Lucas.

Tate handed him the vial, and she watched him closely. I lolled my head against her shoulder and grabbed her face. "You're so pretty. I love your eyes."

She tore her gaze off Lucas to look at me. "Aw, you're so sweet. I love your eyes, too."

Even as she said it, she kept her eyes on my boobs. I wasn't sure if it was the illusion—redirecting her gaze from my face—or if she was that interested in my chest. Perhaps a bit of both.

Lucas faked a dose of nightshade, then handed the vial to me. "Wow," he said, like he was already high. I frowned at him.

"It's really something, isn't it?" Tate asked.

"How long does it last?" Lucas questioned her. "It's my first time."

He was distracting her, while I pretended to place a drop under my tongue. Tate didn't notice we'd faked it.

"A few hours," she said.

I placed the cap back on the vial. "So, this is magical, right? How's it brewed?"

Tate smirked. "Pretty *and* smart. You want to brew some?"

I shrugged. "I'd be stupid not to try."

"Well, I don't know how it's made," Tate said. "I've never asked."

"But someone has to know," Lucas pressed. "I mean, where does it come from?"

Tate laughed. "I don't care, as long as it keeps coming."

Tate was obviously here to party. She didn't know anything.

Shane returned with a cocktail. His pupils were so large that his irises had nearly disappeared. It was a bit eerie.

"Hey, Shane," Tate said. "Do *you* know where nightshade comes from?"

"What?" he asked, like he couldn't believe she'd ask. "No, of course not. Nobody knows."

"Ooh, a mystery," I sang. "Do you have any clues?"

"I don't know anything," Shane said in a clipped tone. "Tate should know better than to talk to strangers."

"Oh, come on!" Tate groaned. "We're having a good time."

I was starting to get sick of this game. It was obvious Tate was clueless. If Shane knew anything, he wasn't going to talk. I really didn't know how we were going to find answers.

I hopped to my feet and grabbed Lucas's wrist. "I love this song! We have to dance!"

I shimmied my shoulders and yanked Lucas onto the dance floor. I waved to Tate as we left. Shane plopped down beside her, but she leaned away from him. Whatever she said to him didn't look pleasant. I think she blamed him for scaring us away.

"Where are we going?" Lucas asked.

"Somewhere else," I said. "Tate doesn't know anything. We can't waste our time down here."

He nodded in agreement. I turned toward the stage, only to run straight into someone dancing. A girl in a navy-blue dress turned, and it took me a second to realize it was Talia. I couldn't tell at first because of the potion, but I recognized her dress. She looked confused at first, then recognition dawned.

"Did you find anything yet?" she asked.

I frowned. "Not anything helpful, but we learned one thing you're not going to like."

She leaned into me to hear better. "What's that?"

I barely heard her over the music. "What?"

"I said, *what did you learn*!?" she shouted.

I still could hardly hear her. I turned to Lucas. "I can't hear anything! I'm taking her to the bathroom to talk."

He saluted me, since we could hardly hear each other. "I'll catch up with you soon."

I dragged Talia off the dance floor, and we entered the bathroom. It was still loud in there, but at least I could hear myself again. I checked the stalls, but we were alone.

"What's up?" Talia asked.

I sighed. "It's your sister. She's here."

I hated to be the one to tell her, but she deserved to know. Talia immediately went rigid. Her voice came out sounding hollow. "She's using, isn't she?"

I grimaced, but I nodded.

Talia groaned. "I *knew* it! I knew she was going to get herself into trouble. This is bad. Tate's not the type to quit."

"Our best way to help your sister is to stop nightshade production all together."

Talia went silent for a few beats. "I guess you're right. You haven't learned anything yet?"

"Nothing. You?"

She shook her head. "There are no other doorways besides the entrance and the bathroom."

My shoulders dropped, and I turned toward the mirror. It was eerie seeing myself in the mirror and not recognizing myself.

"It could be hidden like Grant said," I thought. "Concealed by magic…"

I reached toward the mirror, holding my breath. I thought for certain I was on to something, that my fingers would move straight through it like air. But my fingers met solid glass.

I sighed. "Was coming here a mistake? None of these students seem to know anything."

"Then maybe we have to stop looking at students," Talia pointed out.

"Who else are we going to get answers from?" I asked. "It's not like professors are roaming around the club."

"No, but *someone* must be running it, right? Just like someone is supplying nightshade to the students."

I thought about it. "I always assumed the club was run by students, but someone has to be supplying drinks at the bar. And this seems to be the hottest place to get your hands on nightshade. Someone's bringing it into the school."

"Or brewing it here," Talia added.

"Where, though?" I wondered out loud.

"I don't know." Talia looked as hopeless as I felt when she leaned against the sink beside me. She looked around and scoffed. "This feels surreal. The last time I was in here, I was crying over some loser."

"I'm *so* glad you broke up with him. Cody was awful."

Talia chuckled, like she knew all too well.

"Tal, can I ask you something?"

"Anything, Nadine. You're my best friend."

I hesitated, because I didn't want to hurt her feelings. "You don't have to answer this, and I'm sorry to bring it up, but I've always wondered… why didn't you report him?"

"For what?" she asked, but she knew exactly what I meant. "For manipulation? Coercion? I said *yes*. How could I possibly prove that I didn't want to go through with it? You know as well as I do that nothing happens in this coven without cold hard evidence."

"It's unfair that he got away with it," I said.

"I know," Talia replied, crossing her arms. "I'm just glad I got out when I did. It makes me sad to think of the girl I was. I was so dependent on him. I would literally wait for him to tell me what to do. I even wanted him to tell me who to *be*, like I thought that would make him happier."

"But it never did," I said.

She shook her head. "No. He always just wanted more. It's totally different with Grant. I can be myself and lean on him for support, and we can *both* be happy alongside each other. But I think I needed to learn that hard lesson for myself before I could be with him."

"I'm glad you did," I said. "I think you and Grant are the perfect couple."

She chuckled. "Better than you and Lucas?"

"Hey, now," I teased. "It's not a competition."

"Well, who got further with their man last night?" she asked.

I grinned. "Me."

Talia squealed. "I've been dying to ask! How far?"

"*That* far."

"Oh, my goddess!" Talia jumped up and down. "I want to hear the details."

"Hey! That's private," I said. "But it was amazing. Unfortunately, we don't have time for details. We have to get out there and find more answers."

Talia stood up straight. "Yes. Let's get back out there."

We left the bathroom, and I scanned the club for our friends. It was so packed in here that I barely recognized a single face.

Talia yanked on my arm and pointed toward the couches. "There they are."

I pushed through the crowd toward our friends. We reached them just in time to see Tate lock lips with Shane.

"I think—" Amy started to say, but the conversation stopped dead as she caught sight of Tate kissing Shane. Her expression was the most heartbreaking thing I'd ever seen.

She obviously really liked Tate. It had to be a knife to the gut to see her making out with someone else. I didn't know if Tate had seen Amy there, but it was a shitty thing to do. She'd been leading Amy on all semester.

Mandy's gaze darted toward Amy, then back to Tate. "Oh, hell no."

Mandy's features contorted into rage. She stomped straight up to Tate and tossed her drink all over her front.

Tate jumped away from Shane and leapt to her feet. "What the hell, bitch!?"

"I could say the same to you!" Mandy screamed. "What the fuck is your deal?"

"Me? I'm not the one throwing drinks on people!" Tate snarled. Her eyes were super dilated, and she'd obviously been using all night. "You've been nothing but cold to me all semester. What exactly do you have against me?"

"The way you treat Amy!" Mandy snapped. "It's unfair to lead her on the way you do, then go around making out with other people."

Tate scoffed. "That's none of your business. Amy and I are just having fun."

"Are you?" Mandy challenged. "Because look at her! That's not the face of someone who's having fun. That's the face of someone who's deeply hurt. She *loves* you."

Tate crossed her arms. "Then she can tell me herself."

All eyes turned to Amy. She blinked a few times, and tears rose to her eyes. "Mandy's right. I *am* hurt. I thought we had something together."

"We do," Tate whined. "But I thought we were just—"

"Whatever you thought, you thought wrong!" Mandy fumed.

"Amy," Tate begged, ignoring Mandy's outburst. "Of course we have something special. I just—"

Shane stood. "Hold on, Tate. You're *dating* her?"

Tate's gaze flickered between Shane and Amy. "I'm not dating *anyone*."

Shane just stared at her for a minute. The look on his face very clearly read, *are you fucking serious?*

"I'm sorry—" Tate said, but that apparently wasn't good enough for him, because he whirled around and stormed off.

Talia stepped forward and grabbed Tate's arm. "We need to talk."

Tate shoved her off. "Get off me, bitch. I don't even know you!"

Talia looked shocked for a second, before she remembered she was completely unrecognizable. She looked hopeless, like all she wanted to do was help her sister—and help Amy.

"Apologize," Mandy demanded.

Tate gaped at her.

"Apologize for leading her on!" Mandy yelled. "Amy deserves better than this. She's the kindest, sweetest person I know, and she had her heart set on you. You've been playing her all semester like some fucking toy when she deserves to be treated like a queen. I won't stand here and let you hurt the woman I love!"

My eyebrows shot up, and Lucas's jaw dropped from beside me. The meaning in Mandy's words was clear.

Amy stepped forward. "You… love me? I thought you were straight."

"I thought I was, too," Mandy said. "But seeing you with Tate all semester… I got jealous. I'm still trying to figure out my sexuality, but I know one thing for certain. I love you, and I want you to be happy. You seemed so happy with Tate."

"Well, yeah…" Amy said, taking Mandy's hands. "Tate and I have fun, but she's not *you*."

Tate gaped. "Wait, what?"

Amy dropped her gaze. "I don't know what to say, Tate. It's like you said; we're not *dating*."

"Yeah, but we're still—" Tate cut off. She stared at Amy like she couldn't believe what was happening.

Whatever Tate had tried telling herself, she clearly had deep feelings for Amy. Tears welled in her eyes.

"This wasn't supposed to happen this way!" Tate shoved past them, then hurried in the direction Shane had gone.

Mandy wore a guilty expression. "Should we go after her?"

"I'll check on her," Talia offered. She grabbed my arm and dragged me after her.

I barely had a chance to take in what happened. Lucas and Grant looked super confused.

"Tate won't recognize us," I reminded Talia.

"Doesn't matter," she said. "I know my sister, and I know how she acts when she doesn't get what she wants. She can't be alone right now."

I looked around for Tate, but I'd lost her. My eyes landed upon a guy beside the bar. He was older than us by at least ten years, and he had long hair tied into a low ponytail. My heart stalled. He tossed his head back and placed a drop of nightshade under his tongue. He wasn't even discreet about it. At least most of the students were *trying* not to be obvious. He said something to Alex, then turned away.

I yanked on Talia's sleeve and gestured toward the bar. "One of these things is not like the others."

Talia shot me a glance. "You think we have a lead?"

"I saw him at Wicked Alchemy a few months ago when I went there with Grant," I said. "The lady there called him *David*. He was picking up a package."

"A nightshade shipment?" Talia wondered.

"I'll bet you anything it was," I remarked.

"I think I recognize him, too."

"From where?"

"That night in the alleyway, when we were looking for clues on the missing boys," she reminded me. "He was talking to Professor Daymond. I mean, he was in the shadows, but it was definitely the same build, same ponytail."

"He's involved," I said, knowing it with my full being. "You look for Tate. I'll go after this guy."

"Be safe," Talia said.

I started pushing my way through the crowd, but David was already on the move. He stumbled one way, then the other. He was obviously drunk as well as high. People closed in on all angles, and I could barely keep track of him. I pushed past people. They scowled at me, but I didn't care.

A tall guy walked in front of me, and I practically tripped over him. When I righted myself a moment later, David was gone. My stomach turned to stone as I frantically glanced around the room. He was *just there*. Where had he gone?

I pushed through the crowd again, until it thinned near the bar. But no matter where I looked, I couldn't find David.

Fuck.

I had to get back to my friends. The more eyes we had looking for this guy, the faster we could find him.

"Did you find Tate?" Lucas asked when I reached him.

I shook my head. "Talia's looking for her. I found a lead. Older guy, long ponytail. Grant and I saw him at Wicked Alchemy."

"We'll start looking right away," Grant offered.

We split into different groups. Lucas and I pushed through the crowd, but we couldn't find David anywhere. I spotted Talia's blue dress, but she was glancing around the club hopelessly.

Lucas and I approached her. "Did you find your sister?" I asked.

"I can't find her anywhere!" Talia shouted over the music. "This place is too crowded."

"Let's keep looking," I insisted.

I didn't know how much time passed, but I was getting more and more frustrated. They could've left the club already, and we missed them.

I was about ready to give up when I spotted Tate climbing the stairs to the balcony. She stumbled into people. The poor girl looked like she barely knew where she was going.

"Tal!" I cried. "I found your sister."

We raced after her, but we were swallowed by the crowd. I tried to keep my eyes on Tate, but I couldn't. Lucas disappeared somewhere behind me. It must've taken us five minutes before Talia and I reached the top of the balcony—

And that's when the screams started. My heart came to an abrupt stop.

Two bodies lay sprawled across the floor, unresponsive. My stomach dropped at the sight of Tate and Shane clutching empty vials of night-shade. Talia's high-pitched scream tore through the club, chilling me to the bone. I immediately dropped to Tate's side and felt for a pulse. It was there, but it was faint.

"She's alive, but she's overdosed!" I cried. It didn't matter what Tate had done earlier—she didn't deserve this. *Nobody* deserved this.

Talia's knees buckled, and she pulled her sister into her lap. She shook her, like she might wake up. Talia screamed her sister's name, so loud that I was sure the whole club could hear it over the music.

Panic set in, and my heart began to race. I rushed over to Shane, but horror twisted in my gut when I felt for his pulse...

I felt nothing. It was already too late.

The moment I realized it, the entire club fell silent. Someone had turned off the music, and all the chatter died. The only sound was the terror-filled cries racking Talia's chest. "Tate! No! Wake up! Wake *up*!"

My head spun. I could hardly process that there was a dead body lying in front of me.

"WE NEED A MEDIC!" someone shouted, but I didn't see who. That snapped me out of it, and I began chest compressions on Shane's lifeless form.

Someone rushed to my side—an older girl I didn't know. "We're grad students in medical studies. We can help."

I quickly got to my feet and moved aside. Her friend knelt beside Tate.

The girl quickly assessed Shane, but her features fell. "He's gone."

My hand slapped over my mouth, and I backed up slowly. I didn't even realize how far I'd distanced myself until I stumbled into a group of onlookers behind me. Talia sobbed while the other med student looked over Tate.

"She has a chance, but we have to get help immediately," she said in a rush.

"I'm on it!" Her friend leapt to her feet and raced out of the club.

"She's going to make it, isn't she?" Talia sobbed. "Tell me she's going to make it!"

The med student hesitated. The tears beading at her eyes said it all. *It's going to take a miracle.*

"We'll do the best we can," she said.

People yelled and cursed from behind me. I turned to see my friends break through the crowd.

"Goddess," Lucas breathed.

"What's going on?" Grant demanded. His eyes went wide when he saw Tate lying there.

"Tate's overdosed," I said in a hollow tone.

Amy's hands shot over her mouth. "Oh my goddess!"

"I'm so sorry," Mandy breathed, staring in horror. "I didn't think—"

"It's not your fault," I told her.

Talia's entire body shook as she stood. She stared down at her sister in horror, like she couldn't believe what she was seeing. Slowly, her horror turned to vengeance. Her hands curled into fists, then whirled toward me. "We're finding that dealer. *Now.*"

I stopped her. "Tal, attacking him isn't going to change this."

She glanced around at the onlookers, then yanked me down the hall toward the entrance. Our friends followed.

"Attacking David won't save her, but finding that Wand *can*," she insisted once we were alone. "The Alchemy Wand can affect all Alchemy magic—which means it can halt the effects of nightshade. This was caused by magic, and it can be reversed by it, too."

She was right, but finding the Wand in time could be impossible. "What if we don't find it?" I asked.

Tears streamed down Talia's face. "We have to try!"

By now, the club had returned to chaos. Alex had reached the balcony.

He wailed as he held his brother to his chest. Voices layered over one another, and I could see people on the balcony moving to get a better look. Everyone was trying to get answers about what just happened.

Someone stumbled out of the crowd, making a break for the exit. He stopped in his tracks the moment he saw us blocking his path.

Rage flared in my belly. "That's him," I growled.

David started to back up, but Lucas threw up a shield behind him. David stumbled to the side. He was obviously really drunk and could hardly stand on two feet. Grant and Lucas lunged at him in unison. They grabbed him by the arms and shoved him against the wall.

"Where's the nightshade!?" Lucas demanded.

David's head lolled to the side, and he didn't answer. Lucas wasn't having it. He smacked the side of his face to keep him awake. David's eyes sprang open for a second.

"I'm not going to ask you again," Lucas snapped. "Where's Magnus's operation? Where's he brewing nightshade? Where's the cauldron? Tell me!"

David mumbled something, but I didn't hear it.

"What's he saying!?" Grant cried.

"Get off me!" David sneered. He swung his arm out and knocked Lucas in the face.

That *really* pissed me off. I stomped straight up to him and grabbed him by the collar. "Look, asshole. A student *died* tonight because of your drugs. Another overdosed and may not make it unless we find the cauldron you and your boss are brewing this stuff in."

"You say that like I give a shit," he snarled.

"Look at her!" I screamed. I grabbed his face and turned it toward Tate. She lay just beyond the end of the hallway. The med student barked orders to keep everyone back. "Look at her and tell me you don't care."

David gritted his teeth.

"A death looks pretty bad for your profits, doesn't it?" I said. "Not to mention that I'm a priestess with the power to burn you at the fucking stake. So unless you want to be charged with homicide, I suggest you tell us *exactly* where to find that cauldron!"

David's eyes widened slightly, but apparently not enough to clear his head, because he didn't question whether I was a priestess or not. With the spell I was under, he couldn't recognize me.

His eyes darted down the hall, toward Shane's lifeless body. "Nightshade wasn't supposed to hurt anyone. Magnus promised no one would get hurt."

"It's too late for that," Grant snarled.

"No one else has to get hurt," Talia begged. "Please, my sister's life is at stake."

"Alchemy," David rasped.

"Yeah, we know," Grant said. "Nightshade is made by Alchemists."

"No, no, no." David shook his head. "Wicked Alchemy. It's being brewed there."

I shot a glance at my friends. Magnus owned the shop, but there was no way they were running a nightshade operation out of it. Was he playing us? "There's hardly anything there. That shop is tiny."

"There's a hidden room," David admitted. "It can only be accessed by Alchemists..."

David sagged against the wall in his drunken stupor. I smacked him. "How? A spell, a potion...?"

"Potion... a powder..." he mumbled, but that was all he said. His eyes rolled back into his skull, and his knees gave out. Lucas and Grant dropped him.

"Fuck," Lucas growled. He whirled around and shouted at the med student. "We've got another one! Still breathing, but barely."

"Everyone off the balcony! Right now!" she screamed.

Students clamored down the stairs. The chatter was deafening.

"We have to go to Wicked Alchemy and find that hidden room as soon as possible—" I started, but I cut off when three professors burst through the door.

Professor Richards halted in his tracks. His jaw dropped when he saw the scene at the end of the hall, but his features quickly turned to pure fury. He was always one of my favorite professors, so gentle and kind. But tonight, he looked downright *scary*.

The professors barely looked our way as they rushed past us. A group of nurses came in behind them. They immediately conjured stretchers and got to work.

"Students!" Professor Richards yelled over the club.

The entire crowd froze, and the room went dead silent.

"This party is officially over." Professor Richards's voice boomed over the crowd. "The priestesses have been notified of this incident, and they have decreed a mandatory gathering. This is *not* a request. You will be escorted from these premises and to the lawn, where the priestesses will address this matter. *Nobody* is to return to their rooms."

"But what if we need our coats?" a girl asked. I recognized the voice in the crowd. It was Christine. Her voice shook, and she sounded terrified. I didn't think she nor Ashley knew what had really been going on in this club.

"Yeah," Ashley agreed. "It's freezing out."

"Your rooms are being combed for nightshade," Professor Richards announced. "At this moment, every dormitory at the university is under evaluation. You are not allowed to return until the searches are completed."

Gasps traveled around the room. "They're going to search our stashes, too!" a guy exclaimed.

Professor Richards heard, and he was *pissed*. "You have nothing to worry about if you're innocent."

Professor Richards continued talking, giving students orders to move to the lawn while the nurses lifted the bodies onto stretchers. My friends and I turned toward each other.

Amy shook. "I—I'm freaking out. There's still nightshade stuff in my room from when we were working on figuring out the formula. They're going to find it!"

"Fuck," Grant growled. He obviously felt responsible for leaving it there.

Mandy's voice shook. "What's going to happen to Amy if they find it?"

"Jail time?" Amy guessed. "For all of us, maybe."

"It's too risky to go back to our rooms right now," I whispered. "That could get us into even more trouble, and we don't have the time. Tate's life is in danger. We *have* to get to Wicked Alchemy tonight, and get the Alchemy Wand so we can save her."

"Maybe we can kill two birds with one stone," Lucas suggested. "The Alchemy Wand can remove all traces of Alchemy magic, so even if they find Amy's setup, they won't know it's nightshade. They'd assume it was something else."

"Yes, that's perfect," I agreed. "It's the only way for us not to get caught."

"We just have to find some way to sneak away without being noticed," Talia said.

"Our illusion is still working," Grant pointed out. "The professors may not even recognize us as students."

"Except look at what we're wearing," Talia pointed out, gesturing to her dress.

Lucas lowered his voice. "It's how many of them against all these students? Sneaking away shouldn't be hard."

Amy wiped her nose. "I can't leave Tate. This is my fault—"

"No, it's not," Mandy insisted. "*I'm* the one who started the fight."

"Let's not argue about who's at fault," I said. "Amy and Mandy, you go to the infirmary and stay with Tate. We need someone with her anyway to let us know if the Wand worked. Talia?"

"I can't sit here and do nothing. I'm going to find the Wand. I need to save my sister." Her eyes glistened as she watched them lift Tate's stretcher.

"Wait!" Amy cried. She and Mandy rushed toward the medics. "We're her friends! We're coming with!"

The nurses shot a glance toward Professor Richards. He was an Alchemy professor and had Amy in a bunch of his classes. He knew she was one of the kindest, smartest students at school and that she could be trusted. He gave a gentle nod, and the nurses gestured the girls to follow.

"Wait, hold on," Grant hissed. "How do we know if this will work? We don't even know if the Wand will choose us."

I swallowed the lump in my throat. "We have to believe that it will, because it's our only option."

I hoped our gamble paid off, because if this didn't work, Tate would die… and there'd be no telling what would happen to the rest of us.

TWENTY-ONE

Rocks settled in my gut as we were escorted from The Dungeon by school staff. I couldn't quite wrap my head around what had happened. Shane was with us one moment, then gone the next. And Tate… might not make it. I wanted to hurl, but none of us were given a chance to grieve—or to even process it, really. We had to get that Wand, and we had to do it *now*.

We were herded like cattle to slaughter through the halls of Miriam Mansion. Nobody spoke. All I could hear was the sound of marching footsteps. The whole thing felt ominous and foreboding, so much that the hair on my arms stood. I tried a few doors as we passed, so we could duck inside and sneak out, but they were all locked.

Nadine shot me a worried look. We were nearing the Main Foyer, and we didn't have many more chances to leave. My gaze darted toward the grand staircase, and she nodded. I grabbed her hand, and the four of us ducked behind the staircase. My heart hammered as the students passed by, as if waiting for someone to notice us crouching there.

My heart stalled when I saw who was bringing up the rear of the crowd. Headmistress Verla wore a stern frown, and she kept a close eye on every student. I thought for sure she was going to spot us…

But she passed by without noticing.

I released a shaky breath when the sound of footsteps faded outside. I poked my head around the edge of the staircase and saw we were in the clear. I gestured to my friends. "Come on."

We darted out from under the stairs and sprinted down the hall toward the side entrance. Sneaking out of the school was easy. We crept to Nadine's car, and she kept the headlights off so we would make it off school grounds without being noticed. By the time we lost sight of the crowd, Nadine stepped on it.

"How much time do you think we have?" she asked.

I shook my head. "No idea."

"Let's just pray this works." Talia's voice shook.

Nadine slammed on the brakes when we reached the Catwalk. I shivered in the cold, and snow crunched under my feet as we snuck through the darkness. It was late enough that all the shops were closed, but I kept throwing glances over my shoulder. This place was really eerie in the dark.

Wicked Alchemy appeared ahead, but something hit me just then. "Fuck," I growled under my breath.

"What is it?" Grant asked.

"We didn't think of the wards!" I smacked my forehead. "How are we going to get past them?"

"I can break it," Nadine said confidently. "It's just like breaking a curse, right?"

"Have you ever done it?" Talia asked.

"No," Nadine admitted. "But I just have to move the magic."

"What about the Waning?" I pointed out. "You've been struggling with magic for days."

"It's coming back," she said. "And if the Waning is affecting those wards, it may be a blessing in disguise, the same way Talia obtained those faeshrooms."

We approached Wicked Alchemy, and Nadine raised her hands. "There's a ward, but it's weak. It shouldn't take much…"

A battle orb exploded out of Nadine's palm, and it slammed into the front window. The sound of shattering glass filled the street.

We all froze, but the Catwalk remained silent. No alarms went off. It was rare for the coven to use regular alarm systems, because our wards were better. But not tonight, apparently.

Nadine winced. "Whoops. I transformed the ward into battle magic. I didn't mean to lose control."

"Well, that's one way to get inside," I said as I stepped toward the shattered window.

I kicked a few shards of glass out of the way, then climbed through the window. I helped Nadine over the glass, and Grant helped Talia through. I turned toward the dark shop, eyeing the items on the walls like they might hold answers.

I tossed a light orb into the air. It hovered there, casting the room in shadows. "Where do we start?"

"In the back," Nadine said, starting for the door at the back of the shop. "They must have supplies to brew the potion that will reveal the hidden door—aha!"

She threw the door open and wore a proud smirk. I followed her into the room, my light hovering overhead. The room was small, no bigger than ten feet across, with storage shelves along the outside wall. Between the shelves sat a table with all kinds of potion ingredients.

Talia nearly tripped over the rug in the middle of the room as she entered, but Grant caught her. "Do you have any idea what potion David was talking about?" she asked him.

Grant looked unsure. "I might have an idea."

Nadine hurried over to the potion ingredients. She grabbed a handful of Alchemy stones that lay there. "Then let's get to work."

Grant eyed the potion ingredients. "This. This… and maybe this? No, this!"

"How can I help?" Nadine asked.

"Um… crush this." Grant shoved a mortar and pestle toward her, along with a jar full of herbs. He grabbed a bowl and moved frantically, like he wasn't quite sure what to do.

I hated just standing there. I had to do *something.* I nudged Talia and pointed to a stack of books on a nearby shelf. "Maybe they keep the spell nearby."

"Good idea," Talia said.

We hurried over to the spellbooks and began flipping through them. My eyes scanned the pages quickly, but these were all liquid potions. David had said we had to make a powder. I tossed that book back on the shelf and flipped through the next one. Meanwhile, Grant and Nadine mixed together potion ingredients. Green light filled the room as Grant worked his magic into the mixture, then—

Boom!

The potion exploded. I jumped and looked up to see particles flying everywhere. Grant's face was black with soot, and his hair stood on end. Nadine coughed and fanned the powder out of her face.

Grant cleared his throat. "Well, that was clearly the wrong spell."

"Hold on! I think I found it!" Talia cried. *"Revelare Pulvis.* That means *revealing powder*, right?"

"Loosely translated, yes," Grant said, sounding excited.

Talia slapped the book onto the table, and Grant looked over the spell. "It's a little more complicated than I thought."

"But you can do it?" I asked.

Grant smirked. "I can do it. Everyone stand back."

Nadine came to my side, and I wrapped my arm around her waist as we backed into the corner. Grant worked quickly, but his measurements were precise. This time when his green magic lit the room, it began to swirl into a vortex above him. The powder in the bowl lifted into the air, entangling with his magic to create a glowing powder. Watching him perform the spell was like viewing the Northern Lights. It was beautiful, but we didn't have time to admire it. The magic swirled back into the bowl and dimmed.

"I did it!" Grant cried.

"Excellent. Now how do we reveal the doorway?" Talia asked.

Grant reached into the bowl and grabbed a handful of powder. "We'd have to place the powder over the door to reveal it. Like… here, maybe?"

We all held our breath as Grant tossed the powder against an empty section of wall. Nothing happened.

"Hold on, let's think about this," Nadine suggested. "There's nothing beyond that wall but the forest, right?"

"What if it's a portal?" Talia theorized.

I doubted it. "The coven's portal magic isn't very good."

"A space-bending spell, maybe?" Grant thought aloud.

"It's possible," I said.

"Or…" Nadine stepped to the middle of the room and pounded her foot on the rug. "We need to go *down*."

"Of course!" I grabbed the corner of the rug and yanked it up, tossing it aside.

Grant grabbed another handful of powder and tossed it onto the floor. In front of our eyes, the hardwood floor transformed, revealing a trap door beneath our feet.

"We found it!" Nadine breathed. "The Crock is here!"

I pulled the trap door open and stared into the dark chasm below. "Let's go get it."

I guided my witch light into the hole, and it illuminated a ladder below. I climbed down it first and looked around. The room was the same size as the one above, almost a near replica. It was filled with all types of storage—extra potion ingredients, empty vials like the ones nightshade came in, and a bunch of brooms piled in the corner. But there was no Crock of Death.

"Come on down, guys," I called up to them. "It's safe, but I don't see the—"

I cut off when I turned around. Behind me stood a large door built from worn wooden planks. Large iron hinges stretched across the door, and the big handle looked ancient. A shiver ran down my spine.

Iron... to deter the fae.

We were *definitely* in the right place.

My friends gathered at the bottom of the ladder. "That looks... creepy," Talia said. "Could it be dangerous?"

I stepped forward. "Of course it's dangerous. The Crock of Death is behind there. Magnus did his due diligence keeping it a secret. But we won't know what danger we face until we try—"

"Lucas!" Nadine warned, but I already placed my hand on the doorknob.

I expected a spell to blast me back or something, but instead, a voice filled the room. I jumped back, totally taken off guard. *"I'm the Door of Mystery, from high magic evolved. I open only when my puzzle is solved."*

The voice wasn't male nor female. It appeared to be coming from the door itself.

"A riddle?" I said thoughtfully.

"You speak in strange fragments. You're wasting my time. The Door of Mystery responds only to rhyme."

I pressed my lips together. "Um... okay. *We're seeking passage. Let's meet in the middle. You'll let us through if we solve your riddle.*"

"*You have yourself a deal, as fair as it is. Be quiet, listen closely, for your riddle is this; I'm in the beginning, but I'm not part of time. I'm at the end of everything—now you must solve my rhyme.*"

I turned to my friends, my brow furrowed. "What's at the beginning and the end, but not referring to time?"

"Maybe... it's spatial? Like the beginning and end of a string?" Grant theorized.

Nadine pressed her lips together. "We have to read between the lines. There has to be a clue inside the riddle."

"I can figure it out," Talia said brightly.

"You know the answer?" I asked.

"Not exactly," she admitted. "But if others have answered the riddle before, I can get a vision of it."

Talia walked to the door and splayed her palm across it. She concentrated for a full minute, before dropping her shoulders. "The riddle changes every time. I don't know the answer."

Nadine began pacing. "Hold on. *I'm in the beginning, but I'm not part of time. I'm at the end of everything...*" She muttered the riddle over and over.

"Well, what's at the beginning?" Grant said. "The Big Bang, right?"

"But that's *part of time*," Talia pointed out.

"The beginning of *what*, then?" Grant asked, sounding frustrated.

"The riddle, maybe?" I theorized. "But that makes no sense with the end of *everything*."

"I got it!" Nadine cried. "It's the letter G. It's in the word *beginning*, but not in the word *time*, and it's at the end of the word *everything*."

"Nad, that's great!" I whirled back toward the Door of Mystery. "*You think you're clever, but we solved it, you see. Your riddle is simple. The answer is G.*"

The doorknob clicked. "We did it!" Grant exclaimed.

"Way to go, Nadine," Talia praised.

Nadine shrugged. "Let's keep moving."

The door swung open, and my witch light illuminated the space beyond. A long, narrow hallway stretched so far that we couldn't see the end of it. It had to be a space-bending spell, because nothing else made sense. A vine that looked like black twisted branches grew along the floor and up the walls. Each vine was covered in a layer of slime that shimmered beneath my light.

"Twisted vine," Grant said. "Tons of it."

"The cauldron must be at the end of this hall," Talia whispered. Timidly, she stepped forward, watching carefully to avoid the vines—but they grew too close together. She stepped on one, and my heart lurched.

Everything happened so fast. The vines snapped outward, wrapping around her legs. Talia screamed as the plant yanked on her. She fell flat on her back and was pulled several feet away from me. The vines dragged her down the hall. I lunged for her and threw myself onto the vines. Our hands connected, and Grant and Nadine grabbed my legs to pull me back through the doorway.

"Hold on, Tal!" I yelled. "I've got you!"

I pulled with all my might, but the vines tugged harder on her legs. They began to curl around her middle like snakes looking for their next kill. My heart hammered as I tried to overpower them. Vines grew around my torso, but I ripped them off with my free hand. I conjured a battle orb and threw it into the vines along the wall—the ones that were creeping toward her. The orb sizzled against them, like they vines had been burned. The vines even let out a hiss, as if they were screaming out in pain. It was enough to give us a chance.

"It's working!" Nadine cried. "Do it again!"

I tossed another battle orb at the vines along the opposite wall, and the same thing happened. Grant aimed an orb near Talia's feet, and it struck just inches below her shoes. Several of the vines retreated, but as the injured ones shrank away, more and more came in for the kill.

I let my anger take hold, and I formed a high-powered battle orb in my fist. I grabbed one of the largest vines in my hand and let the battle orb go. It exploded through the network of vines, searing them with rippling purple magic.

My friends yanked on me one last time, and Talia and I broke free. We landed in a heap in the other room, gasping for breath.

"Holy shit!" Talia cried, throwing her hand over her heart. "Someone should've warned me that the twisted vine was *alive!*"

"Of course it's alive," I said, trying to catch my breath. "It's a plant."

Talia frowned. "You know what I meant."

"I had *no idea* it would do that," Grant said. "But we can't walk down this hallway if the vines are going to attack us."

"There must be another way through," Nadine remarked as she got to her feet.

Talia stood and took a cautious step toward the open doorway.

"Be careful," Nadine warned, but the twisted vine didn't reach out for her. It seemed confined only to the hall.

"Maybe I can figure out how Magnus did it," Talia thought aloud. She placed her hand on the door frame and closed her eyes. Her eyebrows knitted in deep concentration.

Anxiety twisted in my belly. I didn't know how much time we had left.

Talia's eyes shot open. "The brooms!"

I looked at the pile of brooms in the corner. "What are we supposed to do? Fly them?" I said sarcastically.

"Yes," Talia said with a straight face.

Holy shit. She was serious.

She walked over and grabbed one. "They must be infused with Mentalist magic, because I saw Magnus riding one in my vision."

"Headmistress Verla said brooms can be enchanted to fly," Nadine said. She took one and spun it in her hands, inspecting it. As if deeming it safe, she mounted the broom and shot me a smirk. "Who wants to go first?"

"I will," I said firmly, snatching up a broom. "It could be dangerous."

"We don't have time to stand around talking about it," Grant said.

I climbed on my broom, but it went nowhere. "How do you do this?"

"Well, it's Mentalist powers," Talia pointed out. "Which means the magic connects with the mind. Just tell it what to do."

I cleared my throat. "Um, okay. *Up.*" The broom tossed me upward so fast that I lost my grip and flew across the room. I landed on my shoulder several feet away.

Nadine slapped her hand over her mouth and laughed. "I'm so sorry! I shouldn't have laughed. Are you okay?"

I grimaced, though I had to admit it *was* kind of funny. "Peachy."

I mounted the broom and guided it up slowly this time, then took off down the hall like a bullet. I moved so fast that my hair blew back from my face. I nearly disappeared into the darkness, before I conjured another light and kept it speeding beside me.

"Whoa! This is insane!" Grant cried from behind me.

"Um, I need to get myself one of these," Talia said.

"Agreed!" Nadine called.

We sped down the long hall, but the twisted vine didn't react like it had before. It was like it didn't know we were there at all.

My light shimmered against something ahead, and I realized we were coming to the end of the hall. The corridor widened to a larger room. I slowed my broom and flew downward. I jumped off the broom as soon as I entered. It was a storage room of some sort, no bigger than a classroom, with tons of shelves lined with potion ingredients, as well as barrels and boxes I couldn't see inside of. My friends landed behind me, and I sent my witch light toward the ceiling to illuminate the space.

My breath hitched when I saw it—a cauldron sitting on a table at the center of the room. It was a decent size, but not huge. It looked like it could hold at least five gallons of brew. It was beautiful, with twisted handles that resembled tree branches and a shiny black finish. It looked exactly as I would imagine a fae goddess's crock would. There was no doubt about it—

We'd found the Crock of Death.

TWENTY-TWO

The magic hit me the second I stepped into the room, tugging at my guts and twisting my insides. I stumbled as I dismounted my broom.

Lucas caught me. "You okay?"

I stood straighter. "I can sense the magic. It's really strong."

Grant stepped forward. "Let's get to work on this brew, so we can get the Wand out."

"Wait!" I cried. All eyes turned to me, and my voice shook. "The magic I'm sensing… it's a curse."

Something Mother Miriam had said to me came back. *The first Wand lies inside the cursed cauldron, as you predicted. You, Nadine, must be the one to pursue the Alchemy Wand.*

"Mother Miriam knew," I whispered.

Lucas eyed me. "What do you mean?"

"She visited me recently," I said. "She said *I* had to be the one to find it. I know why now—because I need to break the curse upon the cauldron."

I stepped toward the cauldron. The magic intensified the closer I got.

"What's the curse?" Grant asked cautiously.

I ran my fingers over the rim of the cauldron, studying the energy signature. "I'm not sure, exactly."

"Let me see what I can learn," Talia offered. She stepped in front of the cauldron. She closed her eyes and flattened her hands on either side of it.

Her eyebrows pinched together, like she was thinking hard. Her eyelids fluttered, and she swayed on her feet. Grant steadied her.

"Tal, you okay?" he asked, shaking her.

She didn't respond, and my pulse quickened.

"Talia!" I yelled.

She snapped out of her trance and stumbled backward. "Whoa. This magic is *very* strong."

"What did you see?" Lucas asked.

Talia's breath wavered. "Nadine's right about the curse. It's ancient. The fae cursed the cauldron to backfire on a witch's brew, and steal your magic."

My eyebrows shot up. "Lucas, do you remember what Hattie told us about nightshade? She said the Elementai had tried replicating the brew, but that something was missing."

"Yeah, the Crock," he said.

"I think it's more than that," I replied. "I think more specifically, this curse is the unique ingredient."

"Like the magic is leaching into the brew, and *causing* nightshade's side effects?" Grant asked.

I nodded. "That must be why the withdrawal symptoms are so intense —why going off nightshade makes you lose your magic. Nightshade wouldn't exist without the cauldron's curse."

The room fell silent for a moment.

"How did your grandpa use the Crock, then?" Lucas wondered. "If it's cursed not to work for anyone, did he actually accomplish what he set out to?"

Worry twisted in my gut when I realized there was a very real possibility that my grandfather's spell never worked. The Wand might not be in the cauldron.

"Let me look into the history of the Crock again," Talia offered. "If Nadine's grandfather made it work, I can see how to make it work for us."

Talia placed her hand on the cauldron again. She stood there for a solid minute, swaying on her feet as her eyelids fluttered. The visions must've been intense, because Grant held her upright. I pressed closer to Lucas, worried about what Talia might find—or not find.

Finally, she pulled her hands away. "Nicholas didn't break the curse, but he tamed it. He used Alchemy crystals to brew the potion."

"So the Wand is here for sure?" Grant asked.

Talia swallowed. "Yes, but to retrieve it—"

"I need to tame this curse," I finished for her. "And my magic is only at half power."

Talia nodded. "But there's more. To retrieve the treasure inside, the person who brews the potion must drink it."

"What happens then?" I asked in a hollow tone.

Talia's tone wavered. "You have to prove your intentions to the cauldron… or suffer."

Grant swallowed. "Suffer how?"

"I—I don't know," Talia stammered. She shook off a shiver. "The vision is unclear. There was just so much screaming."

Grant lifted his chin. "I'll do it."

"Grant, no!" I protested. "We don't know how that potion could affect you."

"The Crock only refuses people who are seeking its material riches, right?" Grant asked. "We're not here for that. We're here to get that Wand to save people—to save Tate, and to end the Waning. I can do this."

"We don't know what the Crock will decide," Lucas pointed out, sounding worried.

"We have to try!" Grant insisted. "Tate might not have much time left, and I'll be damned if I let Talia's sister die without trying to save her. We need that Wand! I've broken down the nightshade formula. I can brew the potion."

"But then you have to drink nightshade!" Talia cried, sounding horrified.

"But it won't *be* nightshade anymore," Grant pointed out. "Not once Nadine breaks the curse. The curse is what made this brew *nightshade* in the first place, right? Please, guys. I can do this. I *have to* do this. I'll suffer if I have to, because the coven needs this Wand."

I hesitated. This was dangerous, but Grant seemed pretty damn certain, and I trusted him.

"We need to make a decision now," I stated. "Not just for tonight, but for the future of every Wand we find. How much are we willing to sacrifice to save the coven's magic?"

The room went silent as we all considered the question. Talia spoke up first. "I don't care about the other Wands. Right now, all I care about is saving my sister. But to ask any one of you to suffer for her in ways I can't imagine… this isn't fair."

"This is our *magic* we're talking about," Grant emphasized. "I waited my whole life to get my magic, and my entire future is based on my powers. I mean, every decision we make about our lives ties back to our magic—what we're going to do, who we're going to be. Hell, half the coven decides who to *date* based on their Cast. I want to be a culinary Alchemist someday. I *love* brewing potions. If you say you don't feel your magic is a part of you, then you're a liar."

"It is," I agreed. "I didn't grow up knowing about magic like you guys did. I wasn't prepared for this. But even losing my magic for a day or two with the Waning is downright miserable. Without it, it feels like I'm missing a piece of myself. We all have unique gifts, and magic is an expression of that. I don't want to give that up."

Lucas cleared his throat. "I spent so much time struggling with my gift, but actually giving it up… I don't think I could anymore. I'm going to be a reaper someday, and if there's no Apprentice, what happens to all those last thoughts? So many more people would be trapped here, and be unable to join Mother Miriam in Alora. It's because of my gift that people can move on. Our magic isn't just our own identities. It's the *coven's*. If we lose our magic, we lose our entire way of life—our whole damn religion. I'll go through hell and back to make sure that doesn't happen."

Talia hugged herself. "The last thing I want is to see any of my friends suffer."

The room went silent, and her words hung in the air. She didn't want to do this?

"But that's exactly what will happen if the Waning continues," she finished, and my shoulders sagged in relief. "To see the coven lose its magic, it would break us. Hell, it's *already* tearing us apart. We just witnessed a hanging. So yeah, I'll suffer to find these Wands and stop this —whatever it takes."

A weight seemed to lift from my heart. "Then let's break this curse."

"How can I help?" Lucas asked.

I glanced around the room. "I need something to shift the magic into. If the curse backfires, then I can transform it into… something reversed. Make water dry up, make fire turn to ice, something like that."

Lucas rushed over to a shelf full of potion supplies. "Here! *Spira cacti.*" He held up a jar with a phallic-looking cactus inside.

"What does that do?" I asked.

"Wards off evil spirits." He paused. "Yeah, probably not the best one. We don't need to *attract* evil spirits."

"I got something." Grant grabbed a jar from the shelf and set it on the table. Inside was a sparkling white liquid. The label read *boneweed juice.*

"What's boneweed?" I asked him.

"It's a plant that grows on the edge of cemeteries," Grant explained. "It's usually used in medicinal potions for enhanced strength."

I eyed the extract. "If this is being used in nightshade, this is what makes your magic stronger when you're on it, isn't it?"

Grant nodded. "I'm certain of it. So if you reverse its properties—"

"I can weaken it," I said. "This will work. I'm ready."

I closed my eyes. I placed one hand on the cauldron and held the jar of boneweed in the other. The curse felt like thick, swirling liquid against my palm—like I could physically touch it, but not grab on to it. I concentrated a while longer, until finally guiding the magic through me—except it didn't budge.

"What's wrong?" Lucas asked.

I opened my eyes. "It's resisting me. The curse is strong, and I'm..."

Lucas placed a hand on my shoulder. "Even with a fraction of your magic, you're a strong witch. Hell, you broke the Reaper's Shadow curse. How does this one compare?"

"It's intense, but it's different," I said thoughtfully. "The way the Reaper's Shadow affected several people... it's like it was rooted deeper. This one is tough, but the curse doesn't run as deep."

"Then the Waning has nothing on you," Lucas encouraged.

He was right. If I could break the Reaper's Shadow curse, I could break this—Waning or not.

"Okay, let's try again," I said. I clutched the boneweed and focused on the magic inside the cauldron. The magic was different than anything I'd ever felt, because it was a fae curse. I'd only worked with witch curses before. It was different, but familiar enough that I managed to entwine my magic with it. I yanked back and drew the magic out of the cauldron, then funneled it into the boneweed. I focused on changing the intention of the spell and reversing the effects of the juice. The more I moved the magic, the easier it became, until every last drop of magic entered the boneweed juice—

Twang!

Like a rubber-band, the curse slingshotted through me and back into the cauldron. I gasped and yanked my hands backward. The jar of boneweed nearly toppled over onto the table, but Lucas caught it.

"What is it?" he asked.

I shook my head. "I don't know. It was going fine, but as soon as I thought I finished, the spell undid itself. It's like the boneweed couldn't hold it."

Talia tapped her chin. "The cauldron is really powerful. Maybe this curse is tied to the magic inside of it?"

"Which means we would need something just as powerful to hold the magic," I thought aloud.

Grant began shuffling through the ingredients on the shelf behind us. "There's nothing here that powerful. The best thing we have is unicorn hair, but that's peanuts compared to the Crock. We'd need a whole damn unicorn."

"What about us?" Lucas asked.

"No," I objected. "I'm not putting *dark magic* into one of you."

"Temporarily," Lucas said quickly. "Until we get out of here and can redirect the magic again. We don't have time for anything else. We need to get this Wand."

"Then I won't do it," I stated firmly.

"Nad, we just said we'd do anything for these Wands," Lucas pointed out. "I can take a little dark magic for a while. You can change the intention to anything you want—as long as it's comparable in intensity, right? I'll be safe."

I crossed my arms. "You're asking me to curse you. I won't do it."

Lucas eyed me a few moments longer, as if waiting for me to change my mind. Finally, he grabbed the boneweed juice and set the jar back in front of me. "Then our only option is to try again."

"Fine," I said. "I will."

This *had* to work, because no way was I putting this magic into one of my friends.

I wrapped one hand around the jar and placed the other on the cauldron, closing my eyes again. This time, the magic came out of the cauldron easier, now that I knew what it felt like. I changed the intention of the magic, turning it into a weakening spell. The magic funneled into the boneweed juice. I pushed harder and harder until I felt no resistance at all.

I breathed a sigh and stepped backward, and the magic remained where I'd put it. "I did it," I said as I opened my eyes.

Horror hit a moment later. Lucas stood there, clutching the top of the jar. With my eyes closed, I hadn't noticed.

"Lucas!" I cried. "You—you—"

"I had to," he said with a heavy sigh. "We need the Wand."

"You stood there the whole time!" I accused. "I funneled that magic into *you*, not the boneweed!"

"I told you I'd sacrifice myself for those Wands," Lucas insisted. "I wasn't lying."

"Well, I never said *I'd* sacrifice you! Let me undo it!" I reached for him.

He jumped back. "Not until Grant brews that potion."

I looked toward my friends. Talia stared in disbelief, but Grant jumped into action.

"I'll get to work right away," he said in a rush.

"I don't know what I've done," I cried, my voice cracking. I reached out for Lucas and noticed instantly how weak and frail he looked. The color had drained from his face, and he blinked slowly. "Lucas... you're so weak."

"I'll be fine," he insisted.

I wanted to believe that, but the second he said it, his legs buckled. I caught him, and Talia gasped. She rushed over to help me guide him to sit on a barrel. I grabbed his face in my hands, and my eyes searched his. He lifted his gaze, but his eyelids drooped. The witch light above our heads dimmed as his magic became weaker.

"You're too brave for your own damn good," I told him.

"Is bravery a bad thing?" he asked.

"If it's going to get you killed, yeah," I said. "How are we doing, Grant?"

"I've got everything!" he cried, tossing an armful of ingredients onto the table.

"How long?" I demanded.

"I—I don't know," he stammered.

Talia rushed over to Grant. "Tell me how I can help."

"Shake this up," he said, shoving a bottle of boneweed juice toward her.

I turned back to Lucas. "I'm so sorry."

"Don't be," he rasped. "I volunteered."

Tears beaded in my eyes. I didn't know how long Lucas could hold on to this magic. "You're lucky I love you, because I'm pissed."

He squeezed my hand, but it wasn't very hard. "I *am* lucky."

Grant lit a fire beneath the cauldron and began mixing the ingredients. Some of the ingredients were benign—things to change the viscosity or potency of the magic. He stirred in the boneweed juice, then added clippings of twisted vine from one of the jars. My eyes widened when I saw the shimmering unicorn hair, which seemed to glow on its own.

As soon as Grant dropped the hair into the potion, it began to bubble. He stirred it a few times, then announced, "It's ready."

We all froze at once. Grant was a great Alchemist. He had no problem brewing this potion… but that wasn't the hard part. He grabbed an empty jar and scooped it through the dark liquid. His hands shook a little as he brought it to his lips.

"Are we sure about this?" Talia blurted. "In my vision, I saw screaming. I saw… madness…"

"I can handle that," Grant said gently. "Trust me, Talia."

No one got a chance to respond, because Grant threw his head back and chugged the potion. The liquid inside the cauldron began to bubble violently, snapping and steaming. Smoke billowed out of the Crock and quickly filled the entire room. It had a strong scent that burnt my nose—like wine, but stronger. My friends and I started coughing. I squeezed my eyes shut tightly and fanned the smoke out of my face.

A deep, animalistic growl filled the room, and my entire form went rigid. My head snapped in the direction of the sound, but I saw nothing except darkness as the smoke dissipated. Lucas's witch light was almost out.

Talia took a step back and stumbled into the shelf behind her. "What was that?"

"Part of the ritual?" I asked breathlessly.

"Or a protector of the cauldron…" Grant squeaked. He tossed a witch light into the air, and my breath hitched.

In the corner of the room stood a monster unlike anything I'd ever seen before. It had the body of a canine, but it had to be the size of a horse. Its head looked like the skull of a deer. There was no fur or flesh—just exposed white bone. Steam puffed out of its nose, and red eyes glowed from its bony eye sockets. But unlike a deer, it didn't have antlers. Instead, large, pointed horns protruded outward, looking like they'd impale anything that stood in the creature's way. Its long tail cracked like a whip, and my heart leapt when I saw there was a spike on the end of it.

"What the fuck is that?" I yelled.

"Uh… that's a cayndor." Lucas's voice shook.

"It's a monster!" Talia cried.

I grabbed Lucas's hand tight in mine, but the cayndor took my slight movement as a threat. It lowered its horns and leapt at us. I immediately yanked Lucas to the side, and we landed hard on the ground. The cayndor plowed straight into the barrel Lucas had been sitting on a moment ago. Its horns pierced straight through it, and dark purple liquid spilled onto the floor.

Talia shrieked and raced to the other side of the room. "What does it want?"

"I think it's pissed that I finished the potion," Grant shouted. "I bet Magnus put it down here to protect his brew."

The cayndor shook its head, then spun toward me and Lucas, eyes blazing red. I quickly tried conjuring a battle orb, but nothing happened. Lucas lifted his hands, but his magic wasn't working, either.

"Fuck!" I screamed.

"Same!" Lucas cried.

The cayndor lunged for us again, swiping out a heavy paw. We scrambled to our feet and jumped behind the table. Wood splinters went everywhere as its claws sliced across the table leg.

"My magic's gone!" I screamed. Lucas and I rolled under the table and hurried to the other side of the room.

"I've got nothing!" Lucas said breathlessly.

"What the hell is happening!?" Talia screamed as she lifted her hands. It looked like she was trying to conjure a shield, but it didn't work. Grant tried, too, but not so much as a spark came from his hands. This was the literal *worst* time for the Waning to hit.

The cayndor jumped onto the table. It growled, sending a shiver down my spine. Sharp teeth seemed to grow from beneath its bony features.

"There has to be something in here we can use!" I cried.

Grant and Talia shrank into the corner. "What are we going to do?" Grant asked. "Strangle it with unicorn hair?"

The cayndor's eyes roamed over us, as if trying to pick its first victim. Its eyes stopped on Grant and Talia. In the blink of an eye, it kicked off the table. I instantly grabbed the first jar my hands could find, and I chucked it at the cayndor mid-flight. The jar shattered over the side of the monster's face, but it didn't do anything to stop its trajectory.

Grant pushed Talia out of the monster's path. They got out of the way just in time for the cayndor to slam into the shelf behind them. Jars shattered, and potion ingredients spilled everywhere. A piece of glass spun across the ground toward me, and I bent to pick it up.

Lucas took a large piece of wood from the broken barrel in his hands. The cayndor was blocking the door to the hallway. Even if we wanted to escape, we couldn't. The only way out of this was to fight back.

Lucas threw a jar at the cayndor. "Hey, you freak! Come and get us."

"Guys, no!" Grant shouted, but it was already too late.

The cayndor's sharp claws dug into the stone floor. He threw himself at us. Lucas swung his weapon, and it *thwacked* against the cayndor's face. The creature became momentarily disoriented, and that's when I lunged. I pierced the sharp piece of glass straight into his chest, then jumped backward. Blood oozed from the wound, but it didn't seem to faze the cayndor one bit.

The monster shook its head, then swiped its claws outward. I heard the tearing of fabric as its claws sliced through the top of Lucas's jeans. My boyfriend cried out in agony, and he fell to his knees. Three long, jagged wounds marred his upper thigh.

I took one look at the blood, then screamed at the top of my lungs. "You fucker!"

I grabbed another broken bit of barrel—one with a sharp, jagged end. I planned to stake him straight through the heart, but I wasn't fast enough. The cayndor threw itself at me and reared its head. A sharp, pointed horn entered my abdomen as he lifted me upward. I screamed as pain seared my belly. The cayndor tossed me to the side, and I rolled across the ground until I came to a stop at Lucas's side. He panted in pain. I clutched my stomach, and blood poured through my fingers.

"No!" Talia shrieked. "It's just like the screams in my vision."

"Get back!" Grant yelled at her. The cayndor must've had one goal—to incapacitate—because once Lucas and I were down, it turned its sights on Grant and Talia.

"We'll kill it together!" she screamed back.

Grant wasn't interested in letting Talia make any sacrifices. The cayndor leapt toward them, growling like it was out for blood. Grant shoved Talia aside, and she tumbled to the ground. He threw himself toward one of the brooms we'd left by the door. He spun around just as the cayndor came up behind him, and he aimed the handle of the broom at its eyes.

I gasped as the broom entered one of the eye sockets and stuck there. The monster stumbled backward, throwing its head in one direction, then the other, as if trying to toss the broom from its eyes.

Talia didn't have time to get up or roll out of the way. The cayndor stepped on her hand, and she screamed in pain as its claws sliced through her skin. The monster began to freak, its tail whipping over and over again, smacking against Talia's side. The pointed end sliced her cheek, and she screamed. Her cries of pain were unbearable, but I couldn't move with the red-hot pain throbbing through my gut.

I caught Grant's horrified features from across the room. I'd never seen him look so pale.

I sucked air between my teeth when I tried to move, but I was in too much pain. The broom flew out of the cayndor's eye, and the creature whirled around toward the three of us. Blood oozed from its eye socket, but its good eye burned an even brighter red. I barely had a chance to take a breath, before the cayndor bared its sharp teeth and leapt in for the final kill. He could take us all three in one blow; I just knew it.

"No!" Grant screamed.

I saw a flash of movement out of the corner of my eye. Grant swooped downward on one of the brooms. He jumped off the broom mid-flight and threw himself between us and the cayndor. Terror leapt in my chest, because I knew the monster's teeth would clamp around his middle, and he'd be gone.

I squeezed my eyes shut tightly. I couldn't watch.

A *thud* sounded, and the cayndor's growls vanished. A beat passed before I truly processed it. I peeled my eyes open, only to realize that the pain in my abdomen was gone. Grant lay in front of the three of us on his side, as if ready for the cayndor's attack—fully prepared to die for the three of us.

But the cayndor was nowhere in sight. I glanced around the room and saw that the shelves were back in order, apart from a few shattered jars that we'd thrown. Anything the cayndor had touched—the barrel, the table, and the shelves—looked like they hadn't been bothered at all.

Lucas, Talia, and I slowly sat up. The confused looks on their faces matched mine.

After a moment, Grant pushed himself up, too. "W-where'd the monster go?"

"It must've been an illusion," I said.

I quickly looked down to my abdomen and ran my hand over the area, but it was fine. I turned to Lucas, but his pants were untouched. Talia was unharmed as well. She lifted her palm, and an orb formed inside of it. Our magic was back, too.

"Of course," Lucas said. "The cauldron belongs to the fae. Illusions are their thing."

"So it was a test," Grant realized. "Magnus didn't put the monster here at all."

Talia got to her feet, though her knees shook. "It must've been."

"Did I pass?" Grant asked breathlessly.

"I don't know," Lucas admitted.

We all stood and hobbled over to the cauldron. My fear melted away when I saw something bobbing up and down inside the brew. The Alchemy Wand floated to the surface. It was identical to my grandfather's drawing.

Grant threw his hand over his mouth. "I—I did it."

"You sacrificed yourself for us," Lucas pointed out. "You showed the cauldron that you would use its treasure for good—that you would die to save the coven."

Talia's worried features transformed into a smile. "Go on, Grant. The treasure is yours."

Grant reached inside the cauldron, and his hand curled around the handle of the Wand. When he lifted it, a breeze swept through the room, rustling his hair. The Wand itself began to glow a bright green. Tendrils of magic swirled out of the end of the wand and twisted up his arm.

"What does that mean?" I asked, glancing between my friends.

Lucas's eyebrows shot up. "I think it means the Wand chose him."

"So Grant has control over all Alchemy magic?" Talia asked.

"I—I guess," Grant stammered, like he couldn't believe it. "I'm going to end nightshade—right now. I'll take only nightshade magic and leave the rest."

Grant spun the Wand, and the tip of it glowed white, intensifying so brightly that I had to cover my eyes. A beautiful note rang out from the Wand, as if it was singing.

Whoosh!

Magic blasted through the room with such power that I had to grip the edge of the table to keep from being knocked over. It was beautiful, incredible magic that seemed so powerful, yet calming.

Once the magic settled, Talia was the first to speak. "Is nightshade over then? Is my sister saved?"

"I think so," Grant said. "Let's call Amy to be sure."

"That won't be necessary," a voice came from the corner.

My heart lurched, and I turned to see a woman step out of the shadows. She donned a black cloak, like the ones the priestesses wore. She reached up to pull her hood down, and my breath hitched when I saw who it was.

Priestess Stella.

My first instinct was relief. Stella was the only priestess I remotely trusted. But the hairs on the back of my arm stood, and I instinctively knew this wasn't right.

"You've done well, students." Stella held out her hand. "Now give me the Wand."

I stepped in front of Grant. "How did you find us?"

"I saw you leaving the school," Stella said. "I was worried about you, Nadine."

I shot a wary glance at my friends. The illusion spell we'd taken earlier tonight had worn off by now, but she couldn't have recognized us when we left.

"She's lying," Lucas accused.

Anger and betrayal twisted in my gut. "What are you *really* doing here?" I demanded.

"Trying to stop this!" Stella insisted. "Nightshade killed a man tonight. It's my duty to protect the coven and bring an end to this!"

I shook my head. It didn't make sense. Why wait until we had the Wand to reveal herself? She must've snuck in while we were fighting the cayndor illusion. Every instinct in my gut told me I couldn't trust her. "I don't believe you."

Stella sighed. "Fine, Nadine. You want to do this the hard way? Because I can play dirty."

She yanked a wand from her cloak and pointed it at me, but my friends and I were just as quick. Lucas and I conjured our wands and aimed them back, and Talia and Grant formed battle orbs.

I couldn't cast strong magic right now. Hell, conjuring my wand felt like casting battle magic. And Lucas wasn't exactly up for spells, either—not with the weakening curse still inside of him. But Stella didn't know that. She stilled when we lifted our wands.

"It was you all along!" Lucas fumed. "You burnt my parents' house down!"

Rage flared in my bones. I had *trusted* Priestess Stella. "You were working with Magnus and framed Professor Daniels, because she was going to expose you," I sneered.

She didn't acknowledge our accusations. Instead, she simply said, "The Alchemy Wand belongs to the Imperium Council."

"The Wand belongs to Grant," Lucas countered. "It chose him, which means it trusts him. If the council cares so much about these Wands, they'd trust him with it, too."

"A *student?*" Stella sneered. "That Wand belongs in the hands of a priestess."

"*I'm* a priestess," I reminded her. "But being a student makes me less, doesn't it? I thought you felt differently about me."

I recalled the heart to heart we'd had that night outside Octavia Hall. Stella had told me how she always felt out of place on the council, because she didn't have as much experience as the others. I thought we had really connected. Now I saw she'd only been manipulating me.

"You *used* me," I accused.

"Please," Stella scoffed. "It's not like I knew you were going to discover the Crock of Death. I already knew *everything* you brought to the council. None of it was useful... though I didn't know the cauldron was cursed. Well done, Nadine."

"Stop it!" I snapped. "Don't compliment me like I did you a favor.

You're admitting you knew about the cauldron before I told the council. You knew the Alchemy Wand was inside. Why didn't you tell the others?"

"Because I was going to find it!" she cried. "I spent years being cast aside as the youngest and least experienced member of the council. I was never taken seriously. When I discovered that the cauldron went missing from the council, I set out to find it. I found out where your grandfather had hidden it—right under our noses in Octavia Hall. That drawing you showed the council wasn't the only clue to what the cauldron held. He left other drawings and notes behind in the Imperium records. When I figured out what he'd done, I dedicated my *life* to acquiring that Wand. When I turn the Alchemy Wand and the Crock of Death in to the council, I will finally get the respect and appreciation I deserve."

"But you're not an Alchemist," I said in a hollow tone. The pieces began to fall together in my mind. "So you hired Magnus to help you."

"Yes. He also proved useful in distribution," she admitted. "*He* was the businessman, but *I* formed the alliance with the Elementai to trade for unicorn hair. I sent Magnus away to protect him."

"So what's nightshade, then?" I asked harshly.

She smirked. "A happy accident. I needed *some* incentive to keep Magnus working for me, and money does quite the talking. But of course, nightshade has its advantages, too. With the Elementai Civil War mounting and the unrest in Malovia, it's only a matter of time before races like the elementals and the fae bring their fights to us. Nightshade could prove to be a very viable safeguard against war. It has quite the effect on the magic of our enemies."

"And the Waning?" I demanded. "Did you manufacture that, too? What was it—a way to sell more nightshade, or a way to draw out the Oaken Wands?"

"I have nothing to *do* with the Waning," Stella growled, like she was offended I'd even suggested it. "But that's exactly why we *need* nightshade and the Wands—to stop what's coming."

"And what exactly *is* coming?" Lucas demanded.

Terror filled Stella's eyes, and I knew this ran a hell of a lot deeper than profiting off nightshade.

"You've foreseen something," I accused.

Her tone became hollow. "Death. Destruction. So much fire, and screams of terror. I sense people's futures, and I know that whatever is coming for the coven is going to tear us apart. We must stop this before it begins."

"It already has begun!" Talia cried. "A boy died tonight because of your nightshade! You hanged Professor Daniels."

"Leila Daniels was an unfortunately casualty!" Stella screamed. "I did what I had to, to protect the coven!"

My stomach twisted. "You planted the evidence on her because she was asking questions about nightshade. She was on to you, wasn't she?"

"Leila Daniels didn't know what she was getting herself into," Stella sneered. "If she exposed me, she risked *everything* I have worked for to protect this coven."

"You don't care about the coven!" I cried. "If you did, you would've told the other priestesses about the cauldron a long time ago. All you care about is your honor and respect, and you've lost it. You're killing people in the name of preventing war, but in doing so, you've *started* one."

I was so disgusted with her that it made me want to hurl. I was ashamed that I ever thought I could trust this woman.

"No!" she shouted. "I'm ending this before it begins! A few sacrifices are nothing compared to the carnage I have foreseen."

Grant's nostrils flared. "What exactly do you think is going to happen when the priestesses find out what you've done?"

Stella chuckled. "Oh, they're not going to find out. I already know how this is going to end. One of you is going to die here tonight, and there's nothing you can do to stop it."

"You're *threatening* us?" I snarled.

"I'm stating a simple fact," Stella said. "I have foreseen it. And the three of you who *do* get out of here won't talk."

"You sound so certain," Lucas said through gritted teeth.

"You already know what lengths I'll go to," Stella replied. As if to demonstrate, she added, "It really is too bad about what happened to your friend—how they found the nightshade in her room, how she was caught dealing nightshade to the boy who died."

My entire form shook with horror. "What did you do to Amy?" I demanded.

"Like I said, sacrifices are required," Stella replied bluntly.

I was done listening to her. She'd framed my friend, and she wasn't going to get away with it. I flicked my wrist, and a defensive spell flew from the end of my wand. But with the Waning affecting me, I had almost no magic left to give. I'd used up all my reserves breaking the cauldron's curse. The spell was a dud.

Stella reacted quickly. A battle orb flew from the end of her wand and slammed into my stomach. I grunted as the air left my lungs. I flew off my feet and landed hard on the ground.

Suddenly, spells were flying everywhere. Grant and Talia threw orbs at Stella the same time Lucas tossed up a shield. Stella's next spell slammed against his shield. He held it just long enough for her spell to fizzle out, but the shield collapsed a second later.

The curse I'd cast on Lucas was getting worse. He couldn't hold his magic for long.

Lucas rushed to my side, and I staggered as he helped me to my feet. Nearby, Talia and Grant threw spells at Stella, but she'd created a shield to protect herself. Each spell bounced off and ricocheted back in our direction.

"You evil witch!" Talia screamed.

"We have to break through her shield and immobilize her!" I cried to Lucas.

"I can hardly cast," he said.

I grabbed a jar from the shelf. We'd have to do this the old-fashioned way—like we'd done with the cayndor.

I hurled a jar at Stella. It shattered against her shield, spraying a gooey black substance everywhere. It didn't hurt her, but it surprised her enough to cause her magic to falter. Grant's battle orb connected with her shield, and the shield shattered.

Talia was so pissed that when she swiped her hand through the air, a cut opened on Stella's cheek. Stella gasped, and Talia's eyes widened, like she couldn't believe she'd managed the spell. It was banned in our classes, but anyone was capable of it if they were angry enough.

Stella touched the wound, and her fingers came away from her face coated in blood. She narrowed her eyes at Talia. "You little bitch."

"Leave her alone!" Grant cried. He threw another spell that buzzed with so much magic, I was sure it could stop Stella's heart. But she tossed her hand upward and created another shield. The spell slammed straight into her shield and exploded.

Stella kept her sights on Talia. She flicked her wand, and Talia screamed. She dropped to her knees and cradled her face in her hands. Lucas and I hurled more glass jars at Stella. Her shield fell. One jar hit her square in the shoulder, and the other connected with her hip.

"Amateurs," Stella scoffed. She thrust her arm out, and a defensive spell hit us like a truck. The spell shot Lucas and me backward. My head slammed into the corner of a shelf, and pain shot through my skull. I heard Lucas grunt beside me. We both crumbled to the ground like ragdolls. Above us, the shelf contents teetered on the edge. I squeezed my eyes shut tightly as jars tumbled to the ground around me, breaking into pieces. I peeked my eyes open to see a large jar land on Lucas's head, knocking him out.

"No!" I screamed. Lucas's chest rose and fell, but that didn't stop hot tears from beading in my eyes.

Lucas and Talia were both down, and I had almost no magic left. We just weren't strong enough to go up against a priestess. She was one of the strongest witches in the coven, and we were barely halfway through our studies. I tried to get to my feet, but pain radiated through the back of my skull.

"You're wicked!" Grant shouted. He blasted another spell at her, but a quick swipe of her hand caused it to fizzle out.

She scoffed. "And you're nothing impressive. I can't imagine why the Alchemy Wand chose *you*."

Stella lifted her palm and spun her wand around at the same time. A spell I'd never seen before blasted from her hands. It touched both walls and spread through the room in the blink of an eye. The blast was so powerful that it sent me rolling across the floor, closer to Lucas. Grant and Talia were both blasted into the walls. Grant slumped against the wall on the other side of Lucas, who lay unconscious beside me.

I clutched my wand tight in my hand, but my head pounded. I couldn't cast a spell, even if I wanted to.

Stella's shoes clicked across the floor as she approached us. Grant groaned, but he winced when he tried to move. Stella leaned down and snatched the Alchemy Wand out of his hand.

"That's not yours!" he yelled.

Stella laughed. "It is now."

Talia sucked a deep breath from across the room. She pulled her hand away from her face, and I saw the damage for the first time. My stomach twisted at the sight of the large gash across her cheek. Blood poured freely down her face.

"You're not going to get away with this," Talia warned her.

Stella clicked her tongue and stepped between Lucas and me. "I foresaw a death, but I didn't think I'd be the one to choose whose it would be."

She sounded pleased, and it made me sick.

"You don't *have* to kill one of us," I said in a strained voice. "You want to change the future? Start right now."

"I can't let you go," Stella said. "Perhaps I'll kill all of you. What a tragedy that would be. A priestess and her friends, killed by twisted vine on their search to end nightshade."

"You want to make me a martyr," I sneered.

"You're right," she said. "Perhaps it's better to make you the bad guy. I'm sure I'll come up with *something* to motivate the coven."

"You're evil," a strained voice came from beside me. I looked over to see that Lucas had come to, but the curse was taking over. All the color had drained from his face, and he could barely move.

Stella threw her head back and cackled. She stopped abruptly, and her gaze snapped in my direction. She leaned down and growled, "You and your friends are naive and *weak*. A priestess always does what has to be done for the coven. If you can't see that, you don't deserve the position you've been blessed with."

Stella stepped on my chest, pressing down so hard that I couldn't catch a breath. I kicked out my legs, but it was no use. I grabbed her leg and tried to yank her off of me, but she wouldn't budge.

My gaze darted toward Lucas. His eyelids drooped. I'd always been so good at puzzles, but I couldn't see my way out of this one. My hand curled tighter around my wand, even though there was no spell I could use with it. But as I clutched it in my grasp, I remembered something.

"No," I told Stella, my voice straining. "I don't kill innocent people. *You're* the weak one."

I curled one hand around her ankle and reached for Lucas with the other that held my wand. My fingers touched his, and I felt the magic in my wand surge. The rainbow moonstone crystal I'd infused with Curse Breaker magic earlier that week began to glow. I used it as a reservoir, draining the magic inside and filling me with the power I'd lost. Magic ignited in my chest, as if my heart had begun beating for the first time in hours. I felt the dark magic I'd placed into Lucas and I latched on to it, funneling it out of him and through me.

Stella's eyes widened when she saw my crystal glowing. She lifted her foot off of me, but I held on as tight as I could. She went to take a step back, but Lucas kicked his leg out, and Stella tripped over him. The Alchemy Wand clattered to the ground. Stella landed flat on her back, but I never let go of her. Magic swelled inside of me, rattling around like it wanted something to latch on to—something powerful, like a witch.

I let the dark magic explode out of me, blasting through Stella and permeating her every cell. Stella gasped as the magic took hold. "W-what have you done?" she demanded.

Stella yanked away from me, but the damage had already been done. Stella had taken on the curse, and it made her weak. She grabbed the edge of the table and hobbled to her feet. She could barely stand.

"*What have you done!?*" she cried.

I pushed myself upright. "I'm taking you to the priestesses. The coven deserves answers."

"I'll be burned at the stake!" Stella screamed.

"I'll fight to prevent that," I insisted. "No one needs to be burned or hanged again."

Stella's voice shook. "That's exactly what's going to happen! It's what I've foreseen."

"Visions can be changed," I said, getting to my feet. My head pounded, but I managed to stay upright.

"No," Stella took a step backward, but her knees shook. "I don't answer to you."

She whirled around and grabbed one of the brooms near the doorway.

"You're not going anywhere!" Lucas shouted. He'd regained his strength and leapt to his feet. I saw the fury in his eyes. Stella had wronged the coven too many times. She would rot in prison for her crimes.

Stella mounted the broom, but Lucas shot a stunning spell across the room. She kicked off, and the spell hit the end of the broom, throwing off her balance.

Stella screamed as she went flying forward. She flipped through the air

—straight into the twisted vine. Her shrieks echoed through the room as the vines whipped around her legs and twisted across her middle.

My stomach lurched, and I raced forward. I grabbed her hand, but the twisted vine was already pulling her down the hall. "Help!" I screamed to my friends.

Talia scrambled to my side, and she yanked on Stella's other hand. Lucas and Grant followed behind. We all pulled on Stella, trying to free her from the twisted vine. By now, the vines had curled around her legs so tightly that I could only see her from the waist up. Terror filled her eyes, and her screams pierced my heart.

"Don't let me die!" Stella cried.

"We won't!" I screamed. "No one else has to die. Hold on. We've got—"

Stella's hand slipped from mine, and my stomach dropped out of my abdomen. The twisted vine yanked so hard that she was dragged several feet away from us. She screamed out in agony, but a vine slapped across her mouth, silencing her cries. Within moments, the vines had grown over top of her and pulled her into their thick roots. Stella had vanished.

I clutched Lucas's shirt and curled into him. He went rigid, then shivered.

"She's dead, isn't she?" I whispered in a hollow voice.

Lucas swallowed audibly and held me tighter. He must've heard her last thought. "She's gone."

Talia and Grant shared a sorrowful look. Everything had happened so fast, and there was nothing we could do to stop it.

Lucas couldn't tear his eyes from the twisted vine. His body trembled, and my heart broke into a million pieces for him. This was nothing like when I'd killed those witches. This was an accident—yet I knew Lucas would spend the rest of his days feeling remorse.

"It wasn't your fault," I assured him. "You didn't mean to hurt anyone."

"No, but I did." Lucas's voice cracked. Apart from that, I couldn't read him. He was a statue, pushing his emotions so deep down that they didn't show. I didn't think he could face it right now, because Lucas got to his feet. His voice became strong as he announced, "We need to get the Wand and the Crock out of here."

I stared up at him, wondering how I was going to help. Lucas just killed somebody, and the weight you carried after something like that never went away. I would know.

But we would have to deal with this later. We didn't have a choice.

"Lucas is right," I said. "We have to move. Stella framed Amy for Shane's death, which means she's in danger right now."

Amy had risked everything to help us find the cauldron, and because of that, her life was on the line. We needed to do whatever was in our power to stop this.

Otherwise, her blood was on our hands.

TWENTY-THREE

The sound of Stella's cries echoed in my ears. I couldn't quite wrap my head around what I'd done. Stella had died because of me.

The weird thing was, it didn't feel like I thought it would. Stella had destroyed my childhood home. She'd killed an innocent professor, and she was responsible for the death of one of my classmates. Daymond was dead because of her, too. She had framed my friend, and only the Goddess knew what danger Amy was in now. It was like death and destruction followed Stella everywhere she went.

Stella was guilty of the most severe crimes against the coven. Perhaps her death was justified.

Conflicting emotions swirled in my gut. It wasn't fair of me to judge Stella and carry out her sentence—but I'd be damned if I wasn't the slightest bit relieved that she was gone. I'd learned to accept Nadine for what she'd done to those witches at Pinewood Manor all those months ago, but I never truly understood it until now. The coven was safer now that they were gone.

Stella had foreseen a death tonight in that basement. She thought it'd be one of us, but it'd been *her* death.

Stella's last thought played through my mind. *The coven will suffer for this.*

The thing was, I didn't believe that we would suffer for her death. We would only suffer for the war she started when she was alive.

I conjured a coat and wrapped it around Nadine's shoulders. I knew how her illness flared in the cold. "It's going to be cold out there. Let's get going."

Grant grabbed the Alchemy Wand and subconjured the Crock of Death. We mounted our brooms and sped down the long hallway. We flew through the Door of Mystery and straight up the trap door. I led the way through the broken window in the shop. I didn't even bother going back to the car, because the brooms would be faster. It was a straight shot back to the school.

We flew over the treetops and high above the buildings. The cold December air bit at my face, but I didn't care. If Stella was telling the truth about Amy, then we didn't have much time.

"What the hell is that!?" Nadine shouted over the sound of the wind.

I narrowed my eyes toward the school. The peaks of Miriam Mansion were lit by an orange glow coming from somewhere on the ground. When I noticed the light flickering, my heart fucking stopped.

"Goddess!" Grant cried.

"It's a *fire*!" Talia screamed.

Horror crept up my spine. We all realized it at the same time.

"Fuck," I growled.

The lawn came into view. I suddenly felt like I'd flown into a brick wall. Below us, students and professors gathered around a huge fire. My heart fell out of my chest when I saw that four stakes had been placed in the center of the flames. The fire must've only just been lit, because it was quickly spreading through the stick bundles surrounding the four stakes. Screams echoed through the night. There was a mix of all types—pain, terror, protest, and even support.

"They're burning people at the stake!" Nadine screamed in a trembling tone that made my insides twist.

"We have to put out the fire!" I yelled back.

I didn't pay attention to what my friends were doing as I surged downward toward the flames. All I could focus on was the four people who were tied to the posts. My stomach lurched as four familiar faces came into view. I took in the scene in mere moments.

Amy trembled from the first stake, and tears streamed down her face as she tried to hold her head out of the smoke. Next to her, Professor Ward had been tied up. She spat profanities at the crowd, as if she wanted them to know how much she hated them.

Beside Professor Ward, two other girls sobbed, begging for their lives—Ashley and Christine. My whole form shook against my broom when I realized what was happening. Stella hadn't just framed Amy for nightshade. Somehow, she'd convinced the council to burn the others. I'd bet my magic it was because they'd been looking into the Oaken Wands.

Three priestesses stood at the front of the crowd, looking on with proud smirks like they'd just caught a gang of serial killers. Police officers surrounded the fire, like they were protecting it from the crowd. Each held a burning torch in their hands. Snow melted and sizzled around the fire.

Several people I recognized stood at the front of the crowd. Miles held back Mandy, who was screaming and sobbing. She looked ready to go on a murder spree, but the police would kill her if she made a move.

"These witches have been charged with conspiring against the coven," Priestess Margaret announced. "They've worked alongside Leila Daniels in producing and distributing a deadly potion called nightshade. A man has died tonight because of them, and the punishment is death."

"Priestesses, please!" Headmistress Verla pleaded. "There must be another way."

"Their sentence is justified," Lilian sneered. "You will stand back and allow this to happen, or you will be charged with treason yourself."

I reached the fire, and I swooped down beside Amy and hovered there. Heat swept over me, and I immediately began to sweat. I conjured my scythe and swung it toward the ropes securing her to the post. A few strands broke, and I swung again.

"Hey!" a deep voice boomed from behind me. "Somebody stop him!"

Spells whizzed by my head, but the smoke was already becoming so thick that I could hardly see through it. I dodged the spells and circled back toward Amy. I threw up a shield that blocked the attack, but it couldn't protect us from the blazing heat.

"Lucas!" Amy gasped through her tears. "Get out of here! You'll be burned!"

"You're innocent!" I screamed back. "You have to fight back. Use your magic!"

"I can't!" she cried. "The cuffs are made of noxite. They've drained my magic."

I noticed for the first time she had metal handcuffs securing her wrists together in front of her. I panicked, but if I cut the ropes free, she could still get away on two feet. But the fire was growing quickly, and there wasn't much time left.

Commotion spread through the crowd. Police officers yelled, but I ignored them. I swung again, aiming the sharp tip of my scythe at the ropes. One of the ropes broke free, but it was immediately followed up by Amy's pain-filled cries. Horror seemed to swallow me whole when I saw that the fire had reached her feet. Ashley and Christine's shrieks echoed across the lawn, but Professor Ward continued her string of curses.

"You will all answer to the Goddess!" Ward shouted. "May you burn in the Abyss for your transgressions!"

Smoke filled my nose and clouded my vision. People shouted from afar, but I couldn't hear any of it over my hacking coughs.

"Leeeaave me!" Amy begged.

"I'm not leaving!" I screamed, but I could barely get the words out as smoke filled my lungs.

Nearby, I heard Nadine's voice shouting over the crowd. "Stop this! They're innocent! I can prove it!"

"We can't stop what's already been done," Priestess Lilian sneered.

"You can't do this!" Nadine screamed. "I'm a priestess, and so is Stella. We weren't here to vote on this!"

"The majority vote rules," Lilian spat. "We needed only three priestesses to sentence them."

Grant and Talia screamed protests nearby, but I couldn't hear what they said. I swung my scythe again, but the smoke was so thick that I could no longer see the ropes. The flames licked so high that they nearly touched my toes. It was so hot that I thought I might pass out.

"*Stop!*" Mandy shouted. A break in the smoke gave me a clear view of her for a mere second. She shoved Miles off of her and sprinted past the police officers. She threw herself toward the burning sticks and plunged her hands straight into the flames. Sparks flew everywhere as she yanked on the burning sticks, like she was trying to dig Amy out of the fire. Her screams tore across the lawn, but a police officer grabbed her and yanked her backward.

Two cats raced out of the crowd behind Mandy. Christine's cat yowled loudly as she watched her owner burn. Stormy jumped into the flames to get to Amy. Her fur caught fire, and she fell into the snow, howling as the flames consumed her.

Amy sobbed in agony as fire licked up her legs. I couldn't bear to look at the pained expression on her face. The priestesses had resorted to pure torture, and it was evil beyond anything I could imagine.

Sweat dripped down my face, and my scythe slipped in my fingers as I swung it. I nearly lost it.

"Hang in there, Amy!" I screamed over the roar of the fire. "I'm getting you out of here!"

Just as I said it, a crackling sound came from behind me. I shot a glance over my shoulder to see that the bristles of my broom had lit aflame. My heart lurched. If I stayed here any longer, I would have no way out. I'd be burned alive, too.

My time was up. The moment the horrifying realization hit me, a shield blasted out of nowhere and slammed into me. I went flying through the air so hard and fast that the air left my lungs. I soared over top of the police officers and landed hard in the snow. I gasped for breath as I came to a rolling stop near the edge of the forest. My whole body ached from the impact, but all I could think of was Amy and the other innocent women being burned in front of my eyes.

I pushed myself upright, groaning. Smoke wafted in front of me as the ends of the broom bristles turned to embers. I'd been blasted back so hard that the flames had been put out instantly. My scythe lay in the snow nearby.

The police had turned their focus on Mandy. No one even looked in my direction.

"Get a shield up!" Officer Baker barked. Within moments, the shimmering outline of a shield appeared around the blazing fire.

Screams of agony went on forever, echoing through the bleak night as the flames licked up the bodies of the bound women…. then they just… stopped. The silence was the most horrifying sound I'd heard in all my life.

Professor Ward's voice entered my mind. *We didn't deserve this.*

I didn't make it, Ashley thought.

I'll miss you, Mom, Christine whispered in my mind.

Finally, Amy's voice came to me. *I hope my death was worth it.*

My stomach lurched, as if twisted vine had taken a hold of me and squeezed so tightly that I could no longer breathe. They were... gone. I couldn't wrap my head around how fast it had happened.

Cries tore through the air, and I finally snapped back to attention. Four limp bodies sagged against the stakes, their silhouettes like omens against the flickering flames. Blackened flesh hung off their bones, and they were no longer recognizable. The stench of burning flesh filled the skies.

I caught sight of police officers shoving Mandy toward the crowd. Grant and Talia caught her, and the terrified look in their eyes sent daggers through my heart.

From out of the darkness, three cats came racing toward me. I recognized them immediately—Oliver, Isa, and Gus. They must've escaped the school while our rooms were being searched. Oliver ran straight up to me, looking relieved to see me safe.

"No!" I shoved him off. "You have to get somewhere safe!"

The cats either didn't care or didn't understand, because they didn't move. I scrambled to my feet and grabbed my scythe and broom from the ground. I quickly subconjured them.

Priestess Margaret stepped in front of the crowd. "The coven is safe now!" she called, lying through her teeth. I saw straight through her—she was trying to control the crowd under the guise of protecting them. It made me ill.

"It's because of *them* that one of your classmates died tonight," Priestess Margaret said. "These acts were necessary. Any student or professor caught brewing nightshade on school grounds shall suffer the same fate, in order to protect you all."

"You're lying!" Nadine screamed. "These women were innocent, and you killed them!"

Fuck, Nadine was going to get herself killed. I had to do *something*.

I raced toward her, the cats following. A police officer tried to grab me, but I shoved him off. The officers must've lost their concentration, because their shield had fallen, and I made it past them.

"Nonsense!" Priestess Lilian snarled. "These were your friends. You're just trying to clear their name."

"I have proof!" I shouted. I pulled my voice recorder from my pocket.

It'd been recording all night, and I had Priestess Stella's confession on tape. I held the voice recorder high above my head. "Priestess Stella framed them—just like she framed Professor Daniels—"

My throat tightened in an instant, as if someone had curled their fingers around my neck, but no one was close enough to touch me. I gasped, and my vision blurred. An invisible force tore the voice recorder out of my hand, and it flew straight toward Priestess Lilian. That's when I realized what was happening. She was choking me with her magic!

This bitch could silence me all she wanted, but the damage was already done. Whispers spread throughout the crowd.

Priestess Stella?

Framed?

Professor Daniels was innocent?

Horror spread across the priestesses' faces. They had no idea what Stella had done, and it terrified them to their very core—because if the coven knew these people were innocent, the priestesses would have to answer for that in the worst way possible.

Lilian lifted her chin. She stared me down as she spoke to the police officers. "Arrest him immediately for attempting to incite a panic."

My heart leapt as the police officers strode forward, but Nadine put up a hand. They stopped mid-stride. They didn't have to like her, but they had to listen to her. It was the way with the coven.

"I am a priestess," Nadine sneered. "You won't be arresting anyone. The coven deserves the truth."

Priestess Margaret's eyes narrowed. She glanced from the fire to the voice recorder, then to Nadine. Then she spoke one single word that chilled me to the bone. "Overruled."

Priestess Charlotte crossed her arms. "The council has spoken. Arrest this man."

An officer lunged for me. Hands curled around my wrists, yanking my arms behind my back. Lilian released her hold on my throat, and I gasped a greedy breath of air.

"They know it's the truth!" I cried. "They're selling you a story so you'll submit to compliance!"

"Please, you have to listen!" Nadine insisted. "These people deserved a trial! Ask yourself why they didn't get one!"

"I believe them!" someone shouted from the crowd. The priestesses whirled toward the voice and glared, as if trying to find the source of the voice. They didn't see her, but I knew that voice.

It was Samantha Stone, the necromancer who'd told me about the Reaper Moon a year ago. I spotted her in the crowd. She held on to two other girls from my classes—Felicia and Darcy. A matching look of terror filled each of their eyes.

The officer holding me muttered a protection charm that would secure my hands behind my back like handcuffs. Magic began twisting around my wrists. *"Conti—"*

He cut off mid-incantation. The burning sticks blasted in every direction, raining flames and embers down all around us. The officer jumped back and screamed as flames landed on his shoulder. The magical restraints forming around my wrists vanished.

"Burn in the Abyss!" Mandy screamed. She charged forward while the officers were distracted. The flames were smaller now, as the blast had spread the fire out, but she sprinted straight through them toward Amy's burnt corpse.

The crowd erupted into a panic. Suddenly, people were moving in all directions, attempting to flee. Magic whizzed overhead, and people screamed as they were hit by rogue battle orbs and stunning spells.

"Stop them!" Officer Baker shouted.

Shields went up, but they came down almost as quickly. Nobody could concentrate amongst the chaos. I grabbed Nadine's hand, and we ducked incoming spells as we raced over the snow.

"I'm sorry!" Nadine's voice trembled as she shot a glance back at Amy. "I had to save you."

"That was *your* shield that blasted me away from the pyre," I realized.

She grimaced. "I had no choice."

"You did the right thing," I assured her. I just regretted that we couldn't save Amy.

Nadine slowed, and she shot a worried glance around the panicked crowd. "Where is everyone?"

"Here!" Talia shouted.

She sprinted toward us, with Grant at her side. Miles clutched Kiki in his arms as he ran behind them.

"There was nothing we could do!" Grant yelled.

"We can't change it," I said. "All we can do is move. We have to get someplace safe."

"Oh, Goddess," Nadine gasped. "Where's Mandy?"

I glanced around, but there was so much chaos. I could hardly see anything through the scrambling bodies and the spells flying everywhere. I looked toward the stake, but Mandy was gone.

"Fuck," I growled. I created a shield and began pushing through the crowd to find her.

"Wait!" Talia cried. "I just saw her! She ran into the forest."

"That's where we need to be," Grant said. "It's not safe here!"

I couldn't take my eyes off the burnt bodies. It didn't seem right to leave them there to continue smoldering. Amy deserved better. I was a reaper, and I needed to stay to help all these people cross over.

But if we stayed, we'd die.

I whirled back toward my friends. "Let's go!"

We hurried toward the trees, our cats following closely behind. But we didn't get to the trees before a blazing inferno swept across the forest. It moved so fast that if I blinked, I would've missed it. It was like magic—except witches couldn't create fire. We stumbled backward before we ran straight into the wall of flame.

"It's Alchemist's Accelerant!" Grant cried.

"What, like gasoline!?" Nadine shouted.

Grant's tone was hollow. "Worse."

The flames engulfed the lawn on all sides, surrounding the school. Snow started melting, creating a slippery slush. The only way out was the front gates. Students began to flock in that direction.

Maniacal laughter met my ears, and I turned to see Ryan standing at the edge of the forest, holding one of the torches the police had earlier. He looked up at the burning trees like a kid who'd just set off a rocket. He was fucking *pleased*.

My heart raced. "Where the hell did Ryan get Alchemist's Accelerant?"

"Probably from Officer Baker himself," Miles quipped, but now wasn't the time for jokes.

On second thought, maybe Miles wasn't joking.

Talia conjured the broom she'd ridden here on. "Let's ride our brooms out of here."

I glanced toward Miles. "We don't have enough for everyone."

"We'll have to hide out in the school until this is over," Miles said.

"No!" Nadine protested. "If the school catches fire, we'll be trapped."

"We *are* trapped!" Miles gestured around at the burning forest.

"We have to get to the front gates before the police do," I said. "Come on!"

We were on the move instantly, but it was like throwing ourselves into an active warzone. Battle orbs exploded around us, and we had to react quickly to avoid being hurt by them. Cats yowled and hissed, and people screamed so loudly that my ears rang. I threw a shield up around us, but I couldn't keep my concentration. Three battle orbs slammed into my shield at the same time, and it flickered out of existence.

Everything happened all at once when my shield fell. Two girls ran straight into me, and the three of us slipped on the melting snow. I landed so hard on my back that the air knocked out of my lungs. Ice cold water seeped through my shirt, chilling me.

Talia screamed the second I landed. I sat up and whirled around to see she had fallen to the ground. Her hand trembled in the snow, and a massive bruise began forming over the back of it.

Grant immediately knelt by her side. "She was struck by magic. It has to be broken."

"Can you move?" Nadine asked.

"I can walk," Talia said through ragged breaths.

The girls who'd run into me both groaned as they got to their feet. They were accompanied by their own cats, but it wasn't until the girls stood that I saw who it was—Chloe and Onyx.

"Fuck. I got hit, too." Chloe's shoulders were hunched as she stood, and I realized one of them was dislocated.

Onyx pressed her hand to the back of her head. She winced as she said, "You need to pop it back in. It'll feel better."

"Pop it back—" Chloe gaped. "Are you insane?"

"I'm serious," Onyx said. "Here, let me help."

Magic continued whizzing overhead. I threw up another shield around us, but it was hard to hold it over everyone. My shield weakened with every spell that slammed into it.

"Make it quick," I insisted. "I can't hold this shield forever."

All around us, the battle seemed to be mounting. Police shot high-powered spells into the crowd. They blasted out of their wands like bullets, and the sound echoed in my ears.

Boom!

My gaze snapped in the direction of a massive explosion on the other side of the lawn. The fire broke for a mere second, and a group of Alchemists led by Stacey and Valerie fled through the trees. Avery Mitchel scampered behind them to safety. They must've used a fire-retardant potion, but it didn't last long. Within moments, the fire was back, blazing around the perimeter of the school yard.

"Ready, Chloe?" Onyx asked. "On the count of three."

Chloe whimpered as Onyx grabbed her arm. "On three."

"One… two…"

There was a grotesque snapping sound, and I winced.

"Gah!" Chloe screamed. "You said the count of three!"

Onyx stepped back, looking proud. "How does that feel?"

Chloe rolled her shoulder. "Better, actually. Tell me that's not the only trick you have up your sleeve. How are we getting out of here?"

"You're on *our* side?" Grant asked in shock.

"Well, I'm not going to stand around and wait to burn to death!" Chloe cried. "Who do you think distracted the police in the first place?"

"That was *you*," Nadine realized. "You blasted all those sticks back with your telekinesis."

Chloe scoffed, looking offended by Nadine's surprise. "I wasn't going to let them arrest you."

Nadine furrowed her brow. "But your grandmother—"

"Is apparently a raging bitch," Chloe said. "I want answers. Whatever is actually happening here, these burnings and hangings aren't the answer. This is wrong."

Nadine hesitated a moment. It was odd for Chloe to be on our side. A year ago, I'd have bet anything Nadine and Chloe would be enemies for life. But things had changed.

"How many people can you lift with your magic?" I asked Chloe.

"None," she replied bluntly. "If I could do that, I'd be out of here."

I glanced around, desperate for a way out. My gaze landed on the priestesses. They'd made it to the front gate with the police. Several people had fled, and a few officers pursued them, but most of the students and professors had hit an invisible barricade. A dozen officers held up their wands, like they were trying to hold a shield. Everyone was trapped.

I caught sight of one of the officers at the end of the line. His hands shook, and he hesitated. Then he did the unthinkable. The officer dropped his hands. He ripped his badge from his uniform and threw it down. Rage marred his features, and he shouted something at the other officers, but I couldn't hear it from this distance. Suddenly, his entire form stiffened. My gaze darted to Priestess Lilian, who held her hands up in his direction.

She was punishing him.

Shock hit several officers' faces, but it melted away as quickly as it came. They put on masks of indifference, knowing that they must comply, or they too would be punished by the priestesses.

My gaze darted around for other options. My eyes landed on Professor Warren across the lawn. He knelt beside a student who screamed out in pain. He looked to be administering first aid.

I spotted Headmistress Verla. She stood at the edge of the school, gazing over the scene with terror in her eyes. Her hair was a mess, and soot was smeared across her face. She spun in a circle, like she was trying to take it all in but just couldn't.

Verla was supposed to protect these students. She was their head-mistress, the voice of the entire student population… and she had failed them tonight. I couldn't imagine what she might be feeling in the wake of this carnage.

Worse than that, she'd seen this kind of thing before. This was the same council that had hung her sister. It was the same coven that couldn't save her stillborn child. We were the people who had failed her time and time again, and judging by the look on her face, I didn't know how much fight she had left in her. Verla had always seemed so strong, but right now, she looked terrified. She lifted her hands, like she was about to cast a spell, but I never saw what she conjured.

A group of Mortana passed in front of me, led by Leroy Benson, the jerk from my Protection Magic class. They ran into a group of Seers racing in the opposite direction. When Leroy saw the Seers blocking his path, black tendrils of magic left his fingers. My stomach twisted as the Seers dropped dead instantly, creating a path for the Mortana to flee. The Casts had begun fighting one another, all in an attempt to escape.

Behind them, another group of Seers moved through the chaos. I spotted Kenna Farlane among them. Her eyes darted around, and she trembled in fear. Every move the group made seemed deliberate. The girl in front held up her hand, and everyone stopped. A battle orb exploded right in front of them. The moment it hit, she gestured her friends forward, and they followed with complete faith. She yelled something, and everyone ducked as another spell flew over their heads. She must've been able to see the spells coming with her psychic powers.

Everything happened in mere seconds. I turned the entirety of my focus back toward my friends. "We have to work together," I said. "If we combine our magic, we can create a shield strong enough to lead us through the fire. Grab hands."

Talia kept her injured hand out of the circle, but she placed her good hand on Grant's shoulder.

"How do we do this?" Chloe asked.

"It's basics of intercast magic," I said, knowing most of them hadn't taken the class yet. "We have to combine our magic and allow it to vibrate at the same frequency. An incantation works best. Repeat after me. *Stronger together, our magic is charmed. Walk us through this fire unharmed.*"

My friends repeated my words. I expected to feel their magic surge through me like I'd practiced in Intercast Magic, but nothing happened.

"Um, is it working?" Onyx asked.

My heart dropped. "Something's wrong."

Grant's eyes darted around our circle. "I've still got magic."

Chloe's features fell. "I don't."

Nadine gritted her teeth. "The Waning!"

I tried to create a protection spell around us, but nothing happened. "My magic was *just* working!"

"You never know when the Waning will hit," Miles said.

"*Everybody's out!?*" Grant asked. He tried a quick spell, and an orb formed in his hand.

Everyone else did the same, but Onyx was the only one who managed to conjure anything. "I'm still good," she said.

"Two Alchemists," Grant sighed. "We'll never make a shield strong enough to hold back those flames."

Chloe whirled toward Nadine and spoke quickly. "Curse Breakers can absorb magic, right? You could restore the power you lost from the Waning. That might be enough to do the spell."

"Supposedly, but I haven't learned how yet," Nadine said. "And even if I could, I'd need at least *some* magic to start with. I'm completely out. We'll have to—"

Nadine cut off as a spell shot between us. I jumped back, narrowly dodging the spell, but it whizzed by me and slammed straight into Onyx's chest. She stumbled back, and her cat hissed loudly.

Onyx blinked a few times, then glanced around frantically. Her chest heaved, and her voice shook. "I can't see!"

"A curse?" I growled.

"I-I don't know," Onyx stammered. "Mentalist powers, maybe? Tricking my brain."

"Then it should wear off," Chloe said, grabbing Onyx's hand. "In the meantime, I'll be your eyes."

"Grant, Onyx," Nadine said. "Can you two create the spell the other Alchemists used to get through the fire?"

Grant hesitated. "Messing with the elements is tough. We'd need a lot more Alchemists."

"Grant," Talia said, like he was missing something. "You have all the Alchemy magic you need."

Grant's eyes widened. "Of course!"

"Let's see what that Wand is capable of," Talia said.

Grant conjured the Alchemy Wand and curled his fingers around it tightly. He drew a deep breath, and the end of the Wand began to glow. Beams of magic connected with the Wand, like it was coming from the surrounding area. I glanced around, and I spotted Headmistress Verla nearby. Her chest glowed, and she stared down at it in horror.

"That's enough," I told Grant. "You're siphoning magic from other Alchemists."

"That should be enough anyway," he said. "Come on!"

Chloe stared at the Wand, like she couldn't believe her eyes. "Is that an *Oaken Wand?*"

"Where did you *get* that?" Miles asked.

"Story for another day," Talia replied.

Grant ran toward the trees, and the rest of us followed. He dropped to his knees and conjured a pile of herbs. He scooped water into his hand from the melting snow and sprinkled the herbs on top. Isa and Oliver rushed up to him and nudged bags of herbs in his direction, trying to help. He moved frantically, pouring the entire contents of the last bag into his hand. He lifted the Wand and spoke an incantation. Alchemy magic twirled out of the end of the Wand, infusing the herbs.

"What's happening?" Onyx asked. She couldn't see a thing.

"Grant's getting us out of here," Nadine said.

"Almost done!" he cried. "Chloe, a bit of help?"

"On it," she said.

Grant drew his arm back, then threw the herb bundle toward the trees. Chloe used her Mentalist powers to propel it faster. The bundle tore apart mid-air and rained down over the flames. An explosion sounded, and the flames died in front of us, providing a narrow pathway.

"Come on!" Grant yelled. "It won't last long."

Everyone rushed forward, but I paused at the edge of the trees. People rushed by so quickly, I couldn't make out their faces. Verla raced over to a group of terrified freshmen. She looked like she was trying to calm them down. Determination was written all over her face, like one way or another, she *would* get them out of there.

"Headmistress!" I shouted. She didn't hear me. "Headmistress Verla! This way!"

She still didn't look in my direction. A hand landed on the back of my shirt and yanked me back. "Lucas, there's no time!" Nadine cried. "We'll find a way to get everyone out, but we have to get to safety first."

It killed me to leave anyone behind, but I couldn't help anyone if I burned to death. We had to get a move on.

I whirled around and raced into the trees. Grant's spell wore off behind me, and the trees crackled. I'd have been burned alive if I stayed a second longer. We ran so far into the trees that the fire wall was long behind us before we stopped to catch our breath. The flames burned so hot that I could feel them on my back even as we escaped.

"What do we do?" Miles asked.

"We have to get the others out," Nadine said through ragged breaths.

"How?" Talia asked.

"Without the support of the police or the priestesses, there may not be anything we *can* do," Chloe pointed out. "They're determined to hold people hostage back there."

"I have the Alchemy Wand," Grant said, holding it up.

"Where the hell did you find that?" Chloe asked.

"It's a long story," Grant said. "But I should be able to restore magic, right? Alchemy magic, at least. It could give some of them a chance."

Grant lifted the Wand, and the end began to glow again, but his eyebrows pinched together the longer he stared at it. "Shit. I can attract the magic, but I can't redistribute it."

"We need all five Wands," Nadine said, sounding certain. "The priestesses mentioned it, that the Wands are stronger together. That's why it's so important to find them all, because the Waning won't end until they're together. Right now, we need to get somewhere safe. We can go to my grandma's. We'll come up with something there."

"Let's get moving," I said. "This fire is spreading fast. We can't stay in this forest for long."

It didn't take long before we reached the edge of the trees and came into town. We snuck onto someone's lawn and around the side of their house. The sound of breaking glass and screams came from up ahead.

When we stepped onto the street, my stomach dropped. The students who had escaped the school grounds earlier had brought their panic into town. Adults and children raced out of their homes. Others threw spells into shop windows, shattering them and looting their contents.

"The Burning has arrived!" someone shouted. "There's no turning back!"

A car sped along the street, and people screamed as they jumped out of the way. The orange glow of fire flickered from inside one of the buildings. Looters chased three girls outside. It looked like they'd ducked inside the building for safety. Their screams echoed down the street as they fled. I realized it was Lena, Gwen, and Camille. They tried to throw spells back at the guys looting the store, but none of their spells worked.

The guys laughed loudly, like they were having the time of their lives. As the fire burned brighter, I caught sight of the symbol on the back of their jackets—a spider. It was the Tarantulas—all of them except Ryan. The four of them continued down the block after Lena and her friends.

I was about to go after them when three guys ran in front of the Tarantulas, blocking them from chasing the girls any further. I recognized

Gregory, Alex, and Brayden. Gregory pulled a wand from his coat and pointed it at Nolan. Alex and Brayden held up their own wands at the others.

"Back the fuck up!" Gregory shouted. He must've grown a spine since I'd threatened him near the Vanishing Stairwell, because he stared down the Tarantulas with murderous intent in his eyes.

"What are you going to do?" Nolan taunted.

"We'll fry your ass, if we have to," Brayden threatened, though his voice wavered.

"You're not going anywhere near those girls," Alex added.

The Tarantulas laughed so loudly that it echoed down the street. "Get 'em, boys " Nolan ordered.

The Tarantulas raised their hands in unison, but the other three reacted faster. Magic blasted from their wands, and the Tarantulas went flying backward, straight through a shop window. Glass shattered and rained down onto the street. The Tarantulas let out strings of curse words.

All around us, the chaos continued. Tires squealed as families fled, and people screamed as the Casts fought one another. Everything happened so fast.

"Dear Goddess," Onyx whispered. She trembled against Chloe, horrified by the sounds.

"How are we going to get across town to your grandma's?" Miles asked.

"Change of plans," Nadine said. "We need to help those people."

Nadine started forward, but Chloe grabbed her wrist. "Without magic? Nadine, these people are terrified. You could get yourself killed."

"It's not *their* fear I'm afraid of," Nadine snapped. "It's the priestesses'. They're killing people in the name of saving them, because they're terrified of the Waning. They're going to be the end of us all."

"And you have to stay alive long enough to fight back!" Chloe insisted. "You're a priestess."

"And it's gotten me nowhere so far!" Nadine cried. "I need to do something—!"

Someone shouted from nearby, cutting her off. "Your Cast is to blame!"

I whirled toward them to see a dozen Mentalists cornering three

Alchemists in front of a shop. I didn't realize until the guy took a step forward that it was James. "You created nightshade!"

"We never touched nightshade," a girl cried. It was Sadie, a girl who worked at The Witch's Brew restaurant on the lake. "I swear!"

"Your word means nothing as an Alchemist," James snarled. "Your Cast is trying to kill us all."

The unthinkable happened. Revulsion festered inside of me as James used his powers on her. The girl dropped to her knees, and her back arched as she cried out in agony. I remembered what it felt when he'd done the same to me last summer. James's magic tricked you into thinking you were in pain—and it was a power he was good at.

I started running, my heart pulsing in my ears. I heard footsteps behind me, but I didn't know which of my friends followed. Oliver sprinted ahead.

The girl's cries were unbearable, but they were over in a second. I barely made it a few paces before her body dropped to the sidewalk.

"What have you done!?" one of her friends cried.

James took a step back, looking horrified. "She's faking it. I'd never—"

"She has a heart condition!" another Alchemist shouted.

Oliver reached James first. He jumped at him, claws outstretched with murderous intent. Oliver scratched James's face, tearing through flesh so fast that blood sprang from his face immediately. James reared back and screamed. He yanked Oliver off of him and threw him against the side of the building.

"Motherfucker!" I growled as soon as I reached him. I didn't think about how I was outnumbered. I barely thought at all. I slammed my fist straight into James's jaw, and he landed flat on the ground.

Miles and Talia raced behind me, their cats following, but they came to an immediate halt when the Mentalists began closing in on us. One of the Alchemy students checked Sadie's pulse, but she was already long gone. The Alchemists took off running before they were killed as well.

"So that's the way it's going to be," one of the Mentalists said, cracking his knuckles. I was preparing for a fight.

The other Mentalists laughed. Kiki, Oliver, and Gus poised for attack, and I was almost certain we were about to be pummeled by their magic—

Then came the sound of sirens, blaring so loud that several people jumped back and covered their ears. My heart lurched as two police cruisers came to a screeching halt beside us. The Mentalists fled in all directions as four officers jumped out of the vehicles. James scurried to his feet and ran.

"Officers! You have to help!" Miles cried. "They killed—"

"Hands in the air where we can see them!" an officer shouted.

My hands shot into the air involuntarily. It was like magic had taken control of my body. One of the officers was a puppeteer. Damn Mentalists.

"Cast a spell, and you'll regret it!" another officer threatened.

My stomach dropped from my abdomen as a shield formed around me and my friends. It was barely big enough to contain us all. We were squashed together.

"Goddess!" Talia cried.

"Fuck," Miles growled.

I could see Nadine on the other side of the squad cars, the flashing lights illuminating her features. Her face had gone paper white. I shot a quick glance to the side of one of the shops, begging her to hide so they wouldn't take her, too.

Nadine got the message. She grabbed Grant's arm and said something, though I couldn't hear what. They fled, and Chloe and Onyx followed. Isa hesitated for a moment, before racing behind Chloe's and Onyx's cats.

The officers slapped metal cuffs onto our wrists. Immediately, my energy drained. These had to be the noxite cuffs Amy had been wearing earlier, because they were definitely magical. If I hadn't already lost my magic to the Waning, then it'd be gone as soon as they put the handcuffs on.

"Move!" one of the officers barked.

Beside me, Talia whimpered as her feet began moving under her without her consent. Gus yowled when she stepped on him. "Sorry!" she cried.

The cats wove between our feet, looking terrified. They weren't affected by the magic, but they couldn't escape the shield, either.

"Where are you taking us?" Miles demanded.

"Back to the school," an officer sneered. He almost sounded amused. "Where the priestesses can decide what to do with you criminals."

"What, like burn us at the stake?" Talia snapped boldly.

An officer laughed. *Definitely amused.* "They'll make an example out of you one way or another."

My blood turned to ice in my veins. It was pretty clear what was happening.

They were marching us to our slaughter.

TWENTY-FOUR

I ducked around the corner of a wand shop, my heart racing. I barely had time to catch my breath. Grant, Chloe, and Onyx hid in the shadows next to me. Isa raced to my side, meowing loudly.

"Shh..." I hissed at her. I couldn't tear my gaze off my friends. Lucas put on a brave face, but I was terrified for him and what the police might do. Hell, it wasn't even the *police* I was worried about. The priestesses would punish him for what he said in front of the coven, and for how he'd tried to save Amy. We had to get him out of there, but I was out of magic. I stood no chance against the police, and they wouldn't listen to me now —not after the council overruled me.

"Grant, is there *anything* you can brew to help them?" I asked.

He wore a calculating look. "I don't know, honestly. With potions and herbs, you actually have to administer it. There's nothing we can do at a distance."

"Can we... cast a curse, maybe?" I wondered. I was out of options.

"That will get us killed," Chloe said. "The priestesses would take it as an act of war."

"This has *become* a war," I insisted. "We already know the coven will kill innocent people. What if our friends are next?"

"We'll think of something," Onyx said.

I hesitated. This wasn't safe for any of us, and I wouldn't put anyone in danger unless they were willing. "Do you really want to go up against the priestesses?"

Onyx scoffed. "Do I *look* like the kind of girl who follows the rules?"

She gestured to herself. Onyx took goth style to the max, with pitch-black hair dyed purple at the tips, knee-high boots, and a velvety black dress. Her features were pale, and her makeup was dark. I always loved her style, but I never took her to be a *rebel*—just a quiet girl with a cool sense of fashion. Though we'd spent a whole semester as lab partners, I realized I didn't know anything about Onyx at all.

"Any one of us could be hanged or burned at the stake," I said. "Is everyone sure they're willing to risk that?"

"Like you said, the priestesses already killed innocent people," Chloe stated. "It seems that we're at risk no matter what side we're on. I'd rather die knowing I was on the side that tried to stop it."

"What about your grandmother?" Grant asked.

"Screw my family," Chloe spat. "I always thought family was the most important thing, but if this is what my family does, then I don't want to be an Olson anymore."

My knee-jerk reaction was to question her. I'd spent so much time fighting with Chloe that it was hard to trust her. We'd worked together to break our family curse, but we weren't exactly *friends*. But Chloe had *always* been against hangings and burnings. She'd told me that when we were tied up in Pinewood Manor together. It was one of the reasons she wanted to become a priestess—to stop it. I had to accept that Chloe was on my side.

"Then let's stop this." I gestured them forward, and we crept through the shadows.

We followed behind the officers at a distance and watched as they marched our friends through the front gates and back onto campus. I caught sight of the priestesses. They wore proud smirks that made me want to hurl. The iron gates shut, and two guards stood out front. I recognized one of them as Lincoln, the guy who guarded Octavia Hall.

My eyes scanned the brick wall that extended outward from the iron gates. "How far does this wall go?" I asked. "It can't surround the whole property." I'd been through the forest surrounding the school many times, and I'd never seen a wall anywhere but at the front of the school.

"It's just at the entrance," Chloe said. "There used to be an iron gate surrounding the property to keep the fae out, but students kept vandalizing it. Now it's more for decoration than anything."

"Let's go this way." I cocked my head, and we headed deeper into the forest, where the guards wouldn't spot us. The scent of a burnt forest filled the air. Embers fluttered to the ground around us, but the raging fire had died. The Alchemist's Accelerant must've reached its limits, and the trees were so wet from the snow that they'd stopped burning. We crept to the edge of the wall that bordered the front of the property.

"I'll boost you up," Grant whispered.

He interlaced his fingers, and I stepped into his hands. My fingers curled around the top of the wall, and I peeked over. My heart jumped when I saw the scene before me. Students had been rounded up in front of the school, and police paced back and forth in front of them. The officers twisted battle magic in their hands, threatening anyone who dared step out of line.

I noticed Professor Wykoff twisting her skirt around in her hands. She stood beside Professor Warbright—the short, stout music professor. They both shared the same worried look, like they wanted to stop this but didn't know how. Not far from them, Professor Warren stood next to a group of students. He kept shooting them reassuring glances, like he was desperately trying to give them hope.

Priestess Margaret looked Lucas up and down as he passed. "People have died tonight because of you," she sneered. I just barely heard her over this distance, but her voice sent a shiver down my spine.

At the stake, Lilian barked orders at professors. She forced them to drag the charred bodies of our friends down from the pyre. I witnessed Professor Richard's trembling hands as he helped remove Amy's body. I winced at the sight of her, and tears beaded in my eyes. I wanted to cry, to break down and scream, but I didn't have the luxury.

The other professors didn't look frightened at all. In fact, they looked like they were hungry for a second burning.

"Priestess, please," Headmistress Verla begged Lilian. "No more burnings tonight. At least give these students a trial!"

Lilian turned away from the Headmistress. "They will get what they deserve."

The following silence was deafening. It seemed that all I could hear was the sound of my friends' footsteps on the lawn. The officers marched them into the school, and I jumped down from Grant's hands.

"It looks like the police are the only ones with magic," I said. "Or anyone who still has it isn't willing to fight back. They've rounded everyone up. I think they're getting ready for a second burning. They've taken Lucas, Talia, and Miles into the school."

Grant swallowed. "What are we going to do?"

"We need to create a distraction and set them free," Chloe said simply, like it'd be easy. "We have to buy enough time that the council will reconsider and give them a trial. Emotions are high right now, and people aren't thinking straight. They'll support a second burning if they have someone to blame. But if we make this last until morning, people will reconsider, and the priestesses will have to plan their next move carefully."

I stared at her. "You're like a chess pro, planning out every move."

"My grandmother has been training me my whole life to become a priestess one day," Chloe said. "You have to know how people work, and you must plan out your moves, or you lose your support. The priestesses have power because the coven gives it to them. If we break your friends out, it gives people time to rescind their support. They got away with this tonight because it was at the school. The priestesses will second guess another public execution, especially after what happened to Professor Daniels."

"Okay," I agreed. "How do we distract them?"

"I might know something," Onyx said.

"Can you do it blind?" Grant asked. "How's your vision?"

"The spell is wearing off," Onyx said. "I can do it."

"I'll go with Onyx," Chloe offered.

I nodded firmly. "Grant and I will sneak around to the back of the school and get inside."

"Hold up," Grant said. "How are we going to break them out? If the police still have magic, they have to be restraining them somehow. They'll be using more than just those handcuffs."

"You know how to break restraints," Onyx said, though there was something in her tone I couldn't read.

Grant gaped. "You're talking about—"

"About saving your friends," Onyx interrupted Grant. "You're the only one with enough magic."

"Can you do it?" Chloe asked.

Grant swallowed. "I think so."

"We'll figure something out," I said quickly. We were running out of time. "How will we know when you're ready?"

"Ooh, you'll know," Onyx said with a slight twinkle in her eye. "I've been wanting to brew this spell forever."

We split up. Chloe's and Onyx's cats went with them, and Isa followed me. Grant and I snuck through the trees and around the perimeter of the property. We moved as quickly as we could without being spotted. We came so close to the pyre that we had to move slowly, or they'd hear us. I stared at Amy's frail, broken body lying in the snow, and my stomach twisted as if I'd just been impaled by a death curse.

Grant choked up and whispered, "She'll be greatly missed."

"We'll hold a proper funeral, but we can't do this right now," I said softly. "There are others who still need our help."

Isa nudged her head against my leg, turning her gaze away from Amy. It was like she couldn't bear it. Hell, I don't think any of us could.

Grant and I snuck to the back of the school, then hurried across the lawn through the darkness. We slipped into the back of the school unnoticed.

"Where do you think they're holding them?" Grant whispered.

"It's gotta be somewhere without windows and no other exits," I said. "So maybe the—"

I cut off when the sound of shouts came from down the hall. "Don't say a word!" someone yelled.

Grant and I exchanged a glance. "I think we found them," I said.

We crept down the hall. I peeked around the corner, but no one was there. I gestured Grant forward, and we continued down the hall until we spotted the Lounge. Two officers stood guard outside the door, and two others paced up and down the hall, as if surveying for threats. I could see the protection spell shimmering in the doorway, locking our friends inside the Lounge. Behind the shield, Lucas paced back and forth. His hands were secured in front of him by handcuffs. Talia and Miles both sat on one of the couches, with their cats in their laps. They looked angry, like they were already plotting their next move.

On the couch beside them sat three girls, each one looking more terrified than the last. They looked up at Lucas with hope in their eyes, like they expected him to save them. I recognized Darcy, Felicia, and Samantha. Each of the girls was hurt in some way. Darcy held her arm, and Felicia had a gash across her face. Samantha propped one leg up on the coffee table, like her ankle was bruised. The priestesses must've had them arrested for speaking up earlier when they said they believed us.

I turned to Grant. "What's the spell Onyx was talking about? How do we break the shield and get them out?"

Grant's gaze locked on the officers. He didn't even blink as he raised the Alchemy Wand and pointed it around the corner. He drew a deep breath, like the thought of casting the spell shook him to his very core. His voice came out as a whisper. "There's only one way to break them. Restraints don't hold if the spellcaster is dead."

My heart lurched, and I grabbed his wrist. "Grant, you mean—?"

"They won't be able to trace the spell back to me," he said quickly.

"But you'll have to live with this," I argued. "When I killed those witches last semester—"

"You saved us," he said firmly. "Lucas killed Stella to save us, too. It's my turn to save someone."

I shook his arm and forced him to look at me. "Grant, are you sure about this?"

"Nadine, you don't understand. It's them, or our friends." Tears rose to Grant's eyes, like he couldn't stand the thought of losing anyone else. "You heard what Chloe said. We have to buy them time if we want them to live. Otherwise, they'll be burned just like Amy. We couldn't save her, but we can save the rest of them."

I swallowed the lump rising in my throat. "What if they find out—?"

A huge explosion sounded from outside, so loud that it shook the walls of the school. I stumbled to the side and caught myself against the wall. Holy crap. When Onyx said she knew a spell, she knew a damn good one. My ears rang from the sound.

"What the fuck was that!?" one of the officers shouted.

I peeked around the corner to see two of the officers grab their wands and race toward the Main Foyer. Two officers remained. They stood guard outside the Lounge, glancing up and down the hallway.

Grant lifted the Alchemy Wand, and my stomach twisted. The end of the Wand began to glow.

"Wait, Grant," I said, but it was already too late.

"I know what I have to do," he said boldly. "But I have to get closer."

He straightened his shoulders and stepped out from his hiding spot. The officers noticed immediately. My heart leapt into my throat when they grabbed their wands and pointed them at Grant.

"Grant!" I cried.

"Drop your weapon!" one of the officers yelled.

"You drop yours first," Grant threatened. "I'll give you one chance to drop your shield and walk away. I don't want to do this."

It happened so fast. The officers waved their wands, and lights blasted from the ends.

Pop! Pop! Pop!

A sound like gunshots filled the hall, and my heart stopped. Grant turned to a statue, and I was certain he'd been hit. Time halted, and the whole school spun around me.

Grant waved the Alchemy Wand, and the officers stumbled back. They began coughing in unison. They dropped their wands and doubled over. Blood sprayed from their mouths as they heaved, and they cried red tears as they collapsed to the ground.

All I could do was stare. Isa meowed as the sound of their dying coughs filled the school. My friends stood in the doorway of the Lounge, staring out into the hall at the horrifying scene before us.

Then all at once, it was over.

The coughing stopped, and the hall filled with silence. The officers' bodies lay in pools of their own blood. The shimmering spell blocking the doorway dissolved, and my friends rushed out of the Lounge.

"Grant!" Lucas cried.

Grant's face paled, and his eyes glossed over. Lucas caught him as he collapsed, but he couldn't hold him upright with his hands bound together. He lowered Grant to the ground. Oliver rushed to Grant's side, pressing his paws to his shoulder like he was trying to wake him.

"Goddess!" Talia cried. Her broken hand trembled, and Gus meowed at her feet.

"Grant! Bro!" Miles shouted as he dropped to his side. Grant groaned at the sound of his name.

Samantha gasped, and Felicia took her hands. Both of them appeared sick, eyes stuck to the officers' corpses.

My stomach clenched. Blood oozed from a hole in Grant's shoulder. It looked like a bullet wound, but it'd be cast by magic. A sheen of sweat coated his forehead, and all the color left his lips.

Miles pressed his hand over the wound, but blood poured through his fingers. "What did you *do*?"

"I poisoned their blood," Grant admitted in a rough tone.

Felicia's jaw dropped. "That's impossible!"

"Not with the Alchemy Wand," I said quickly.

I scrambled toward one of the officers and yanked a set of keys from his belt. I quickly began freeing my friends from their handcuffs. As soon as I touched the metal, I started swaying on my feet.

"What are these?" I asked. They were definitely magical.

"Noxite cuffs," Felicia said as I undid her cuffs. "They're made with some sort of magical metal that drains your magic."

"Could noxite be causing the Waning?" I asked as I moved on to Darcy.

Felicia shook her head. "No, it would need to be administered somehow, and if they were poisoning us with it, we'd be knocked out as soon as we lost our magic."

I pulled Talia's cuffs off next. "We have to get out of here," I stated firmly. There was no point to what Grant had done if we got caught.

"Where are we going to go?" Darcy asked.

"Anywhere but here," I said. "Hopefully somewhere we can get Grant some help." I glanced around the group. Almost everyone seemed to be injured. I quickly added, "Somewhere we can get everyone some help."

Lucas looked up to me. "The headmaster's abandoned mansion. We'll call Helena."

"Yes," I agreed.

"What about Tate?" Talia asked. "She's gotta be in the infirmary."

"She's recovering," Lucas pointed out. "We can't move her right now. She's not a threat to the priestesses. She'll be safe."

I nodded in agreement. Tate was better off with the doctors than with a bunch of fugitives. "Let's get moving."

Miles and Lucas helped Grant stand. Grant sagged against his brother as we left out the back of the school. Grant clutched the Alchemy Wand tight in his hand, as if he was ready to use it again if need be. Talia held Gus to her chest with her good hand, and tears beaded in her eyes. Felicia and Darcy helped Samantha as she limped down the hall.

"Stop," I hissed, holding up a hand. I peeked outside the door, and I spotted a pair of professors gathering sticks and taking them back to the pyre. As soon as they disappeared around the side of the school, I gestured forward.

Everyone was gathered at the front of the school, so no one saw us as we snuck out the back. We hurried across the snow and into the forest, our cats following close behind. When we reached the trees, two shadows appeared. I gasped, but a voice quickly cut through the darkness.

"It's just us!" Chloe said as she came out from behind a tree.

"You got them out," Onyx added in relief. Her sight had finally returned.

"Yes," I said. "But we have to move. It won't be long until they come looking for us."

"Where are we going?" Samantha asked, her tone a few pitches higher than normal.

"Somewhere safe," Lucas said.

I held my breath the whole way to the hidden mansion, but we reached the clearing without being spotted. I burst through the front door. My whole body gave a jolt when I saw a figure in the hallway. Someone shot to their feet, and a battle orb formed in their hand. When I saw her face, relief flooded through me.

"Mandy!" I cried.

When she saw it was me, Mandy dropped her hand, and she burst into tears. "Thank Goddess it's you!"

I rushed over to her, and Mandy threw her arms around my neck. She sagged against me, sobbing into my shoulder. I rubbed her back.

"I'm so glad you're okay," I said.

Mandy shook as she drew away from me. "And everyone else?"

"We're alive," Lucas said in relief. "But not everyone was so lucky."

"Come on." Mandy ushered everyone through the door. "There's room down the hall."

We entered the living room. Lucas quickly got to work building a fire. I noticed there was a fresh pile of wood there. He must've restocked since the last time we'd been here.

"I wasn't sure whether to start a fire," Mandy admitted. "I thought someone would find me here."

"This place is enchanted," Lucas explained. "If anyone seeks to harm this place—or us—they can't find it."

Mandy's shoulders sagged. "Thank the Goddess."

"I need a phone," I announced. "Is anyone's conjuring working?"

Grant winced as Miles helped him sit down, but he conjured his phone and handed it to me. I stepped into the hall as everyone got settled in around the fire. Isa looked up at me with sad eyes.

"Nadine?" Grammy asked breathlessly when she heard my voice. "What's going on at the school? I've been trying to get in touch with you all night. I was so scared."

"I'm safe, Grammy," I told her. "But my friends need help. We're hiding out at the old headmaster's mansion. Bring as many healing herbs as you can."

"I'm on my way," she said immediately.

The atmosphere in the living room was melancholy when I returned, but I finally felt like I could breathe. Darcy, Samantha, and Felicia sat one side of the room, inspecting each other's injuries.

"I was so scared," Darcy admitted, wincing as she moved her arm.

"Why would they arrest you?" Chloe asked curiously. She sat next to Onyx, stroking the top of her cat's head.

Samantha's gaze dropped. "We were trying to stop the fires. As soon as everything broke out, we grouped up and tried to get a hose from the greenhouse, but everything got out of hand."

Darcy shivered. "I thought for sure I was going to die. The spell that hit me knocked me out for a while."

"Some asshole walked right up to me and did *this*," Felicia said, gesturing to the gash on her face.

"I tripped and got trampled," Samantha said.

Chloe frowned. "I'm sorry. I'll do everything I can to convince my grandmother to give you a trial."

Darcy pushed her red curls out of her face and shot Chloe a smile. "Thank you."

I walked over to Lucas and collapsed onto the ground beside him. He draped an arm around my shoulder and pulled me close. I sagged against him, and fatigue finally had a chance to set in. All I wanted to do was close my eyes and sleep until this was all over.

"You okay, Nadine?" Talia asked. Grant winced from beside her, but he already had a t-shirt pressed to his wound to slow the blood loss. There was nothing we could do except wait for Grammy to arrive.

"I'll be okay," I said. "I'm more worried about you and your broken hand."

Talia grimaced. "It'll heal."

"Assuming I still receive my dialysis treatment after this, I'll be okay," I said.

Silence settled over the room, and Grant was the first to break it. "Where are we going to go?"

"What do you mean?" Chloe asked. "You want to *leave* Octavia Falls? How will we fight back if we leave?"

Talia wore a worried expression. "You might be able to stay, but the priestesses have already arrested us. I don't know if we stand a chance."

"What if they came after you?" Onyx asked.

"Would they, though?" I wondered. "The priestesses only have jurisdiction inside Octavia Falls. They'd be better off making a political statement out of us leaving. I don't like the idea of them using us, but at least we'd be safe."

Lucas reached out for me. "But your treatments…"

"I can find another dialysis center," I said, but my throat closed up around my words.

I didn't *want* to leave. Chloe was right. We couldn't help the coven if we weren't here. If we left, it meant that we'd failed. We'd be leaving behind everyone who needed our help—people like Samantha, Darcy, and Felicia. We'd be abandoning all the people who couldn't help themselves, like the children and the elderly. I thought of Rose, the woman from the nursing home. Leaving meant putting her fate—and everyone else's—in the hands of the Imperium Council. I didn't want to go, but I also knew my friends and I could die if we stayed.

"What about your kidney transplant?" Lucas pointed out.

Chloe's jaw dropped from across the room. "You need a new kidney?"

I pushed my hair behind my ear. "I have one. Lucas and I are a match. Problem is, I don't have a doctor who will perform the surgery. If we left, I'd have to wait on the transplant list—and I may never get a kidney."

"Lucas could still give you his." Chloe sounded honestly concerned. "You can find another doctor."

I frowned. "His therapist won't approve him, and he can't convince her. That's on his record now. The only way to sway the doctors is with the help of the Imperium Council. They said if I hand over an Oaken Wand, they'll help me get the transplant."

Chloe looked speechless. "I had no idea you were that sick."

I shrugged. "I haven't exactly made it public."

"Ow!" Samantha winced as she tried to move. Chloe rushed over to help, and I turned back to my friends.

Grant cleared his throat, and he held the Alchemy Wand out to me. "Here, take it."

I gaped at him. "Grant, I can't."

"You need a kidney. Take it," he insisted.

"So the priestesses can control Alchemy magic?" I asked. "No. We're not handing any of the Wands over. It chose *you*."

"Right, and I get to choose what to do with it," he insisted. "The Wand is mine, which means the priestesses can't use it."

"Unless it changes loyalty," Lucas pointed out. "That can happen. But I agree with Grant."

"You what?" I asked.

Lucas shifted. "If we hand over the Wand, you get your kidney. We can always get the Wand back, but we can't get you back if you die."

I gaped at him. "Yeah, I want a new kidney, but I won't die without one."

"Unless the priestesses threaten your dialysis," Lucas said. "That's a bigger deal, because this transplant is a one-time thing. They can use your dialysis to control you over and over again. We know they're powerful. What's to stop them from preventing your treatment, even if you're getting it somewhere else?"

"They'll arrest us if we stay," I pointed out.

"Not if you hand over the Wand," Grant said. "Use the Wand to pardon yourself and Lucas, so that you can get your transplant. The priestesses want the Wand more than they want to hang either one of you. Plus, they still need you to find the other Wands. You two have been chosen. You *have* to stay. Talia, Miles, and I will skip town as soon as we're strong enough to travel. We'll take Felicia,

Samantha, and Darcy far away—and anyone else who wants to come."

The thought of tearing our group apart seared me to the core. We'd already lost Amy. I couldn't imagine losing anyone else.

Lucas and I *were* chosen, but only because *we* chose to stand up and fight. We could still change our minds. And yet, how could we abandon our own people?

I choked up. "This isn't fair."

"No," Lucas agreed. "It isn't fair, and it isn't easy, but it has to be done."

I swallowed the lump in my throat. "I'll have to think about it."

"Take it," Grant begged. He pushed the Wand toward me. "Please, just take it."

That's when I realized he wasn't asking me to take it for *me*. He was asking me to take it for *him*. I knew what it was like to take a life—even to save another. Grant couldn't bear to look at the Wand right now, not after he killed those officers. My heart shattered for him.

Gently, I took the Wand from his hand. He sagged against the wall, like I'd just lifted a fifty-pound weight off his chest.

A door burst open from down the hall, and I heard the sound of a cat meow. Isa and Oliver both bristled, then raced out into the hallway.

"Isa!" I called.

"It's just me!" Grammy's voice came back.

I was so relieved. I didn't have the energy for anything else tonight. "In here, Grammy!"

Grammy rushed into the room, and she stopped dead in the doorway when she saw us. Her gaze immediately went to Grant. The t-shirt Miles had given him was soaked in blood already.

"What kind of spell?" she asked.

"I've never seen it before," Miles said. "It was like a gunshot."

Grammy winced. "This will be a tricky one."

"But you can help him?" Talia asked hopefully.

Grammy nodded, but her gaze darted toward Talia's broken hand. "I can help, then I'm helping you. Lucas, I need your help."

Onyx stood. "I'm an Alchemist. My magic's still good."

"Perfect, dear," Grammy said. "Come on over."

Grammy gave Lucas orders, and Onyx helped crush herbs to brew a numbing potion.

"Anyone want to tell me what happened?" Grammy asked as she worked on Grant's shoulder.

"It's kind of a long story," Talia said.

Grammy shrugged. "I have time."

"I'm dying to know, too." Chloe held her cat close to her chest and came to sit by me, like she was a kid listening to a bedtime story.

Talia shot a glance around the room.

"It's okay," I said. "We're all on the same side."

She sighed. "Ever hear of the Oaken Wands?"

"The Oaken Wands are a myth," Felicia insisted, like she knew better.

"Are you sure about that?" I asked, holding up the Alchemy Wand.

Soon, everyone was gathered around the fireplace as Talia and Lucas took turns telling the story. I was too exhausted to chime in. Once Grammy stitched and bandaged Grant's wound, she moved on to Talia's hand, which she wrapped in leaves and ointment that would heal her broken bones in a week.

Grammy continued administering first-aid well into the early hours of the morning. Onyx looked thrilled to be brewing potions, and the other girls seemed so invested in our story that they seemed to forget their own injuries.

Mandy sat in the corner, her eyes locked on a spot on the floor. She looked so frail and broken, and I felt awful for her.

"I miss Amy already," I said once Talia reached the end of the story. "I honestly can't believe she's gone."

Talia frowned. "I agree. She was a really good friend."

I sniffled. The reality of everything that happened tonight only now just seemed to be hitting me. "She was kind and passionate. She wanted to study supernatural history. She thought history could teach us something, so that we'd never repeat the Great Supernatural War ever again."

Miles stared off into the distance. "For them to target her—such a kind, pure soul... it's sick, really."

Grant swallowed. "I can't help but think that it was my fault."

"No, Grant," Lucas said quickly. "You can't blame yourself."

"But I left the nightshade in her room," he said. "If we'd cleaned up earlier—"

"You didn't," Talia cut in. "It doesn't matter how much you go over it in your head. It won't change what happened."

An uncomfortable silence settled over the room. Lucas cleared his throat. "Amy brought me crystals for my depression. I don't know if I ever told anyone that. I still have them. She always asked about my therapy sessions."

"She made me a cream for my arthritis," Miles stated sadly. "She came up with the recipe herself."

My breath caught. "She always brought me gifts on my birthday. Amy really was one of the kindest people I knew. She was just… incredible."

It hurt to talk about her in the past tense.

"Amy was kind to everyone," Lucas added as he helped Grammy with Samantha's ankle. "I literally never saw her say a bad thing about anyone."

Chloe hugged her knees to her chest. "She was almost kind to a fault, to be honest—"

"Shut the fuck up!" Mandy cried from the corner of the room. It caught us all off guard. She shot to her feet and rounded on Chloe. "Don't you talk about her like that! You didn't give a fuck about Amy. You conned her into helping you brew a potion to turn me into a frog!"

"Which is how you two became friends," Chloe pointed out. "I know you're hurting right now. I don't blame you for being mad at me. Maybe sometime we can talk about this, but I've changed. I regret what I did."

"Good!" Mandy growled. "You should! You don't get to treat her the way you did and then grieve over her with us. You're a bitch, and we all know it."

"Mandy." Miles rose to his feet and walked over to her. He wrapped his arms around her. Her bottom lip trembled, and I wasn't sure if she was about to cry or scream. I wouldn't blame her for either option.

"I loved her!" Mandy cried. "And I didn't get my time with her! She's the *last* person who deserved to die tonight! Fuck you, Chloe, and fuck your grandmother! I hope you and your whole family burn in the—"

"Come on, Mandy," Miles said firmly. "Let's take this to the next room."

Mandy broke down into tears. She sobbed so loudly that she started hiccupping. I couldn't understand anything she was trying to say. I started to get to my feet, but Miles stopped me.

"I've got this," he said. "Everyone else should rest."

I knew Mandy, and Miles was right. She'd do better one-on-one. I sat back down, knowing there was nothing I could possibly do to help

Mandy right now—to help anyone, really. The silence in the room chilled me to the bone. I sat close to the fireplace and held Isa's warm body in my arms, and it still wasn't enough to ward off the cold.

"I'm almost done," Grammy said softly. She dabbed ointment over Felicia's face. "But Miles is right. Everyone should get some sleep here tonight. We'll see what things are like in the morning and go from there, okay?"

No one had the energy to argue.

Lucas finished helping Grammy, then came over by me. Grammy went around the room, conjuring blankets and handing them out. Talia and Grant curled up together under one of them, and Lucas and I snuggled under another. The floor was uncomfortable, but as soon as I laid my head on his chest, I didn't care. Isa and Oliver curled up at our feet, purring.

"I'm so sorry about everything that happened tonight," I whispered.

Lucas stroked my hand. "You couldn't have known."

I sniffled. "No, but I wish things turned out differently."

Lucas let out a wavered breath. "The only thing we can do is fight this, to be sure things never turn out this way again."

He was right. I only worried what else we might lose before the fighting ended.

On any other night, it'd be next to impossible to keep my eyes open. I was so tired, but I couldn't sleep with the rage flaring through my bones.

I waited until everyone had fallen asleep. Grant snored from nearby, but otherwise, the room had gone silent. Lucas's breathing had slowed. It was near torturous to peel myself away from him, but I slid out from underneath the blanket and snuck out of the mansion.

My friends would never let me confront the priestesses on my own. It was too dangerous right now. But I knew this night wasn't over.

I couldn't explain how I knew. It must've been my intuition. The Imperium had said at my induction ceremony that my intuition would be stronger once I became a priestess.

I had to convince them to pardon my friends before they made other plans—and acted on them.

I marched up the stairs to Octavia Hall. The cold bit at my fingers, but it didn't bother me. I was too enraged to care. I didn't bother knocking before storming into the Imperium headquarters.

"Our next move is to call off the nightshade deal with the Elementai for good, and we must bring the next Seer priestess onto the council immediately—" Priestess Margaret cut off when the door burst open. All eyes turned cruelly upon me.

"I believe I have a say in these plans," I said boldly.

The three priestesses stood around their meeting table, looking agitated. Margaret's face fell when she saw me, but Priestess Lilian narrowed her eyes.

"Please, Nadine," Lilian sneered. "Spare us the theatrics. You know as well as the rest of us that you are on this council only for appearances. You don't actually deserve to be here."

"Yet here I am," I replied. "Council law dictates that I get a seat in these meetings."

Lilian scoffed. "Whatever your plan is, you'll be outvoted."

"But I still get a say," I said. "You know, for *appearances*. That's why you haven't killed me yet, right? Because regardless of what the coven thinks of me, it would look awfully bad to hang the only Curse Breaker in the coven."

Lilian gaped, and Margaret rushed to say, "We thought you'd be long gone by now."

I scoffed. "I'm not going anywhere. And if you think you can get rid of me, you're wrong."

Lilian pursed her lips. "What exactly is it that you want, Nadine?"

"The same thing you want," I said. "I want to bring an end to the Waning. I want peace among the coven. I want to prevent a war. But that means that we have to work together. Stop the burnings and the hangings. Give the people a fair trial."

Margaret's features darkened as I spoke. "You fail to understand the political pressure the coven is under right now. We *are* saving the people by taking extreme measures. It's the only way to prevent a war."

"A war that you started!" I snarled.

"The coven must respect us!" Priestess Charlotte snapped.

"Killing them isn't going to earn you respect!" I growled. "You're making people fear you, so that they will bow down to you. That's not respect!"

"We are doing what must be done," Margaret snapped. "Controlling the people is the only way."

My nostrils flared. I couldn't believe that in their sick, twisted minds, they actually thought they were doing the right thing. "You will get yourself killed before the coven recovers from this."

Lilian narrowed her eyes. "Is that a threat, Nadine?"

"That's reality," I told her.

"No," Lilian snapped, slamming her fist onto the table. "The reality is that you are going to do exactly as you're told, or you'll be hanged for treason. Hand over the Alchemy Wand, Nadine."

I swallowed. "Not without a deal."

Lilian laughed, like my attempt at negotiation was comical. "We know you have the Wand, and we know your friend used it tonight to kill several officers."

My heart lurched. Grant had assured me the spell couldn't be traced back to him. "I don't know what you're talking about."

Priestess Charlotte pursed her lips. "Lying to the priestesses will earn you a charge of treason without a trial."

"We have the recording, Nadine," Priestess Margaret reminded me. "Stella's confession isn't the only thing we have on tape. We know your friend Grant Bryant retrieved the Alchemy Wand. We know he used it against those officers. The magic was too great for a single Alchemist. He will be burned for these murders."

I didn't let my features falter for a moment. "And how exactly is that different from the murders you sanctioned tonight? He had the best intentions, too. You'd have murdered my friends otherwise."

"And we still can," Charlotte threatened.

"Unless of course, you hand over the Wand," Margaret added.

I crossed my arms. "And how long does that earn them immunity? How can I trust that you won't turn your back on this deal and arrest them anyway?"

"You have our word," Priestess Margaret said—like it meant something to me. "We will offer your friends a trial in exchange for the Wand and the Crock."

"No," I objected. "I want their charges wiped out completely—every single one of them, including Darcy, Samantha, and Felicia. And I want the kidney transplant you promised me."

Lilian burst into laughter. "You overestimate your power in these negotiations, Nadine. You get one or the other."

My entire world seemed to flatten. This was just too unreal. A kidney… or my friends?

Lilian tapped her foot, like she was getting impatient. "If you find a second Wand, *then* you can have your kidney. We're not giving you everything you want for a single Wand."

Fuck her.

"I want everyone pardoned completely," I said firmly. I wouldn't settle for anything less.

Lilian eyed me. "You do realize that should we wipe their charges, it provides them no protection in the future. The minute you turn your back on us, or once your friends step out of line, we *will* take action."

I hesitated. I didn't know if it was enough. I couldn't stand back and watch the priestesses hurt more people. I had to fight back.

"We can agree to pardoning you and your friends for these crimes," Charlotte said. "You will retain your seat on the Imperium Council. In return, you will hand over the Alchemy Wand and the Crock of Death. Lucas will destroy all records of the article he's been working on regarding nightshade. He will not publish it."

I gaped. Lucas had been working on his article all semester. He was almost finished. I didn't even know how they knew about it—until I realized that he'd submitted a proposal to Professor Daniels, and they'd seized all her records when they hanged her.

When I didn't say anything, Priestess Margaret turned to using threats. "It shouldn't be hard to rally the coven and drag Grant Bryant to the gallows. After all, he killed two respected officers of the force. I suggest you take the deal."

The witches were pure evil, but I had no choice. Even if my friends left, the council would use their crimes to smear their names, ruin their reputation, and twist the story to gather supporters. The coven would crumble if I didn't do this.

My stomach twisted as I forced the word through my teeth. "I'll take the deal."

Lilian wore a smirk.

"Oh, and one more thing," Margaret added—like I had no choice, because I'd already agreed. "You're going to make a public statement clearing Priestess Stella's name. You and Lucas will take back everything you said about her in front of the pyre."

"But she was behind the nightshade production," I argued. "She went behind your back and lied to you for years. Aren't you *pissed*?"

"It doesn't matter," Charlotte said coolly. "The people need to trust us. If they believe Stella was evil, they'll believe that any of us can turn dark—including you."

"This is for *your* benefit, Nadine," Margaret said. "If you want the coven to trust you, you cannot let them believe that a priestess can turn her back on the Imperium Council."

"So it's all about appearances again?" I demanded. "We have to play nice."

"Yes," Margaret said bluntly. "Unless you want the coven to turn against us all."

I didn't want to do it, but they left me no choice but to agree. "Okay. I'll lie. But let me make one thing very clear."

I pulled the Alchemy Wand from my coat and marched straight up to the council table. I slammed the Wand onto the tabletop. I leaned toward the priestesses with death in my eyes. "You can take this Wand from me, but the second you touch me or my friends, I'll fight back. My *friends* will fight back. I'll make public everything you've done, and the coven will know exactly what's gone down this semester. You can hang us from the gallows, but the moment you put a noose around our necks, you put one around *yours*."

I swore to the Goddess the priestesses trembled. In that moment, one thing became very clear to every person in the room.

I would burn the council to ashes for the people I loved. If they wanted to take us down—take *me* down—then so be it.

They were going down with us.

TWENTY-FIVE

I woke to the feeling of cold air brushing against my side. I'd fallen asleep with Nadine in my arms, but she wasn't there anymore. The sound of the front door clicked, and my heart lurched when I realized Nadine was leaving the mansion.

I got to my feet and hurried outside behind her. I spotted Nadine disappearing into the trees. I called her name, but she didn't hear me over the sound of the wind. I wrapped my arms around myself and followed her, but I lost her in the trees.

I began running, searching the forest and calling out her name. But Nadine didn't hear me.

Fuck. Where had she gone?

I didn't know how long I'd been searching for her. It had to be fifteen minutes by now, at least. I was getting really cold, and I didn't know how much longer I could stay outside. I began to panic. I tried to put myself in Nadine's shoes. What would possibly possess her to leave the mansion tonight? It was our one safe place in the entire town.

Nadine wasn't the *stay safe* kind of girl, I realized. She was the kind of girl who ran into danger. She'd said that to me when we first met.

Nadine was going to see the priestesses.

The school grounds were quiet when I passed them. All the students were gone—probably escorted back to their dorms by police. The pyre remained empty, and a lingering burnt scent filled the air.

I didn't have any magic, so I couldn't conjure my broom, nor car keys to drive into town. I shivered in the cold as I made my way into town on two feet.

I rushed into Octavia Hall and took the stairs two at a time. Nadine's voice sounded down the stairwell.

"You can hang us from the gallows, but the moment you put a noose around our necks, you put one around yours."

I caught the end of her speech, and my jaw dropped as I slowed outside the door. Nadine was a force to be reckoned with, and I was certain the priestesses feared her more than the Waning itself. They couldn't touch her, because if they did, they fucked themselves over.

Nadine stopped in her tracks when she burst out of the Imperium headquarters and saw me standing on the landing.

"Lucas?" she breathed, looking shocked.

"I'm sorry," I said. "I had to follow you. I had to make sure you were safe."

She shot a glance back at the door. "I made a deal, and we're safe for now. We can stay in Octavia Falls. We have to go tell everyone."

Nadine started down the stairs.

"Nad, wait," I said as I followed her. "Tell me you got your kidney."

She stopped on the lower landing. "I didn't have a choice. I could pardon everyone, or I could get the transplant. Those were my options."

"This is bullshit," I growled.

"What part? The part where the priestesses started a war, or the part where they forced me to hand over the Alchemy Wand?"

"All of it is bullshit!" I cried. "They can't hold your kidney hostage like this."

"They can, and they are," Nadine pointed out. She shook her head, like she didn't know what to make out of any of it. "The prophecy about us is bigger than nightshade and the Waning. We were careless, and that's why Amy died. We need to find the rest of the Oaken Wands before the Imperium does, or they'll make this worse."

Nadine looked totally defeated. I wrapped her in my arms, and she sagged against me. She was wiped, and I lowered her to the ground. Nadine leaned her head back against the wall.

"We'll do everything we can," I told her firmly. "There's no other option. We *will* fulfill this prophecy and bring an end to the witch trials. But first, we have to get you your kidney."

"Lucas," Nadine tried to stop me, but I already whirled around and started back up the stairs. I didn't think she had the energy to come after me.

My hands curled into fists as I marched up the stairs. I had every intention of giving the priestesses a piece of my mind. They *would* convince the doctors to go through with this transplant. Nadine *would* get her kidney.

But the second I reached the landing, my heart stopped. Angry conversation drifted through the door, which had been left open a crack.

"Nadine is out of control," I heard Priestess Margaret say. "We must take drastic measures before she breaks this coven apart. We need help from the other side. It's our last resort."

I crouched down and peeked through the crack. My heart hammered as I spied on the council. The three priestesses sat around the table, their hands joined in the center.

"Where do we find the next Oaken Wand?" Lilian asked, but it didn't sound like she was asking the other priestesses. She spoke like she was asking someone I couldn't see. Their hands moved in unison over the tabletop, and it was only then that I saw the planchette beneath their fingers. My breath caught when I realized what was happening.

A Ouija board.

Priestess Charlotte read the words slowly as the planchette moved over the board. "Let... me... show... you..."

The moment she finished, the atmosphere shifted. Hair stood on my arm, and my pulse quickened. Air whooshed through the council head-quarters, sending papers flying and the priestesses' hair billowing around their faces. An ominous red glow filled the room, and the entire area darkened.

My blood turned to ice when I witnessed a portal appear. The black depths of the Abyss shimmered through the spatial anomaly. I couldn't move—couldn't even breathe—as I witnessed a figure step through the portal. He had the body of a man but the face of a ram, with long, curved horns growing out of his head. Where his eyes should've been were nothing but empty sockets dripping with blood. Sharp claws grew from his fingertips. My entire form trembled as I took in his cruel, haunting figure.

A terrifying, disembodied voice spoke. *"Let's make a deal."*

Air blasted across the room as the portal closed. The door slammed shut, and I stumbled backward in horror.

I didn't have time to process what I'd just seen. I had to get out of here, before the priestesses found me sitting in the hallway trembling. I scrambled to my feet and sprinted down the stairway. Nadine and I had to get the *fuck* out of here.

The priestesses had gone further than I ever thought possible. They'd summoned a demon, and there was no going back now. If they were willing to resort to such deep, dark measures to find the Oaken Wands, then we were totally screwed. It wasn't just our lives on the line anymore. Nothing was safe—

Not even our souls.

END OF BOOK THREE

Continue on to read a special excerpt from book four: *The Demon's Spell.*

HIDDEN LEGENDS

Read more from the Hidden Legends universe! Each Hidden Legends series takes place within the same world, but in separate and unique societies. Every series stands on its own, and they can be read in any order.

☾

ELEMENTALS, DRAGONS, & MORE

Academy of Magical Creatures by Megan Linski & Alicia Rades

☾

SHIFTERS, FAE, & SORCERESSES

University of Sorcery by Megan Linski

☾

SUPERNATURAL PRISON

Prison for Supernatural Offenders by Megan Linski & Alicia Rades

☾

Never miss a new release! Join our newsletter at www.hiddenlegendsbooks.com/fanclub

THE DEMON'S SPELL
CHAPTER ONE

Lucas

Summoning a demon was a recipe for disaster, but disaster had already struck—and it was time to raise some hell.

My pulse quickened as I snuck into Miriam College of Witchcraft. A dark hall loomed ahead, and a shiver traveled down my spine. I listened closely, but I didn't hear anything.

Over a week had passed since the Burning. The priestesses had burned Amy alive on school grounds, along with two of our other classmates and one of our professors. Riots had broken out, and at least a dozen people had died. The school was supposed to be closed for winter break, but the magic surrounding it had been weak since the night of the fire. It wasn't hard to get through the wards and sneak inside.

I created a light orb and shone it down the hall. "Clear," I whispered, gesturing my friends forward.

The snow crunched under Nadine's feet as she tiptoed through the darkness. Talia and Grant crept closely behind her. Our three cats—Isa, Oliver, and Gus—slunk along at our feet, moving so quietly that I couldn't hear them.

"I'm not sure about this, Lucas," Grant hissed. "This isn't a good idea."

"We don't have any choice," I replied.

Nadine stepped into the deserted hallway. "We need answers, Grant. The school's library is the only place we're getting them."

"There has to be another way," he insisted.

"There's no time," I said. "The priestesses summoned a demon a week ago. Doesn't it bother you that nothing has happened since then?"

I shivered just thinking about it. I'd only witnessed the demon for a mere second, but the sight of his hollow eye sockets still shook me to my core.

"Isn't that a good thing?" Grant asked. "I mean, we don't *want* anything bad to happen."

I shook my head. "It means the priestesses have bigger plans. They didn't summon that demon on impulse; otherwise, chaos would've broken out by now. We know they're using this demon to find the Oaken Wands, and once they have all five, they're going to control the coven's magic. But there's gotta be more to it. Demons don't do favors. The priestesses have already proven that they'll kill innocent people for their cause. We need to find out what else they're willing to sacrifice. Whatever deal they made with this demon can't be good."

"But summoning a *demon* for answers?" Grant sighed. "What if we're not strong enough to talk to this guy? What are we going to do—persuade him to our side? Demons can't be reasoned with."

Nadine bit her lower lip. "It's risky, but Lucas is right. Another demon will know what kind of deal the priestesses made. They could have answers about the priestesses' plans. We need to figure out what we're up against. Talia, what do you think?"

Talia took a deep breath, and her gaze roamed over Grant. "If we have any chance against the priestesses, we need to be a step ahead of them. I'm willing to go through with this ritual… if you are."

Grant reached for Talia. Her hand had been broken by a rogue spell the night of the Burning, but Helena's herbs had sped up the healing. "This could be really dangerous," he said. "People keep getting hurt."

"That's why we *have* to do this," Talia responded. "We need to know what the priestesses are up to so we can stop these witch hunts. My broken hand is nothing compared to what they did to Amy."

The hallway went dead silent when Talia mentioned Amy. My stomach churned. The sight of our friend's burning body was seared into my mind. Images from that night flashed behind my lids, and I thought I was going to hurl. We'd held a private memorial, but it wasn't anywhere close to the closure we needed.

I couldn't save her… but maybe I could stop future burnings. It was the only way to make up for my failure that night.

"Okay," Grant said, looking defeated. "Let's keep moving. For Amy."

We crept down the hall. Floorboards creaked beneath our feet, and the cats sniffed the air, as if they might be able to detect incoming threats. I looked around corners, but I never saw another soul. We made it to the library undetected.

The library was filled with two levels of bookcases. Tall, arching windows filtered in light from the quarter moon, and wind whistled from outside.

"What are we looking for, exactly?" Grant asked.

"A ritual to summon demons," Nadine said casually, like we did this every day.

"Our professors don't teach demon summoning," Grant pointed out. "It's forbidden, because of how dangerous demon deals can be. Are you sure they'd keep those kinds of books here?"

"The college library is open to the public," I reminded him. "There has to be something here. The coven summoned demons for centuries. There's no way it's been erased from our history."

"If there's anything, it's a restricted-access book." Talia stepped up to the nearest bookcase and ran her fingers across the spines. "They're marked with black dots. I remember when I found a book on hauntings for one of my classes, and the librarian wouldn't let me check it out. She said it was for professors and alumni only."

"Then we're looking for any restricted demonology book," I said. "Let's hope this doesn't take us all night."

I stepped down one of the aisles to begin my search, but before my hands landed on a book, a *crash* sounded from the upper level of the library. I froze.

"What was that?" Grant hissed.

I listened closely, and though it was faint, I caught the sound of footsteps upstairs.

"Someone's here," Nadine whispered.

"Do you think someone followed us?" Talia asked, sounding worried.

I glanced toward the doors. There was only one way in and out of the library. "No. They were here before us."

Nadine sighed, and she stepped out into the center of the room. "Okay!" she called up the stairs. "You can come out now."

"Nad," I hissed. For all we knew, it was one of the priestesses. But Nadine was fearless.

When no response came, Nadine raised her voice further. "I am a high priestess of the Miriamic Coven. I demand that you show yourself at once, or suffer the consequences."

Someone huffed, and footsteps sounded as they emerged from the shadows. A tall, thin female stood at the top of the balcony, and the shadow of a cat prowled beside her. She held a thick book in her arms. I couldn't tell who it was in the darkness, until she spoke.

"There's no need to be so dramatic, Nadine," Chloe said. "It's just me."

Grant conjured a battle orb in his hand within a second, and my fingers sparked with magic. I moved to Nadine's side in an instant.

"What are you doing here, Chloe?" I demanded.

She strolled along the balcony casually, like she didn't find Grant's magic to be a threat in the slightest. "The same as you—looking for answers."

"Answers about what?" Nadine asked curiously.

"The Waning," Chloe stated as she descended the stairs. "Our magic is disappearing more frequently, and for longer periods of time. Things have been worse since the Burning. It's too weird that all our magic went out at the same time that night. I thought if there was a way to end it, perhaps everything else could be solved, too. But now you have me curious about demons. What exactly do you know?"

The four of us hesitated, and Nadine shot me a nervous glance.

"Like we'd tell you," Grant sneered. "You'll run off and tell your priestess grandmother."

Chloe stepped into the moonlight, and I caught the scowl on her face. "Did I not prove myself to you during the Burning? I'm on your side."

"We were all desperate that night," Grant pointed out. "You've been nothing but mean to us otherwise. Hell, you tried to *hang* Nadine!"

"When I was *cursed*," Chloe reminded him.

"But it was still your choice," he shot back. "You called me Hispanic scum."

"And you have every right to be mad at me about that," Chloe said. "Look, I know I can't make up for the past. I can't say sorry and hope that it will magically fix everything. Come on, Lucas. I was at your Evoking Ceremony."

"Because you wanted to make Ryan jealous," I reminded her.

"Ryan and I are *long* over," she assured me. "I know what kind of bitch I was, but I've changed. Please let me show you that. All I ever wanted was to protect the coven, and I know that's what you want, too. I'm here doing research just like you, so let me help."

I'd never heard Chloe beg the way she was pleading with us now. I was skeptical, but I heard the truth in Chloe's words.

"Well, you can't help us," Grant insisted. "Tell her, Lucas."

I hesitated. She *had* helped us escape arrest the night of the Burning. "It might be useful to have a Mentalist on our side."

"Lucas!" Grant balked.

"I'm serious," I said. "Chloe's passionate, driven, and manipulative—"

"Which is why we can't tell her anything!" Grant cried. "She already knows too much."

"Or it's why we need her," I countered. "But we can't work with her unless it's unanimous. Nad?"

Nadine hadn't taken her eyes off Chloe. She studied her, as if searching for the lie behind her words. Isa stepped forward and sniffed Chloe's cat. The cat sniffed her back, and the two began purring and licking each other.

Chloe gazed down at them. "Marley agrees. He likes you guys."

Talia frowned. "We're not taking opinions from your cat."

Nadine turned to me. "I think Lucas is right. We need a Mentalist. The Oaken Wands will work best if we have all five Casts working together."

"But *Chloe*?" Grant whined.

"Chloe's as headstrong as I am," Nadine said. "If we're going to butt heads, we might as well do it on the same side. Once this is all over, the coven will have to make amends with each other. If we can't do that with Chloe, the coven has no hope. We have to be the start of that. I vote to work with her. What's your vote, Tal?"

Talia eyed Chloe curiously. "She does seem... different. And she did help us during the Burning. She wouldn't have done that if she wasn't on our side. I don't like the idea, but Nadine's right. We need to start forming alliances, or we don't stand a chance."

Grant scowled. I didn't blame him. Chloe had been awful to all of us, but a grudge wasn't going to win us this war.

His eyes darted toward the cats, who were purring. That must've persuaded him, because he said, "It's obvious you care deeply about the coven… and we could use your help."

Chloe opened her mouth to say something, but Grant cut her off.

"But if it even *looks* like you're about to betray us, so help me, you'll be standing at the gallows next," he threatened.

Chloe crossed her heart. "I wouldn't dream of it."

The strange thing was, I believed her. Chloe honestly wanted to work with us.

"So what's this about demons?" Chloe asked.

"Oh, boy," Nadine sighed. "There's a lot to catch you up on."

Chloe shrugged. "Then let's get started."

We sat around one of the study tables, and I told her how I'd witnessed the Imperium Council summon a demon at their headquarters. They were looking for answers about where to find the Oaken Wands, and the demon wanted to make a deal. I hadn't learned what deal they'd made, but we came here tonight to figure it out.

Chloe blew a breath when I finished, like she couldn't quite believe it. "I never thought my grandma would resort to demon deals, but this… ooh, this is bad."

"In what way, exactly?" Talia asked curiously.

"Demons can make all sorts of contracts," Chloe pointed out. "One of the things they often trade for is souls, but you can't just give them the right to anyone's soul. It has to be yours… or your kin."

Nadine's jaw dropped. "So you could be at risk? You don't think your grandma would make that kind of trade, do you?"

Chloe looked worried. "After the Burning, I don't think I know my grandmother at all. I honestly don't know what lengths she'll go to anymore. We need to figure that out."

Chloe dropped the book she'd been holding onto the table. "Luckily, I ran across this just before you showed up."

My eyes scanned the thick tome. *Advanced Demonology.*

"You were looking into demons before we arrived?" I asked.

Chloe nodded. "I'm exploring all angles. The Waning could definitely be caused by demon magic."

"It is demon magic, actually," Nadine said. "The Imperium made me do a spell with them to figure it out. They confirmed it's demon magic, but there's no way to know if it's a deal, an artifact, or if a demon is working independently."

Chloe's lips curled back. "We need to find out. Problem is, this damn book won't open!"

She tugged on the front cover, but it didn't move, as if it'd been glued shut.

"Let me see…" Nadine slid the book across the table and splayed her palm over it. She pressed her lips together, like she was concentrating hard. "This ward is a joke. I can break it no problem."

Nadine closed her eyes, and black magic billowed out of the pages, swirling up her arm. As a Curse Breaker, Nadine had the unique ability to move magic from one place to another. It was what allowed her to break curses, but it had other perks, too, like breaking wards. Most wards were too strong for a single Curse Breaker to break, but Nadine was getting better. I was confident she could break this simple ward with ease.

She transformed the ward magic into a battle orb. It crackled in her palm for a second, then shot out of her hand and whizzed across the library. It slammed into a nearby shelf and knocked a bunch of books to the floor. I winced as the sound filled the room.

"Whoops," Nadine said. "I really need to work on that."

"You don't think anyone heard that, do you?" Grant asked.

"Relax." Chloe said. "No one's here."

Nadine opened the book to the table of contents, and Talia leaned forward, her eyes bright with interest. "Let's see…" Nadine mused. "Demon summonings…"

"This looks promising," Talia said, pointing.

Isa peeked over the edge of the table and hissed, as if warning us not to go through with this. Nadine stroked her fur. "It's okay, girl. We'll be careful."

Isa let out a low growl, but Nadine ignored her and turned to the spell Talia had pointed out. She studied the page for a moment before saying, "This looks simple. All we need to do is draw a sigil and speak an incantation—oh, wait. This spell uses blood magic."

"So?" Chloe asked.

Talia gaped at her. "Blood magic is *bad*."

"Why?" Chloe challenged. "If I cut my hand open, I'm not hurting anyone but myself. I don't see the problem."

"Because it's tricky and can backfire on you," Nadine pointed out.

Chloe shrugged. "Same with summoning a demon. You know the real reason the coven doesn't sanction blood magic, right?"

I eyed her curiously. "What are you getting at?"

"Blood magic is powerful," Chloe pointed out. "We're like magical reservoirs—batteries that can be recharged. That's why your magic returns every time you're affected by the Waning. Our magic comes from Alora, but once we're recharged, we hold our magic in our blood. The coven doesn't want us using blood magic because they don't want us to know how powerful we really are. They're afraid of it, plain and simple."

Talia narrowed her eyes. "That has to be a conspiracy theory. The coven banned blood magic to protect us."

Chloe shrugged. "Believe what you want, but I'm convinced. You already know the priestesses aren't above lying. Is it so hard to believe they would lie about this? *Of course* blood magic is going to backfire the first few times you use it—just like *any* magic. They tell you it's dangerous so you won't ever use it and realize how strong you really are."

Chloe made a good point, one I had never considered before. I used to trust the priestesses. I didn't anymore.

"I think it's worth a shot," I said.

Grant crossed his arms and leaned back in his chair. "Perhaps we should let Chloe do the honors."

He was testing her, trying to see if she was bluffing. Chloe was more than up for the challenge. "I don't mind," she said.

Nadine nodded. "Then let's begin."

She conjured a marker and began drawing the sigil on the tabletop, glancing at the book every now and then to make sure she got it right. It was a circle, with a five-pointed star inside and all sorts of runes surrounding it.

The moment Nadine finished drawing the sigil, an icy chill filled the room. I shivered and wrapped my arms around myself. "Does anyone else feel that?"

Talia shot a glance around the room. "Definitely weird."

"Well, we *are* summoning a demon," Grant said. "It *should* be weird, shouldn't it?"

"Grant's right," Nadine said. "Let's keep going."

Chloe conjured a pocketknife. As she lifted her hand above the sigil, her cat hissed and ducked under her chair. Chloe pressed the blade to her palm—

Wind swept through the library so fast that the demonology book slammed shut. Chloe squealed and leapt backward. Her blade thudded to the ground. The cats all hissed and huddled together under the table. Grant grabbed Talia. She buried her face into his chest, while Nadine and I leapt to our feet.

I pulled her closer to me, but my gaze darted around the room. "It can't be a demon," I said breathlessly. "We didn't finish the summoning."

"*Something* is here," Nadine emphasized in a wavered breath.

"What, like a ghost?" Talia squeaked.

An ominous scratching filled the room. My pulse quickened when I looked down at the table. I grabbed Nadine tighter and pulled her close to me. Lines appeared on the tabletop, as if someone was carving them into the wood right in front of me, but no one was touching the table. Letters formed in front of my eyes, breaking the sigil and spelling out words.

My mouth went dry as I read the words aloud. "*History will repeat itself. He has come to kill. Return to the past to vanquish the demon for good.*"

I barely finished reading the words before a white, ghostly figure appeared. All I saw was the outline of a woman before a high-pitched shriek filled the library. My friends and I slapped our hands over our ears. The ghost swooped across the table, air billowing out from the hem of her dress. The gust was so strong that it nearly knocked me over.

The ghost slammed straight into Talia, and she was blasted backward. Talia screamed as her chair flew across the library. Her chair toppled over near the entrance, and she rolled across the ground. The ghost vanished, but Talia lay on the floor, unmoving. I raced toward her. Grant and I reached her at the same time, and we gently rolled her over.

"Tal!" Grant cried. "Talia!"

She groaned, but she gazed up at the ceiling with an empty gaze, like she was slipping in and out of consciousness.

Nadine stood over us, her hands slapped over her mouth. "Dear Goddess."

Life returned to Talia's gaze, but she gritted her teeth, like she was in pain.

"What hurts?" I asked.

"Ugh, everything," she complained. "I'll be fine, though. Just one hell of a bruise."

Grant helped her sit up.

Talia pressed her hand to her forehead. "What the hell was that?"

"A warning," Chloe stated.

My blood chilled. I knew Chloe was right. "Whoever that ghost was, she didn't want us summoning a demon. She came to deliver an answer herself."

"But what does it mean?" Nadine asked. "*Return to the past*? I thought witches didn't have time travel magic."

"We don't," Chloe said. "You'd have to be a demigod, at least, to perform that kind of magic."

"We don't need that kind of magic anyway," I said, rising to my feet. "*History will repeat itself*. It's obvious, isn't it? This demon has been here before. We just have to figure out when and why, and we'll find the answer to getting rid of him."

The library fell silent. None of us wanted to acknowledge the last part of the warning. My heart hammered as the words repeated in my mind. *He has come to kill.*

This demon had been set loose on the coven by the priestesses. There was only a matter of time before he claimed his first victim.

Continue The Demon's Spell to vanquish the demon!

BONUS OFFERS

Find coloring pages, games, quizzes, and bonus content at hiddenlegendsbooks.com.

Join the *Orenda Academy: Hidden Legends Fan Group* on Facebook for all things Hidden Legends!

Check out the *College of Witchcraft Official Playlist* on Spotify!

Never miss a new release! Join Alicia's email list at aliciaradesauthor.com/newsletter.

ABOUT THE AUTHOR

Alicia Rades is a USA Today bestselling author of young adult and new adult paranormal fiction. When she's not dreaming up magical stories, she's either binge-watching Netflix, meditating, or spending time with her family. She has an unhealthy obsession with psychic characters and writes with a deck of tarot cards next to her computer.